The VIXEN

The Love of a Rogue
Loved by a Duke
To Love a Lord
The Heart of a Scoundrel
To Wed His Christmas Lady
To Trust a Rogue
The Lure of a Rake
To Woo a Widow
To Redeem a Rake
One Winter with a Baron
To Enchant a Wicked Duke
Beguiled by a Baron
To Tempt a Scoundrel

Lords of Honor

Seduced by a Lady's Heart
Captivated by a Lady's Charm
Rescued by a Lady's Love
Tempted by a Lady's Smile

Scandalous Seasons

Forever Betrothed, Never the Bride
Never Courted, Suddenly Wed
Always Proper, Suddenly Scandalous
Always a Rogue, Forever Her Love
A Marquess for Christmas
Once a Wallflower, at Last His Love

Danby

A Season of Hope
Winning a Lady's Heart

Brethren of the Lords

My Lady of Deception

Nonfiction Memoir

Uninterrupted Joy

The VIXEN

CHRISTI CALDWELL

Montlake
Romance

Text copyright © 2018 by Christi Caldwell
All rights reserved.

Published by Montlake Romance, Seattle

www.apub.com

Amazon, the Amazon logo, and Montlake Romance are trademarks of Amazon.com, Inc., or its affiliates.

ISBN-13: 9781503902251
ISBN-10: 1503902250

Cover design by Erin Dameron Hill

Cover illustrated by Chris Cocozza

Printed in the United States of America

To Reagan and Riley: my strong, loving, courageous,
intelligent, compassionate girls.
Never doubt your worth. Always know your strength.
You can and will do anything in this life.
Absolutely no one can or will stop you.
Ophelia's story is for both of you.

Prologue

London, England
1812

The boy was in her territory.

Nay, no place in London truly belonged to anyone but *him*, the Devil incarnate, Mac Diggory.

Regardless, she answered to that blackhearted bastard and, just like everyone else, paid the price for his discontent. As such, she'd fight for these cobbles with her own life. Hers was forfeit anyway, if she did not.

Anticipation of the battle thrummed in her veins. She wove through the throngs of lords and ladies on their way to the theatre. All the while she kept her gaze trained forward on the gangly boy at her corner.

Nearly six inches past five feet, he had the height of most men and would surely grow to be a bear.

She didn't care if he was boy, man, or giant; he threatened her safety and security.

She'd be damned if any interloper did. Especially not a boy pick-pocket, and a lousy one at that.

He paused, his nervous stare darting about.

Tamping down her sound of disgust, she eyed her opponent.

Fidgeting with the hat that tipped low over his brow, he couldn't be more obvious if he'd streaked across London with his bare arse hanging out.

The pathetic excuse for a street rat would be lucky to survive another week, let alone a year.

She ducked inside the alley, shot a hand out, and yanked the taller child by his threadbare shirt.

He gasped, stumbling back into the darkened recess. He made a grab for his knife.

She already had her dagger out and against his throat.

The muscles there convulsed as he went absolutely still.

"These streets ain't yars," she snarled, nicking him. A crimson drop beaded on his flesh. She forced him back against the wall, knocking his hat loose. "They're—"

Her words trailed off as she stared, riveted by the small mark etched above his right eyebrow, an engraving left in his flesh.

The air hissed from between her teeth as a memory echoed around her mind.

"Oi'm not doing it to 'elp you," she snarled.

"Then, why are you not turning me over?" he asked quietly, searching her face.

Why, indeed? When she'd see herself slain for betraying Diggory's orders?

Footsteps sounded over her shoulder. She gave Connor a hard shove. "Unless you wish to be carted off to Diggory with yar entrails for his supper, go."

That was all it had taken. He'd gone.

And now here he was.

"The one who got away," she whispered. *Connor O'Roarke.* One of Diggory's street boys, he'd escaped long ago and remained as elusive as a ghost.

Connor grinned coldly. "Still a slave to Diggory," he taunted, and her neck fired hot.

She hated the slight tremble to her hand that came from his derision. "Ya don't know anything about it," she growled, pressing the blade deeper.

The muscles of his throat moved, and with a braveness she'd not seen even in Diggory's most ruthless guards, he smiled mockingly at her. "You aren't going to stab me."

How did he know that? Unnerved, she firmed her grip. "Shut yar mouth," she warned.

"So what are you going to do? Are you going to force me back?"

For his brave show, there was a spark of fear in his eyes.

As there should be. Since she was a small child toddling about, she'd heard the name Connor O'Roarke—the one who had *slipped* free in the dead of a night, made off with a hefty purse, and pillaged these same streets owned by Diggory. *And Oi found 'im . . . again.*

Feeling his eyes on her, she swallowed hard.

"This time I should turn you over," she growled, as much for herself as for him.

Or better yet, she should let him get himself hanged so she could get on with her business and reclaim her streets. Connor O'Roarke wasn't her business. He wasn't part of Diggory's gang, and he certainly wasn't her friend or family.

"Or mayhap you won't," he murmured. He'd sensed her indecision. She heard it in his cocksure tone and saw it in his hardened gaze. "Mayhap you fear I'll tell him of the other times you—"

"Shut yar damned mouth, bastard," she hissed, reapplying pressure with her blade.

"What are you going to do, Lagertha?" he challenged.

She gritted her teeth. There it was. That name he'd tossed as casually as those lords did a purse to the boys who held the reins of their mounts.

Do you want to know why I call you that, Lagertha?

She had. She'd wondered it in the time since she'd last seen him. But she'd not, despite the curiosity that had gripped her then, conceded that weakness, and she wouldn't now. Even as the need to know was as strong . . . nay, stronger.

She slowly let her arm fall. "Ya're a fool." Or a lackwit. "Ya want to get yarself caught by him. That's the only way to explain it. Go . . . or next toime Oi *will* bring ya to him." For if she didn't . . .

She shivered.

The ghost of a smile on Connor's lips hinted at one who'd spotted the lie.

Why had she always been a bloody fool where this boy was concerned?

Her feet twitched with the need to flee, hating that he saw too much, despising that she'd allowed him an upper hand in any way. "Go to 'ell, Connor O'Roarke." Jaw tightening, she darted from the alley, leaving him alone—again.

Ya're a fool. If Diggory knows what ya'ave done, and that ya'ave done it twice now . . .

A chill scraped its way along her spine as she tasted the same fear she'd smelled from Connor O'Roarke when she put a blade to him.

She had to find a fortune this night. Had to keep Diggory appeased, not happy, because the Devil was incapable of anything but cruelty.

Frantically, she searched the streets. Searching. Searching. Searching.

Her gaze landed on a gentleman striding with easy steps toward the theatre. She squinted, bringing every detail into focus: the stranger's fine black cloak, his collar adorned in velvet. Everything about the man, from his garments to his stride, spoke of wealth.

Connor O'Roarke forgotten, she sprang into movement, starting through the crowds. At any time she despised her size for the easy way

Diggory and his men managed to beat her down. Yet sometimes that smallness served a benefit. This instance, weaving between lords and ladies, a mere slip of a ghost, being one of them.

The nob paused to consult his gold timepiece, the metal shimmering under the street lamp he stood beneath.

But she didn't have want of that watch. That was merely the distraction she required, for the real item he'd only briefly flashed as he'd descended his carriage.

She crept forward.

The moment he turned, she sidled closer.

From across the way, she felt eyes on her. She picked up her head, and her gaze locked on his. Connor O'Roarke gave a slight, warning shake of his head.

She frowned. This blighter would give her warnings? This, the same man who didn't know that this territory belonged to Diggory, and if he were discovered here, his entrails would be ripped through his slit throat and fed to him as his last meal?

Jutting up her chin defiantly, she moved. She had her hand in the nob's cloak and his velvet purse in her hand without even breaking stride. Stuffing it inside her front pocket, she paused to shoot Connor a triumphant look.

"You bloody street rat," someone cried. A large hand wrapped around her wrist. Wrenching it back, a man forced her to the ground.

She tamped down the cry that sprang to her lips and knelt before the two men.

"What is the meaning of this?" the gentleman barked.

The constable stuck an accusatory finger at her. "The girl was stealing from you."

Surprise lit the nob's face. He felt around his jacket and opened his mouth. When he turned his attention back, she braced for a blow.

Except the gentleman stared contemplatively down at her. "What is your name?" he asked quietly.

Her name? He'd ask her bloody name? She trembled; the shake started in her toes and set her whole body to quaking. The shiver had nothing to do with the stinging pain of flesh scraped bloody from her fall.

Never show fear . . . never let them see . . . or Oi'll cut ya loike Oi did yar sister.

The constable yanked her up from her knees. "What's your name, girl?" he barked, giving her a hard shake.

Yet for the numbing dread, she'd been whelped and reared by the most ruthless blighter in East London. She shrugged her shoulders.

The crimson-haired constable looked over at the fancily dressed nob she'd nicked from with confusion in his eyes.

The pair exchanged a look.

"His lordship asked you a question," the constable growled. Dragging her up by the front of her threadbare shirt, he shook her so hard her teeth rattled. "Answer the bloody question."

Her lower lip quivered, and she bit it. She might hang for her crimes here, but she'd be damned if she let a constable break her.

Growling, she brought back her foot and kicked him in the shins with the tip of her worn boots.

He hissed. Using his distraction, she brought up her other leg and caught him square between the legs.

The constable's eyes bulged in his face, and then releasing his tight grip, he went down hard on his knees, clutching at himself.

Heart thundering, she sprang forward, when a hard hand settled on her shoulder, killing her flight.

She hissed and snarled. So this is 'ow the cat her sister had insisted on fighting to make a damned pet had felt. Cornered. Terrified. *Trapped.*

The nobleman, well over two feet taller, may as well have been the giant in Diggory's employ who roused terror just by his appearance alone for the way he now towered over her.

Hair greying at the temples, a diamond pin stuck in his snowy-white cravat, he'd the look of a king studying his subjects. He passed an unreadable gaze over her person, and she shivered. The fear of no reaction, she'd long ago learned, was far more perilous than a telling fury. One knew one's opponent would ultimately attack. But when? How? All the questions added to the terror.

She gasped as she was wrenched back by the constable. The panting bastard brought his arm back, and she hunched her shoulders, braced for the blow.

The nob held up a staying hand, and she started, concealing her surprise at that brief show of mercy. "You won't tell me your name," he repeated, rubbing at his chin.

"Go to 'ell," she snarled. Glaring at the fancy gent, she tossed back her head and spit at his feet, marring the gleaming heeled shoe.

The constable tangled his fingers into the hair she'd knocked loose in her fall a short while ago and yanked so hard tears sprang to her eyes. How had she made that bloody blunder? She never made a mistake. She knew the repercussions. She'd just believed the greatest danger came from Mac Diggory, the leader of these dark streets. *Oi was wrong. The bloody law . . . it's the law to fear.*

"Newgate for you, girl."

Vomit stung the back of her throat. "No," she begged. "Please." *I don't want to die.*

A shout went up. "Wait."

As one, they looked across the street. Connor weaved between passersby and observers taking in the display between her and the gent.

"Who in blazes are you?" the constable muttered, dragging her closer like one who sensed a trap.

With a dangerous glint in his street-hardened eyes, Connor took a threatening step closer, so close he knocked into her and the bastard with a strong grip on her.

"Watch what you're doing, boy—"

"What are you doing with her?" he demanded, his tones not the rough Cockney of her and her siblings.

It was just another reason she'd always hated him. Always thinking himself better than the rest.

"On your way, boy," the constable barked. "It's not your affair. Unless you care to see yourself in Newgate like this one." He shook her so fiercely her neck whipped back.

She cried out, hating herself for that pathetic display. Crying was weakness, and weakness got one killed. It was a rule ingrained into her since she drew her first miserable breath.

Again the nob lifted a silencing hand.

Connor narrowed his eyes into thin, menacing slits. "It is my business."

The nob and constable spoke in unison, one man in his coarse East London tones and the other with the King's English better suited for the palace.

"Your b-business, you say?" the constable sputtered.

"Your business?"

By God, he'd always been arrogant; his conceit was enough to have earned the ire of Mac Diggory. Connor's gaze met hers. "Yes, my business."

As the two men in control of her fate exchanged looks, she ignored them, lifting her chin in furious anger toward the boy opposite her. Hating him for being free. Hating him for having managed to escape . . . in every way that she'd been unable to. He'd been one who'd gotten away . . . and remained elusively so.

"On your way, boy." Angling his shoulder dismissively, the constable dragged her with him. "I'll see this one to Newgate, my lord. My apologies that you've been abused by this trash—"

Connor stretched out an arm, and a monogrammed velvet bag twisted back and forth between his fingers, bringing the two men to an immediate silence.

What? She swiveled her gaze from her front pocket to his fingers and then to Connor's eyes. Her lips parted.

If she weren't so befuddled by the unlikeliest of rescues, she'd have been bloody enraged over the fact that her pocket had been picked.

"Impossible." Despite his earlier confidence, the constable wavered. He lightened his grip but still retained a determined hold on her.

The gentleman in his fancy cloak frowned. "You took my purse," he said slowly.

"Let her go."

Why? Why would Connor O'Roarke do this?

At last the nob nodded slowly, breaking the impasse. "You heard him. Release the girl," he ordered with an air of finality.

Just like that, one's future had been saved and another's fate sealed.

The constable let her go with such alacrity she stumbled back and landed hard on her arse. She lay there, briefly frozen, as the constable dragged him off with the nob matching their strides.

Connor shot a last glance over his shoulder.

"A debt paid," he mouthed.

It was the motto ingrained into every one of the boys and girls miserable enough to find themselves in Diggory's clutches.

A debt paid.

Chapter 1

London, England
Spring 1826

One of the luxuries of being the most successful investigator in England lay not only in the wealth one possessed but also in one's ability to accept or decline whichever case one chose.

There could not be any doubt. Connor Steele had built a vast fortune through his work.

As such, he'd considered not coming.

When the note had arrived on his desk, he had contemplated tossing the missive into a dustbin.

In the end he'd granted the upcoming audience not because of monies needed, but because one was wise to gather information. From each appointment he could decide what to do with a case, but he'd not flourished as the head investigator by turning down assignments from the wealthiest, most powerful peers in London.

Despite the presence of two uniformed servants, a heavy silence loomed in the soaring foyer.

While the surprisingly fresh-faced butler examined the card he'd handed over, Connor touched his gaze on the grand space, from the white Italian marble floor to the sweeping red-velvet, carpeted staircase and the crystal chandelier that hung overhead. Aye, the gentleman who sought to utilize his services was deep in the pockets.

"If you'll follow me?" The tall, ginger-haired servant murmured the only words exchanged since he'd opened the door and Connor had offered over his card. After handing Connor's cloak to the footman, the butler started down the corridor that intersected the foyer.

Connor glanced over to the liveried servant who, garment in hands, melted into the shadows.

Keeping a slower pace behind the butler, Connor followed after him. The most skilled of investigators, he missed nothing and saw all. It was a lesson not known by most, and one Connor had come by not in the ten years since he'd established his own business but rather from the years he'd spent living on the streets.

To miss a detail could see a man with his throat sliced. It was a rule of life Connor was not so naive to believe was reserved only for the streets of East London, but for all of England, from its dark alleys to its glittering ballrooms.

The butler looked over his shoulder and then adjusted his pace as he led them down a bisecting hall. "This way, Mr. Steele," he muttered, and then another blanket of silence descended as Connor was ushered along.

While they made the long journey through the Marquess of Maddock's Mayfair townhouse, Connor cataloged every detail, ultimately settling on the single most defining element of the palatial residence.

Silence.

It was the single word that defined this household and the staff contained within. A manner of quiet that felt sharp in a person's ear and discouraged discourse, all the while punctuating what otherwise would have been mundane sounds: the distant tick of a clock, the tread of a quiet footfall, the groan of a floorboard.

The young butler slowed his steps, bringing them to a stop. He paused, waiting until Connor reached the heavy oak panel before rapping.

That pressing silence remained.

And then a harsh voice sounded from within the room. "Enter."

The efficient servant was already twisting the door handle, allowing Connor entry.

Doing a sweep of the room as he stepped inside, Connor at last settled his stare on the figure seated at the desk. Head bent over whatever task occupied him, the man didn't even deign to look up.

The butler cast an apologetic glance in Connor's direction and then cleared his throat. "My lord, Mr.—"

"I know bloody well who it is," the man seethed. From where he sat at his desk, a ledger open before him, and by both his command of the room and the fear he evoked, there could be no doubting the man's identity. "Get the hell out, Quint."

The butler may as well have been politely dismissed for the grace with which he exited.

"And close the door after you've gone," the gentleman whispered, still not bothering to lift his head.

The young servant inclined his head.

Once the man had gone and the room was quiet, Connor strode forward, uninvited. With every step that carried him closer, he intensified his study of that figure who'd long been whispered about amongst Polite Society: the Mad Marquess.

And with his unkempt blond hair hanging over his face and his frenetic assessment of that page, there could be no doubting the man's insanity. The Mad Marquess's wife had been burned alive while he'd remained remarkably untouched and conveniently out the night she'd been ravaged along with their child.

Connor, however, had dealt with demons in the streets and men and women bound for Bedlam. He'd long been jaded to fear or feeling anything around men such as the marquess.

"You came," the marquess observed in the rough tones of one unaccustomed to speech.

Taking that as his invitation to sit, Connor claimed the chair closest to the gentleman's desk. Not bothering with permission, he tugged it out and sat, his fingertips leaving trails upon the dusty arms.

Minuscule specks danced around in the air, the uncared-for offices at odds with the gleaming mahogany furniture outside these rooms.

Connor measured his words. He nearly hadn't come. His wealth afforded him decisions in the cases he took on. However, even in the earliest days of his career, he would have sold his soul to work on the case of a child killer. "You expected I would not," he settled for, gauging the other man for any reaction.

Not breaking his study of the ledger, Lord Maddock flipped the page. "I don't hold any expectations anymore, Mr. Steele," he said in deadened tones. While the marquess worked his gaze over the paper, Connor straightened his neck, studying the words written there.

Name after name filled the rows. Some of the names held stars beside them.

At long last the marquess set aside his book and picked up his head. He glanced, almost bored, at the *D* carved just above Connor's brow. Where most in Polite Society swiftly averted their horrified stares, Lord Maddock's lips turned up in a grim smile. "Do you know who I am?" he asked with an almost sick relish.

Connor narrowed his eyes. He'd survived hell on the streets. The last figure that could ever rouse a hint of fear in him was the Mad Marquess. "I've not come to be toyed with. You sought my services, and I've come to hear you out. So say what it is you'd say."

Another mirthless smile that would have withered a lesser man curled life-hardened lips. "I would hire you to oversee a case." Reaching inside his desk drawer, he withdrew a single sheet. He pushed it across the desk.

Connor eyed the page a moment and then picked it up.

"It's what you stand to earn," the marquess explained, sitting back in his carved mahogany King Lion throne chair.

Connor skimmed the paper.

One hundred thousand pounds.

Mayhap years earlier, he would have been impressed by that exorbitant sum. It was a fortune greater than that of most kings and princes.

"I don't decide upon my assignments by the size of the purse to be obtained," he said bluntly, shoving the sheet back.

"You're a fool, then."

No, he was a man with some integrity. Or rather, one who'd sought to reshape himself from the cutthroat he'd once been. "I'm a man who has means enough that I don't need to take cases unless I wish." He sharpened his gaze on the marquess's face. "Particularly by one who insults me."

A brief war raged in Lord Maddock's eyes.

"You want to tell me to go to hell," Connor observed, further establishing his foothold. "You want to toss me out on my arse, but you cannot." Because he required his services.

Despite his relaxed pose, the marquess's shoulders went taut. "It is about a child," the marquess said gruffly, a faint glitter of triumph in his eyes. "A boy."

Connor steepled his hands and continued studying the other man. "Dead or alive?" he asked bluntly.

A muscle ticked at the corner of his mouth. "Alive." Just that. One word and no further details.

In a bid for nonchalance, Connor drummed his fingertips together.

Children. They had forever been Connor's weakness as an investigator; those cases presented to him that involved a child were ones he'd been hard-pressed to decline. It was a detail that too many had gleaned and had resulted in impoverished mothers and desperate fathers appealing to him for rates that would see no man rich. He finally stopped his distracted movements. "You wish me to help you find a child," Connor waded through in measured tones.

"My son." Speaking in that cool, emotionless way, the marquess may as well have referenced the way he took tea or the bloodlines of his mount.

"Your son was killed," he said, training his gaze on the other man's face.

The marquess chuckled, the coarse sound of empty amusement filling the office. "You have done your research, Mr. Steele."

It was a story still occasionally whispered about in ballrooms: the remembered tale of the blaze set by the marquess when his wife, expecting their second child, and his son and heir had slept following a violent row between the husband and young mother.

Then all feigned hilarity withered as a dark, somber mask settled over the marquess's heavy features. "My son was stolen."

Mayhap this was the man's madness at play, a bid to reshape and twist his past to make it more bearable for his moments of lucidity. "Your child is gone seven years, and you're now making claims he's been kidnapped," Connor said, letting his incredulity seep in.

Lord Maddock pursed his mouth. "I didn't have reasons to believe he was alive." He paused. "Until now." He dangled that pronouncement.

A familiar hunger to know more gripped Connor.

For him it had been a lifelong compulsion. He'd sought it as an eager student with his long-dead mother, who'd been his first tutor. Then as a student at Cambridge . . . and ultimately as an investigator working the streets of London. It filled him even more now.

When Connor spoke, he did so with a matter-of-factness. "What information have you discovered that should lead you to believe your child survived a fire?" *A fire you set.* It hung unfinished, as real as if it had been spoken.

Ice frosted over Lord Maddock's brown eyes.

He grabbed a small leather journal at the corner of his desk and held it out. "There are names."

Wordlessly, Connor accepted the book.

He opened it and caught the pages sloppily ripped from gossip columns, slightly faded and showing the beginning signs of age.

"Begin with my notes," the marquess ordered as one accustomed to being obeyed.

Connor removed the miscellaneous sheets and set them aside. He quickly worked his gaze over the first page.

Names. Just like the ones scratched in a sloppy hand upon the marquess's journal that still rested open.

Only these were well-known ones, more recently spoken of and written about in Polite Society.

Helena Banbury, the Duchess of Somerset.

Ryker Black, Viscount Chatham.

Connor paused, his gaze lingering an additional moment on the information gathered on the viscount: his gaming hell partners. Nay, one in particular.

Niall Marksman.

Ya'ave to do what 'e says, Connor . . . just loike Oi did . . . unless ya want to end up loike Ryan. Just shut yar mouth and do whatever he tells ya to do.

He blinked, keeping his head down, as he attempted to reorder his thoughts. He'd not thought of Niall or any of the boys and girls he'd served with in the streets of London.

Nay, he'd not allowed himself to think of them. The demons intruded enough, where keeping his memories buried had proven far safer.

Thrusting them back once again, he finished reading.

"They were taken," the marquess spoke, bringing Connor's attention from that sheet. He jabbed a finger at the newspaper clippings. "It took time for me to make sense of it," he said like one possessed. "The Duke of Wilkinson's two children turned over to Diggory. It was all just useless gossip, and then with every lurid story, the pieces began to fall into place."

"The pieces?" Connor echoed slowly. They claimed the man was mad, and the frenzied glitter in his eyes lent those whisperings credence.

The marquess's words rolled together in a frenzy. "Children, taken. Stolen. Used." He stopped abruptly, his stare moving through Connor, beyond him, to a point only he could see. "Until it all made sense," he finished on an eerie whisper.

Connor, who'd long believed himself immune to unease, was proven very wrong in this instance. Shivers raced along his spine. "What did?" he urged, reaching for the stack of clippings.

The marquess blinked slowly, and it was in that moment Connor knew he'd forgotten another's presence—until now. "Why . . . he was taken by someone in the streets. Sold, perhaps."

Despite his earlier aloofness, pity tugged. Yes, perhaps it was easier for the gentleman to explain away his own crimes with a re-created imagination of what had truly taken place that December night.

"I didn't kill my son," Lord Maddock said, unerringly following Connor's thoughts and revealing an unexpected cogency.

Connor lifted his head. "What of your wife?" he asked quietly. He accepted cases for even a sliver of the amount he'd been extended, to aid those parents and kin searching for answers about lost or murdered children. But he did not take on the coin of murderers. "Did you kill her?"

A desolation reserved for those who'd given up on life flickered in the marquess's eyes. "Her death I am responsible for," the marquess said flatly.

Connor made to stand, the meeting concluded. But something gave him pause.

Her death I am responsible for.

It was a statement of ownership but devoid of an outright declaration of murder.

He searched his mind for everything he recalled about the Marquess of Maddock, sifting through the nuggets of gossip and digging for more. And wishing for the first time he'd paid more attention to the sensational case that had riveted the whole of England, long after the marquess had been exonerated and the cause of the fire attributed to an unknown arsonist.

Of course, it was far easier for the *ton* to contend with a nameless arsonist than to accept there was a killer in their midst.

Or that is what Connor had accepted as fact.

But what had he truly known of the case?

"Did you kill your wife?" he repeated.

"I gave you my answer," the marquess said, unflinching in the face of Connor's probing gaze.

"I'd have you say it aloud." Take ownership of the actual crime of which he'd been accused and then later acquitted.

"I've already said it; my wife is dead because of me. I'll not say it another way to appease you. Will you take my assignment and . . . find my son?"

"Is this the only evidence you have to suggest he might be living?"

The marquess's silence served as his answer.

Children were taken every day in the streets and made hired thieves, killers, and whores for the lords of the underbelly. Connor wore the mark upon his brow as eternal proof of that very truth. And yet—he directed his focus to the sheet—the cherished children of lords and ladies weren't the ones who found themselves as pawns to grow those ruthless bastards' power. They were boys and girls who'd had the same modest beginnings as Connor—some born to whores and sailors, others orphaned by a cruel fate, and others made orphans by the men who ruled their world. "Your child is . . . different from the men and women listed here," he said at last, setting the book down on the marquess's desk. "These are orphans—"

"Chatham—"

"The viscount's mother was a duke's former mistress who became the lover of a gang leader," he cut in. Everyone in London had recently discovered the tale of the Banbury mother.

The marquess frowned; his confidence flagged.

Determined to press his point and disabuse the marquess of any desperate or foolish hopes, Connor pointed to the Duchess of Somerset's name. "She is Chatham's sister and thus connected by blood. The other names here . . ." His gaze was drawn, unbidden, back to the middle of that page. "They were all common street orphans. There is no noble blood amongst them."

He made to stand.

Lord Maddock held up a hand. "You are wrong."

In his career as an investigator, those three words had proven foreign to Connor, who'd been accustomed to only success.

Still, Connor wasn't one with an overweening pride. He'd seen too much, done even worse, that any slight had long ago ceased to matter. "Rarely," he countered, coming to his feet. "I am rarely wrong."

"We are all wrong on occasion," the marquess said gravely, again a man lost in his own musings and regrets.

Connor took a step.

"But in this you are," the marquess snapped, bringing him reluctantly back to face him. Lord Maddock layered his palms to the desk, and the parchment wrinkled noisily under that pressure. "Tell me . . . were you the son of a whore and sailor? Common street blood, as you call it?"

Connor went still.

He is here . . . good God in Heaven, Connor, he is here.

He stared blankly at the marquess, whose lips turned up in another smirk. Society often whispered of and wondered after the young man marked with a *D* who'd been adopted by the Earl of Mar. But no one knew all. No one amongst Polite Society knew any of it.

Or that is what he'd believed.

His jaw tightened.

"You see, Mr. Steele, I, too, have heard rumors . . . of you." The marquess flicked his finger over the precise area of his brow where Connor's scar stood out, a stark reminder of his past. "Tales of how you were once with a different sort, saved by the Earl of Mar."

"My past is none of your affair," he said, infusing a steely edge to that threat.

"But it is," the marquess persisted. "In the sense that you, too, found yourself separated from your kin."

This is yar lucky day. It turns out Oi'll 'ave a use for ya, after all.

"And where did you go? Who did you live with on those streets?" Lord Maddock asked in the way only a predator who'd sensed weakness could.

Connor stood there for a long moment, motionless, the marquess's words whipping through him, challenges that forced Connor's past back to the present. "You believe your son is alive," he put forward so the other man might hear the words aloud and realize the improbability of them. "It is likely he is dead."

A paroxysm contorted the marquess's face, the first crack in his hardened composure. "But there is a possibility he is alive."

Which was more likely? That the Mad Marquess, who'd not denied killing his wife, believed his dead son was alive, or that the child had perished along with his mother that long-ago night?

And yet Lord Maddock had pulled forth the one word that kept Connor rooted to the narrow hemlock floorboards.

A possibility. *The chance that something may happen or be true.*

It was an essential word for all investigators for the reminder it served . . . and yet there was more.

In the court of public opinion, the marquess had been found guilty of wrongdoing. What if he were not the monster Society made him out to be but simply a father who'd gone mad with grief?

Again, even as it was . . . unfeasible, it was . . . possible.

But if it were true, that would also mean there might be a boy still living in those miserable streets Connor had been unfortunate enough to call home . . . and a nobleman looking for him . . . when none had ever looked for Connor.

The marquess narrowed his brown eyes into slits, a challenge and a question there . . . and something more: *a plea.*

Connor pulled out the chair and sat.

Chapter 2

Ophelia Killoran's father, Mac Diggory, the most ruthless blighter in all of London, used to say night was when the Devil came to play.

Darkness proved little shroud of the evil that unfolded amongst England's most desperate souls.

Ophelia, however, had come to appreciate the dead of night and the thick London fog as a reassuring cloak that offered protection no weapon, or person, could afford.

The rain? It made it all the safer to slip about unnoticed . . . and it also made fancy nobs, who shrank in the rain, careless.

Ophelia surveyed the streets, touching her gaze on the passersby hurrying toward the Devil's Den and the corners of buildings. She continued her search, and the horror-filled words shared between several servants in her family's clubs whispered forward.

He finds them in the Rookeries. When the rains come, and the fog's thickest, he's always there.

That telling, both haunting and ominous, conjured the oldest, darkest memories. The ones that refused to stay buried.

Do not think of him . . . do not think of him . . . focus.

Closing her eyes, Ophelia counted backward. *Three. Two. One.* She opened her eyes. Breathing slowly through her lips, she tugged her cap low and ducked away from the safety of a conversant alley and into the precarious streets of London.

The stench of St. Giles flooded her nostrils, and she let the scent fill her lungs, finding a calming effect from the familiarity to be found here. It was the only home she'd ever known, and when so many others had fallen in these streets, she'd not only survived alongside her siblings but also thrived. That reminder chased away her demons and restored her strength.

Ophelia slipped through the shadows, measuring each footstep, avoiding well-traversed paths.

He lures 'em into the alleys. No older than twelve, if they're a day . . . inside the sewer, he takes them.

Hatred singed her veins.

And where there should be fear at what the implications would be, should she be discovered, the sense of right was stronger.

Ophelia reached the juncture of Great Russell Street, that place where thieves and murderers had swung hundreds of years ago. The place London's poorest still called home. She glanced about. Heart racing, she hefted a grate aside and slipped through the narrow opening. She felt around with her feet and found purchase on the ladder. With one hand she drew the metal back into place. It settled with a heavy clank that echoed damningly around the dank sewers. Once she'd scurried quickly down the ladder, Ophelia's feet sank silently onto the floor.

Blinking to adjust her eyes to the dark, she hurriedly withdrew the dagger from inside her boot.

The acrid sting of waste slapped at her senses. No matter how accustomed one was to this world, the smell of rotting shite and death was one that could never be truly purged. Swallowing back the bile in her throat, she inched over the slick ground, measuring each step.

The squeal of rats echoed off the sewer walls.

"My, how pretty you are . . ."

Ophelia froze, going still, as those cultured tones pinged quietly ahead.

I am not too late.

Her feet twitched with the need to fly forward.

Haste, as Diggory had schooled, made waste. And though she hated the man who'd birthed her with an intensity that showed the darkness in her soul, she also recognized that certain lessons he'd passed down had value.

Keeping her breaths slow and even, Ophelia tiptoed through the sludge, keeping step in time to the conversation unfolding up ahead and the unexplainable groans of the sewer.

"Very lovely . . . my, how . . . so very lovely . . ." That hated voice grew closer and closer, and Ophelia stopped.

Though his back was presented to her, the dark did little to conceal the quality of that wool frock coat. Hatred scorched her tongue, burning her with the ferocity of that emotion. Was it arrogance that made a nobleman believe he needn't bother to disguise his wealth and rank when assaulting a child? Or was it simple carelessness?

Either way, it ultimately made her work this night all the easier.

Ophelia continued forward.

A child's whimper echoed throughout, that plaintive sound faintly muffled by the whine of rats scuttling about.

"It will not hurt one bit. I promise," the nob promised on a husky whisper as he fiddled with the girl's skirts. "And there will be a nice treat for you when it is done."

Brandishing her dagger, Ophelia lunged. *Riiiip.* The whine of her blade shredding that fine garment pealed around the sewers.

His breeches shoved low, the nob was slow to move. "Wh-what?" he shouted, stumbling. He ambled about, whipping his head all around the sewers as he sought her out.

Ducking low, Ophelia darted around him. She sliced a hole down the back of his jacket.

The vile lord's breath coming fast, he spun.

His previously gleaming boots slicked in excrement, he landed with a noisy thud in the shite.

Ophelia withdrew her pistol and leveled it at his chest.

"M-my God, you c-cannot shoot me," he sobbed. "Please, do not," he wisely amended.

"Ya're a child fucker," she taunted in graveled tones, relishing the way the color drained from his cheeks. "Wot would yar fancy wife say? Or does she know?" she continued, moving her pistol lower to the open front fall of his breeches. "Oi wager she's relieved to 'ave ya out o' 'er bed that she wouldn't care that ya 'urt a child."

"I don't hurt children," he cried. "She wanted it." *You want it, you little whore . . . you street rats are all the same.* "Followed me of her own will, she did. Ask her. Ask—"

Ophelia cocked her pistol, and that decisive click reduced the lord to a pathetic round of inane ramblings. "Shut yar bloody mouth," she warned. Not taking her gaze from the letch at her feet, she moved closer to the quaking child.

Her buttons undone, the tattered garment hung loose about her gaunt frame.

Please, please, do not touch me . . . don't . . .

Ophelia's heart lurched as her past merged with this little girl's present.

The gun in Ophelia's hand shook, and the nob brought his hands over his ears, cowering. "Do not hurt me," he shouted hoarsely. "I'll give you whatever you want. Name the price."

She flattened her lips. "Shut yar mouth, bastard," she hissed. While most errant cries went ignored, those shouted in cultured tones often brought constables and intervention from men and women of the streets eager for the coin that could be had in *saving* a nob. "Another word an' Oi'll shoot it off." She waved her gun meaningfully at the front of his breeches. Backing up, she edged closer to the girl.

"The Devil's Den 'as been known to 'ire children in trouble," she said from the corner of her mouth in hushed tones meant only for the child. "Go there."

Wide-eyed, the girl nodded. Then, clutching her garments close, she took a wide berth around Ophelia and the nobleman at their feet and bolted.

As soon as she'd gone, Ophelia kicked out her boot, catching the nobleman in the side.

He hissed, rolling over to cradle his ribs.

Using that distraction, she stomped on his groin.

An ungodly cry ricocheted around the sewer. "Oi said shut yar mouth," she warned as he writhed and moaned at her feet.

"Please, God. Please," he entreated, clutching at himself.

Her breath coming hard and fast from her exertions, Ophelia leaned over him, sticking her lips close to his ear. "There's no God in these sewers. There is no God in these streets. Next time you think to put your hands on a child, think of what's been done to you this day." Catching his head, she banged it against the ground once.

The nobleman's eyes rolled back.

She cursed that slip in her Cockney. Bloody hell. She'd been careless. "My lord?"

Her heart thudded to a quick stop and then resumed an accelerated cadence.

Bloody, bloody hell. She glanced down at the nobleman prone at her feet, knocked senseless at her hand. It wouldn't matter to the world if he'd been about to bugger a child or gut her to keep her silent of his sins. All Polite Society ever saw was a people higher and better than street scum like Ophelia and her siblings.

"My lord?" That voice drifted closer, along with the clumsy footsteps of a man unfamiliar with these sewers, increasing her heart's beat. "You there." A crimson-clad footman rushed forward.

He launched himself and caught Ophelia's right calf.

Her leg buckled, and she cried out.

Ophelia came down hard on her hands as the dagger flew through the air. It struck the stone pipe with a damning clang.

Both froze, staring down at the crimson knife.

Then, using the man's distraction, she scrambled to her feet and kicked him hard between the legs.

His shout of agony went up around the sewers.

Panic knocking around her chest, Ophelia looked over her shoulder to the tunnel connecting the sewer and ducked inside. Her feet sank into the water, soaking the soles of her boots. The chill penetrated the thick leather. Damning the loud echo of her feet kicking up water, she raced deeper and deeper in.

Terror choked off her airflow as she stumbled into the next connecting tunnel. She strained her ears for a hint of the man following her but maintained her frantic pace. Slowed steps were the most dangerous ones, nearly as dangerous as a false sense of security.

Ophelia continued running until a faint shaft of moonlight beckoned, spilling from the opening that connected the sewers. She broke free, welcoming the refreshing coolness of the nighttime air as it slapped her face.

She paused to catch her bearings.

The gallows that had long defined Charing Cross glowed under the moon's pale light.

Bloody, bloody hell.

At her quickest pace, she could make the return in twenty minutes. Having pushed herself to evade capture, it could only be longer.

Of course, at midnight her brother's club, the Devil's Den, was overflowing with patrons. Nothing could pry her brother from the gaming floors at this hour, and he'd certainly not question the whereabouts of Ophelia . . . or of any of the Killoran siblings. Nay, he'd be monitoring tables and watching to see the serving girls and prostitutes weren't mishandled, but he would never seek out the private suites and look after sisters who'd been looking after themselves since long before he'd ever entered their lives.

A hackney rattled along the cobbles, and Ophelia stepped into the shadows.

She adjusted her cap, miraculously still in place despite the trials she'd put her pins through this evening.

The bloody letch in the sewers had deserved a far worse fate than the one she'd handed out.

"Please, don't. Don't touch me . . . please."

Her stomach muscles tightened.

Do not think of it . . . do not think of it.

No good could come in thinking of that long-ago night. Particularly not here, amongst the Rookeries, with the constables no doubt already called and searching the streets for the one who'd assaulted a precious peer.

Ophelia turned at the end of the street. Relief eased some of the pressure in her chest at the familiar sight before her.

Home.

Awash in the glow of candlelight, the Devil's Den pulsed from the raucous activity spilling out each moment the doors were opened.

Oh, it was hardly a place that any person would think of as home, but it had been the only one she'd truly known. It represented security and safety. Another carriage rolled noisily along, and she hunched her shoulders. Never before had that proven more true.

Head down, Ophelia surveyed the busy streets, waiting for a break in the steady stream of patrons entering the club. For a handful of moments, not a carriage, horse, or stranger passed.

She bolted.

Pulse pounding the same frantic rhythm as when she'd made her escape from the sewers, Ophelia wound her way through the crowds to the adjacent building purchased by their family and linked to the club. Making use of the narrow alley that ran between, she picked her way over trash and a swarm of rats eating whatever treasure they'd found here.

She wrinkled her nose.

By God, she needed to speak to Broderick about tending this space. Connected as it was to their club, it deserved the same attention as the Devil's Den. Ophelia found her way to the expansive mews connecting the properties and slipped inside through the servants' doors.

As soon as she'd closed the oak panel behind her, Ophelia leaned against it. Her shoulders sagged.

Safe.

"Trouble."

She gasped.

The panicky whisper at the entrance of the kitchens brought her eyes flying open.

Her sister Gertrude, bent over, resting her hands on her knees, panted. "Trouble," she rasped again.

Ophelia's stomach flipped over itself.

She knows. How could she know? Neither Gertrude nor Stephen nor Broderick nor Cleo, when she'd been living here, had ever made mention or come upon her after one of her midnight jaunts. And on the heels of that was a gripping terror. "What manner of trouble?" she asked steadily. How was her voice so calm?

Her breath settled into a normal cadence, Gertrude rushed over . . . and then stopped. Wide-eyed, she looked Ophelia up and down, her stare lingering on Ophelia's mud-stained boots and breeches. "What—?"

"We have rats," she blurted. Which was not an untruth. They did. A sizable number of the miserable rodents.

Gertrude cocked her head.

"Large ones," she finished lamely, gesturing with her hands to indicate an exaggerated size.

Her far-too-compassionate sister clutched at her throat. "And you were out . . . *killing* them?"

By the horror in that question, Ophelia may as well have been accused of slaughtering the queen. "I was out . . . clearing them," she settled for. Why, why, had she mentioned the rats? She could have gone with mucking the stables or tending the gardens, either of which would have elicited far fewer questions from her tenderhearted sister.

Suspicion filled Gertrude's right eye; the other had long ago been lost to a brutal fist to the head. A familiar guilt sank deep in Ophelia's heart.

"What does that mean, precisely?" Gertrude dropped her hands on her hips. "Clearing them?"

Ophelia sent a prayer skyward for patience. She should have known that her sister, a lover of rodents, with a dratted mouse of her own, should take umbrage at Ophelia's supposed *handling* of the creatures. "Gertrude," she said warningly, "what trouble?"

Her eldest sibling blinked slowly, and then the earlier panic filled her tone. "Someone arrived a short while ago," she whispered, taking Ophelia by the hand. "Demanded to see Broderick."

Oh, God. "Who?" She forced the question out.

"An investigator."

Ophelia stumbled.

Gertrude caught her by the waist, steadying her.

Fear kept Ophelia rooted to the floor, unmoving. "What?" she whispered.

Gertrude took Ophelia's hand once more and forcibly tugged her along. "Will you focus? His name is Mr. Steele. He is an investigator," Gertrude reiterated. "And . . . and . . . you cannot be discovered looking"—her sister wrinkled her nose—"or, for that matter, *smelling* like that."

Her heart pounded frantically. Leave it to Gertrude, who when worried or anxious tidied everything from the rooms to her younger sisters' appearances. "I hardly believe this merits me taking a bath." No matter how desperately she wished it and how very much she longed to sink her aching muscles into the hot water.

"No, there isn't time for that." Gertrude set her jaw at a determined angle. "But at the very least we can make you presentable."

And as she allowed herself to be pulled along, Ophelia very much felt like the sacrifice being readied for an offering.

"When did he arrive?"

With a like terror reflected back in her sister's always steadying gaze, Gertrude swallowed loudly. "Not long ago. Broderick turned him away, but he . . . insisted on being seen."

Their brother had been unable to send him packing? Oh, bloody hell, this was bad. She'd been discovered. There was no other accounting for his appearance here at this given moment. She slowed her steps. "D-did he indicate what the meeting is about?" What else *could* it be about?

Gertrude shook her head once. "They did not speak in my presence."

A startled gasp burst from Gertrude's lips as Ophelia grabbed her by her shoulders and gave a slight shake. "Surely you listened at the door?"

Her eldest sister shook her head again. "No. I have been searching for you."

And Ophelia had been sprinting all over the Rookeries, avoiding capture.

Through the terror clogging the corners of her mind, she struggled to find a semblance of rational thought. There could be any number of reasons for the investigator to be here, all of which might have nothing to do with Ophelia slipping around the Rookeries, assaulting treacherous lords.

Oh, bloody hell. What else could it be?

The wisp of a shadow flitted over the crimson satin paper. Ophelia found the small figure before he'd even stepped out of the shadows.

"'e's 'ere for me," Stephen whispered, blocking the path to their rooms. Terror spilled from his eyes. "Oi know it. It's because Oi burned down the 'ell and Sin an' almost killed Cleo and Thorne an'—"

"Shh," Ophelia whispered. Pulling free of Gertrude, she dropped to a knee beside the ashen-faced boy. "The Blacks pledged to keep that secret. They refused to involve the law." Were those assurances for him or for herself?

In his bid to end the alliance between their families and bring Cleopatra home, Stephen, who'd always had a terrifying appreciation for and ease with fire, had set one inside the rival club. What if her brother was correct and the other family had reneged? Cleopatra loved Adair Thorne and vouched for the newly forged alliance, but what if they'd all been wrong?

"Ya're scared. Oi see i-it," Stephen charged, his lower lip trembling. "Ya ain't Cleopatra. If ya were, ya wouldn't show that, and ya'd make 'im go away, an'—"

"Stephen," Gertrude admonished.

Ophelia gathered her brother by the shoulders and drew him into her arms. "Look at me," she commanded, framing his small face between her hands. Even as she knew his were the words of a hurting child who missed the sister who'd been more like a mother for him, his charges stung. "I will not let anything happen to you. Do you hear me?"

"Ya ain't a match for a constable, let alone a damned investigator," Stephen cried, wrestling against her.

Dropping her hands to his forearms, she tightened her grip upon him. Too many times he'd slunk off and couldn't be found, except on his own terms. "We do not even know why he is here." He might be here because of Stephen. *Or what if you were spotted in the streets after knocking a nob unconscious?* A chill scraped her spine at both prospects.

"Come," she said softly as he trembled. "We've outsmarted plenty of constables in our existences," she reminded him.

"That ain't a word." He dusted the back of his hand over his nose. "Don't try to distract me." With Cleopatra gone and his schooling being undertaken by Gertrude, all the Killorans remaining inside the Devil's Den had taken to infusing those lessons into his daily speech. "An' anyway, this one is different," he insisted. "This ain't any sloppy constable in the street." He dropped his voice. "This is the Hunter."

At that ominous hushed whisper, gooseflesh dotted her arms.

She looked to Gertrude.

Her sister lifted her hands and gave her head a slight shake.

Retraining her focus on Stephen, she compelled him with her gaze to say his piece.

"'e's only the most powerful investigator in London. Ruthless. 'asn't ever failed a case." A waif-thin boy, he'd always managed to slip between crowds and guests, escaping notice and gathering information. "They say 'e puts a notch in a belt whenever 'e brings a blighter in St. Giles to justice." Stephen rounded his eyes. "Say 'e has ten belts and settles for nothing less than a 'anging for the men, women, and children he catches." His pronouncement ushered in a heavy pall.

Despite herself, Ophelia shivered. "Do not be silly," she urged, for hers as much as for Stephen's benefit. "No investigator can be *that* skilled." She'd a lifetime of experience with the men in those posts to know they could be outraced, outwitted, and outplayed.

"This one is different," Stephen insisted.

They looked between one another.

Disquiet swirled through Ophelia. She had never been one for false assurances, particularly when the Killorans knew themselves to be guilty of any number of crimes. "Go to the attics, Stephen," she said quietly.

Immediately, color splotched her youngest sibling's cheeks, and his earlier nervousness was replaced by a familiar show of bravado. "Oi ain't scared of 'im!" He pounded a fist against an open palm. "'e's just a man. An' Oi'm a man marked by the Devil."

No, he was just a boy who also wore one of Diggory's scars upon him—Devil horns carved into one knee, as a vicious reminder of who his sire was.

From over his head, Ophelia caught Gertrude's eye.

Her eldest sister immediately sprang forward. Taking him by the shoulders, she pointed him to the doorway. "The attics, Stephen."

Until she ascertained for herself both why the investigator was here and just how skilled he was, she'd not take any chances.

This time Stephen went without protest . . . tangible evidence of his fear. Good. They should all be cautious.

Ophelia had not survived as long as she had in the streets of St. Giles by making faulty miscalculations, and she did not intend to now.

Certainly not for a damned investigator who knew nothing about her world.

Chapter 3

The sins and strife of St. Giles never left a person.

It just drove one in different ways.

Some were content to thieve and kill in rat-infested alleys for every last scrap.

Others rose up to become lords of the underbelly, kingpins in the cesspool of these streets.

Then others, like Connor Steele, resolved to rid London of all that evil: those men who'd prey, those women who'd lift their skirts with one hand and stab a client in the belly with the other.

He intended to leave St. Giles better than it was—an easy feat if it were not for the scum who inhabited this cursed corner of England.

Escorted into the offices of the head proprietor, Connor entered, coming face-to-face with one of those very blights on St. Giles— Broderick Killoran.

The same burly guard who'd escorted Connor in now quietly closed the door behind him.

For a long moment, Connor and the proprietor of the Devil's Den studied each other, sizing each other up in the primitive way of when men had warred with their hands and there was only room for one to emerge triumphant.

Connor's gaze was unflinching.

So this was the man Diggory had made his heir. He wore his arrogance and conceit boldly, with a loud, embroidered waistcoat revealed by his slightly gaping jacket. From the tailored sapphire frock coat to the diamond stud neatly positioned at the center of an immaculately tied cravat, Broderick Killoran fairly oozed the wealth he'd built from vice and corruption. Of all the ruthless, coldhearted bastards, Diggory had selected the one before him.

Under Connor's intense scrutiny, Killoran thinned his eyes. "Mr. Steele," he said with a street-hardened grin. "You are nothing if not persistent."

No, Connor had never been one to falter. "And you are remiss with your correspondences," he returned, dusting those words in ice. Without awaiting permission, he claimed a chair.

Killoran's expression toughened, but then that fleeting annoyance faded, his false grin in place once more. "May I offer you a brandy?" He motioned to his fully stocked sideboard.

"This is not a social call."

The casualness of Killoran's steepled fingers and the smooth grin on his face belied the hard glint in his eyes. "It is an honor to have one of London's finest investigators inside my club." He laughed as though he'd delivered the most hilarious jest. "I'm lying," he whispered. "Your being here is bad for my business."

There was a warning in the words that Connor would have to be deaf to fail to detect.

He inclined his head. "Then it would be wise to take my meetings rather than ignore my missives."

A vein bulged in the corner of Killoran's brow. "Are you threatening me?" he whispered.

"I'm explaining to you how I conduct business." Connor withdrew the small leather notepad and pencil from inside his jacket.

Killoran flicked a dismissive stare over the book. "Your business," he sneered, "does not affect me. You are neither Bow Street nor a constable. I am under no obligation to answer to you. So if you would? I have—"

"Patrons?" Connor put forth menacingly. "Men, as you pointed out, who are even now asking questions about my appearance here." That vein pulsed all the more. "You see," Connor went on, pressing his advantage, exploiting the other man's weakness, "appearances . . . they matter here. You know that. Your patrons, powerful lords, will toe the line of danger . . . but they won't cross it."

The proprietor layered his palms over the arms of his chair; those long, scarred digits curled like claws. "My patrons' safety here is assured at all times."

"Is it, though?" Connor lifted an eyebrow.

Killoran said nothing for a long moment and then cursed blackly. "What do you want?"

"I have questions for you."

Killoran reclined in his seat. "I cannot promise I have answers."

"You hire children," he said, shifting to the reason for his visit.

Killoran reached for his nearly untouched brandy. "That does not strike me in tone as a question." He swirled the contents in a smooth, fluid circle.

"All of London is aware you . . . keep children in your employ."

In your employ. Bringing them into this pit of vice and sin, a kingdom built by Mac Diggory. Loathing unfurled in his gut.

"Many establishments do," the other man pointed out, sipping at his spirits. "Are you taking umbrage at my offering employment to children? Are they better off in the streets?"

"I'm questioning where you find these children, and I'd like to speak to them."

Killoran froze, his glass pressed against his lips, and then belatedly he completed that swallow.

It was always in a person's eyes—the extent of one's evil. One's guilt or innocence. One's unease or fear. All were revealed within the glints or glimmers of one's irises.

Killoran, however, shuttered his, revealing nothing.

And it was all the more dangerous for what it suggested . . .

Complicity.

The facade of affability now gone, Killoran set down his drink hard and leaned across the desk. "What are you suggesting?" the proprietor finally asked in steely tones.

"Suggesting? I am asking questions." Connor grinned coldly. "Unless there are reasons you might feel guilty?"

A flush marred the other man's cheeks. "I hire children in need of employment, Steele. Poor ones. You want to speak to them about their pasts? Allow me to save your valuable time. They are boys and girls without families, some without names, who've done what they can to survive. If my hiring them is a crime, that is the least of my offenses."

Men who bragged over their treachery and evil . . . it was the mark of the streets, one Connor was still immersed in for the work he did, but he had separated himself from it in every other way.

"Where do you find them?"

"The streets," Killoran said with a flick of his hand.

Connor scrutinized the man across from him.

When he comes, Connor . . . you hide . . . and if there is no place to hide, you run and you never look back.

He concentrated his attention on his book, pushing back that memory. They would always be with him, and yet how much stronger they were here in this place built by the man who'd destroyed Connor . . . and those he'd loved. And now he sat before the man's former apprentice of evil and heir turned king of this dark world. Hatred singed his veins, and he lifted his head. "Who brings these boys to you?"

"One of the members of my staff is responsible for interviewing and then hiring them." That admission came as if dragged from the other man.

"Come," he scoffed. "You expect me to believe you don't do the hiring of every person who has employment here?" In East London, a man had enemies all about, ready to plunge a blade in one's back. Rising as Killoran had to kingpin of the underbelly didn't make him immune to those dangers; it increased them. "You wouldn't be foolish enough to turn that over to someone else," he said bluntly.

The ghost of a smile curled the other man's lips in his first real expression of amusement. "You don't know the 'someone else' in my employ."

"I want that someone else."

Killoran's humor died. "You aren't interviewing my staff."

"I don't need your entire staff, just the person who brings the children into your clubs."

"Go to hell," the other man spat.

"Very well." Snapping his book closed, Connor stood. "Perhaps your patrons will have answers."

The proprietor leaned forward in his seat. "I'll have you thrown out on your bloody arse before I allow you to interfere with my club," he whispered, that hushed sound more menacing than had he thundered it.

Connor grinned, a rendition of the other man's previous smile. "Killoran, I've conducted work on behalf of some of the most powerful noblemen in England and even for the king himself. Do you truly believe I cannot secure the necessary means of moving in here, should I wish, and carrying out my business?"

The color leached from Killoran's cheeks. "I'm listening," he shot back, his tone weaker, hinting at a man wise enough to know when he'd been defeated.

"I've been hired by a gentleman who is looking for his child."

It did not escape his notice that Killoran spoke over the latter question. "Who is the gentleman?"

Connor leveled a searching gaze on the other man. "That is confidential."

Several lines creased Killoran's high brow, the only marked shift in his composure. "Is it a patron?"

"What of the 'someone else'? The one who brings you your children," he asked, ignoring Killoran's question.

"They are not my children," Killoran gritted out. "They are orphans, hired by my establishment."

"Do you require my help with the overseeing of your club?"

The proprietor looked at him as though he'd sprung a second head. "You, help me?" he scoffed, and a rusty laugh startled from him.

Connor flattened his mouth. "Then do not presume to tell me how to complete my assignment."

The other man's laugh abruptly ceased.

With every moment that ticked by, however, it became increasingly clear by the proprietor's evasiveness: he was protecting someone.

But who? And to what purpose? "I'm waiting, Killoran," he said, tugging out his etched gold watch fob. He consulted the timepiece. "And I've just the one case that I am currently working on. Your move."

"There is nothing underhanded in how my"—Connor sharpened his gaze on the other man—"staff member finds these children."

"And yet you don't know how?"

"I know enough," he gritted.

"Do you know the *person* enough?" he needled.

Killoran glanced down at the clock, and then, in a dismissive movement, downed the remainder of his drink. "It seems we are at an impasse, Steele. I'll not subject any of my staff to a baseless inquiry. So if you will excuse me?" The other man shoved to his feet. "I have an establishment to run."

Connor masked his surprise. As one of the most ruthless men in St. Giles, it was no secret that Broderick Killoran had devoted himself to growing the late Diggory's already successful venture and turning it into one of the greatest clubs in England. He remained seated and, in a deliberate challenge, folded his palms and rested them on his flat belly. "I trust you've dealt with all manner of men in these streets. However, I understand you don't know me, so let me be abundantly clear. I'll have my interview . . ." He paused, letting that silence stretch on until tension pulsed in the room. "Or I'll not only secure the king's permission to do so"—a favor he'd surely grant because of his client's lineage and Connor's connection to the nobility—"but also make myself a fixture here until every last dandy, lord, or fop in London finds their pleasures elsewhere." He forced his lips into a jeering grin.

Standing outside her brother's office with her ear pressed to the door, Ophelia's stomach sank.

He knows.

There was no other accounting for the muffled words she'd managed to make sense of through the heavy slab of oak.

Dread spiraled in her breast, threatening to consume her.

And yet . . . *which* had he discovered? That Stephen, her brother the arsonist, had burned down the Hell and Sin Club twice now and, through those blazes, had also destroyed four other establishments in St. Giles?

Or does he know of your crimes a short while ago?

A man known as the Hunter. He was as ruthless as her brother and sister had whispered of a short while ago. Here only a handful of hours and he'd threaten their very security . . . just to have his interview.

Her palms moistened, and she dusted trembling fingers along the sides of her skirts.

I would rather it be me.

Nay, she'd rather it be neither of them . . . her nor Stephen.

But her young brother, jaded by his years with Diggory, still afraid to believe there could be safety and security in life, would be crushed under the evil of Newgate. There would be no recovering for him.

"So what is it to be, Killoran . . . ?"

That low, faintly lilting baritone slashed across her panicky musings.

"Who does the hiring of the children inside your club?"

Worry brought her eyes closed. Oh, God. *It is me the investigator seeks.* Coward that she was, her feet twitched with the need to take flight. Indubitably, it was an inherent part of survival existent to all in these parts. And yet Ophelia would never be one to sacrifice the possible safety and security of her kin . . . or the people dependent upon the club because of that elemental need.

Still, she briefly considered the path of escape down the opposite end of the hall, and with her gaze found Gertrude waiting, her head ducked around the corner.

Her eldest sister jammed her fingertip toward the floor. "Get over here," she mouthed.

Only . . . Ophelia had been the one to go out into the streets and find the children to employ. It was a responsibility she'd all but entreated her brother to turn over to her and he had given, despite the reservations he'd always shown toward her. Nay, reservations he'd always shown toward her and anyone who was not their capable sister Cleopatra.

And now I've gone and brought the law down upon the club.

If he hadn't been wholly determined to see her off and married before, this would assuredly seal his aspirations for Ophelia's future.

She reached for the door handle; Gertrude's gasp ricocheted around the empty halls.

Ophelia glanced over, an apology in her eyes.

"No," Gertrude silently mouthed, giving her head a firm shake. "Do not—"

Even as her sister took a flying step forward, Ophelia let herself in.

The tense discourse instantly ceased as both men were on their feet with weapons trained on the door—on her, to be specific.

The moment Broderick's gaze registered his recognition, fury that would have withered most men roared to life in his eyes.

Deliberately turning her shoulder in a disdainful rebuff of the man who threatened her and her family just by his presence here, Ophelia trained her gaze squarely on Broderick's face.

"You summoned me." She offered that as a statement.

Her brother's face turned a mottled red, and had he been any other man, the murderous rage seeping from his eyes would have sent terror through her. Broderick, however, had never lifted a hand to her or any of her siblings in violence, and she trusted him as she did her blood sisters. "No," he said slowly, a warning in his hard stare. "No. You were mistaken."

"Yes, you did."

They locked in a silent battle. She tipped up her chin.

Her brother was the first to look away.

Feeling the eyes of the investigator on her, she glanced over. "I understand . . . *y-you* . . ." Distinct, slate-grey eyes met hers squarely.

All coherent, logical thought fled.

Four inches taller and with more muscle to his powerful frame, the man before her bore little trace of the "boy who'd gotten away." Those thick, loose curls hung unfashionably about his shoulders, falling over his brow. She peered at him, willing to shove those locks back so she could find that mark, a hated one worn by too many, so she might confirm that she didn't, even now, imagine him. Even as his harsh, heavy jaw and crooked nose served as all the proof she needed. That he was real before her.

The one Diggory had been obsessed with finding and who she'd both resented and cheered for the freedom he'd found . . . until Diggory had reminded her that he always triumphed in the end.

*Ya let 'im go, ya fucking fool . . . ya'll pay for it . . . Now, to make
you pay.*

Her fingers curled reflexively. All these years she'd believed he'd been
hanged, saving her. Ultimately, that last exchange with him had brought
down Diggory's fury and seen Gertrude beaten and then blinded. And
for the weight of guilt that had followed her, there was a peace in knowing that Connor had survived. "You are alive," she whispered.

The ghost of a smile graced his lips. "And should I not be . . .
Miss . . . ?" He spared a questioning look for her brother.

"Ophelia?" At her brother's perplexity, she blinked slowly.

Then a wild rush of color blazed across her cheeks. "Forgive me.
I . . . You had a familiar look," she finished lamely. It was a lie. With his
swarthy features and gypsy looks, he was unlike any she'd ever known.
All the while she peered at the towering figure beside her brother,
searching through that tangle of black curls over his brow for the mark
that would give the most definitive confirmation.

"Allow me to present," Broderick gritted out, "my sister Ophelia
Killoran."

"Your . . . sister?" He curled a dry edge around those two words
that called her brother a liar . . . because, of course, having lived on
the streets, he very well knew the Diggory-gang girls had never had a
protective older brother about.

"Yes," she snapped, taking a step forward. Just like that, the inso-
lence of Connor O'Roarke, who'd always thought himself their better,
raged to life. "I am his *sister*." She might not have Broderick's blood in
her veins, but he'd been like a father when her own had no use of her
other than the coins she could earn and as a convenient figure to whip
about when angry or frustrated.

Once more, her perceptive brother did not miss the palpable
tension between Ophelia and Connor. Frowning, he moved his stare
back and forth between them. He finally spoke. "Mr. Steele is an

investigator who has questions about the children we've employed in the club."

"Is he?" she snorted, and the ghost of a dangerous frown hovered on the hard flesh of Connor's lips. Ignoring that latter part, she focused on the lie her brother had unwittingly uttered. "Mr. *Steele*," she greeted, placing a heavy emphasis on that name she knew to be false.

His gaze narrowed all the more. "I had questions for the man who does the hiring of the children here."

Her insides twisted into vicious, painful knots, and just like that, she was recalled to the purpose of his being here. "The *man* who does the hiring?" she asked coolly.

Broderick regained his footing as they connected with a shared mockery for the interloper endangering all they'd built. He tossed his arms wide. "Allow me to present *her*."

Connor narrowed his eyes. "You would be the first proprietor I've dealt with who's ever given such responsibility to a woman."

Her brother smiled, and unlike the practiced gestures of before, this contained a whisper of mirth. "I am the only proprietor to have sisters like I do."

In a bid to hide the tremble to her fingers, Ophelia dropped her hands on her hips. "What do you want?"

Connor honed his piercing gaze on her face, and for an uncharacteristic moment of cowardice, she wished she'd remained silent. Wished she hadn't taunted this older, harder, more unforgiving version of the boy she'd kept safe. Then he spoke. "I would like a meeting."

That was all? Brother and sister exchanged a look. It could never be that simple. Not with any man on his side of the law.

Broderick's mouth went taut, and he reached reluctantly for his chair.

"With your sister," Connor said coolly. "Alone."

"Absolutely not," Broderick barked. The muscles bunched under his sleeves; he was a man prepared to fight.

Were it any other man before them, she would have not doubted Broderick's ultimate triumph. But two inches taller, and with a solid wall of muscle, in this man Broderick had met his match. As if in silent testament to that supposition, Connor flicked a restrained, bored glance at the other man.

She gnashed her teeth. He'd always been a blight upon her existence. "You have twenty minutes," she announced. "Leave us, Broderick."

Chapter 4

It was her hair.

It may as well have been a calling card, as defining as it was of the young woman before him.

With hair so pale it was nearly white hanging loose about her back, there was an ethereal, otherworldly quality to her.

Aye, such hair would forever make it an impossibility for the spitfire to have anonymity . . . anywhere, regardless of the passage of time.

If there had been any doubt, however, that the woman before Connor was anyone other than the girl loyal to Diggory, who nonetheless had spared Connor's life, the effortless way she ordered Broderick Killoran from the room, and his compliance, served as all the confirmation Connor needed.

Killoran paused as he reached Connor's side. "You have twenty minutes." With a sharp, warning look at Connor that promised death, he stalked from the room.

As soon as he'd gone, Ophelia Killoran drifted closer, all the while keeping a slight distance between them.

She walked a slow path around him, the same girl who'd caught him unawares more times than he'd deserved to survive, assessing him with her clear blue eyes, watching.

Her incisive stare periodically returned to his brow.

Through her scrutiny, Connor remained motionless. In the past he'd lived in the shadows, carefully skirting all members of the Diggory gang. Frankly, his life would have been forfeit had he been discovered.

As such, he'd studied them all—including this woman before him.

Ophelia Killoran had been angrier, fiercer, and more terrifying as a slip of a child than most grown men in St. Giles. She proved all that and tenfold as a woman. And while she examined him, he used the opportunity to study her in return.

He passed his gaze over her satin-draped figure; the fine lace trim of an expensive gown was better suited for a lady than any common street pickpocket. Though a hideous shade of brown, there could be no mistaking the quality of that modest dress. Nay, she'd done more than survived. She'd flourished and thrived as one of the Diggory gang. He trailed his gaze up and down her tall frame. Just a handful of inches shy of six feet, she was a medieval warrioress. Her gown clung to a generous bosom, trim waist, and lush curves that would make a saint into a sinner.

Nor had Connor ever been confused with the former.

His breath stuck oddly as once more the truth pierced him— Ophelia Killoran was no longer the snapping child of the streets but had grown into a carnal siren. Hers was the haunting beauty that those foolish sailors would thrash themselves happily against rocks for should she wish it.

She finally stopped, a mere handbreadth between them.

Her large crimson lips curved up in a smirk, and that cynical expression suited to one twenty years her senior knocked out the lustful musings. "Steele, is it now?"

He touched an imagined brim, specifically that spot where he'd been marked as a mere boy of eight, revealing his scar. "If it is not Lagertha," he murmured. A lifetime ago it had been a utilitarian name he'd given this woman. Back when she refused to share her real one with him, he'd assigned her one. One that had been drawn from old books read to him by his mother.

Lagertha—*Ophelia*—had survived. A ball of emotion stuck in his throat.

These streets aren't yars . . . they'll never be yars . . . now go before he foinds the both of us.

Coming around him, she hitched herself up onto the edge of her brother's desk, an incongruity of lady and street rat. "Last I saw of you, you were carted off. Never to be seen again," she said. Her hushed, smoky tones barely reached his ears, and he drifted closer.

How different this sultry woman's tones were from the guttural Cockney of her childhood years.

He stopped with the leather winged chair between them and placed his scarred palms along the back. "Did you look for me?" He met her question with one of his own.

Her eyes darkened. "Why would I have looked for you?" she asked with nothing more than a faint curiosity so that he may have imagined that fleeting grimness.

And more . . . why should he have asked? The question, irrelevant to the case he'd taken on, hung on his lips and remained unspoken.

"Why would you?" he murmured to himself. God, she'd always been more stubborn than a mule. She'd not give him a single answer, and he knew Ophelia enough over the years to know they'd stand here until the earth ceased spinning before she ceded a proverbial inch. "I'm an investigator now."

"An investigator," she repeated, those two words rolling from her tongue as if foreign ones she puzzled through and, by the souring of her expression, had found wanting. "*You* became an investigator."

"That is so hard to believe?"

She lifted her shoulder in a defiant shrug. "Given the last I saw of you, you were stuck between a nob and a constable, yes, it is."

He searched for a hint of undeserved regret or guilt from that long-ago day, but her expression was as empty as a slab of uncarved stone.

She leaned forward, her long, graceful neck arched as she strained toward him. "How did you get away?" Silver flecks within her irises glittered.

In other words, how had he escaped the filth of St. Giles and eluded a ruthless Mac Diggory? "Luck." He finally settled for that vague but accurate reply. "Which I trust you know something of." He glanced pointedly about the mahogany Chippendale furniture better suited to a nobleman's Mayfair offices than to a gaming hell . . . and then Connor touched his eyes on her fine gown.

The young woman followed his stare, briefly grazing her fingertips along the lace overlay at her flat stomach. Those long digits fluttered back to her lap and curled into defensive fists.

"After all, your brother is now the owner of Mac Diggory's impressive gaming establishment," he persisted.

"Yes, it would seem we've both been . . . lucky."

Adopted by the same man he'd rescued Ophelia from, and supplied with tutors and a Cambridge education, Connor had certainly made out better than most any other child in East London. He knew that. And was grateful every day for the gift he'd been given that day outside the Covent Garden Theatre.

"Is this why you're here?" she asked, sotto voce. "To fondly chat over the past and reminisce over lost years?" Ophelia looked briefly across the room to the clock ticking away louder than their actual words. "Because you're already down five minutes, Mr. *Steele*."

Connor drifted around the chair until they stood so close their knees touched. "I'm searching for a child."

Her shoulders went back. "A child?"

Whatever she'd been expecting, it had not been that.

"Did you think I'd come to bring you and your kin to justice for past crimes?" Committed so they might survive. Ruthless acts he himself was as guilty of as any member of the late Diggory's gang.

She leaned forward. "How adorably naive of you," she said. The scent of her apple blossoms conjured the fields of his father's property in Lythe Valley. "To assume the Killorans are now free of sin."

"Still attempting to intimidate me, Ophelia Killoran," he murmured, trailing his gaze over the heart-shaped face that had always been set in a perpetual scowl.

She quickly drew back, retreating. "Four and ten minutes," she warned, her husky contralto gruff.

Connor reached into his pocket and withdrew the notepad and pencil tucked away there. "I'm looking for a child," he repeated, opening the book.

"Yes, you said as much." She followed his movements guardedly. "And you believe me and my family guilty of an underhanded operation of harming children?"

"That was your *brother's* assumption," he clarified. Though every instinct that had served him well since his parents' murder told him she would not harm a small boy or girl, from his own dark existence he well knew what any person was capable of. "I merely explained I had questions about the person responsible for bringing the boys and girls inside this establishment."

"Man."

Connor creased his brow.

Ophelia angled her head back to better meet his stare. "You wanted to put questions to the man responsible. Not person."

She missed nothing.

It was why she'd endured. Always tripping up one's opponent was the key to survival in St. Giles, and her presence here, despite the peril she—they—had faced, was a mark of her strength. It was also likely why her brother had ceded responsibilities over to her when nearly all men—regardless of station or birthright—rarely entrusted women with any.

"How long have you been accountable for hiring the children employed here?" With Diggory dead only these past four years, she could not have found herself with power during his reign of terror.

A muscle in her jaw twitched. "Just a handful of months."

Questions swirled. If she'd only recently taken on that task for the club, what had been her role before that?

"I suggest if you have another question, you ask it, O'Roarke. Ten minutes," she warned, ticking down his remaining time allotted.

"Steele," he quietly corrected. Connor O'Roarke had been reborn again under the care of the Earl of Mar; the name of his birth represented a connection to the darkest time in his life and the evil he'd carried out to survive.

"Ah, yes, of course," she said, as if she could see. As if she knew. When she didn't. When no one, not even his adoptive father, could begin to speculate about the horrors that linked back to that birth name. "A fancy investigator now. Are you trying to erase the streets from yourself, Steele?" she persisted, dangerously accurate in her supposition. "Still haven't figured it out, have you?"

She was baiting him. It was there in the spitfire's eyes and tone and insolent smile.

Do not take it . . . do not take it.

"I trust you intend to tell me, Miss Killoran?" he asked with that same rash impulsiveness he'd managed to quell over the years that had seen him rush headfirst into Mac Diggory as a boy of eight, riddled with rage.

"It will always be part of you. No matter"—Ophelia flicked at the lapel of his jacket—"the fine garments you wear," she taunted.

He'd always thought himself better than Ophelia and her family.

He'd believed himself better than any of the people in St. Giles.

When everyone well knew one's survival was dependent upon the bonds formed with other unlucky souls in the streets, he'd slunk off and lived on his own, a phantom in the shadows that Diggory had failed to bring to heel.

Now, with his finely tailored double-breasted tailcoat, he'd stand inside her family's home and put questions to her like she was again in the streets and he with the influence to bring her down.

Always keep 'em 'appy . . . Don't give 'em anything other than pretty words.

It was one of the earliest instructions beaten into her by Diggory when she'd been trained for her assignment as a palm reader. And if the miserable blighter were still drawing breath, in this instance he would have bloodied her senseless for engaging an investigator within this club.

By the slight flaring of his nostrils, there could be no doubting—she'd insulted Connor O'Roarke. Or Steele. Or whatever else he went by these days.

"Was that admonition for me? Or yourself, *Lagertha*," he murmured.

Lagertha. Until now, she'd forgotten the name he'd assigned her in the streets. Unnamed by Diggory, Connor O'Roarke had unwittingly given Ophelia her first. Secretly, she'd craved that identifying gift. Only now he uttered those three syllables in a low voice, even deeper, but smooth like that warmed chocolate her brother had spoiled Ophelia and her siblings with when he'd first taken ownership of the Devil's Den.

She blinked slowly.

What madness was this, waxing on about Connor O'Roarke's bloody voice?

A flush crept up her cheeks. "Bugger off, Connor." She knew precisely what she was. She knew the stench of the streets would remain upon her skin no matter how many times she bathed or how much fragrance she dabbed on her person. "Ask whatever questions you have, and get yarself off," she snapped, slipping into her coarse Cockney.

He narrowed his eyes. "I am looking for a child."

"One? In all of London?" she snorted, giving him a once-over. "You might be the skilled investigator they say, or you may not, but you expect to find one child gone missing?"

"He is a marquess's son," he said quietly.

Ophelia opened and closed her mouth several times. *Well.* She hurried to mask her surprise. "Is that supposed to impress me?" She hopped down from her perch and wandered over to the windows that looked out onto the same streets upon which she'd once slept. Peeling the edge of the curtain back, she passed her gaze over the rain-dampened cobblestones. When she spoke, she infused a boredom into her tone. "And here I thought it was only the rotters of East London who went about *losing* their children." Which invariably was what drunken da's and ma's who didn't need another mouth to feed did with their babes. Conveniently lost them or left them or sold them, uncared for, prey for the Mac Diggorys of the world.

"He has reason to believe his son was not lost. He believes the boy was stolen."

The floorboards groaned, indicating Connor had moved.

From his reflection in the crystal windowpanes, Ophelia followed his relaxed steps. In this instance, with those slow, languid movements, lazy enough to trip an unsuspecting prey into misstep, he was very much the Hunter her siblings had earlier spoken of.

This Connor O'Roarke—lethal, with power and influence to his name and five stone more in the weight of muscle to his person—was far more dangerous than the street rat she'd saved who'd then returned the favor.

"And you believe we stole this child?" she asked carefully, keeping the annoyance from her tone. He'd accuse her of the same type of evil Mac Diggory had demonstrated.

"I believe members of Diggory's gang were, and remain, children of the streets. That has not changed with his death."

She stiffened, and avoiding his gaze in the panel, Ophelia trained her stare on the dandy below stumbling up the steps through the rain. The doors were thrown open, admitting the inebriated fop. The raucous din of drunken revelry spilled out, climbing to where she stood, before those heavy panels closed once more.

They hadn't known each other, Ophelia and Connor. Not truly. Theirs had been fleeting moments where their paths had crossed and their exchanges kept short for what discovery would have entailed—for the both of them. Yet his willingness to believe her capable of such treachery grated.

She released the curtain, and it fluttered back into place. "And this nobleman?" she asked, turning back to face Connor. "He simply lost his child."

"Seven years ago."

She choked. "Seven years?"

He confirmed that query with a nod.

"Seven years a nob's son's been missing, and you truly believe he survived here?" she asked incredulously. "In St. Giles?" Ophelia gave her head a bemused shake. "Then you are even more foolishly optimistic than you were as a boy."

"Why?" he tossed out. "Because I thought I could survive without Diggory? Because I thought I could escape? When I did just that?"

His words struck like a lance to the chest. For she *had* believed him a fool. Had urged him back into the fold of Diggory's gang because a life on the run from him would have seen Connor O'Roarke with a fate worse than death. In the end it was as he'd said . . . he had escaped.

While you remained, a prisoner, until the day the bastard died.

Bitter, she glanced beyond his shoulder. "So the child has been missing seven years," she said, dragging out the reluctant words. "Who is the father?"

Connor hesitated.

She folded her arms at her chest. "You come here, threaten my family and club, put questions to me, and don't feel you need answer any of mine in return?" A sound of disgust escaped her. "My God, you are as insolent as ever, Connor O'Roarke," she said, purposefully using the name he'd once gone by.

She made to step around him, but Connor shot out a hand, catching her gently by the forearm.

Ophelia started; odd little shivers moved through her at that bold touch. She went absolutely still, transfixed by his hand upon her person: large, coarsened fingers belonging to a man unafraid of work but also surprisingly gentle in his hold.

"I am asking for your assistance, Ophelia," he said in quiet tones.

"Who is he?" she repeated.

Connor released her. "He is"—something flashed in his eyes— "something of a recluse."

"A recluse," she repeated slowly. There was more there.

His expression closed up. "I don't discuss the details of my case with anyone."

She jutted out her chin. "I'm not just anyone. I'll have his name, Connor."

He remained mutinously silent.

As a boy making his own way in the streets, he'd always been a stubborn blighter. He proved even more so now. "I can find out everything without your providing another detail," she snapped. "Or mayhap we should just call this the end of our meeting?" Ophelia took a step toward the door.

"Wait," Connor called out, staying her.

She faced him once more. "Well?"

A muscle twitched at the corner of his mouth. "I've been hired by the Marquess of Maddock."

She searched her mind and came up empty. "I've never heard of him." The gent wasn't a member of her family's clubs, and those gentlemen were the only lords she knew or cared anything about.

Connor looked her squarely in the eyes. "Lord Maddock was accused of murdering his family."

She swallowed wrong and dissolved into a choking fit. "F-forgive me," she sputtered without a hint of true remorse there. "You come here on some noble bid to unite a child with a father who is purported to have murdered that same child?" Ophelia continued, not allowing him a chance to edge in a word. "My, Connor Steele, how very far you've come in the world. From street rat to hand for the nobs."

Ire flared in his eyes—a burning, seething sentiment so strong her bravado faltered. Ophelia took a hasty step away from the towering figure until her back rattled the crystal panes. She swallowed around a sudden, unwelcome ball of unease in her throat. After all, what did she truly know of Connor O'Roarke? Yes, they'd moved within the same streets, but they'd never truly been allies, or friends, or even really acquaintances. She skittered a nervous gaze to the door. Broderick was there. One shout from her and he'd bring hell and fury down on Connor's dark head, regardless of the other man's connection to the prince, the king, or any peer in between.

When he at last spoke, she braced for a derisive response but was brought up short once more. "You don't like me," he said. His voice suited a curious scholar puzzling through an ancient text. "You never did."

No, she'd hated him. Resented him. He'd looked after only himself. He'd never cared about finding friends or family in the other boys and girls who'd been subjected to the same fate as he had been. *Or do you hate him for having managed what you were unable to?*

Fighting back that useless, silly question, she tilted up her chin.

"And now you'd judge me. Why?" he asked. "For the work I do?"

"On behalf of the peerage," she spat.

"On behalf of what is right," he corrected.

A jaded laugh tore from her lips. "A murderer?" she managed around her dark amusement. "By your own accounts, you aren't doing the work of what is right." What did that even mean in the world they'd been born to? "You are doing it for a man with powerful connections." *Just like my brother would kiss the feet of the peerage.*

Unnerved, she swatted the thought back.

Connor passed a long, sad, lingering look over her . . . and contained within his smoky-grey eyes was something more—pity.

It soured her belly, that sentiment. She brought her shoulders back.

"The marquess was exonerated of any wrongdoing," he said quietly.

"Power and influence can buy anything." She paused for emphasis. "*Including* a pardon for killing one's family."

"A fire claimed the lives of his wife and unborn child. He believes his son lived."

She drew her brows together. Set blazes had been one of Diggory's calling cards, and yet he'd not dared enter the fancy ends of Mayfair and Grosvenor. He'd been content with the empire he'd carved out of East London. "How old was the boy?" she asked reluctantly.

"Just three."

"A babe," she murmured. She gave her head a pitying shake. "Then if he is not a murderer, the gentleman is delusional. For no babe could have escaped a fire when his wife was unable to." Ophelia spared another glance at the clock. His allotted time was nearly up.

She took a step toward the door, but Connor matched her movements, blocking her.

"He doesn't believe he escaped," Connor said quietly.

"Well, then, I suspect that is the quickest assignment you've ever handled. Case closed." She took another step.

He prevented her escape once more. "He believes the fire was intentionally set and the child stolen."

That gave her pause. Stolen children and deliberately lit blazes were as routine in her world as Sunday sermons were in the world of the nobility. And yet . . . "It is impossible," she finally said. "Diggory was many things." Cruel. Violent. Evil. "But he was not stupid. He knew better than to torch a nob's residence, and he certainly wasn't fool enough that he'd nick a child."

Ya 'elped 'im escape, ya little bitch . . . ya want to know wot 'appens if ya do that again, girl.

The whistle of a lash sailing through the air, and then the crack of it striking flesh, slid around her mind like a venomous serpent, spreading the poisonous memories of long ago.

Bile churned in her belly, and she forcibly swallowed it back as it climbed her throat. "We're done here," she said flatly, wanting Connor and every last hated, unwanted memory he'd roused with his talk of Diggory gone.

"We're not," he countered, blocking her retreat once more.

She tossed up her hands in exasperation. "Even if Diggory was involved, it was years ago. Nearly all of the men and women who served under his command are either dead, imprisoned, or turned out by my brother. No one is here who would recall a babe from seven years ago, Connor," she said impatiently. "Or any babe, for that matter." Diggory had employed ruthless fiends who cared for nothing but their own survival.

"But you and your family know children of that age." He honed his gaze on her face. "The boys and girls who belonged to Diggory's gang, others you're responsible for hiring . . . How many years are they generally, Ophelia?"

They were near in age to the missing child he sought. She went tight-lipped. Did he think she'd betray anyone in her family's employ simply because he did the work of a nobleman?

Connor dipped his head close. The hint of bergamot and sage filled her nostrils, flooding her senses with the crisp masculinity of it. So very different from the drunken patrons with liquor on their breath and sweat on their skin.

"Well?" he urged, and that prodding broke that maddening pull.

"You're on a fool's quest for a case that cannot be solved. The child is dead." This time Ophelia slipped out from behind him and started for the door.

"What if he's not?" Connor called after her, staying her movements. "What if the child is alive and is even now living on the streets or employed in this very club?"

The possibility whispered around her mind. A child with a future outside this world—safe, cherished, pampered. Everything she and her sisters never had been.

He spoke of elusive gifts, more dreams than reality for those in St. Giles.

"It would be impossible to even know, Mr. Steele," she said, erecting a wall of formality between them. "It would be finding a proverbial needle in a meadow." She tightened her mouth. "And given what you've revealed about your employer, it is a needle that would be better off hidden."

"You don't know that," he shot back.

Your kind always wants it. Ophelia clenched her hands into fists. "I know enough about the nobility."

He scoffed. "Because you see them lose their fortunes at your tables?"

He knew nothing, this smug bastard before her. "Go to hell, Connor," she said, her throat thick. She made to step around him, but he blocked her path once more.

"The marquess, as you said, is likely wrong, and yet there is the slight chance he is correct. You claim it is impossible to know whether the child is alive, but if I put questions to the children who've belonged to Diggory's gang, I'll possibly learn something."

She gnashed her teeth. "My God, you are unrelenting." And how easily he trusted an exonerated lord. "You think I can help? Why? Because we have children in our employ? *Many* clubs do," she went on before he could speak. "The Hell and Sin, to name one." As soon as the name of that rival establishment slipped out, she bit her tongue hard.

"I've already questioned the owners there. They also allowed me free access to speak with each member of their staff."

Of course they had. What else had they revealed?

She searched him for signs of knowing about her brother's actions, but Connor's face remained a carved mask, a study in chiseled stone.

Ophelia held his piercing stare. "Continue your search elsewhere, Mr. Steele; I know how to locate children of these streets no better and no less than anyone else." It was a blatant lie she tossed him. She knew St. Giles and the Dials together better than she did the lines on her palm. "Even if I did, I'll be damned if I aid you and a nob accused of murder." Ophelia knew firsthand the treachery those lords were capable of.

She curled her hands into tight fists.

That is it. Open your legs for me . . . let me slip it in.

Her breath came loudly.

Connor interrupted her tortured memories. "You and I both know your claims aren't altogether true. As part of Diggory's gang, you are in far greater possession of information than most."

Diggory. The demon who'd spawned her. A hatred so sharp buffeted her senses, proving her very much the Devil's daughter for the darkness within her. "Then, speak to my sister Cleo. I trust she'll prove more accommodating." The very one who'd abandoned St. Giles and effortlessly established a new life in Grosvenor Square.

She turned to go.

"According to your brother, Mrs. Thorne was never the one responsible for hiring the child staff. *You* are."

"We're done here." She cursed him all over again for forcing her past upon her. She swept over to the door. "Now if you will excuse me?

It is late, and a man mindful of societal ways should honor respectable calling hours."

On perfect cue, the door opened.

Her brother filled the doorway, a steady, reassuring presence in the face of the tumult roused by Connor O'Roarke.

Connor lingered, his jaw muscles moving.

What did he wish to say? To challenge her? To threaten her? She braced for it. Welcomed it. Because it was those ruthless sentiments she recognized and knew how to handle.

He nodded once, proving as frustratingly unpredictable as ever. "Miss Killoran," he murmured and, not sparing a glance for Broderick, stalked off.

Yet as he left, why could she not shake the unease slithering around that she'd not seen the last of Connor O'Roarke?

Chapter 5

One.

Two.

Three.

Four.

Five.

"What in blazes was that?" her brother exploded.

Ophelia yawned. "Do you know you are unarguably predictable with the amount of time you wait for a person to leave before you begin speaking? At the very least, you can vary your number count. Of course"—she nibbled at the tip of her finger—"Mr. Steele is a stranger, so he surely doesn't yet know all your nuances, but—"

"For the love of all that is holy, Ophelia, would you be silent?" he barked.

"You certainly shouldn't be yelling," she scolded, wagging a finger. "Why, if I know investigators, they'll move at a snail's pace so they might linger and listen."

Her brother immediately went tight-lipped.

As strong as Broderick was, and for all the power he'd amassed, he had still not been born to the streets as Ophelia and her blood siblings had. Though Broderick did not speak of his past, and had certainly never confirmed or verified her suspicions, he needn't have. His appreciation for the nobility and his periodic missteps marked him one not wholly of this world.

Since the day he'd entered their midst with his fancy speech, she'd known precisely what to say to push him to the brink.

One. Two. Three. Four—

"First"—he stuck up a finger—"you are never again to storm into my meetings. Are we clear?"

She silently noted his amended counting. That was why Broderick had found himself accepted and then respected amongst Diggory's gang. For anything he hadn't known, he'd committed himself to learning and then changing as he needed for his own survival.

She folded her arms. "Do you truly believe I'm one who'll take to being ordered about?"

Naturally, that was always the limited opinion the world—her brother included—had of her. A pretty face and little more, only recently charged with meaningful responsibilities.

"I was being truthful with him, Broderick," she protested as he beat a path over to the sideboard. "I was not meekly accepting his midnight appearance as his due and his insulting questions of how I conduct myself, hiring the children I do." She leveled him with a stare. "Not from Mr. O—Steele."

"You are familiar with Steele?"

Her mind stuttered to a stop. What had he heard? Or had he picked up on that slight misstep when she'd entered the offices and first caught sight of Connor? Ophelia wet her lips. "I . . ." She shook her head, unable to get words out. Broderick grabbed a bottle of whiskey, assessed the label, and then poured himself a drink. She gave thanks for his distracted movements. What was she to do? Admit her connection to

Connor O'Roarke? Explain that in helping him escape Diggory, it had been not Ophelia who'd paid the price but another of their beloved siblings? And now Connor was back in their lives—a threat to the Killoran world.

After he'd set aside the bottle, Broderick shot her a puzzled look.

She scoffed. "Of course I don't know him," she lied through her teeth. "How would *I* know a detective?" And more . . . how had he become the ruthless investigator feared by all in their years apart? How, when their kind dealt in vices that destroyed men and did not serve on the side of law that sought to bring justice to an unjust world?

"You wouldn't." He paused, midselection of a bottle. Her brother briefly lifted his head and tossed her a penetrating glance over his shoulder. "Unless you were in trouble with the law."

Which she had been countless times. This, however, was not one of them. "I'm not," she snapped. "You know my role. I find children to work here." As she spoke, she neatly left out the truth of *how* she located some of the young ones in their employ. "And that's the extent of my involvement." Her sole focus was on saving them from the perils that existed for orphans. From there, those boys and girls fell to Gertrude's care.

Broderick lingered a probing stare over her.

She forced herself to go absolutely still under his scrutiny.

At last he returned his attention to the sideboard. "I assigned you that role in the club." He grabbed a decanter and considered it. "I did not, however, give you carte blanche to insult an investigator who could ruin us," he muttered, settling on the French cognac.

He poured himself a drink. "It is in our best interest not to anger the man threatening our club."

His was a valid point. And yet . . . "We know nothing, and as such have no reason to fear him."

He scoffed. "Surely you don't believe that? Do you think a bloody investigator would trust one of us?"

No, she didn't. Particularly not Connor O'Roarke. Having moved within their gang and then escaped, Connor knew precisely the type of people Ophelia and her siblings were. "It doesn't matter that he would not find anything." For he wouldn't. In this, they'd done nothing. "If he so wishes, he could cast aspersions upon the club that we wouldn't recover from."

A shadow settled over her brother's eyes. Then where would they be? It hung real and unspoken between them.

Ruined. They would be ruined.

She shivered. For they might have the luxuries of the Devil's Den as their residence, but when they set foot onto the streets, war raged all around, and they were even less safe than they'd been years earlier before their climb to security. They could not go back to that.

"This is why you should not have stormed in." His jaw flexed. "Damn your impulsivity."

That stung. It was a condemnation that had never, nor would ever, be tossed out at Cleopatra. *Cleopatra would never taunt and bait a detective. She'd know better.*

Shoving aside that needling thought, Ophelia planted her hands on her hips. "He asked if I knew anything. I told him I did not," she said, impatience slipping in.

From over the rim of his glass, he frowned. "He will return with questions for you."

At that ominous prediction, an eerie echo of her earlier thoughts, another shiver iced Ophelia's spine.

Her brother shook his head and, with an air of finality, strode over to his desk and sat. "It is time."

"Very well." Ophelia turned, relieved to be done with this exchange. Her stinging palms still required tending, and her brother still had not noted the injury.

"You misunderstand me," Broderick called after her.

She continued on, but his words registered, bringing her to a slow stop. Warning bells went off in the back of her mind. Ophelia turned. "What is that?" she asked guardedly, fearing . . . and knowing, all at the same time. Her palms made reflexive fists, and she winced as her nails grazed the wounded flesh.

"We require that match, and you fielding questions from an investigator"—Broderick took a sip, the insolent calm of him setting her teeth on edge—"will help nothing. It will only hurt." He met her gaze. "His presence here has only highlighted our need for noble connections."

There it was.

All the air left her on a whoosh.

As he sat sipping his brandy and wisely avoiding her eyes, the weight of his betrayal hit her squarely in the chest.

Of course, it had been inevitable. She'd always known his plans and intentions . . . for her and the entire family. And yet, with the additional responsibilities he'd ceded, she'd been lulled into a false sense of peace.

As her brother set aside his drink in favor of a sheet of parchment and pen, Ophelia watched on, feeling like a voyeur in someone else's life.

That rapid click of his pen struck the page over and over, near deafening in the thick silence, until she wanted to clamp her hands over her ears.

She, who'd not fainted after some blighter had cornered her in an alleyway and yanked up her skirts, or faltered when Diggory had beaten her senseless for an imagined slight, felt her legs shift under her. "What?" she whispered breathlessly, the steady beat of her heart drowning out that muffled demand.

"It's overdue, Ophelia," he said, not deigning to glance up from the task that occupied him. "You know that."

Ophelia surged forward. Planting her palms on the surface of his desk, she leaned forward. "I will not do it." In that, mayhap, she'd proven the reason all power and confidence had been given to Cleopatra. For even she had attempted to fulfill the expectations Broderick had for their family.

Broderick lifted his gaze not higher than her white-knuckled grip. "Very well."

Very well? She furrowed her brow. She'd not survived by being lulled into a false sense of security. The one time she had, it had found her against a wall and a nobleman with his hands under her skirts.

Her mouth went dry as the hated memory slipped in. She desperately fought it back.

Focus. Do not let him in . . . not now . . . not when my brother has waged war and I need my wits about me.

Ophelia slowly straightened. "Very well?" she repeated, examining him closely.

"Yes. Very well, you may oversee your responsibilities, and you are absolved of joining Cleopatra and . . . and"—he grimaced—"her husband for the London Season."

Under any other circumstances she would have found hilarity in his inability to bring himself 'round to using the name of their longtime rival and now brother-in-law, Adair Thorne. "It cannot be that easy." He'd never abandon his goals.

"Yes. Sometimes it can." He grabbed his glass and took a long swallow. "This is one of those times," he said after he'd set the tumbler down.

Her heart quickened. Ophelia swept her lashes low. "What game do you play?"

"*This* is no game," he pledged, adding his flourishing signature to the bottom of that sheet.

She'd have to be deaf not to hear the emphasis placed there, one that suggested they spoke of something so much more than a London Season and her being spared from taking part in it.

As he lifted the lid from the crystal bottle and sprinkled pounce upon the ink, Ophelia squinted, attempting to bring those words into focus.

Cleo,
Tomorrow, I will be sending . . .

Ophelia saw, tasted, and heard red. It flooded every corner of her, an all-consuming fury and rage. With Cleo recently married, Broderick had wasted no time. She whipped her head up so sharply the muscles wrenched down her neck. "Gertrude?" she screeched, trying to order her spiraling-out-of-control thoughts.

Broderick flicked his hand. "In the event you are unable to join Polite Society, Gertrude indicated she would spare you from going and see to it herself."

"Did you just . . . flick your hand?" That callous gesture restored order to her jumbled mind.

He'd sacrifice Gertrude . . . Gertrude, who'd already lost so much. *Because of me . . . she lost so much because of me.*

He wisely lowered his palm. "I have already spoken to her."

"I don't believe you," she shot back. He'd ceded even less control to their eldest sister than he had to Ophelia. His was surely nothing more than a street trick to gain her acquiescence. "When did you speak?"

"After Cleo's wedding."

She rocked back, feeling like one who'd taken a bullet to the chest. They had spoken of it then. They had both assumed Ophelia, with her disdain for the peerage, would be unable to move forward with Broderick's plan and discussed Gertrude's alternate role?

Bitterness tasted like vinegar in her mouth.

First Cleopatra should have their brother's ear, and now he'd bypass Ophelia for Gertrude. It didn't matter that Gertrude was the eldest; it mattered that Ophelia had forever been overlooked by all—her blasted kin included.

What was worse . . . they'd both believed she would be unable to go through with something, and another would have to act in her stead. She fell back a step, and another, and another, and then stopped her retreat.

Frantically, she scraped her gaze over Broderick's immaculate office. How to make him see that it was not about her being unable to enter the world of Polite Society. It was about having a choice. Choosing something more than a path Broderick thought was their only one. Choosing a future of purpose that she made for herself. Simply . . . choosing.

But did it truly matter?

For now she'd been given the ultimate choice—control of her fate and future, or to sacrifice her sister Gertrude.

Ophelia made a final attempt at reasoning with him. "Why is this so important to you?" she pleaded. "We have wealth. We have power."

"And we have already seen how easily it can crumble," he put forward with an uncharacteristic gravity.

The Hell and Sin. First by the proprietors' marriage to ladies of the *ton* . . . and then by fire.

She looked away.

The quiet shuffle of her brother folding that page that would seal her sister's fate was the only sound.

Ophelia closed her eyes.

The obstinate part of her that had never bowed to him or anyone wanted to tell him to go hang. And yet there was something else there, too: fear. Her stomach muscles clenched, and she folded her hands over her belly to ease the tension there.

Her efforts proved futile.

Could she do it? Could she bind herself to a nobleman? One of those lecherous, vile lords? Her chest moved up and down quickly with the force of her rapidly drawn breaths.

Take 'is lordship back there and read 'is palms. Yar da would wont it . . . Get back there.

Ophelia's gaze went to that glass of spirits on Broderick's desk as past lines blurred with present ones, together melding to create a horrifying future.

The stench of brandy. A hand scrabbling with her skirts.

You want it, my lovely. Now spread your legs for me . . . Ah, you like it rough, then, do you? Even better.

Ophelia's breath rasped loudly in her ears.

"Ophelia?"

Broderick's concern-laden tone yanked her back from the brink.

What is he saying? What are we debating?

Then it came back to her. Connor's visit . . . and the chore her brother would turn over to Gertrude.

Nay, he'd do so only if Ophelia was unwilling.

I'm going to be ill.

She focused on Broderick's lips as they moved but could not make sense of the words coming out.

Rubbing the ache at her temples, she wandered over to the windows. Peeling back the rich gold-brocade curtains, she looked out into those darkened streets she'd raced through only a short while ago.

Her brother would bind Gertrude or Ophelia to one of those reprobates. Men who took their pleasures where they would. She pressed her forehead against the cool pane.

Ultimately, her brother would not be swayed. He might speak of Connor's visit and the threat he posed, but it all came down to what Broderick sought—not just a connection to the peerage . . . but a respectable nobleman.

A link to a lord.

Leaning back, she stared blankly at the slight fog her breath had left upon the glass. With the tip of her finger, she traced a teardrop in that stain.

Broderick coughed, bringing her blank gaze to his. "I believe we are done here?" There was an infinitesimal pause to that question that hinted at the very game he played. The weakness he used against her.

Her spirit blazed back to life, and she opened her mouth to deliver another blistering diatribe.

Her brother's visage pulled into focus. The worry stamped in his features reflected back. This was an unfamiliar side of Broderick. One he shared with none and carefully concealed under the veneer of a practiced grin and urbane charm.

If it is not me, he very well will use Gertrude as his pawn. "The London Season," she forced herself to say. Her tongue heavy in her mouth made the words garbled to her own ears. Ophelia turned back. "I will do it."

Broderick started. "You will?" A pleased grin flashed briefly on his lips before he swiftly concealed it.

I'm going to be ill.

"But I am not living in Mayfair," she said quickly, claiming some control of the arrangement.

Her brother shook his head. "Absolutely—"

"I am not. And you'll allow it. Let us not play games. You always wanted me to go." Back when he'd sent Cleo, it had really been Ophelia—never either of her siblings. Because to those in this gang, Ophelia was always the one for sale for her face alone.

A guilty blush splotched his cheeks. "I sent Cleo first."

He made no attempt to deny it. That willingness to sacrifice her because he saw Cleo's worth stung. "Because she demanded it." She pinned him with her gaze. "Just as I am demanding it now." As she should have done for her younger sister and now did for Gertrude. Guilt snaked around her insides. It didn't matter that her sister had come out happy for her arrangement; it mattered that Ophelia had sacrificed her. "So I'll have a Season and make a match, but on my own terms." She proceeded to lift a finger as she enumerated her list. "I'll live in the Devil's Den." The only place she'd ever been comfortable.

"I'll decide on whom I . . . on whom I"—she strangled out the vile epithet—"*marry*. If I don't wish to attend a certain event, I shan't. I'll be afforded the same freedoms as I am inside the club."

"Fine." Surely it could not be that easy? Broderick matched her movements, ticking off on his callused digits. "Marriage to a lord. You choose the gentleman. You'll be free to decline an invitation unless it is a respectable lord or lady issuing the invite." He paused to adjust his already immaculate cravat. "I'll not have the *ton* say we're ungrateful."

"Oh, never that," she drawled.

He went on talking over her droll interruption. "No breeches. New dresses." She glanced down at her modest, high-necked gown.

Her stomach flipped over itself. Over the years she'd taken to wearing drab gowns which concealed her frame. Now, her brother would take away that layer of protection, too? "No."

Broderick flicked a pained glance over her skirts. "*That* is not negotiable. Furthermore . . ."

The argument over garments instantly forgotten, she braced herself, knowing what was coming even before he uttered it.

"You are not living at the Dev—"

"I am not going anywhere. Or there is no deal."

She held her breath as they met at a tense impasse. Brother and sister, both warriors of the street, refusing to cede victory.

He threaded a hand through his hair. "Oh, bloody hell. Very well. You may remain."

Ophelia released a sigh she hadn't even realized she'd been holding. For the first time that night, a smile won out. It was quickly dashed at his next set of terms. "But you are to at all times act the part of a lady."

Act the part. "At least you recognize this for the farce it is," she muttered.

"It is scandalous enough, your living here and having a bloody Season. One misstep and your trunks will be packed and you'll be sent to Cleo's."

"Cleo's new home in Grosvenor Square?" she snorted. "I'd rather live in the hovel I was born in."

Broderick held her gaze. "Are we clear?"

Resentment surged through her. As much as she wanted to send him to the Devil with his ordering her about, she knew how very easily he could simply abandon the agreement and send Gertrude. "We are." Before she could change her mind and consign herself to the hated fate she wished to escape, Ophelia swept over to the door.

"Ophelia?"

She stopped, her fingers poised on the door handle, and for a fraction of a heartbeat she clung to a hope: that he'd abandon his plans. That he wouldn't ask either her or Gertrude to sacrifice themselves in this way—or any way.

All hopes were dashed with his next question.

"What happened to your hands?"

Her mind stalled, and she looked blankly down at her scraped palms.

Ophelia smoothed her hands down her skirts and winced at the sting of her scraped hands. Oh, bloody hell. He had noted.

The floorboards shifted once, marking his path over. "What is this?" he murmured. Taking her palms, he inspected them alternatingly.

"I fell," she squeaked, praying he mistook the pitch of her voice as one of pain. "We have a problem in the alley. Rats. A lot of them."

"*You* were cleaning the alley?" he asked, his voice rich with skepticism.

He knew. Knew of her loathing for the alleys and the speed with which she raced through them. Though not he, nor anyone, knew the reasons why. Or had he known . . . and it was simply impolite for a brother and sister to speak of that? Ophelia concentrated on drawing in steady, even breaths. She gave a negligent shrug. "It needed to be done."

"In the middle of the night?"

Ignoring the question there, she stilled.

Broderick nodded slowly. "That will be all."

Feeling his searching gaze on her nape, Ophelia twisted the handle and let herself out.

The moment she closed the panel, putting much-needed space between them, her shoulders sagged, and she borrowed support from the door.

Given all the ominous possibilities of what had brought Connor to their club—Stephen's burning of the Hell and Sin Club, Ophelia bloodying a nob senseless—the evening could have most assuredly gone worse, much worse.

Only why, as she at last found the sanctuary of her rooms and braced for her entrance into Polite Society, did she find she would far rather face the prison of Newgate than the one her brother would have her enter into?

Chapter 6

Having once slept with the dank London cobblestones as his only bed, Connor had come to appreciate that there were different levels of misery.

Existing on the streets of London had been a special kind of study in torture.

Attending *ton* functions represented an altogether different sort.

His visit to the Devil's Den completed—with unsurprisingly little assistance from the proprietor and his kin—Connor, in a proper change of garments, strode through his father's residence toward the kitchens.

Not for the first time since he'd taken leave of the Devil's Den, thoughts of Ophelia whispered forward in his mind.

A *she* who, at last, had a name.

Of course she had one . . . even the basest-born street criminal was given that simplest of gifts. She'd been the one who could have turned him over to Diggory years earlier and instead had spared him. He'd risked his own life for hers in return . . . a debt paid . . . that vow of Mac Diggory, a code of street ethics honored by all those unfortunate enough to call St. Giles home.

He'd never known her name . . . until now.

Now, the young woman was as irascible, spirited, and angry as she'd always been. Instead of her child's tones of long ago, the vitriol on her tart tongue rolled forward with a husky contralto, reminding him that Ophelia Killoran was no longer a child. Dangerous as a girl, she was lethal as a woman, but in ways that had nothing to do with something as elemental as his survival.

"Mr. Steele." That cheerful whisper brought him up quick, and he glanced back. "Never tell me you are going to the kitchens."

Alas, she'd always known him too well.

Mrs. Fearson: stout, short, and with the roundest, reddest cheeks, the only thing fearful about her was her name. She smiled widely.

"Mrs. Fearson," he greeted, doubling back to meet her as she waddled his way. A loyal member of his father's household since the day Connor had entered it, she'd been one of the few members of the staff who'd not eyed him like he'd come to slit their throats as they slept. Or make off with the family's silver—as they'd openly accused—before the earl had sacked them.

"No need to come meet me, dear boy," she panted, out of breath from her minimal exertions. She planted her hands on her knees and puffed loudly.

Leaning down, he bussed her on the cheek.

She swatted at his arm. "Enough of that. The kitchens?"

If he'd been a proper sort, he'd have managed at least a hint of a hangdog expression. Instead, he grinned and shoved open the doorway to the room over debate and made for the long oak table filled with platters. "Ah, and never one to disappoint, I trusted there would be platters still." Of food. Heaping mounds of it that his father's guests hadn't finished but would have been enough to feed countless starved mouths in the streets.

It was surely an evening spent revisiting his past and those closest to the Diggorys, but as he slid onto one of the long benches, guilt needled at him.

"Never one to disappoint?" Mrs. Fearson snorted, and then, in her usual manner, grabbed a plate from the counter and proceeded to put together a dish. "Tell that to your father, who has been awaiting your arrival all night."

"I can see to that myself," he protested, plucking a plum tart from the table and dusting it off in one bite.

She swatted at his hand as he made to gather the dish from her hands. "Let the earl's son make his plate?" she groused under her breath. "I'd sooner retire before I was charged with that."

By terms of service and the pension offered, the grey-haired woman should have hung up her proverbial apron a decade ago. Instead, she'd remained on, overseeing the earl's household and being a motherly figure to Connor when he'd first entered it as a lonely boy.

Connor stared expressionlessly down at his plate.

"Now, now, no need for the frown," Mrs. Fearson murmured, misinterpreting the reason for his grimness. "The earl has done fine enough this evening, and he understands what keeps you away."

The devoted servant was correct. When most other noblemen would have turned their noses up at Connor's work, the Earl of Mar had not only supported him but also expressed his pride. As such, he would understand that it was a case that had kept Connor away.

Before.

Another rush of guilt for altogether different reasons.

With a sigh, he shoved aside his plate. "Is it too much to hope I at the very least missed the dancing portion of the festivities?" he ventured, climbing to his feet.

Mrs. Fearson's lips twitched. "I have it on the authority of several maids that his lordship intended to delay, in the hopes that you should arrive."

"Bloody wonderful," he muttered.

"You can find him along with the other gentlemen in the card rooms set up." Her laughter trailed after him.

Lifting his hand in thanks, a short while later Connor found himself outside the Blue Parlor. The irony was not lost on him as he entered a room full of his father's Whig friends that the same men who'd devoted themselves to abolishing vice should sit and take part in games of—Connor did a search of the rooms—whist and loo.

He instantly found his father engaged in a game with Lord Dapplewhite. The earl glanced up and, with a quick word for his partner, tossed the cards down.

Grinning, he shoved to his feet and cut a path around the tables neatly arranged. An inch over six feet, broad of shoulder, and in possession of the same shock of thick hair, the earl may as well have been a replica cast of when he'd plucked Connor from the streets and given him a home and a new beginning.

He arched an eyebrow. "I'd begun to doubt you would come, my boy."

Known as the Hunter to everyone in London—except this man, who'd only ever spoken to and with Connor as "my boy" or "son"— Connor smiled, grateful for the diversion from thoughts of the Killorans. "The irony of the very men attempting to eradicate vices from London meeting over brandy and cards has ever escaped me."

His adoptive father slapped him on the back. "All in moderation, my boy. All in moderation. Join me," he urged, motioning him to a vacant table.

They made their way past the throngs of assembled guests. All powerful players in Parliament, they were respectable gentlemen known for their upright reputations and their charitable endeavors.

Still, for that integrity, they were also the same men, along with their wives, who'd forever stolen side-glances at Connor and whispered about him.

Several lords paused in the middle of their wagering to look over at him as he passed. The irreverent stares he'd acquired had been the least of the discomforts he'd suffered. They hadn't mattered when he'd been a beggar, pleading for their coins and being met with a slapped hand, and they mattered even less now.

He and his father slid into the two chairs set before a folding oak table.

Wordlessly, the earl collected the deck, neatly shuffled, and then returned them to the table.

Connor drew first.

Ace of diamonds.

His father chuckled, reshuffling the pile. "You always were luckier than me in this."

Yes, it would seem we've both been . . . lucky.

What had been the reason for the slight hesitancy in that pronouncement? One that suggested she'd mocked with her words and that they'd held a heavily veiled hint of her own past.

"Connor?" his father implored, swiftly dealing out the remainder of the deck and turning over the final card, a seven of diamonds.

"Forgive me. I was distracted," he murmured, directing his attention to the thirteen cards in his hand.

Connor played his first card, a king of hearts.

His father swiftly tossed down his queen in that same suit.

Winning the trick, Connor claimed the trumped-up ace of diamonds.

"Your latest case," his father said, taking the next card.

They continued in silence, alternating wins.

Something was coming. Even as there was a relaxedness to his father's movements, tension fairly spilled from the earl's frame.

Connor lowered his cards. "What is it?"

Some of the tension lifted from the earl's only faintly wrinkled features. "You never did miss anything, did you?" he asked softly, as if only to himself. "Since the day I found you." Nay, this man had rescued him. Given Connor hope and a new beginning that did not include murder, thievery, and mayhem.

For that, he'd called him "Father" when the one Connor had so loved had been viciously cut down.

"It is why you are so very good at what you do," his father said, pride rich in his voice as he settled back in his chair. He clasped his hands at his belly. "I am proud of you every day, Connor Steele. The work you do"—a smile lit his face—"has kept so many safe. It is good work. Important. The most important: making the world a better place for all."

For every negative word whispered about the peerage, there then proved men like the one before him: a childless lord who'd taken Connor in, given him his name, and led a crusade to improve the lives of other orphaned boys and girls. It had restored the hope of a snarling, snappish, angry boy who'd resented the world with a hatred better suited to an aged man at the end of his years.

"Why do I suspect there is a 'but' contained within that?" he drawled, blunting that with a grin.

The twinkle gleamed brighter in the earl's eyes. "Because you have always been a keen boy. I applaud your work, and yet, Connor"—his father leaned forward—"you have dedicated your life to improving the streets at the expense of truly living."

"This from a man who gave all of himself in Parliament for those same causes," he said gently, a reminder to the earl, who'd never married.

"It's how I know you'll have regrets," the earl said with his usual pragmatism. "You can make a difference . . . outside of your cases."

His father had supported Connor early on when he'd established an inquiry agency. Over the years, however, his support had . . . wavered.

"If you were anyone else, I would take that as a lecture."

"You know I am not one to do that."

"No, you are not." His adoptive father had never lectured. He'd patiently instructed Connor, allowing him to falter without admonishment. He'd encouraged him to make his way for himself in the world as a detective, applauded it, and never acted as though what he did was somehow less because of the self-made man he'd come to be. Rather, he'd lauded him for the future he'd created; however, increasingly of late, he'd begun to question Connor's role within Bow Street.

"This is all you do. All you are now . . . and soon I fear it will be all that you ever are."

"I can make a greater difference by taking to the streets—"

"And risking your life." That charged statement exploded from his usually collected father.

"There are risks," he quietly acknowledged. He'd never lie to his father. Nor would his father be naive enough to fail and see the threats Connor faced. "But there is a greater need to see that children in those streets don't suffer the same fate . . ." *As me.* After his parents' murder, Connor had been forced into Diggory's gang. How many children lived a like existence?

His father's throat convulsed. "I will admit my own selfishness, Connor. As I age, I confront how empty my life would have been if you were not in it."

His chest tightened.

"I do not want you to give every day of yourself and someday look back, wishing you had . . . more." The earl spoke with a certainty of one who knew.

"And you wish that you did." He said the truth aloud.

His father's gaze grew distant. "Never once did I regret the time I dedicated to Parliament and the crusades I overtook in the House of Lords." He met Connor's gaze. "But that is only because of you. There should have been a wife. Alas, I was"—he swatted his hand in Connor's direction—"entirely too busy. I did not have time for a courtship or a betrothal. I was making the world better for others." He chuckled. "Or so I told myself. Children . . . they leave and make a new life for themselves. And what is left for an old man but an empty household . . . and wonderings about what life might have been for the both of us had you had a mother and I a wife. You can have both. You can make a difference by taking a seat in the House of Commons and marrying." There it was. His father's hope and his tenacious bid for Connor to tender his resignation. "Lord Middlethorne was unable to attend this evening. He was not feeling himself," he said in an abrupt segue.

Viscount Middlethorne, his father's closest friend, an equally respected vocal Parliamentarian who'd long championed the plight of the poor. Connor frowned. "Is he—?"

"Insists he is fine," his father said with a wave of his hand. He paused, giving Connor a meaningful look. "Lady Bethany is in attendance."

Unnerved still by the never plainly stated talks of a union that would join their family to Viscount Middlethorne's, Connor glanced briefly at the ormolu clock atop the hearth. "I trust the lady is well?" Lord Middlethorne's now widowed daughter had been the only friend Connor had known when he was taken in by the earl . . . and then she had become the woman he'd hoped to one day marry.

Until she'd wed another, and Connor realized the truth: to her and her father, Connor would always be just a boy from the streets.

"She asked after you during the dinner," his father continued, relentless.

"Oh?" He flipped another card.

His father huffed impatiently. "She was your friend for a lifetime, Connor. Is this because she wed another?"

At one time in his life, it would have been. Childhood friends, she'd spoken of one day marrying him. In the end she'd accepted the offer from a duke. "It is because we'd never suit," he settled for.

"That's rubbish, Connor. You suit more than most."

Aye. Connor had long admired Bethany for her philanthropic endeavors. He appreciated her. But never had he been overwhelmed with any real passion for the lady. Not the way Ophelia Killoran had sent desire coursing through him just a short while ago. Neck heating, he made a show of studying his cards. "I've other responsibilities commanding me now that are vastly more important than marriage," he substituted. "As such, I cannot be the husband she deserves." Even if Lady Bethany weren't a paragon amongst Polite Society, marriage to her was no longer an option. Connor would not commit himself to Bethany—nor any woman—when his work commanded his days and nights.

"She was young."

"Eighteen," he reminded. She'd hardly been a child when she'd married the Duke of Argyll, but rather a woman grown. At the time he'd mourned the loss of what could have been. Now, he recognized his hopes of a match had merely been based on grand illusions built by a boy with aspirations of the love his parents had shared.

"She understands you, Connor," his father persisted, setting down his hand. The pair at a nearby table paused to look over, interest in their eyes. When he spoke, the earl's words came quieter. "She understands what motivates you and where you've come from." Did she? Did his father, for that matter? Aside from the sparse details he'd handed over of his parents' murder, not another word had been spoken of Connor's past, nor a question asked. "She will make you a good wife." The earl tacked that on almost as an afterthought.

Will. Not *would.* Because regardless of Connor's lack of a pledge, there remained the expectation that they would join . . . if for no other reason than the like goals they shared.

It was far more a connection than most marriages in Polite Society were built on.

And yet . . . it was also far less than the love that had driven his own mother to forsake her family and good name to carve out a life for herself with a poor Irishman who'd nothing to offer her but his heart.

His father spoke, bringing Connor back from poignant musings of the parents who'd birthed him. "I encourage this match . . . not because I desire a connection between our families"—lifelong friends since Eton, both powerful nobles had together worked to improve the lots of the poor—"but because I know you . . . and I know Bethany."

Connor turned over the next card.

Yes, with their shared vision of a different London, they certainly had more than most marriages within the nobility.

A fancy investigator now. Are you trying to erase the streets from yourself, Steele? Still haven't figured it out, have you? It will always be part of you, no matter the fine garments you wear.

His lips twitched.

Nor would Bethany be one to burn him up with her caustic tongue as Ophelia Killoran had always been able to.

His father tossed his cards down. "Come," he said, shoving his chair back. "We should continue to the dancing portion of the festivities."

Oh, bloody hell.

Mention of Bethany, Connor's bachelor state, and dancing . . . The Earl of Mar could not be any clearer than if he'd dragged out a betrothal contract with Connor's name etched alongside the lady's and asked for his signature.

Reluctantly, Connor stood.

Suddenly, it felt a good deal safer returning to St. Giles and facing a spitfire like Ophelia than Bethany . . . and his father's expectations.

Chapter 7

Since Ophelia Killoran had taken her first steps, she'd been groomed, trained, and sent out into the world as a pickpocket. From East London to West, she'd learned every crevice and every nook of every stone.

Now, she moved along those same streets not as a thief . . . but as a woman playing at being a lady.

All because of her blasted brother.

Lingering at the corner of Madame Bisset's, Ophelia surveyed those very streets. Fancily clad couples with their arms linked passed by, along with other solo passersby, young women with maids and footmen trailing close.

Trapped.

They were all, regardless of station, trapped—in different places, but invariably it remained the same.

"What of this one?" Gertrude called out.

In the crystal pane, her sister's visage along with the plump shopkeeper's reflected back. The smooth, clear glass served as a window in which the proprietor's pursed lips revealed precisely what she thought of waiting on the Killorans.

Shopping. Just one more aspect of her life which had been changed. Where before milliners and dressmakers and seamstresses had been paid substantial sums and brought within the Killoran world, now they'd be forced to step into theirs.

It was one thing for those sought-after proprietors taking the fat purses and secretly cladding the Diggory gang. It was altogether different for Ophelia and her siblings to enter their shops so all the *ton* knew whose money they took.

"Ophelia?" her sister pressed, shaking a bolt of fabric.

"Fine," she gritted out. "It is fine."

It was all irrelevant. Fancy garments, ornate bonnets, extravagant jewels. It changed nothing before the eyes of Society. Nor did Ophelia care whether she was or was not accepted by the *ton*. She did care that her entire world was about to be upended.

"You did not even look," Gertrude protested, waving the swatch again.

Tossing a requisite look over her shoulder, she assessed the ice-blue satin. "It is fine," she repeated, glancing out the window once more.

Several ladies at a nearby table made little attempt to conceal their whisperings.

"The nerve of them . . . believing they could ever . . ." The rest of that uninventive charge was lost to a flurry of giggles.

Ophelia slid a cool look in their direction. The pair, not many years older than Ophelia and her own sisters, instantly fell silent.

Lifting the edge of her skirt, she displayed a blade she'd commandeered from one of the guards and now wore strapped to her lower leg.

The ladies shrieked and tripped over themselves in their haste to exit the shop.

"My ladies," Madame Bisset cried, abandoning Gertrude. She flew after those fleeing customers. "Pleeze, zees is a misunderstanding. Do not—"

Gertrude caught Ophelia by the forearm and dragged her into the corner. "Bloody hell, can you not at least feign an attempt at civility? By God, even Cleo did."

Even Cleo . . . which suggested Ophelia was somehow the lesser of the sisters. Yet—she lifted her chin—"Cleo is also the one who's forgotten where she's come from."

Her eldest sister glared. "Why? Because she's made an attempt at creating a new life for herself?"

Yes, that was precisely why.

With Madam Bisset still at the front of the shop pleading with her outraged clients, Gertrude dropped her voice. "This is happening. Either you go along with what Broderick wishes or you do not. But if you enter into this agreement and join the *ton*, you might, like Cleo, find you do not mind the world as much as you believe you do," she said in a hushed whisper.

Ophelia snorted. There was a greater chance she'd develop a taste for spit-roasted pig dipped in chocolate.

"Now," her sister said, pointedly ignoring that outburst, "what about this one?" She held the swatch of satin so close to Ophelia's face she went briefly cross-eyed.

Burnt orange. "It is fine."

Gertrude's frown deepened.

"It is . . . not fine?"

Growling, Gertrude stomped off.

Her sister once again preoccupied at the table full of material, Ophelia returned to looking out the storefront windows and the lords and ladies bustling along the pavement, longing for home. *I should be overseeing my responsibilities.* Instead, she was wasting her hours on inane tasks suited to proper misses and not street rats.

Her gaze wandered out to the busy thoroughfare, instantly locating a small waif with threadbare garments, dirty cheeks, and eyes that revealed his hunger.

Ophelia's perusal came to a stop at the gaslight, and she continued to study the small boy. Near in age to Stephen, he wore the same angry expression upon his gaunt cheeks that any who'd been born on the streets did.

She should be helping him. Helping so many. Instead, she'd be suffering through fittings, selecting fabrics she didn't give a jot about for garments expensive enough to keep twenty or more of those street urchins clad and warm.

Madame Bisset's increasingly strident tone cut across her musings.

A moment later the bell affixed to the door was set ajingle as her upset clients stormed from the establishment. No doubt, her *former* clients.

"That izz it," Madame Bisset cried, storming back to Gertrude. She cast an impressively black glower in Ophelia's direction. "I have outfitted your family over zee years, but this?" she squawked, sweeping a hand in Ophelia's direction. "Is too much. Too much." Her voice pitched to the ceiling. "They say your sister threatened zem with a knife."

"I'm sure my sister did not . . ."

While her sister launched into a fiery debate with the proprietor, Ophelia looked out, again, searching for the boy.

And found him.

Ophelia blinked.

Found him speaking to a broad, towering figure.

Found him speaking to a broad, towering, and *familiar* figure, to be precise.

She swiped her hand over her eyes. Surely she was merely seeing things. Surely after his unexpected resurrection and then appearance in her family's club the evening prior, she was seeing him everywhere. There was no other accounting to explain why Connor O'Roarke was even now in discussion with the street urchin outside Madame Bisset's.

She honed in on his lips, trying to make sense of his words. Annoyance sparked to life, healthy and familiar where this man was concerned. There could be no reason that an investigator known as the Hunter could be talking to a child who'd been moments away from picking a nob's pockets.

Taking advantage of her sister's escalating debate with the French modiste, Ophelia strode to the front door and carefully opened it, mindful of that blasted bell. When no hue and cry went up from her sister, Ophelia did a sweep of her surroundings—instantly finding Connor and the boy walking off side by side.

Over my bloody body.

Surging forward, Ophelia wound her way through the busy crowds, her muslin skirts bright and cumbersome. She damned the garments, longing for her breeches. All the while she followed Connor and the boy, she kept her gaze trained on their backs, keeping them within her sights while also maintaining a measured distance. They continued walking until the clean, crowded streets gave way to dank, less-traveled cobbles.

The pair stopped, and Connor motioned the child down an alley.

Ophelia staggered to a jerky stop, her heart plummeting to her stomach and churning up nausea. *Do not be a bloody coward . . . you are Ophelia Killoran.*

For the hell visited upon her in one alley, she'd escaped and survived. She'd only become stronger over the years. She'd be damned ten times to Sunday before cowering as she was while Connor did . . . did . . . whatever it was he sought from that street waif.

Energized by that, Ophelia pressed herself against the brick wall. Bending, she discreetly plucked free the knife she'd flashed to the shop ladies. Dagger in hand, Ophelia glanced about the streets. There was an eerie emptiness here at this end of Oxford Street; it chased a chill down her spine and iced her from the inside out.

She swallowed hard.

Before her courage could desert her, she dipped around the corner.

Empty.

Impossible . . . and yet, as someone who'd dwelled in alleys, she'd come to know there was oftentimes more to them.

Her fingers curled reflexively around the hilt of her dagger, the carved wood biting into the fabric of her leather gloves. Damning the silly articles that could get a person killed in a street fight, she paused to tug at one with her teeth. She made quick work of the other glove and shoved the pair into her cloak pocket.

She inched down the alley, her eyes everywhere. *Do not think of it . . . do not think of him.*

Take 'im down and read 'is palms, girl.

With every step, the memory streamed closer and closer to the surface, forcing her back into her past, to the smells of that day: whiskey on his breath and the strong scent of leather as he'd smothered her cries.

She tripped and shot out her spare hand, searching for purchase.

Why else would a girl take a gentleman down an alley?

Ophelia sank her teeth into her lower lip, for he'd been right. There could come no good in venturing down an alley alone . . . and even less so with or after a man.

As you're now doing.

Only, this was Connor. How many times had she come upon him in these very places?

But he was a boy then. *All these years have passed, and what do you truly know of him?*

"Focus," she mouthed, forcing her feet onward.

It was as though the pair had simply vanished . . . or she'd imagined the two together. Ophelia stopped suddenly. Her gaze caught on a doorway at the back of the brick structure.

Heart speeding up, she cast a look to the front of the alley and then at the handful of steps between her and the opposite end.

Trapped.

Stop it. You chose to come down here. No one knows you're here. No one has lured you here.

It recalled her pursuit: Connor . . . and that child.

Drawing a long, slow breath between clenched lips, Ophelia crept the remaining distance. She hesitated at the edge of that solid oak door, lingering.

Now what?

The panel flew open, and she turned to flee.

A body slammed into her with such force it sucked the air from her lungs and killed the cry on her lips.

Her knife clattered uselessly to the ground as Ophelia came crashing down, her stomach connecting with the harsh, unforgiving stone floor. Pain exploded throughout her body. Agony, sharp and vicious, screamed in protest of the weight crushing her to the ground.

"What do you want?" he rasped loudly against her ear. Collecting her wrists in one hand, he rendered her defenseless while the other did a search of her person.

Tell me what you want.

She whimpered, bucking and thrashing wildly against her captor's hold.

A sheen of tears blurred her vision, those crystal drops blinding.

Once more she was trapped.

Since he'd gone off with the street waif, Ned, Connor had sensed the threat in the shadows.

The miserable years he'd suffered in the streets and then his years working as an investigator had ingrained in him the peril in ignoring one's gut warnings.

He'd been followed.

There could be no doubting the soft figure he'd taken down, which was now gyrating under him, was female. Blood pumped fast through his veins, as it always did from the threat of danger; this time there was more. His body reacted strongly to the lush, generously curved buttocks rocking against him.

"Be still," he growled, tightening his mouth.

The woman only rocked her hips all the more, grinding against him.

Connor steeled his resolve.

He'd seen sirens bury blades in the bellies of unsuspecting men and as such learned long ago never to underestimate someone because of their gender, age, or size.

"What do you want?" he demanded again, dragging up her skirts. He scraped a hand over her muscular calves, one at a time. They were strong legs, the flesh surprisingly soft, a contradiction to the work-roughened palms in his hand that marked her of the streets. His fingers curled reflexively around her lower right leg.

She hissed. "Bastard."

That breathy voice, threaded with panic, froze him on the spot. "What the hell?" he whispered incredulously, flipping her over. Shock brought his mouth open. *Impossible. "Ophelia?"* And then a slow dawning horror. "Did I hurt y—?"

Ophelia shoved her knee hard between his legs.

All the air slipped from him on a sharp gasp. Stars dotted his vision, but he retained his hold.

"Get. Off. Me," she panted, her chest moving up and down at a frantic pace. He'd seen Ophelia in many forms over the years: angry, outraged, disgusted, mocking.

Never had he seen her fearful. Now, it rolled off her trembling frame in waves, seeping from her eyes.

"Will you stop fighting me?" he managed to rasp out through the agony of her effectively landed blow.

She jerked her other knee up in reply.

Anticipating that strike, Connor caught her leg and forced it back to the earth. "You vixen," he muttered. Her hands still clasped between his, he struggled awkwardly to his feet, dragging her up with him.

"Bastard," she hissed again.

"I hardly think you've followed me from Mayfair to Oxford Street and down this alley all for the purpose of challenging my parentage," he said dryly, issuing a frosty warning to that statement, one that demanded answers.

He should have known better where Ophelia Killoran was concerned. "Go to hell, O'Roarke."

"If I'd had a pence for every time you've uttered that in the course of my life, I would have lived the life of a king."

She spat at his feet, spittle landing on the tips of his black boots.

Connor narrowed his eyes. "Or am I to gather you're still picking pockets?"

Ophelia moved for her knife, and he dove for the blade, reaching it first. He examined the crude hilt, the sharpened blade. It was a quality weapon, and yet . . .

"This is hardly a dagger fit for the Jewel of St. Giles," he murmured, turning it over.

Eager fingers shot out, and even while he told himself to look away, he stared on, riveted as she tugged up her skirt and strapped the blade to a shapely leg. A leg that just moments ago he'd been exploring. Another wave of hunger went through him. He fought back a groan.

"I lost mine."

Connor didn't miss the way she briefly avoided his eyes, and he easily spotted her lie.

"You?" he countered, steeping his voice in disbelief. "*You* don't lose anything. You were never without that knife. After all, I had it pressed to my neck enough times to recall its importance to you."

Ire blazed to life in her eyes. "What did you do with that boy?"

He creased his brow. What was she on about?

"The boy, on North Bond Street," she clarified in crisp tones. "What did you do with him?"

Connor's mouth moved, but no words came out. He tried again. Why . . . why . . . ? His ears went hot. "What in blazes are you accusing me of?"

"Where is he?" she whispered, taking a threatening step closer, and by the saints in heaven, she had a look of the furies to rouse terror in any sane man's chest.

A muscle jumped at the corner of his eye, and for a long moment he considered telling her to go to hell and sending her on her way. Only . . . what about the boy had brought her following after him? He swept his hand toward the doorway.

She wetted her lips. Darting a stare over her shoulder, she briefly considered the opposite end of the alley. Then, adjusting her cloak and bonnet, she swept ahead.

She stepped inside and then stopped. Her slow, widening gaze took in the young boy, Ned, seated at the table.

Ned glanced up from the plate of bread he currently devoured. "Who are ya?" His voice emerged muffled around his bite. He yanked free another piece and then jammed it into his mouth.

Ophelia peered over her shoulder.

Ignoring the question in her eyes, Connor closed the door behind them and joined the boy.

"A childhood friend," Connor supplied when Ophelia let that question go unanswered. He picked up a pitcher and filled an empty glass.

"She's yar *friend?*" the boy asked, incredulity rich in his voice. "Looks loike a fancy lady to me."

"Don't be deceived by fancy garments," Ophelia put forward in her Cockney.

The boy's eyes went round, and he looked to Connor.

Ophelia lingered at the doorway, fiddling with the fabric of her cloak.

Catching his gaze on her, she stopped that distracted movement. She had the look of one sorting through pieces of a puzzle, attempting to make them fit into something of sense.

"Ophelia, allow me to present Ned. Ned, Miss Killoran."

The boy stopped midchew and then swallowed down that too-large bite. "Killoran?" Wariness settled in his gaunt features. "Diggory's Killoran?" Cheeks pale, Ned shoved back his chair.

Connor handed over the glass of water.

The child hesitated, and then thirst won out over fear. He audibly gulped down his drink, all the while keeping a wary eye on Ophelia.

She frowned.

Did she take offense at that deserved reaction elicited by the gang she'd belonged to . . . and, by her place within the Devil's Den, still did?

"Miss Killoran saw us on North Bond Street," he explained for the lad's benefit.

The mistrust only deepened in Ned's eyes. He wiped the back of his hand over his mouth. "And followed us 'ere?"

Connor slid a lingering glance in Ophelia's direction. "Indeed." Color flooded her cheeks. "Why don't you continue eating while I see what pressing business Miss Killoran sought with me this afternoon." He motioned to his office door.

Ophelia hesitated and then followed him into the spacious rooms. Leaving the door open so he might survey both the boy whom he'd been questioning and the woman who'd been following him, he propped his hip on his desk.

Ophelia did a small circle. Her eyes missed nothing, touching on every detail of the room: the gilded figural clock atop the mantel, the pair of leather library armchairs, his brown leather-top desk. "What is this place?" she asked slowly as she came back to face him.

"My offices, madam."

She tipped her head at an endearing angle, and the pale strands that had been knocked loose fluttered at her shoulder. "Your offices?"

Connor laid his palms on the edge of his desk, opening his body's positioning. Years of posing questions had given him the appreciation and value of what one's body could convey . . . and, more important, what it could elicit. "Mmm, madam. My turn. Why were you following me?"

"I . . ." Ophelia looked over her shoulder to where Ned still sat, shoveling bread into his mouth again. When she turned back, she spoke in hushed tones. "I . . . wanted to be sure he was . . . safe."

It shouldn't grate that she believed him capable of hurting a child. After all, he very well knew from the worst possible ways the evil the orphaned boys and girls of London suffered. "And you intended to help him?" he countered without inflection.

Her narrow shoulders moved up and down in a little shrug. "If he required it." She took a step forward and folded her arms at her chest. "My turn." With the fire in her eyes and her proud, regal carriage, she had the bearing of a seasoned military commander. She was magnificent in her fury. "What are you doing with him?"

"I'm questioning him."

She pursed her lips tightly. "Questioning him on behalf of your Mad Marquess?"

He lifted his head in acknowledgment.

"You'll ask him about his . . . past?"

A past, present, and future that was certain to include a litany of crimes that could not be forgiven in a lifetime. "Will I ask him which street gang he's belonged to?" he murmured and then answered his own question. "I will." Nor could there be any doubting the child had allegiance to some street tough. Those men and women owned the orphans of East London the way the nobility had stables of horses.

Ophelia surged forward and quickly sank back. "I'm taking him with me."

"You're—?"

"Taking him with me," she elucidated in slow, drawn-out tones. The young woman tilted her chin defiantly.

"I assure you the boy is indeed safe in my care. Far safer than . . ."

The color on her cheeks deepened at that unfinished slight. "One who'd sell his services to a murderous nob," she sneered. "I hardly think so. You're not questioning him."

Over Ophelia's shoulder, he stole a look in Ned's direction.

His neck arched, he craned his head, taking in the exchange. The original unease he'd watched Connor with since he'd approached magnified in his expressive eyes.

He silently cursed. "Bloody hell, Ophelia. I'm not going to turn him over to the magistrate for crimes he was forced to commit." Ones he himself was guilty of. Furthermore, why was he answering to her when he answered to none on matters of his investigations?

"Very well," she conceded slowly. "You may ask him your questions. But I am remaining with him through your interrogation." He was already shaking his head. No one, unless he'd orchestrated their presence for a reason connected to his case, sat in on an interview or interrogation. "I'm not asking you," she said bluntly. "I'm telling you. If you wish to speak to him, then you'll have me here, and if not, then you can take your damned case"—she shoved the sizable file on his desk closer to him—"and stuff it up your arse."

In the course of his life, since he'd been rescued by the Earl of Mar, no one had ever dared speak to him so. Oh, they'd whispered about him and sneered, but none had dared challenge him to his face, and in such a flagrant way. Not a single person had dared hurl such a stinging delivery.

But then, he'd wager there was no one quite like the fuming woman before him. A smile tugged at his lips.

Squinting, she narrowed her eyes. "Something funny, O'Roarke?"

He schooled his amusement. "Very well," he conceded. "You may remain."

She sprang forward on her heels and then sank back. "What?"

So she'd expected a fight from him.

He, however, knew better that there were more benefits to be had by meeting her demands. This was one of them. If he'd not capitulated, she'd have only made his work here all the more difficult.

"You may sit and observe." Connor gathered his belongings . . . when he registered the silence. He glanced up. "What is it?" he asked impatiently. "Do you have any other requirements or demands?"

Ophelia remained frozen.

He arched an eyebrow.

"No. No questions."

"Then, shall we begin?"

Chapter 8

Life—more specifically, men—had given Ophelia countless reasons not to trust their motives.

He'd agreed to her demand.

Oh, when she'd bit out the vow to remain through his interview, she'd thought hers was a futile bid.

Commanding, self-possessed, he was an investigator who'd never willingly relinquish so much as an inch of his investigation.

But he had.

At her demand.

She didn't trust that too-easy capitulation for a bloody instant.

As they returned to the main rooms where Ned sat, his bread gone and half the pitcher of water empty, the child looked up.

Ned whipped a terror-filled gaze in her direction.

Hers. Not Connor's. The boy's earlier mention of Diggory and the antipathy etched in his weary features said he trusted her less than he would the Devil. It hit her like a kick to the stomach.

Everything she'd done had been to spare the innocents on the street from suffering at the hands of ruthless lords, and yet she'd never before seen that which was before her—until now. *They fear me.* They feared Ophelia and her family because of the ruthless reputation they'd earned for their rank and role in the late Diggory's gang. A boulder was weighing on her chest, restricting airflow.

This is what the Killorans had become?

Nay, this is what they'd always been.

"Miss Killoran?"

Connor's murmur cut across her horrified musings. She started and, averting her stare, seated herself on the cane and gilt-wood chair in the corner.

Connor pulled out another chair, the legs scraping along the oak floorboards. "Thank you for your patience, Ned," he said in gentle tones . . . ones she'd expected a man such as him incapable of. Ones she'd expected *any* man incapable of.

Ned chewed at a fingernail. "Ya talk loike the fancy blokes." He spat the nail on the floor. "Ya a nob?"

At that wise—and previously neglected—detail on her part, she started. For Connor did speak with the cultured English of the finest lords and not the tones of one born outside the peerage. He always had. Not for the first time, questions whirred about his past.

Connor leaned back and laid his arms on the sides of his chair. "Far from it. Miss Killoran saved me." His gaze locked with Ophelia's.

"And wot's she doing here?" The boy turned around and jabbed a finger in her direction.

How very much like her this child was. Wary. Mistrustful. Direct. Only . . . as Connor had accurately pointed out, she'd emerged on the other side of evil to find wealth, security, and power.

"Miss Killoran?" Connor asked as if there was another present. "She wanted to sit in. Look after you."

"Her? Look after me? Or kill me?" The child glared at Ophelia once more. "Does she have to be here?"

Those insults struck like a barb to the chest, with well-placed arrows left there to burn. All these years she'd seen the good her family had done and yet had been blind to the fear her kin inspired because of their birthright . . . and the things they'd done to survive.

"Miss Killoran is not the Devil you fear," Connor assured.

She sat motionless. For . . . she was. She'd killed and stolen and maimed men.

She was undeserving of that defense.

"I'll get my coins when ya're done with yar questions?" the boy groused, Ophelia seemingly forgotten.

Oi'll get my coins when I'm done?

Her mouth went dry as memories tugged at her.

All you need to do, gel, is take my palms . . . read them.

Fighting back the always present demons, she focused on the boy.

A faint tremble racked his frame. The tips of his shoes barely brushed the floor, highlighting the great disparity between the two: Connor, an imposing wall of strength, power, and confidence; and Ned, scared, small, and uncertain.

"You'll be richly rewarded for your time and answers," Connor quietly assured. "In no way will you be punished for anything you reveal."

From under a tangle of red curls, Ned peered at Connor. "This a trick? Ya gonna turn me over to the law?"

"There is no trick here. I'm simply looking to gather information to help my investigation."

The boy puffed his chest. "And ya think Oi can 'elp?"

"I certainly hope you're able to," Connor said somberly, picking up the glass Ned had been drinking from. Instead of pouring another, he weighed the small tumbler in his left palm.

The boy watched Connor's every movement. "Oi can't stay long." Ned wetted his lips. "Oi've . . . moi business to see to."

No doubt a gang leader he answered to.

Her heart ached all the more.

"I suspect you've seen much in these streets," Connor noted, passing that glass back and forth between his hands.

Ned pumped his legs, a childlike movement at odds with the hardened glitter in his eyes. "Oi 'ave." Planting his hands on the table, he leaned forward. "Oi ain't snitchin' on anyone, if that's wot ya're lookin' for."

That fierce devotion to one's gang leader came not from love or any true loyalty; rather, it was inspired by fear.

Connor fished inside his jacket, and as he pulled out his hand, a flash of metal glinted.

"Have you held a gold full guinea in your hands?" From between his ink-stained fingertips, Connor offered the coin for the boy's inspection.

Ophelia studied the exchange with an intensifying wariness. Where in blazes was he going with his questioning?

Ned didn't spare the coin in question a second glance. "Plenty o' toimes when Oi'm . . ." *Stealing.* Flushing all the way to the roots of his hair, Ned abruptly closed his mouth. His waiflike frame shook wildly under what he'd nearly revealed.

"Then you know a real one versus a fake that someone tries to foist off on you," Connor went on, giving no indication he'd noted the boy's fear. He flicked the coin through the air.

Ned shot a palm open and easily caught the piece.

"Well?" Connor encouraged.

Reticently, the boy forced himself to examine the coin.

"Is it real?"

At Connor's probing, Ned turned the King George III guinea back and forth, assessing it. "Yes," he acknowledged and returned the shining coin. "If ya can't tell a fake coin from a real one, ya ain't know nothin' in the streets."

His attention reserved for the boy, Connor's lips formed a smile, and the amusement there colored his voice. "Aye, you would be correct on that score."

Aye.

It was that lone lilting word that sang as he spoke, hinting at the faintest of brogues.

Who was Connor Steele? Refined Englishman who spoke like a noble? An Irishman? A Scot? After all, how very easily Ophelia had shed her own street speech for the proper sort.

"I am skilled enough to identify a real coin." That modest statement didn't fit with one who'd earned a reputation as a ruthless Runner who'd never failed a mission. "However, I wanted to see if you were able to." Again picking up the empty glass, Connor held it aloft in one hand and the coin in other. He tapped the bottom three times, the guinea clanging loudly, and then it emerged from the bottom of the crystal tumbler.

Both Ned's and her gasps filled the offices. Why . . . why Connor's was a skilled trick suited for the circus act her brother had sneaked Ophelia and her sisters into years earlier when he'd joined their gang.

"How . . . what . . . ?" the little boy stammered.

Grin widening, Connor wordlessly turned both over, and where before there had been a guardedness to Ned, now he eagerly grasped the glass.

The boy dumped out the coin and, squinting, held the tumbler close to his eyes. "How'd ya do that?" he demanded. From the inside and then out, Ned poked the bottom of the glass. "Ya're a wizard," he answered before Connor could speak.

"If I were, I'd certainly have a good deal more of those gold guineas." Connor again winked, and that subtle gesture softened him, made him real and approachable and a figure not to be feared.

Ned chuckled and turned the coin back over.

Her heart did a little somersault in her chest.

Or mayhap that gentle teasing made Connor a figure to be feared for altogether different reasons.

A grinning Ned settled back in his chair, all his earlier worry washed away.

The truth slammed into her. Why, that is precisely what he'd sought to do . . . put Ned at ease. Was it merely an investigator's strategy to lower a person's defenses, to wheedle information? And yet Ned had been a stammering, frightened child moments ago. Had Connor wished, his ruthlessly cold demeanor could have as easily managed that feat.

Struggling to make sense of his efforts, she scrutinized the nuances of the exchange unfolding before her.

The pair spoke as more a casual dialogue between equals than the most formidable Runner in England and a slip of a child.

"You were familiar with Mac Diggory?" Connor was asking. That hated name raised the gooseflesh on her arms and doused the room in cold.

Ned hesitated, glancing briefly at Ophelia before continuing. "Aye."

"Were you a member of his gang?"

"Was, until he died." He spat on the floor. With the hatred that burned in the boy's words, they might have been spoken by Ophelia herself.

Only . . .

Her heart squeezed sharply.

It had been her father who'd terrorized this boy.

"How did you come to be in his gang?"

"Me da sold me to 'im."

Sold him.

He was just another one of so many boys and girls who'd been bartered, used, and traded as slaves . . . but her stomach pitched anyway, as it always did at the evidence of that suffering.

To keep from giving in to that nausea, she focused on the exchange between investigator and street waif. Through the course of the relaxed interview, she hung on Connor's every word. By God, he was bloody good at what he did. Far more impressive than she wanted to credit . . . and certainly more than she wanted him to be. Ophelia could handle coldhearted, sloppy Runners who didn't give a jot about the unfortunates in St. Giles. She knew less what to do with a man who occasionally slipped in and out of a lyrical brogue and who sought to allay a child's fear.

With his thumb, Connor artfully flipped that coin in a distracting turn. Perhaps this was what made him so skilled an investigator. This ability to ask questions and distract. Ophelia sat there a silent observer, desperately trying to find the path Connor was leading the boy on.

"Do you know many of the boys bought by Diggory?"

"Oi do, sir."

Connor held up a palm. "I'm no gentleman. I'm from the same streets you are. I'd like to hire you as part of my staff, Ned."

The boy jolted. "Beg pardon, sir—Mr. Steele?" Hope blazed to life in his eyes . . . dashed a moment later by mistrust. "You having a laugh at me, sir?"

"Not at all." He proceeded to share minimal details, painting a portrait of a heartbroken father and a beloved child lost in St. Giles.

Ophelia pointed her eyes to the ceiling. As much as she could admire his assuaging the boy's worries, she took exception with him presenting a ruthless lord as anything less than what he was.

Connor tossed the coin, and Ned caught it once more. "Those are all the questions I have for today, Ned."

The child's eyes formed round saucers, and as if he feared Connor would change his mind, he stuffed the gold King George III into the front pocket sewn on his shirt. "Sir, thank you," he said, a smile dimpling his cheeks, highlighting the thread of innocence that still lived within the boy.

Connor reached inside his jacket, withdrew a card, and handed it over to the boy. "I need you to take this. Bring it to the Eve Dabney Foundling House."

Furrowing his brow, Ned turned the small scrap back and forth.

"You will be given shelter there for as long as you shall need it. I'll visit sometime this week to again speak with you."

Ned hopped up. "Thank you, sir. Thank you." With the same trust that had led Ophelia down an alley with a nobleman, the boy scampered off.

After he'd gone, Connor returned his attention to his notepad. His pencil struck the small leather book, filled the room, as Ophelia sat there—forgotten.

Nay, mayhap the word was *invisible*. It was an unfamiliar state . . . one she'd always craved but had never been afforded. Instead, she'd been pinched and fondled for the unsavory attentions shown her. Even with the safety afforded her as Broderick's sister, there wasn't a day she wasn't leered at or whispered to less than carefully as she walked by patrons.

Until this man.

Surely that was all that accounted for this ease in his presence?

He briefly glanced up, a question in his nearly obsidian gaze.

"Thank you," she said quietly, "for allowing me to remain." Even the child had looked at her for the Devil she was.

Her throat felt tight.

Connor tossed his pencil atop his book and slowly stood. "Come, Ophelia," he said, rolling his shoulders. "Do you take me for a monster? Did you expect me to harm the child? Threaten him to get the answers I seek?"

How was it possible for this man, a stranger, to know her thoughts? For that was precisely what she'd believed.

Disconcerted, she wandered over to the table and ran her fingers over the scalloped edge. "Oi don't know ya enough to say if ya would or would not," she said softly. Life in the streets killed the humanity in most of them. "If ya did 'urt 'im, ya would hardly be the first." She winced, hating that she'd inadvertently slipped into that coarsened, vulgar Cockney. She'd long associated that speech with the ugliest time in her life, and it served only as an unnecessary reminder of Mac Diggory and his gang. Concealing it had also become a means of killing her bastard of a da's memory. At the protracted silence, she stole a peek at him.

Connor's expression darkened. Was it her retort? The reminder of her birthright? Disgust? Loathing? Anger? What was it?

"I am not that man," he said quietly, drifting closer, erasing the space between them. Heat rolled off his powerfully muscled frame. "I am not a bully, and I'm certainly not one to terrorize a child."

Dangerous warmth stirred in her heart.

She'd been propositioned by lords in the street . . . and witless patrons in her family's club—who'd had their memberships revoked by Broderick for those offenses. Not a single one of those material offers of diamonds, garments, or a fancy townhouse of her own had ever held the sway that Connor's grave assurance did. "Oi don't know that about ya, either." Her voice emerged with a shameful throatiness that brought his thick black lashes sweeping down.

A gypsy's lashes that most ladies would have sold their souls for.

She swiftly averted her eyes, taking in his room once more. "After all, ya're the law now. Even less reason to trust ya than before." As such, he could have her thrown in Newgate for having dared touch a nob . . . and stabbed one long ago.

She shuddered. Through the fabric of her cloak, she rubbed at her arms.

At his silence, she glanced over and abruptly stopped, letting her arms fall back to her sides.

A smile grazed his lips. "I'm hardly the law, Ophelia," he assured, resting his hip on the table.

"So what are ya, then?" she asked, moving around the opposite end, touching her fingertips to the gleaming mahogany. "Ya've fine stuff like a nob."

"As do you," he pointed out, pivoting to face her while she continued her slow move.

"Not the same. Mine came from . . ."

"Theft?" He winged an eyebrow.

Murder. Mayhem.

"The boy was roight. Ya talk loike a fancy gent." She chewed at her lip. "But you always did." Ophelia suddenly stopped. "How did you do it?"

He shook his head.

She strode around the table to face him. "How did ya escape?"

"Without your help?"

"Oi didn't say that."

"What if I said a benevolent lord?"

She snorted. "No such thing." She'd known a lifetime of suffering and disdain at their hands; she knew better than to believe that twaddle squat.

He bowed his head. "Then we shall call it luck, madam, and leave it at that."

Leave it at that. Because there was no reason for their paths to again cross. Not when she'd declined to help him on his futile mission—one on behalf of a ruthless lord who'd offed his wife.

There was an air of finality to that decision that filled her with a peculiar melancholy. Perhaps it was because, ultimately, the sacrifice she'd made that had resulted in Gertrude's partial blindness hadn't been in vain: Connor O'Roarke's life had been spared.

Ophelia fiddled with the strings of her bonnet. "Oi'm . . . 'appy ya didn't 'ave yar neck stretched."

He shoved away from the table and drifted closer. "Come now, Lagertha. I'm going to come to think you actually like me."

His words called forth that long-ago exchange. He remembered, too. "Don't be getting foolish thoughts in yar head."

They shared a small smile.

I should go.

"Yes, you should."

Ophelia started. She'd spoken aloud?

"You did," he murmured, his baritone thick and warm and dangerously hypnotic.

He touched his hooded gaze upon her face, lingering that piercing stare on the slight tilt of her nose, then on the teardrop-shaped birthmark to the corner of her right eyebrow, and ultimately on the mouth she'd long lamented as too full.

Lips made for wickedness and sin.

How many times had that accusation been hurled at her by Diggory's men, an invitation they'd made themselves to debase her with their taunts?

Connor dipped his head and then stopped. He lowered it a fraction more, so close his quick, ragged intakes of air stirred her cheeks. His lemon-and-coffee scent melded the bitterness of that brew with a delicate sweetness at odds with the liquor-soaked patrons inside this club.

A little fluttering unfurled in her belly, like a thousand butterflies set free.

How much more wonderful that sensation was than the fear . . .

Her chest moved in time to his own as their breaths mingled.

I want to explore it. She wanted to know if she was capable of feeling everything a woman should be capable of feeling: desire, hunger, and passion . . . without being consumed by shame and fear.

Ophelia darted her tongue out and trailed the seam of her lips.

Connor's eyes darkened as he took in that subtle movement.

His Adam's apple bobbed in his thick neck.

"I want to kiss you."

Now who did that whispered admission belong to? All sense and order had ceased to be, and Ophelia continued on in this nebulous state.

Fluttering her lashes closed, she tipped her head back.

His mouth touched hers, and there was an unexpected softness to his hard lips.

For an instant, panic slammed into her as this moment blended and melded with another long ago. The sound of her own screams, muffled against a punishing hand. The stench of brandy and turmeric, peppery and robust as it clogged her senses.

I wouldn't kiss a street whore . . . I'll have your mouth elsewhere.

God help her . . . Her breath came in frantic spurts. The keeper of her past, in all his infinite vileness, had proven correct in this—there was a searing intimacy in such a meeting.

Ophelia tangled her hands into the front of his jacket to push him back. Only it was not the satiny softness of French silk under her palms but rather a coarse wool—garments worn not by a gentleman or lord but a man unafraid to work with his hands.

"Connor," she whispered against him, a reminder to herself that he was not a stranger of long ago but a stranger of a different sort.

He groaned and then palmed her gently about the nape, angling her head to better avail himself of her.

I am safe.

It was a foreign concept, surely steeped in madness to find a sense of safety in her childhood nemesis's embrace.

Yet as Connor slanted his lips over hers in a masterful stroke, it blotted all fear and rekindled the earlier warmth in her belly. Heaven help her, she wanted more. She dimly registered her bonnet sailing to the floor and landing with a soft thump.

She wanted the burning heat of his mouth upon hers and the hot desire thickening her veins. She wanted all of it. To be a woman, capable of passion.

How much more glorious this heated connection was than the fear.

She closed her eyes and surrendered herself to simply feeling.

Ophelia climbed her fingers up the broad, muscled wall of Connor's chest, questing higher to tangle in the unfashionably long strands of his hair. Going up on tiptoe, she pressed herself against him, meeting each increasingly hungry slant of his lips over hers.

Their chests rose and fell in a frantic rhythm, deepening their connection.

She panted, her lips slightly parting, and he swept the inside of her mouth with his tongue.

Her legs weakened under her, and she dimly registered him catching her about the waist and anchoring her close. He slid his palms lower, cupping her buttocks.

Dampness settled between her legs, and with it a throbbing, tingling ache.

A moan climbed up her throat, that wanton sound swallowed by Connor's kiss. Since that long-ago day, no one had intimately touched her again. This embrace, however, was altogether different from that one stolen from her. This exchange was one she freely gave, and she wanted the moment to continue forever.

Their tongues met slowly at first, with a hesitancy, and then with increasing ardor. It was the feel of being branded, burned, and marked by him.

His breath rasping loudly in a tantalizing, erotic haze, Connor shifted his attentions lower, to her neck.

Ophelia's head fell back, and an endless moan escaped her as he tenderly placed his lips to the place where her pulse beat wildly for him and his embrace and this moment.

This is what the other women in the club had spoken of . . . this was the splendor and bliss she'd mocked as a delusion or a harlot's trick, and how gloriously wrong she'd been.

Connor brought a hand between them, and he filled it with the plump flesh of her right breast. Through the fabric of her satin day dress, the tip pebbled and puckered. "So beautiful," he breathed against her neck, and delicious shivers danced down her spine.

Biting her lower lip, she tipped her head to allow him a better vantage to taste her. For when he uttered those words, they were a prayer of sorts, and not the empty, emotionless platitudes tossed at her by powerful lords.

For he wasn't. He was . . . he was . . . Connor O'Roarke, the ruthless investigator threatening her family's clubs.

A gasp exploded from her lungs. Ophelia stumbled back, tripping over herself in a bid to put space between them.

Connor's ragged breath filled the offices, and as the thick haze of lust clouding his vision receded, only horror remained.

What have I done? Ophelia touched shaking fingertips to her tender mouth. *I'm a traitor to my family* . . . "My God," she whispered. "I . . . I . . ."

But what was more, she'd wanted to continue in his arms.

His own lips that he buried behind a steadier palm than hers were damp and swollen from their kiss and surely a mirror reflection of her own. "Miss Killoran—" he began hoarsely, shattering the brief illusion of closeness and recalling the madness in desiring, of all men, this one.

"D-do not," she said tightly, the timbre of her voice trembling. She wanted neither his apologies nor his explanations. Not for what they implied: a mistake.

When everything about his embrace had felt—right. "Stay away from me," she snapped, illogical in that command. Knowing she'd been the one to follow him. Knowing she was the one guilty of this embrace.

Proving herself an even greater coward, Ophelia grabbed her bonnet and fled.

A short while and a miserable hackney ride later, Ophelia hurried down the alley beside the Devil's Den.

Oh, God. What would her brother and sisters say if they knew she'd chased after Connor O'Roarke and, worse, melted in his arms? Fingers shaking, she fiddled with the door to the kitchens. Only it wasn't her fear of alleys that sent her into a panic.

She cringed. *I kissed him.*

And you enjoyed it.

At last, managing to let herself in, she stumbled into the kitchens. And into the fire.

Broderick stood, arms folded, brow furrowed.

Her stomach sank. "B-Broderick." Around them, the bustling kitchen staff scurried about, stealing sideways looks at brother and sister.

"Leave us," he quietly ordered.

The men, women, and children all abandoned their tasks and filed from the room.

She forced herself to remain absolutely motionless as Broderick passed a probing gaze over her disheveled hair and rumpled cloak, damp from when she'd been knocked down. Which only conjured images of Connor covering her with his broad, powerful frame—her breath caught—and the feel of his mouth on hers. Which hadn't been at all vile. It had been . . . magic. It had been . . .

Broderick lingered his eyes on her lips. Thoroughly kissed as she'd been, the heat of Connor still imprinted upon her person, surely her brother could see that brand left?

Heat scorched her entire body.

"You ran out of a shop."

She bit down on the inside of her lower lip. "I'm not a child in need of lecturing."

He went on. "The most celebrated modiste in London, and only *after* you threatened a lady."

"It was two." Her brother stitched his eyebrows into a single line. "Ladies," she clarified. "Nor did I threaten them," she said on a rush. "I merely"—she waved her hand—"revealed my knife." Or rather the one she'd relieved one of the guards of. She took care to leave that detail out.

Broderick covered his face with his hands and inhaled loudly. He let his arms drop to his sides. "We had an agreement." Her every muscle tensed. "You honored it . . ." Her brother yanked out his gleaming timepiece and consulted it. "Less than fifteen hours ago," he confirmed, snapping the case closed. He tucked the fob back inside his jacket.

No.

"Reggie is seeing to your things."

Ophelia fluttered a hand to her throat. "Seeing to my things?" Her voice emerged faint.

"Your trunks. I've sent word to Cleo and . . . her husband that you'll be arriving."

A tortured little moan left her lips. "But . . ."

"Your word is your bond," he reminded, killing her useless appeal.

She tried again. "But . . . but . . . my role here." The control she'd wrested for herself could not be this fleeting. Bloody impetuous self. Why had she gone after him? *Because you were worried about the child.* A child who'd burned with his hatred of her and hadn't even wanted her underfoot anyway.

"Your role will be overseen by another."

Think . . . think . . . She inhaled slowly. He sought to protect . . . which had always been Broderick's way. First Ophelia and her sisters in the streets, and Stephen, their brother . . . then the men, women, and children employed by the Devil's Den. It was an inherent part of his character he could not divorce himself from. He sought to scuttle her away for her own protection. "I've done nothing wrong, Broderick," she said with equanimity, meant to reassure. "I am safe." She gave him those three words. That one he'd been single-mindedly fixed on since he'd entered their midst a scared but determined-to-survive orphan.

Broderick paused. "No one of our station is ever safe. Not truly."

It explained his hungering for a connection to the nobility that he was determined to secure at the expense of her happiness and future.

"You leave tomorrow." Without another word, her brother left.

And her fate was sealed.

Chapter 9

Once, Ophelia had been saved by her brother, Broderick.

Only to be sacrificed by him all these years later.

"A dinner party," she muttered.

From where she stood, on the fringe of Calum and Eve Dabney's parlor, Ophelia scanned the crowded room.

Under any other circumstances, the fact that she'd set foot in the home of her family's rivals would have been reason enough for the unease churning in her gut. But everything had changed. Through the marriage of her sister, the once-hated family had become an unlikely ally . . . and was the reason she was able to be presented before Society even now.

Footsteps sounded in the hall.

Her back went up.

One had to always be prepared for battle.

An older white-haired gentleman entered the room as bold as if he owned the space. The smile on his face was a contradiction to the harsh glowers she'd come to expect of the peerage.

There'd been enough nobs with that same type of smile . . . and there had been nothing but treachery in their black souls.

You like it rough, do you? All the better, my naughty little girl.

Her stomach pitched, and to keep from giving in to the nightmares, she breathed in slowly through her nostrils.

"'is Lordship, the Earl of Mar," the coarse butler announced in street Cockney.

Ophelia shook her head hard, fighting back the memories and focusing on Dabney's servant.

Street rats holding doors and announcing lords. When had the world gone topsy-turvy? Ophelia made to look away from the stranger even now being greeted by their host, but something about the older lord called her back.

Furrowing her brow, she studied him, searching her mind. A wide smile wreathed the gentleman's face, an expression unrestrained and sincere in its warmth.

Had he been a member of the Devil's Den? There was an odd air of familiarity to him that she could not place.

She scoffed.

Don't be silly.

Of course she didn't know the nob. Bored in her examination, she shifted her attention out and sighed.

So this is why her sister had sneaked out and returned home after her presentation to Polite Society. It had made sense before, but it made even more sense now on a level Ophelia could personally commiserate with.

Praying for a swift end to the night, Ophelia searched out the ormolu clock atop the mantel. A different gentleman, tall and smartly dressed, stood between her and that piece that could provide her a glimpse of just how much more of this misery she'd have to suffer through. Ignoring the bald stares shot her way, Ophelia angled her head.

Move, will you, already?

She arched her neck back and forth.

The gentleman touched a surprised hand to his chest, and then a pleased and pompous grin curled his lips.

"Move," she mouthed.

His smile froze in place.

"Move," she repeated, and then when he remained motionless as a lackwit, she made a slashing gesture across her throat.

Blanching, the gentleman scurried out of her way, allowing Ophelia an unfettered view of the clock.

Ten minutes.

She and her sister and brother-in-law, and former enemy, had been here ten minutes. Her eyebrows shot to her hairline. That was all? She knew even less than nothing about Polite Society and the silly events they assembled, but she'd wager her family's club that those affairs lasted a good deal longer than—Ophelia stole another peek—eleven minutes. Now, eleven minutes.

Ophelia tamped down a groan.

After a week's time of living with her sister Cleopatra and her husband, Adair, it could be worse.

Liar.

"It could be worse," a voice whispered against her ear.

Gasping, Ophelia spun to face her sister Cleo. "Bloody hell, Cleo," she muttered, her neck burning hot. That curse earned several censorious stares, which both sisters ignored. She'd been caught. It was an unpardonable sin to commit, even with one's own sibling. Tasked with presenting Ophelia before the *ton*, who in St. Giles would have wagered that it was the ruthless Cleo Killoran who would pave Ophelia's proverbial way? "You do not go sneaking up on a woman," she groused. "Any person," she amended, lest her sister had forgotten all the ways of the streets.

A wicked glimmer danced in Cleo's eyes, and she winked slowly. "And you certainly don't allow yourself to be sneaked up on."

Of course, her sister was right. A wise person bent on survival didn't let his or her guard down—be it an alley in St. Giles or outside the theatres at Covent Garden . . . or in this case, Calum and Eve Dabney's Mayfair residence. Not unless one wished to find oneself cut down by one's enemy. Her stare collided with a slender, dark-haired woman eyeing her from over the rim of her fan. The stranger swiftly snapped it shut and jerked her attention elsewhere in a clear redirect.

There could be no doubting . . . there were enemies all around, and of every station.

Cleo looped her arm through Ophelia's, and startled, Ophelia stared down at that unexpected contact. Her sister had never bothered with shows of affection—and certainly not public displays. "It really could be," Cleo explained through her surprise. "Worse, that is."

"I rather doubt that," Ophelia mumbled.

"Oh, certainly," her sister said, demonstrating her lifelong irascibility. With her spare hand, she proceeded to mark off a list on her fingers. "You could find your first foray in Polite Society to be a ball full of leering lords"—yes, that would have been a good deal worse—"but only after you are formally presented to all, with the entire room's eyes upon you."

Ophelia shuddered. "I concede the point." Cleo was correct. It was, however, a possibility that would become an eventuality.

Cleo arched an eyebrow. "It does bear mentioning that such a fate was the one I suffered through when I was presented to the *ton*, and I was not in the presence of a sibling or friend . . . but rather alone. On my own. With our enemy."

"Very well, your point has been made," Ophelia cut in to that accurate and humbling set-down.

Cleo grinned and fell silent.

They stared at the guests assembled thus far for the Dabneys' dinner party.

With the exception of her sister and kin by marriage, there wasn't a soul she recognized within the room. It was an odd occurrence for a Killoran to not identify a single patron.

"They are all reformers," Cleo said, following the precise thoughts her mind had wandered to. For the first time in the whole of their sisterly existence, her sibling avoided her eyes.

"What kind of reformers?"

But then, were there any other kind? Cleo gave a negligent roll of her shoulders. Making contact with her husband across the room, she lifted her hand in greeting.

Anticipating the step before she even took it, Ophelia shot a hand out, capturing her forearm. "What kind of reformers?" she repeated, a warning there.

"Ones against spirits."

Ophelia released her sister and jammed her fingertips into her temples. So this was why not a single person here, outside the Black family, was familiar. "What else?" she gritted, because as skilled as her youngest sister had always been at dissembling, Ophelia knew that look in her eyes.

"And they *might* be opposed to . . . gambling," Cleo mumbled. "*Are* opposed," she reluctantly corrected herself. "They are opposed."

Mad. The world, her kin included, had all gone mad, and Ophelia was the last Killoran to have maintained her sanity. "We are keeping company with . . . r-re-re—?" She choked.

Her sister patted her on the back. "Reformers," she repeated with far too much tolerance, by Ophelia's way of thinking.

"S-surely you see the absolute ridiculousness in this," she hissed.

"Hush," Cleo muttered, slapping her all the harder, this time in warning more than an effort to help.

Through tear-filled eyes, Ophelia glared at her sister. These were the manner of people her sister sought to introduce her to? Men and women who'd not only look down on their livelihood but also seek to destroy them?

"You are mad," she whispered. Clutching her sister by the elbow, she dragged her from ear's reach of a gaping matron. "You are attending events hosted by—"

"By the Dabneys," her sister protested with a frown.

"By our rival, who's given up his gaming club?" Now his reasons for doing so made sense. She blanched.

God would cart her off to Newgate to pay for her crimes the day she sold her soul on the altar of the peerage.

From across the room, Adair stopped midconversation with his brother, Calum, and met Cleo's eyes. There was both a tenderness and possessiveness to that stare that Ophelia had to look away from. "Your husband awaits," Ophelia said.

Cleo held her elbow out, but Ophelia waved her off.

"I'll join you later." After she settled her outrage at the discovery tossed out in this public setting.

Except instead of rushing off, her sister lingered, and when she spoke, there was a newly acquired hesitancy there. Sadness slipped in, chasing off her earlier annoyance. It served as just one more mark of the ways life in Mayfair had wholly changed her sister and made them more strangers than anything. "Those who live here . . . the lords and ladies of the peerage, they are not all bad. Some are good."

You little street slut . . . open your legs . . . you want it . . . you always want it.

Bile climbed up the back of Ophelia's throat, and through it she forced a grin, wanting her sister gone, needing to be alone—as one might manage in a stranger's parlor filled with guests. As her sister reluctantly took herself off, she stared after her.

Ophelia had fended off attacks from strangers in the streets; she could certainly make it through a dinner party.

Hovering at the edge of the parlor, Ophelia forced her feet to remain rooted to the Aubusson carpet of Calum Dabney's Mayfair residence and made herself as still as possible. If one made oneself still, the world forgot to pay note, and one was spared attention and notice.

With the festivities continuing in a whirl around her, and she on the fringe of it all, how eerily similar this moment was to so many of her past: on the outside, surrounded by nobles.

Nay, that wasn't altogether true. She was not surrounded solely by fancy lords and ladies with fancy titles that went back to the first king of England.

As if in mockery of her own discomfort, a full, unrestrained laugh bounced around the room, echoing off the walls, bringing Ophelia's attention to the owner of that joyous expression.

Cleo.

Only Cleo as Ophelia had never seen her. As she'd never known her. Comfortable, casual, engaging in discourse with those same privileged peers she'd once vowed to gut if they stepped too close.

And smiling . . . she was also . . . smiling.

It was a warmer, softer, more tender version of her sister.

Amidst a room full of strangers staring baldly back, Ophelia had never felt more lonely.

In that instant, she confronted her own ugliness as a person and as a sister, for she resented Cleopatra. Resented her for fitting in this world they'd once hated with equal measure.

So that is what love did?

It melted a person's hatred and turned them into a vague shadow of the person they'd always been.

Just then, Cleopatra's husband, Adair, whispered something in her ear, earning a blush.

A bloody blush? Not the soft, pink, so-faint-it-might-be-nothing-more-than-a-play-of-the-lighting blush . . . but the crimson, fiery sort.

Ophelia choked on her swallow.

What in the Devil alternate world was she living in?

In the past they'd been unsuspecting of her presence. Now, they knew of it. When before she'd only been invisible to them. And knew it in the way the ladies curled their lips in disdain and whispered around their delicate satin fans.

It could be worse. It could be worse.

Those words rolled around her mind, a silent mantra.

It could be—

Connor entered the room.

Ophelia went absolutely still.

Surely her eyes were merely playing tricks in the candles' light.

After all, she had been gripped by thoughts of their embrace since she'd fled his presence. Her pulse quickened. Hot energy speared through her, burning her with the memory of those hard lips on hers. The taste of him. The corded power of his muscles. His . . .

"Mr. Steele," the butler thundered in his roughened street tones.

Well, bloody hell, she'd been otherwise wrong—the evening had just gotten worse.

Why in blazes was he here, of all places?

Why else do you think he's here? He'd discovered her attack of a lord that night. Her *assault* of the man had been splashed upon the gossip columns, warning the nobility of the peril in the streets. *No. No.* There could be any number of reasons he was here. *He could . . . or he might . . .* There could be no other explaining his presence.

With all the stares now securely reserved for the beautifully rugged guest at the front of the room, Ophelia searched for an escape.

Tall and in command, he strode deeper into the parlor with purposeful steps, a man on more of a mission than any soldier in the King's Army. Ophelia darted her gaze about as a flurry of whispers followed Connor's wake.

That strangely familiar gentleman alongside Calum Dabney approached him.

It was with years of relying on another's unspoken body movements to survive that she noted the easiness of that trio's exchange: the lack of tension as they shook hands, the older man's laugh . . .

Why . . . why?

Ophelia furrowed her brow.

He knows them. There was a familiarity with which that group spoke. As she watched on, her mind raced.

Connor O'Roarke, the Hunter, an investigator feared throughout London, had been invited by Calum Dabney.

Which meant he was going to be dining at the same table she was.

Swallowing a groan, she searched the room, the urge to flee even stronger. All of a sudden she found herself preferring his formal questioning to a sure-to-be-mocking reaction to her attending an event hosted by Polite Society.

Nodding his head at something one of the pair speaking with him now said, whatever Connor's reply was earned a laugh from Calum Dabney.

She edged backward, wanting to slip behind the curtains.

Just then, he looked up, and his eyes collided with hers.

Even with the distance between them, she registered the surprise in his gaze. A slow grin tipped his lips at the corners. He winked.

She flared her eyes. "Did you wink at me?" she mouthed. That almost-taunting-but-wholly-teasing gesture. Damn her heart for tripping an erratic beat.

He responded with another wink before his attention was called by the kindly looking gentleman who'd snagged Ophelia's notice earlier.

Ophelia stood there in silent tumult.

Before Broderick had taken over control of Diggory's streets, everyone had been too terrorized to feel any emotion except hatred and fear. After that miserable blighter had kicked up his heels, the men within the gaming hell had treated her and her sisters as though they were of an exalted station.

Yet Connor had teased Ophelia. Had done so when no one else before him had.

Ophelia found Connor precisely where she'd last spied him, along with the familiar stranger and their host, and now the addition of a new person.

This one . . . a lady.

Taller than many, Ophelia had always thought herself to be of a considerable height. She'd lamented it as a child for the fact that she'd not possessed the small stature of her sister Cleo, who'd been stealthy in her thievery because of it. The woman, two inches shorter than Connor's six feet four inches, was a veritable giant.

Only a slender, small-hipped sort.

Her thick black curls, elegantly gathered and held in place with diamond butterfly clips, were a perfect complement to the man beside her. They were a gypsy couple in full command.

And by the way the woman periodically swatted at his arm and leaned into him, they were very much a couple.

Who was she? His lover? Moving freely about the gaming hell floors over the years, Ophelia was certainly no innocent to the ways of the *ton*. Lords visited their clubs and bedded their whores while their wives took on with others. Is that what Connor was? Some noblewoman's lover?

It would just be another sign that Connor O'Roarke thought himself better than the world he'd been born to, carrying on with a lady. It was surely that which accounted for the uncomfortable sentiments swirling in her gut . . . ones she could not name or identify, nor wished to . . . in Calum Dabney's parlor, no less.

"Dinner is served," a servant announced from the front of the room.

Dinner with her childhood nemesis Connor O'Roarke and his noble friends . . . and his fancy lady.

Panic mounting, Ophelia darted into the adjourning room. The echo of the other guests' voices grew increasingly distant until Ophelia was left alone with a safe silence.

She paced, cursing Connor's reappearance in her life as an age-old resentment for him was kindled anew.

He'd been the boy who'd gotten away and thought himself better than anyone. He'd only grown into an equally pompous man. It had been resentment of that fact that had pulled the bitter reply off her tongue. The work Connor did now for men of power, and his attendance at *ton* events, flirting with ladies and chatting with lords, only highlighted that exalted place he'd always claimed for himself in St. Giles.

In the days when she'd allowed herself to think of Connor and her role in ensuring his freedom, she'd alternated between revering him for what he'd accomplished . . . and hating him.

Ophelia stopped abruptly, her skirts swirling angrily about her legs.

Is it really Connor you hate? Or yourself for having sacrificed one sibling to secure his future?

Because each time she saw him again, she was confronted by all the ways she'd failed her sister.

Ya found 'im and let 'im go . . . ya'll pay for that . . . now how to make ya pay.

A fine sheen developed over her eyes, and she furiously blinked it back. *Bloody dust.* There was no other way to account for her blurred vision. For she certainly wasn't one given to waterworks. She dashed a hand angrily over her eyes. One would expect a duke's daughter, even one married to Calum Dabney, to have servants to see to the blasted dusting.

Yet if Connor were the pompous bastard she'd always taken him for, what was to account for the offense he'd taken at her words? Nor could there be any mistaking those sentiments before he'd stood and stalked off.

In the silence of Calum Dabney's room with all the guests thankfully gone, she accepted the needling in her belly for what it was—guilt. *You bloody fool.* What in blazes did she have to feel guilty for?

The facts remained:

One, Connor O'Roarke had escaped St. Giles and somehow made a life for himself outside of East London.

Two, he worked for those same fancy lords who thought nothing of battering and abusing the children who lived on those streets.

Three, he'd sought to force her hand in his investigation by threatening her club . . . and through that, her family.

She wrinkled her nose. Was there a fourth? Ophelia fished around her brain . . . and came up empty.

There needn't be any more than that. The latter reason alone had been enough to hate him outright.

I wouldn't be so foolish as to laugh at the Jewel of St. Giles.

There hadn't been a thing sardonic or biting about that statement. Instead, he'd spoken with a respect and admiration that she didn't know what to do with.

"Wot in 'ell are ya doing?"

Gasping, Ophelia whipped up her head.

Caught.

Her sister Cleo cursed a stream of invectives that would have set a sailor to blushing. "Wot in blazes are ya doing?" she demanded again, storming into the room.

"I'm not stealing from Dabney, if that is what you're worried after," she muttered.

"Oi'm worried about what they'll say about ya being caught sneaking about Calum's home."

Calum. Another of their lifelong rivals whom her sister now spoke of and about with such ease.

"Is that what you care about now? The gossips?" My God, what had happened to her fearless, unrepentant sister?

Except she had cowed to Broderick's wishes and expectations. Was it a surprise she should continue to falter before that world her brother had thrust her into?

"Don't look at me like that," Cleo snapped.

"Like what?" she asked, lifting her chin in a challenge.

Her younger sister's eyes formed small slits. "And do not presume to play the lackwit with me. You know precisely what I'm talking about." With a reassuring show of her old spirit, Cleo growled. *So she hadn't been wholly crushed.* "You look at me differently."

"You are different," Ophelia said softly. She'd simply believed her sister hadn't noted the changes.

Cleo's waiflike frame jerked erect in the same way it had on the cusp of a street battle. Her sister dropped her voice to a hushed whisper. "You look at me as though I'm weak and you're somehow stronger."

She made a sound of protest. "Don't be foolish." Having had her face against a brick wall while a nobleman had pawed at her, Ophelia had no misconceptions of her own infallibility.

"Let us be clear, Ophelia, as you stand here the proud Killoran, resolute in the face of the *enemy* . . . you've also been ordered about by Broderick, and not unlike me, you are here now, just as I was." She jammed a finger toward the gleaming oak floors. "You also gave in to Broderick. Why? To prevent him from using Gertrude in your stead?"

That is precisely what it had been. Only . . . "It's not the same," she said through gritted teeth, eyeing the doorway. Her sister had once been more careful. Careful enough that she'd not risk an exchange that could be overheard by those lurking in the shadows.

"Very well, then. How have I changed, hmm? Do you see me as weak now?"

"Never that," Ophelia said at last. She'd endured too much and defeated foes two times her size when she'd been a mere girl. They all had. Those experiences left a person stronger in ways they'd previously never been. That could not be undone, any more than the evils they'd endured to survive could be erased.

"What, then?" Her sister dropped her hands on her hips and angled closer. "A traitor to the Killorans?"

There it was. The wedge that had divided them since Cleo had returned to the Devil's Den and professed her love for a man they'd spent their young lives hating as an enemy. Unable to meet her sister's too-knowing eyes, Ophelia glanced to the doorway. After dreading dinner with a room full of nobs and her family's rivals, she found herself wishing she'd followed the guests to that damned dining room.

The fight drained from her sister's taut shoulders. "That is why you don't come around," her sister noted, and had there been fury and condemnation in her tone, it would have been far easier to take than that whisper of sadness. It was the rawest, most real she'd ever recalled her sister being in any discourse . . . and she didn't know what to do with this stranger.

But then, that is what she'd become in so many ways—a stranger.

Ophelia swiped a hand over her eyes. "I have my work at the club now." Or she had. Before she'd been ordered away and had ultimately chosen to save Gertrude over all the waifs in the street in need of saving.

Through her smudged spectacles, Cleo's regretful eyes met her own. "You could do both," her sister pointed out.

Ophelia stared at her quizzically. What was she talking about?

"Visit me, and see to your work at the Devil's Den."

She scrabbled with the sides of her skirts. For though she had been consumed with her role in helping the children of St. Giles find safety and security, she could have, as her sister argued, *come 'round.*

But Ophelia had been unable to enter Adair Thorne's household, even with her sister living there. There were too many years of hatred and mistrust.

Cleo gathered her hands, squeezing them tightly. "My God, they forgave our family for burning down their clubs, Ophelia. Yet you still cannot see past your hatred. They were not wrong all these years. Our family was—"

She recoiled. "Do not," Ophelia rasped. It was enough that Cleo had tied herself to the Blacks. It was an altogether different matter to have that same sister now question who the Killorans had been all these years and what they'd done to survive.

Releasing her, Cleo gave her head a shake.

"I am here now," Ophelia said lamely.

Her sister smiled, a pitying one that cut to the quick. "Yes. Yes, you are . . . here." Precisely where Cleo had been and would forever remain.

Had her younger sibling spoken them, the words couldn't have been clearer.

They stared at each other, neither conceding another word or emotion.

Cleo was the first to look away.

She glanced to the clock. "Come." Cleo held out her arm. "As it is, with the both of us gone, they'll no doubt wonder if we've made off with Calum's silver." She followed that with a smile, a hesitant bid at returning them to normality.

Ophelia looped her arm through her sister's and allowed her to lead her to her first societal event . . . within the enemy's lair, with Connor O'Roarke seated at the opposite side of a supper table.

Connor with his steel-hard eyes, who'd teased her. It was an incongruity that didn't fit with the cold investigator who'd threatened her family's livelihood.

Too soon, Ophelia and Cleo arrived in the Dabneys' formal dining room.

All eyes swiveled to the doorway, equal parts fascination and revulsion spread amongst the respectable guests.

Ophelia curled her toes so tight her arches ached.

"You can do this."

Did that muted whisper belong to her sister? Or was it merely a product of her own silent thoughts?

Tilting her chin at a defiant angle, she glowered in return, daring the crowd with her eyes, moving her stare down the length of the table—and then colliding with the empty seat alongside an unsmiling Connor O'Roarke.

Oh, please, please, saints above, let the seat belong to my sister. Please. "Miss Killoran."

She stiffened as that gentle and cheerful voice sounded from the head of the table.

Mrs. Dabney, the sister of a duke whose cultured tones and graceful movements were so at odds with the man she'd wed. Waving off a servant's offer to assist, she hopped up from her seat and joined Ophelia and her sister. "Allow me to show you to your seat."

No. Please. No. She allowed herself to be pulled along past lords and ladies and Blacks, feeling like one being led to one's executioner.

Mrs. Dabney escorted her to that blasted open seat beside her lifelong nemesis.

Connor, with a gesture better suited a gentleman, climbed to his feet.

If she had any inclination of the palpable tension between them, their hostess hid it and beamed, glancing back and forth between Ophelia and Connor. "Mr. Steele, please allow me to introduce you to Miss—"

He settled an inscrutable stare on her face. "I have had . . . the pleasure."

Whatever their hostess and the assembled guests close enough to hear that statement had been expecting, it assuredly had not been that. Mouths fell agape, and looks were exchanged.

As Ophelia claimed the seat next to Connor, she silently cursed a day that had gone from bad to worse—and was now a disaster.

The vixen was miserable.

Which shouldn't matter. This was an altogether different misery from what he'd come to know from the heated spitfire.

Shoulders bent, she devoted all her attentions to the contents of her white soup, the way a clergyman attended his morning prayers.

As she had since it had been set down before her nearly fifteen minutes earlier.

It doesn't matter to you.

She was quite clear in her opinion of him and his company. She detested him—as she had since she'd found him in the streets, a boy fighting recapture.

Or it shouldn't matter. Only, he'd been her. New to Society, whispered about by all and respected by almost none. It had taken him years to let those insults roll off his person and become content in who he was.

Oh, she might believe herself different from him, but the truth remained: given the crimes they'd committed and the evil they'd witnessed, they'd always be alike—whether either of them wished it or not.

It was surely that reason alone which counted for the need to see her usual spirit restored—even if it was to the spitting and snarling creature she'd always been around him.

"I believed it was palms."

Slowly lifting her head, she met his gaze squarely. "Beg pardon?" She begged no person's pardon, and she certainly never had his.

Connor gestured to the gold-filigree Limoges bowl. "I've seen you study a hand with such intensity only when telling the future."

Her eyes went wide, and her lips moved, but no words came out.

He winked and spooned some of the light broth into his mouth.

"You know that," she whispered. Given the fact that before he'd been plucked from the streets, he'd existed as nothing more than a shadow hunted by Diggory, hers was a fair query. "*How* do you know that?" Her returned question was heavy with skepticism.

Lowering his spoon, Connor placed his lips close to her ear. "I may not have been as skilled at subterfuge as you, Ophelia Killoran, but I did manage on occasion to survive, unseen, without your help."

It still did not diminish the great favors she'd done him. She had been the only one of Diggory's gang whose path had crossed his. And for all her shows of hatred for him, she'd never turned him over, and for that he would be forever grateful.

She wrinkled her pert nose, indecision warring in her eyes. "I haven't read them since I was a girl. I have no intention of ever doing so again."

She didn't trust him. It was there clear for him to see, an indelible part which every person who'd lived in St. Giles would carry. ¡

Then she collected her spoon, dipped the silverware inside, and drew a circle in the broth. He expected a stretch of uncomfortable silence from her.

"You never explained why you are here."

But then, he should always know better than to make assumptions where Ophelia was concerned. "You never asked," he reminded. He took a long swallow from his crystal goblet. All the while he studied her over the rim.

Ophelia paused with her distracted movements. "Your investigation?"

He lifted his lips in a droll grin. "It's hardly an equitable trade to offer details about my presence when you have proven less than accommodating to discuss why you are here."

Had he not been studying her so closely, he'd have failed to miss her long fingers tightening around the stem of her spoon and the way the blood drained from those digits as she kept a death grip upon it.

She no more wanted to be here amidst Polite Society than he himself had all those years earlier. She'd the same look of one poised to take flight. For the tension that had always existed between them, he felt a kindred connection to Ophelia in this instance.

"Am I to expect you, the great investigator, knower of all information, has failed to see all the stories about me splashed upon the gossip pages?" she asked, bitterness making her tone sharp.

Setting aside his glass, Connor reclined in his chair. For the majority of rot published in those pages, there was occasionally a snippet of information that had helped him solve cases. As she'd predicted, he was one who gathered details and filed away that which could benefit whichever case he'd taken on. "You are correct. I did read the gossip." Ophelia's full upper lip curled. "Of course you did."

"You judge me for being cognizant of what is being said? Yet never did I claim to take the words written in those sheets as fact. Are they true?" he asked curiously. It was surely a curiosity about the minx from his past and nothing more. "Are you here to make a match with a nobleman?" If so, she was no different from the Lady Bethanys of the world. All his oldest annoyances boiled to the surface.

A footman inserted himself between them, and Connor silently damned the gold-clad servant now clearing away the first course of the evening meal.

After the next dish was placed before them and the servants returned to their positions against the wall, Connor redirected his attention to Ophelia.

"Well?" he asked, as though there hadn't been so much as a break in their discourse.

She grabbed her fork and knife, and he tensed, warily eyeing those makeshift weapons.

The ghost of a smile graced her lips. That slight expression of mirth softened her features, chasing away the unfortunate cynicism that had marred her since she was a girl. "Do you think I'm going to carve you up?"

"You certainly suggested you'd do it."

If ya know what's good for you, O'Roarke, ya'll stay away from me and mine, or Oi'll cut ya up and feed ya to the dogs in St. Giles.

Ophelia briefly dipped her eyes, but not before he spied the darkening there. Was it regret he observed in them? He studied her bent head. The chandelier's glow cast a soft light upon her pale strands, adding to the otherworldliness of this woman. No. It wasn't possible. She'd never been anything but unapologetic where he'd been concerned. "What have you heard?" she asked gruffly.

"What have I *read*?" he corrected. "That you have your eye on a title."

"And what do you think?"

It was on the tip of his tongue to ask her whether it mattered . . . when it never had. She'd been the proverbial oil to his water. Only—

If he spat that retort, that would undoubtedly be the end of their discourse.

"I always believed you'd rather cut a lord than marry one."

A smile dimpled her cheek and lit her eyes, and by the softening of her expression, he may as well have plucked a star from the heavens.

All of a sudden, that soft amusement withered. "My brother," she conceded, shoving the tip of her fork at the ragù of veal on her plate. He hurried to mask his surprise at her forthrightness. She abruptly lifted her head, and her next words came out underscored with a defensive edge. "My *brother* wants the match," she said softly from the side of her mouth. "*Not* me." As soon as that revealing bit slipped out, she went tight-lipped.

He flicked his gaze briefly to Bethany, though he was wholly engrossed in his discussion with Ophelia. *My father insists I make the match, Connor. What else can I do?* It was all women ultimately desired. It was why he'd never wander down that perilous path of love again.

"And only nobility will do for the Jewel of St. Giles?" he murmured.

"According to my brother."

Oi would have made ya moi wife. Oi've a special spot for ladies.

The distant screams of his mother melded with her pleading echoed at the back of his mind where the darkest demons would forever linger.

The lively discussions and periodic peals of laughter occurring about the dining room heightened the viciousness of the crime that had seen Connor an orphan. Three crimes committed that day that had seen Connor shattered and alone.

Hatred sang in his veins for Diggory and the men who'd helped him amass his power, Broderick Killoran being the greatest one. In his craving for a link to the peerage, Killoran proved himself very much the Devil's apprentice.

The young proprietor was too blinded by his lust for power to see: no lord in London could ever be a match for the Jewel of St. Giles. With her contempt for the peerage, no nobleman could ever make her happy; nor would those gents understand her and the life she'd known.

"Well?"

Brought back to the moment, he arched an eyebrow.

Ophelia lifted her shoulders. "I told you my reason for being here. What is yours?"

Again, Connor leaned forward. "The truth?"

A snort escaped her, that inelegant sound attracting several disapproving stares. Connor and Ophelia ignored them. "It's a certainty that I wouldn't have you lie to me."

"I'm a guest."

"*You're* a guest?" she echoed, incredulity in her eyes. "Of Calum *Dabney?*"

He frowned. She didn't know. Ophelia truly had never gathered what had happened to him that long-ago night. Didn't know that when he'd stepped in to forfeit his life so she might be spared, he'd been saved in every possible way by one of those noblemen she so mistrusted. "You find that so hard to believe?" he evaded.

"You, an investigator, keeping company with a proprietor of a gaming hell?" Her words came to an abrupt stop. Understanding dawned in her eyes. "I see."

"What exactly do you believe you see?" he asked, wondering which path her clever mind had traversed.

"He supplies you with information about St. Giles."

"Calum Dabney has been forthcoming with the information that would be helpful to my case, but I am not here on a matter of official business."

"Then, why are you here?" she asked with a frankness he appreciated.

He considered her question a moment. "You asked how I survived . . . that day. How I escaped the constable and gentleman who dragged me off." He paused. "I was saved."

She tipped her head at an endearing little angle. That movement sent a white-blonde curl toppling over her eye. "What?" She swatted the strand back, but the stubborn lock persisted.

Connor's fingers ached with the need to gather the loose tendril. "I was adopted . . . by a nobleman."

Her crimson lips parted. "A nob?"

"Aye." He hesitated. The day he'd interceded on her behalf, Connor had confined her to a life of continued misery, while he had the world laid out before him without ever an empty belly and day of fear again. Pain twisted in his chest as that long-carried guilt whispered around once more. "The lord whose pocket you nicked spared me the hangman's noose . . . and brought me home."

Ophelia's jaw went slack, and she swiveled her head to the opposite end of the table where Connor's father sat speaking. "It is him," she said as a person who'd at last put together the pieces of a complicated riddle.

He searched for a hint of resentment and found only curiosity. "The earl had no family. He took me in his care. Gave me a home." A two-story townhouse that had been a palatial mansion to a boy accustomed to hovels and alleys. "An education." What had become of Ophelia in their years apart? His gut clenched.

"It is why you're now 'Steele,'" she said, more to herself.

"It is why I'm now Steele," he echoed, directing that to where his father sat conversing with Bethany.

She followed his stare. "Why are you telling me this?" she asked with guarded eyes as she looked back. "What do you want?"

How suspicious she'd always been. "What do I want?"

"People always want something."

Aye, that usually held true. And given her part in Diggory's gang and then at the late bastard's club, working with the children there, she represented access to countless boys he might interview on behalf of Lord Maddock.

"I would have you know that not all noblemen are evil. Some, like my father"—he edged his chin in the earl's direction—"are good."

Her mouth tightened. "And some are murderers, too . . . like the nob you're serving now."

"He was declared innocent," he said quietly. "I should think as someone who's so often judged and condemned before Society, you'd be more forgiving."

Ophelia scoffed. "Come, Connor. You know I'm more guilty than not of the crimes Society has accused me of." She picked up her knife and passed it back and forth between her hands. *"Worse."*

A pang struck his chest. Since he'd first met her, he'd always taken Ophelia as one made of steel, so jaded by life that she had erected walls that protected her from any and every hurt.

"You did what you had to, to survive," he said somberly. "We both did." She, however, failed to realize it all these years later.

Ophelia ceased her deliberate movements. "We're not the same, Connor. We never have been."

"Tell me, Miss Killoran," a singsong voice intoned from down the table. In unison, Connor and Ophelia swung their gazes across the table. "Are you enjoying your time in London?"

The previously noisy table fell silent.

From where she sat diagonal to Connor and Ophelia, the young duchess smiled. Hers was the practiced grin of a lady, one that did not strain the muscles of one's cheeks, and yet, unlike most of the women of the *ton*, her eyes sparkled with kindness.

At his side, Ophelia slowly set her fork down. She dabbed her napkin slowly at the corners of her lips before responding. "I've always lived in London," she finally said.

"Ah, yes. Forgive me. That is correct." Viscount Middlethorne's daughter lifted her head in apology. "I am ever so fascinated by life in St. Giles." She dropped her elbows to the table and rested her chin atop interlocked fingers. "Won't you tell us about your experiences?"

Her experiences. Connor ground his teeth. Bethany broached the subject of Ophelia's life as though they discussed the young woman's embroidery skills.

All eyes remained on Ophelia.

Ophelia lowered her hands to her lap, and from the corner of his eye, he took in the way she clenched and unclenched those callused digits. "What do you wish to know?" she asked in the flawless, clipped tones to rival the King's English.

He pressed his lips together. As long as he'd known Lady Bethany, she had very much been enthralled by the plight of those who dwelled outside of Mayfair. Hers, however, had never been the cruel searching that came from busybodies who didn't give a jot for those men, women, and children suffering. Rather, she'd devoted her time, resources, and energies to improving the lot of those like Connor and Ophelia. As much as he'd always admired the lady's altruism, in this, with Ophelia splayed open before a sea of curious onlookers, he felt a sharp sting of annoyance.

At the silence, Bethany's smile dipped. With one hand still tucked under her chin, she waved the other. "Oh, I do not know, Miss Killoran. All of it. Any of it." She stared back through innocent eyes, round like saucers. "I wager there is a table full of guests very much eager to learn whatever it is you would share. Were you a pickpocket? Is that what I've heard?" She glanced around the table as if seeking confirmation from another guest present. "Am I correct? One never likes to rely upon the gossips, isn't that true?" A nervous tittering went up around her.

Ophelia's expression hardened, and she remained mutinously silent.

Had he not stolen another sideways glance, he'd have failed to see the quake in her fingers; that slight tremble belied the brave show she now presented.

At the opposite end of the table, a growl rumbled from Connor's chest.

"Miss Killoran saved countless boys and girls in the streets of St. Giles back when she was merely a child herself, and even more now with the work she does for her family," he said. His deep, rumbling pronouncement blanketed the room in a thick tension.

Lady Bethany widened her eyes. "Indeed?" she said, in awestruck tones. "How very thrilling your life has been, Miss Killoran," she said with a small clap of her hands.

At her side, Connor's father said something that called her attention back, and the table resumed their previous discourses.

Connor's jaw clenched with frustration.

Precarious. Ruthless. Unforgiving. Ophelia's life, just like Connor's own, had been any number of things. Thrilling never had been one of them.

But then to those who'd never walked through the fires of hell as they had and lived to fight the nightmares, neither Lady Bethany, nor any other philanthropic guest here at Calum and Eve Dabney's behest, would ever understand. By the very nature of their fortunate existence, they were removed from the streets of East London.

"I'm sorry," he said quietly.

Ophelia raised her gaze to his.

"About . . . that questioning. Even as some of them, Lady Bethany included, mean well, there is . . ." He searched his mind.

"An insensitivity?" Ophelia supplied, distractedly trailing her fork around the perimeter of her porcelain plate.

"There is that." At best. Cruelty at worst. Connor reached for his glass.

"Connor?" Ophelia said, freezing his movements. "Thank you."

He lifted his tumbler in unspoken acknowledgment, and even though silence fell between them, Connor could not help feeling an unspoken truce had been struck.

Chapter 10

Ophelia's first appearance before Polite Society had been deemed a success by the gossip columns, but it had been bloody miserable.

As she was ushered through the Duke and Duchess of Somerset's residence later that week, it was a certainty that Ophelia's next foray could only prove to be even more horrid.

For this evening, there would not be a mere dining table full of vipers to face but an entire ballroom of them.

Trailing along at a slower pace than the one set by her sister and brother-in-law, Ophelia swallowed hard, as with each slow step that brought her closer toward her grim fate, reality settled firm around her mind.

There would be fancy lords who'd sign the silly card strapped to her wrist and then put their hands upon her.

Sweat beaded on her forehead.

Do not think of him . . . do not think of him.

For mayhap there wouldn't be. Mayhap those bloody nobs would treat her with their usual disdain and find themselves too pompous to taint their bloodlines with a bastard born in the streets.

As soon as the hope slipped in, it died.

If her sister's Season had proven anything, there would always be wastrel lords so in need of a fortune that they'd be willing to sell their names, bodies, and titles to ones such as the Killorans.

Yes, there would be dancers. Men who settled their hands at the small of her back and waist, forcing her fingers onto their shoulder . . . maneuvering. Manipulating. Controlling.

Just as he'd been.

You will do whatever I ask, you little slut . . . because that is what I paid good coin for . . . and that is what my right is.

She faltered and shot out an arm, steadying herself. Perhaps it had been a naïveté she hadn't believed of herself, or perhaps it had been wishful thinking, or mayhap even hope. But until this instance, she'd not considered the very real possibility that their paths would cross: hers and the gentleman's who would always own a horrifying place in her memories.

Ophelia abruptly stopped, motionless while her sister and Adair continued on ahead, and she gazed vacantly at their backs.

Of all the balls and soirees, what was the likelihood that of all people, she would come face-to-face with him?

I'll kill you for this, you little slut.

Ahead, she dimly registered her sister and brother-in-law looking back.

She stopped and gave her head a little shake.

I cannot do this. Not even for Gertrude. Be it a mark of her selfishness or weakness or cowardice—none of it mattered. The only thing that did was retaining her razor-thin grasp on sanity.

Cleo said something to Adair. He nodded once, and with a final concerned look in Ophelia's direction, he continued onward, allowing the sisters privacy.

Her sister sprinted down the hall. "Wot is it?" she demanded before she'd even come to a stop. Her words came muffled as if down a long, narrow corridor.

Unable to get words out past her thick throat, Ophelia shook her head.

Frowning, Cleo slapped her palm gently against Ophelia's cheek. "Please, don't tell me ya're going to faint on me?" In the past there would have been annoyance at the possibility. This newer, more tender Cleo entreated with her eyes and pulled Ophelia from the brink.

She inhaled slowly. "I don't faint," she managed, her voice weak to her own ears.

"Is this because of last evening?" Her mind blanked. They'd not spoken of Calum Dabney's dinner—until now. More specifically, they hadn't spoken about anything last evening or really at all since Cleo had moved out and Ophelia had moved in.

"Last evening?" she ventured cautiously, weighing her words. Had her sister noted her stolen exchanges with Connor? *And if she did, what would she say of your history with him and . . . what you did?*

"The Duchess of Argyll," her sister pressed, "and her public questioning."

That steadied her. So the young widow with a possessive gaze on Connor was . . . a duchess. A step below royalty. Is that what her sister believed? That Ophelia had been thrown off-kilter by a nob fascinated with the life of a street rat?

"It is no less than I expected." Talk of that idealistic lady was far safer, as it didn't involve discussions of the past and decisions Ophelia had made that had resulted in tragic consequences for one they loved.

That immediately earned a small, disapproving frown, again highlighting the marked shift that had occurred in Cleo. As one who'd hated the nobility with a vitriol to rival Ophelia's, even that had changed.

"Not all of them are unkind," her sister proceeded to point out. "The duchess, as I understand it, gives of her time at Eve's hospitals."

"That'll feed an empty belly," she muttered sarcastically, earning a frown from Cleo. Her sister's defense of the young widow was not unlike that of another. How highly Connor still thought of Lady Argyll, even after her betrayal.

Why should that rub Ophelia's last nerve raw?

Perhaps it was just that Connor had proven the unlikeliest of her defenders last evening when the Spartan beauty had dug her claws into Ophelia's flesh.

Ophelia bit at her lower lip. For there had been another time when he'd come to her rescue . . . years earlier. He'd allowed himself to be carted off to Newgate in her stead. The outcome didn't outweigh his sacrifice that day.

Who was Connor O'Roarke? Pompous hand of the nobility who didn't give a jot about the plight of those in St. Giles? Or respectable investigator with honorable intentions for all, regardless of station?

Her sister stuck an elbow in her side, and she grunted. "What in blazes was that for?"

"If you were anyone else, I'd say you were woolgathering."

Which was actually what Ophelia had been doing. Her cheeks heated, and she gave thanks for her sister's erroneously drawn opinion. "I don't give a jot about what that woman had to say; nor do I care about anyone else's opinion," she weakly offered. They'd faced Society's ill thoughts since they'd first drawn breath, and that disdain would follow them, regardless of the wealth they'd acquired.

"I know you," Cleo said quietly. "It bothers you that the nobility should be pardoned their crimes when we wear ours like a mark upon our skin."

The *D* carved above Connor's brow flashed to her mind's eye; that mark of ownership was etched into nearly all of Diggory's boys and girls, an indelible part that could never be erased. Yet Connor had somehow risen outside of the filth of St. Giles, the only place Ophelia and her kin would or could ever comfortably belong.

"I promise, for the manner of people such as that nasty harridan last evening, there will be others who speak on your behalf," her sister assured, mistaking the reason for her contemplativeness. "Honorable people like that Mr. Steele." Did she merely imagine the probing look her sister shot her? For it was gone so quickly it may as well have been a trick of her imagination. A mischievous twinkle sparked in Cleo's eyes. "Even if he is a bloody investigator," she said on a hushed whisper.

She forced the requisite grin and allowed her sister to lead her to the Duke and Duchess of Somerset's ballroom—and the miserable future her brother insisted she forge for the family.

As Connor entered Lord and Lady Somerset's ballroom, it became apparent with one glance that Ophelia Killoran had taken the *ton* by storm.

Just not for the reasons that the gossip columns had predicted. They had anticipated Ophelia would be met with closed doors, empty dance cards, and the scorn of all.

The swell of gentlemen in the corner of the room now swarming the pale-haired beauty made a mockery of any such forecast.

Having spent the day conducting interviews with the children who comprised the staff at Black's club, Connor had arrived conveniently late enough that he was spared the receiving line. From where he stood at the front of the ballroom, his gaze remained fixed on that blonde hair swept up into an artful chignon. Held loosely in place by rubies that glittered under the candle's glow, the coiffure gave the illusion that one slight move would set those strands tumbling free.

His breath hitched in his chest.

Bloody hell if he didn't want to see her hair flowing about her shoulders and waist as it had in Broderick Killoran's offices more than one week earlier.

The young woman's shoulders went taut, and she arched her long neck, glancing about.

Her gaze collided with Connor's.

She widened her eyes. "You," she mouthed.

He touched a hand to his chest and dropped his head in a deferential bow. "The very same."

Even with the length of the room between them, he caught the errant smile grazing her lips. She swiftly attempted to hide it with her hand.

"Quite a crowd," he articulated carefully, nudging his chin at the loudly dressed dandies surrounding her.

She cast her eyes to the ceiling and shook her head.

They shared a smile, and he started forward. Moving along the perimeter of the room, past elegantly clad lords and ladies, he continued on to Ophelia.

A tall, satin-clad figure stepped into his path, and he silently cursed. Bethany leaned negligently against a pillar, arms folded at her chest. "My, my, I'd begun to believe I'd only imagined our more than ten years of friendship," she drawled. Over the ruffled rim of her ivory fan, a teasing sparkle lit her green eyes. There was something else there . . . a smoky desire.

As a young man, he'd all but panted from one of those tempting come-hither looks she'd cast.

Now he found them pathetically coy.

"Ten and four," he corrected, looking in Ophelia's direction to those bloody swains now surrounding her. He forced his attention to the woman before him. He dropped a respectful bow. "Duchess."

With a snort, she snapped her fan closed. She glided over and swatted at his sleeve. "Hush with your meticulous accounting of our friendship. You are making me feel positively old, Mr. Steele."

"Never," he demurred, raising her fingers to his lips for a requisite kiss.

"Come, walk with me," she cajoled, slipping her arm through his, making the decision for him.

He cast a last regretful glance in Ophelia's direction and proceeded to walk Lady Bethany about the room.

"I understand you are busy with another case," she murmured.

"I am." His responsibilities as an investigator were just another reason why he could not fulfill the expectations that she and their families had for them.

That is not solely the reason. Despite each of their fathers' expectations of and for them, Connor had long ago ceased to see Lady Bethany in any romantic light. She'd come to simply be the wide-eyed girl who'd declared him her friend . . . and proceeded to pepper him with questions about his life in St. Giles.

The viscount's daughter eyed him. "I've heard your investigation has taken you into the Devil's Den. Is it as wicked as they say?"

For her philanthropic endeavors, she'd also always been fixated on the world of East London as if it were more of a story in a gothic novel than real life. "I was otherwise focused on my assignment and not the vices to be explored." Whereas Ophelia Killoran . . . she appreciated and understood the world precisely for what it was and sought to improve the lives of the children in her charge.

Bethany stopped in the far corner of the ballroom, forcing him to a reluctant halt behind the Doric column. Before he could respond, she looked off pointedly in Ophelia's direction. "I trust it is your work that accounts for the attention you've shown the young woman."

He flashed a grin. "Come, Bethany, you've been many things where I'm concerned, but possessive was never one of them."

"Is she . . . important to you?"

Connor carefully weighed his reply. "She was my dining partner."

"How very . . . convenient," she commented, leaning against that marble pillar. Then her mouth formed a perfect circle, and she placed an artful gloved palm over it. "I see."

"And just what is it you think you see?"

"She is part of your investigation," she ventured, unerringly close. "It explains your . . . interest in the young woman."

His interest, as the lady put it, went beyond Ophelia's role at the Devil's Den. They had a shared history . . . often tense and mostly dark. But she'd also been the one to save him . . . more times than he'd deserved. How had she fared after the Earl of Mar's rescue? It was a question he'd not allowed himself to entertain, for selfish, cowardly reasons. Now, shame soured in his stomach.

"I trust Mr. Dabney knew what he was doing when he seated you beside the creature," Lady Bethany was saying.

Connor flattened his lips, unsure of which insult to take offense over on Ophelia's behalf: that disparaging title affixed her by Bethany or the claims that Ophelia's invitation last evening had been doled out as a way for him to interrogate the lady. Nonetheless, it was safer leaving Bethany to her erroneous opinions. "Come, you were never one to treat a person differently because of their birthright," he mocked, edging that reminder in steel.

Her lower lip quivered. "I've insulted you."

"Not at all." She'd annoyed him. Bethany layered hidden meanings within her questions and statements that grew tiring.

Unlike Ophelia, who'd only ever been given to blunt honesty.

A servant found them and proffered his silver tray of champagne. Connor waved the footman off and briefly considered the point of escape beyond Bethany's shoulder.

The duchess touched her fingertips to his sleeve, forcing his attention back. "I'm not cruel. I'm realistic of a person's motives," she went on, relentless. "And I've learned about the young woman's family in the papers. They are not to be trusted. She is not to be trusted."

It spoke to the lady's tenacity that she didn't show even a modicum of remorse over his previous rebuke.

"I do not make a habit of placing overly much credence in the gossip columns," he said frostily. The only use he had of those newspapers was as a means of obtaining information related to men or women involved in his cases. Beyond that, the *ton* was full of rather useless drivel.

"No, you never did," she said bemusedly. Going up on tiptoe, she whispered boldly against his ear. "It is just one of the many things I've come to admire about you, Connor," she murmured, commanding his Christian name. With a smile, Bethany sank back on the soles of her satin slippers. "The gossips were right about one thing where the young woman was concerned." He stiffened. "She is as lovely as they claimed."

More so. He grunted. Widowed two years now, Lady Bethany had become more dogged in her hope of a match between them. Had she always been this ruthless in her pursuit?

She formed a slight moue with her lips and gave him another tap with her fan. "It does not escape my notice that you did not refute it." The perfectly even-toothed smile she flashed did little to blunt the sharpness of her chastisement.

Yet why should he? Connor dealt in facts, and there could be no disputing that Miss Ophelia Killoran had a siren's allure.

The orchestra concluded the lively reel. As the polite applause of the partners went up, he searched out Ophelia once more. Which swain would be escorting the spitfire for the next set? A fancy lord who'd put his hands on her trim waist, and—

An uncomfortable knot tightened in his belly.

He jumped as Bethany rapped her fan against his sleeve.

"You are not paying attention," she pouted. All earlier hint of displeasure faded under a coy smile. "You may make it up to me with a dance."

A dance. Once, he'd been so desperate for her affections it was a morsel he'd craved from this woman . . . a public showing that she was unashamed of him—and more, that he had a claim to a future with her. "You know I'm rot at dancing." She'd often reminded him of that very fact as a way of explaining away her unwillingness to engage in a single set. "It is because I call you friend that I will not ask you to suffer through my plodding."

"Oh, hush, you are ever graceful on your feet," she protested with her usual fawning nature. He would have appreciated her more had she maintained the correct opinion of his dance skills from their youth.

Ophelia would *never* be one to ever praise him for the travesty of his steps on the dance floor and offer false compliments. Why, he'd wager the sterling reputation he had as an investigator that she'd as soon as stick a blade in his belly before allowing him to sign her dance card.

And the prospect of drawing her lush form into his arms was appeal enough that he'd be willing to find out.

Bethany planted her hands on her hips. "Do you intend to make me beg for a dance, Connor? Tsk, tsk, that is not very gentlemanly of you."

It was the one leveled charge that always had the ability to scrape at his conscience. It was an unwitting reminder of the life of crime and evil he'd lived before he'd entered the world of Polite Society, determined to be better and do more.

The couples filed onto the floor for the next set, a waltz. He found Ophelia precisely where he'd last spied her. Intrigued that she, too, remained on the sidelines, he made his excuses. "Duchess, please forgive me. I should pay my respects to our host." Connor sketched another bow and started across the ballroom, his gaze solely focused on the spitfire now surreptitiously inching around their host's ballroom.

Chapter 11

The night had been bloody miserable.

Until he'd arrived.

Which was surely a hint of her own desperation in being thrust into Polite Society that Connor's presence alone had managed to chase off the tension that had dogged her since her gown had been pulled into place and her hair arranged.

Following their brief, silent exchange from across the room, she'd been certain he'd been coming to join her. After suffering through the company of the wastrels in debt to her family's gaming clubs, she'd welcomed rescue where she could take it.

Then he'd gone and joined his fancy piece in the corner. With her fan, and wicked eyes, and ruthless jibes last evening, she could be a match for any ruthless sinner of the streets. "Nasty tart."

"Uh . . . I beg your pardon?"

Dragging her attention away from Connor, she forced her gaze back to Society's leading rogue. Lord Landon, the tenacious gentleman who'd positioned himself at her side since her arrival, blinked slowly. In dire financial straits and in desperate need of a fortune, the miserable blighter had gone from courting Cleo . . . to now Ophelia. She shoved to her feet. "I said, this is where we must part." She might be willing to make a match to save Gertrude, but she drew the proverbial line at a bastard who'd shift his attention from sister to sister.

A flurry of protests went up.

Lord Landon stepped into her path. "But our waltz is coming shortly," he purred.

"Step aside, Landon." Lifting her skirts slightly, she revealed the dagger positioned at her ankle. "I see my sister motioning." She pointed to the couples whirring across the duke's Italian marble floor.

The collection of gents gathered all looked in unison to the lone sibling in question. The very same one now being elegantly turned about the dance floor by her husband, both with matching besotted expressions. Expressions that indicated neither Thorne sought the company of anyone beyond their own.

Lord Landon smiled wolfishly. "She looks otherwise engaged," he persisted.

Betrayed by a second Killoran.

Ophelia sighed. She'd always looked after herself. Certainly she'd never required saving from anyone. "Look again," she growled, and this time when Lord Landon and the other nobs looked off, she ducked around the group and lost herself in the crowd.

With careful steps, she clung to the fringe of the room, dogging the footsteps of unsuspecting servants. The din of guests blurred with the whine of the orchestra's instruments in a cacophony of sound.

Her fingers twitched with her need to clap her palms over her bleeding ears. How she ached for the familiar sounds of St. Giles. The clink of coins striking coins. The—

A tall figure stepped into her path. "Miss Killoran, we meet again."

Ophelia shrieked, that soft cry muted by the din of the ballroom. She shot out her arm reflexively.

Connor easily caught it, deflecting the blow.

Heart racing, she forced her breath into an even cadence. "Bloody hell, O'Roarke, you know better than to go sneaking up on a person."

First her sister had managed the feat, now Connor O'Roarke? She groaned. Bloody hell, she was going soft.

He grinned, still retaining his hold on her arm.

She braced for the usual fear and horror that came from any such grip.

Little shivers of warmth radiated from his touch, foreign and so unexpected she was secretly loath for him to relinquish her.

Inevitably, Connor had never done as she'd asked or expected. He let her arm go, and she swiftly drew it close to her chest.

"I trust you are enjoying yourself."

She snorted. "Hiding in the shadows? I gather we have a like appreciation for the event."

He grinned again, flashing his even white teeth. "You would be correct on that score."

Her heart tripped a silly little beat.

Over Connor O'Roarke? Nonsense. It was merely the familiarity of suffering through *ton* events with someone who'd lived on the streets of St. Giles—even if it had never truly been with her.

He propped a hip against the wall and folded his arms at his chest. "Given we'd both sooner steal again in the streets of St. Giles than take part in the festivities, perhaps I can instead convince you to answer some questions."

Her smile froze in place.

That was all her every exchange with him came down to. Given what Gertrude and Stephen had shared about Connor's reputation as the Hunter, coupled with his own insistence since their reunion, she should expect nothing more.

So how to account for the disappointment that settled in her stomach?

He lifted an eyebrow. "Am I to hope that is a yes?"

She tried to pull forth her usual flippant "Go to hell" but couldn't manage it. For the truth she could at least admit to herself in her silent musings, was that after his defense last evening, she'd expected . . . more.

What she'd hoped for she could not say, and her mind shied away from any answers as to what it could possibly be.

"Miss Killoran!" They glanced off to that loud shout.

Whisperings went up loud enough to rival the whine of the orchestra as the crowd looked to Lord Landon. One arm up, he moved at a determined clip across the dance floor.

"Oh, bloody hell," she muttered.

"Lord Landon?"

She tensed her jaw. "The same." He hadn't left her alone this whole night. Nor by the determined glint in his eyes did he intend to. Under the thin leather gloves, her palms moistened. Another fancy lord determined to put his hands on her . . . "Dance with me." Hers was a harsh order.

Connor blinked slowly. "I don't . . . I . . ." He held up his palms.

She grabbed his hand and dragged him toward the dance floor. "Consider this the second debt paid," she muttered, yanking her reluctant partner along.

"The debt was paid when I stepped between you and a constable."

"There were others." Must he be difficult in this? She peered toward the resolute swain.

Lord Landon skidded to a stop in the midst of the ballroom and held a hand to his furrowed brow. Nearly trampled a moment later by a waltzing couple, he hurried from the floors.

"Put your hand on my waist, O'Roarke," she clipped out. When Connor tossed a desperate look over his shoulder, she muttered, "Oh, blast, I'll do it myself." She guided his hand to the point just above the small of her back and rested her other palm on his left shoulder.

With a sea of dancers whizzing past, Ophelia waited.

And waited.

Ophelia squeezed his fingers. "Well?" Even as the question left her, a slow, horrified understanding dawned. "You cannot dance."

The Duke and Duchess of Somerset knocked into them. Connor righted Ophelia. That graceful couple made their swift apologies and wisely adjusted their steps away from the still-motionless couple.

"I received lessons," he said grudgingly.

"The earl," she remembered. His adoption. How greatly their lives had diverged after that night when he'd been escorted off.

"Very well," she conceded. "You dance with me, and I'll answer three questions from you."

He froze.

"But we complete the set," she warned.

Without hesitation, he guided her slowly through the steps of the waltz, his large hand heavy at her back, reassuringly strong and warm.

She beamed. "You were being modest. You aren't nearly the—" His heel came down hard on her foot. Ophelia winced. "I cannot determine if that was on purpose."

"It wasn't," he mumbled, silently mouthing the one-two-three of the gliding dance.

"Yes, I see that now." Or he was determined to punish her feet for commandeering the set.

Connor's firm lips counted off the movements.

Ophelia shook her head. "Don't think of it in terms of numbers. Think of picking pockets." He stepped on her foot one more time. They stumbled, and with a curse, Connor tightened his hold on her, steadying them.

"Picking pockets?" he repeated incredulously, still counting that one-two-three pattern.

"Well, thievery we understand." Numbers, like words, had been irrelevant to them as children of the street. When Broderick had entered their fold and insisted she and her sisters be schooled in more than those dark acts, her only points of reference had remained her street experiences.

"You're mad."

"And you're going to find yourself counting a useless pattern, not having asked a single question before we're through."

He fell promptly silent.

"Do you see Lord Rothesay?"

Looking to where the dandy stood on the fringes, arms planted on his hips, a glower on his face, Connor nodded. "Left and center." His expression darkened, and were he any other man holding her so, with the harsh glint frosting his eyes, she'd have been riddled with terror.

But this was Connor O'Roarke.

"He shall be our constable," she explained as they slowly ambled through the movements. "The doorway in the far-right corner of the duke's ballroom shall be our escape."

His lips twitched.

She brightened. "See, you are enjoying yourself."

Connor scowled. "I am decidedly not."

Wrinkling her nose, Ophelia gave a toss of her head. "Very well. Forward-side-close. That's what you follow. Not your useless—"

"Ophelia—"

"Yes, yes. Of course. We move forward toward escape, slip sideways, and then close." While they drifted through the motions of the waltz, Connor instead repeated back her pattern.

"Is our constable staring?"

He stole a quick peek. "Indeed."

"So then we retreat: back-side-close."

They continued through the motions slowly, and with every repeat movement, she felt an increasing confidence in Connor's hold and steps. "I'm right," she said with a grin.

"You might be," he conceded, glowering over her shoulder at their improvised constable.

They settled into a companionable silence, and while she allowed Connor to concentrate on the new rhythm, her mind wandered back to his previous revelation. His earlier admission should not come entirely as a surprise. From her earliest memories of Connor, he'd always spoken in cultured tones that hinted at more than the street rat she herself had always been. "You've had dancing lessons."

He gave a slight nod. "I have."

That was it. Nothing more. For the rules of the streets that dictated a person not pry, questions hovered on her lips. Questions about not only what had become of him after his capture but also who he had been . . . before. Before he'd found himself in Diggory's clutches.

As the set continued, Connor relaxed the death grip he had upon her. With a gentler touch, he whirled her in neat, sweeping circles.

"They were my favorite lessons," she softly confided.

Connor tripped and quickly caught himself. He held her eyes, and in that instant all words and thoughts fled.

In the glow of the candles, and no more than a handbreadth between them, Ophelia appreciated the harshness of his heavy features. Had she truly believed him ugly? The pugilistic jaw of a fighter and the small bend in the middle of his nose from one too many breaks marked him as a warrior, unafraid of the battle.

"Which were?"

She studied his lips as they moved, hearing those words and slowly attempting to make sense of them past her muddled thoughts. "M-my dance ones. My lessons, that is," she elucidated. Her instructor had been five inches shorter than she'd been and hopelessly in love with the head guard at the Devil's Den. She'd never felt safer with another man . . .

Until Connor.

Ophelia stumbled, and Connor righted her. "It appears my own inadequacies are having a dangerous effect upon your own talents," he murmured. The hint of mint that clung to his breath caressed her face.

"Hardly." Unrecognizable. Did that breathy utterance belong to her?

"You enjoyed dancing?" he asked with a deserved incredulity.

There'd never been a thing fanciful about her, and yet . . . "There was something so thrilling in it," she said softly. A smile pulled at her lips. "After I'd mastered my lessons and my instructor, Monsieur La Frange, had gone, I would on occasion lock my chamber doors and waltz myself about my rooms." She'd forgotten about that detail until now. She glanced up, braced for his mockery.

Instead, he stared back with a tenderness that caused her heart to quicken. "Sometimes," she confided, when she'd shared no parts of herself with even her siblings, "I would pretend if I twirled fast enough, I might . . . disappear." From the dank apartments she'd called home, from the streets of St. Giles, from Diggory's gang. From all of it.

Feeling his piercing eyes on her face, she cleared her throat. "Yes, well, they were my favorite because those lessons were the closest I could get to scaling buildings and weaving between constables." Because of it, she'd felt less inadequate than she had for her failings where words and numbers had been concerned.

The orchestra concluded their playing, and as Connor and Ophelia stopped, the couples around them politely clapped.

They remained frozen as they were, hands upon each other.

She didn't care.

Didn't care because there'd never been a thing proper about her and never had, and never would she make apologies for it.

Didn't care because his touch burned through her gown and didn't inspire the fear and horror that had followed her these past thirteen years.

His gaze dipped to her mouth, and reflexively she wetted her lips. *He is going to kiss me here, with a room watching on, and help me for the whore another insisted I was, I want this man to do it.*

Connor's thick black lashes swept low, proving little shield for the heat within the grey depths of his eyes.

His expression grew shuttered.

Puzzling her brow, Ophelia followed his stare, and the intimate moment shared was broken.

Lord Landon strode purposefully through the crowd, his gaze trained on Ophelia.

"Bloody hell," she muttered. He was unrelenting.

"Determined suitor?" Did she imagine the steely thread to that query?

"Wastrel indebted to my family's club," she clarified. How easily Landon had shifted his attentions. But then, did it truly matter which Killoran he wed? Their fortune was all the same, and his purpose single-minded.

"Make your escape now," Connor whispered. "I'll meet you shortly."

"Where . . . ?"

"Go," he urged. "Unless you care to take the next set with Landon." Needing no further urging, she rushed off.

With the same steps that had saved her as a girl, she wound her way through the throng of guests, hiding behind pillars, ducking behind servants, until she managed to sneak from the hall.

The din of the crowded ballroom emerged muffled behind her as she crept through the Duke of Somerset's corridors. Footsteps sounded down the hall. "Miss Killoran."

She stiffened and briefly contemplated the path forward before reluctantly turning to face the owner of that voice.

The Duchess of Argyll sailed over with great, graceful gliding steps. The smile on her perfectly bow-shaped lips dimpled both plump cheeks. She reached Ophelia slightly breathless, a mark of her privileged lifestyle. "I do hope you do not mind me following after you. I have desperately been seeking a word with you since we first met."

"You're desperately seeking a word with me?" she said gruffly. She may not have been born to the same world as this regal creature before

her, but she knew enough that polite meetings didn't happen in empty corridors, away from Society's eyes.

The young widow beamed, collecting Ophelia's hands between her own gloved palms. "I could not help noticing your . . . familiarity with Connor." She paused, her cheeks reddening. "Mr. *Steele*, that is."

Ophelia hooded her eyes. So this was the reason.

"Do you know each other from the streets?" the duchess asked with the same wide-eyed innocence she'd shown while putting questions to Ophelia at their last exchange.

Was the woman Connor's lover? Her stomach muscles clenched. *Why should you care anyway?* "Mayhap you should put your questions to Mr. Steele." She made to go.

"Please, do not!" the duchess entreated. She held up a staying hand. "It was not my intention to . . . offend you."

"I don't offend," she said bluntly.

Dropping her arm to her side, the duchess's smile was firmly back in place. "Splendid." Looping her arm through Ophelia's, she dropped her voice to a conspiratorial whisper and urged them farther down the hall. "I must confess, all the stilted exchanges and measured words are a bit cumbersome. It is just . . ." The woman scrunched her brow, and had she been anything other than the blatantly transparent young woman before her, Ophelia would have taken that contemplativeness as a show. The young woman brought them to a stop and turned to face her. "It is just . . ." Would she get on with it? "It seemed you and Connor . . . *Mr. Steele*, that is, know each other, and as he is someone very special to me, Miss Killoran"—Ophelia's muscles tightened all the more—"then that would mean you, too, would be special." The duchess's cream-white cheeks fired red. "To me, that is. Not that you aren't special." The woman continued her ramblings and then stopped. She released Ophelia and fiddled with her flawless satin skirts. "You see . . . Connor and I have been friends for a lifetime."

Odd. Ophelia had known Connor when he was a boy, scared shite-less by the same demons Ophelia herself had battled when this princess was no doubt fed with a golden spoon. "I . . . see," she said, when in actuality she saw nothing.

"As you're not of our station, you might not know that since we were children, it's been expected we'll wed."

Taken aback, Ophelia hurriedly masked her surprise. Connor O'Roarke wedded to this woman? A lady of the peerage? Each revela-tion from the duchess only deepened the riddle of what had become of Connor after a constable had hauled him off. And yet . . . "Though I'm not of your station"—she took care to use her flawless, cultured speech ingrained by a determined governess—"I can still say how *odd* it is that given those expectations, you now carry a different name than his, as well as the title of duchess."

The other woman lowered stricken eyes to the floor. "It has . . . complicated the history between us." She raised her head. "Do you have feelings for each other?" she finally blurted, the most direct and concise bit she'd managed since cornering Ophelia.

Ophelia opened and closed her mouth, and then a great big belly laugh burst from her lips. "You think that I . . . that Connor Steele and me . . . ?" Unable to get the words out, she dissolved into another fit. "Ya people of the *ton* may 'ave money and power, but ya don't 'ave two thoughts to rub together to form a scrap of common sense."

The duchess cocked her head. "So you do not have any . . . feelings for Mr. Steele?" she asked. Relief flooded her eyes.

Dusting back the signs of her amusement, Ophelia looked down the empty hall, eager to be rid of the young duchess. "You are welcome to the *gentleman*."

A relieved little smile curled the duchess's lips. "I am very glad to have had this . . . talk, Miss Killoran. And will be happy to call you friend." As if registering the impropriety of their meeting, the duchess cleared her throat. "I shall leave you to your . . . uh . . . yes. Well, it was a pleasure." With a jaunty little wave, the woman sashayed off.

Ophelia stared after her. The ladies of the *ton* were as possessive as the gents they set their marital caps on, the way a pickpocket staked out a corner. Both were ruthless, but one wore a smile through it. "A pleasure, indeed," she muttered with a wry shake of her head after the lady had gone.

"Was that reserved for me or your most recent company?" a voice drawled over her shoulder.

She gasped and whipped around.

Connor lounged against a wall with a negligent ease.

"Both," she muttered, even as her heart did a little leap at the sight of him. Attired in a double-breasted black jacket and matching midnight trousers, there was a devastatingly handsome appeal to Connor O'Roarke. Her belly fluttered.

And here, all these years she'd believed herself incapable of feeling anything but fear where a man was concerned.

"Is that the manner of people you've been keeping company with since you climbed out of the gutters?" she asked, jerking her chin in the direction of her recent visitor. Her words came as more a reminder for her than a question for him.

"Amongst them."

How vague and veiled. Two words that revealed everything and nothing, all at the same time.

"Should you be here? Not sure it's safe with your lady if we're caught talking."

Connor grinned wryly. "My lady? I don't have any lady."

He hadn't gathered the duchess had designs upon him? Or was it that he did not care?

Either way, Ophelia released a breath she hadn't realized she'd been holding. "Then, wot would ya call her?" Ophelia bit down on the tip of her tongue. Where in blazes had that question come from? And why did his answer matter so much?

Connor stuffed his hands in his pockets, contemplating her query and the path the Duchess of Argyll had strode a short while ago. "A friend," he finally said.

Ophelia snorted. "Men and women can't be friends."

He bristled. "Of course they can." As he and his young widow were.

"No, they can't." The Duchess of Argyll was proof enough. She bit her lip to keep from mentioning the lady's barely concealed interest.

"You speak as someone who knows."

She shrugged. "Because I do. My brother appointed a friend as his right hand within the club."

Connor eyed her like she'd sprung another limb. "And?"

"*And* the servants or prostitutes at the club strike a friendship with the guards or other servants, and . . . it *isn't* possible." Were men truly so obtuse? But then, hadn't her brother, Broderick, proven equally thick on the matter of men and women? She sighed, trying to make him see reason. "It always becomes . . . complicated. Someone ultimately confuses friendship, and everything becomes jumbled, and . . ." She gave her head a decisive shake. "It just doesn't work."

"What does that mean for us, then?"

She started. "What?" she blurted.

"Well, we aren't lovers."

She sputtered, heat burning up her cheeks. "C-certainly not." Only, the unfamiliar stirring low in her belly made her question whether it would be so horrifying to know more than Connor O'Roarke's kiss.

"And you've already pointed out numerous times that you've no intention of helping me in my investigation."

"For a nobleman? No." He'd been taken in by a kindly gent. The actions of that one nobleman didn't erase the countless horrors Ophelia and her kin had known at the hands of other lords.

"Very well," he murmured, drifting closer. "What does that make us?"

Her mind came to a jarring halt. She stood there attempting to make sense of his question and to come up with a suitable answer. What *was* Connor to her? He was certainly someone she felt comfortable around. A person whose presence she enjoyed. But friends? She scoffed. They would never be anything more than childhood nemeses. As it was, his desire for respectability and his appreciation for the peerage made anything else between them not only unlikely—but also madness. Unlike his fancy duchess. "The duchess didn't talk about ya like ya were just friends," she said instead, deliberately reminding herself that Connor had, and always would have, an undeserved appreciation for people Ophelia despised.

Even in the darkened corridors, she detected the flush on his high cheekbones. Drifting closer, Ophelia studied him, awaiting his reply, and still when it came, it knocked her off balance.

"I'd intended to make the lady my wife."

She missed a step.

That somber pronouncement killed her jesting. "Oh," she blurted. For what did one truly say to that revelation? An intimate part of one's life when those pieces were never freely handed out. And yet . . . Connor had. She studied the same empty hall a moment. "*That* woman?" Cheerful as the summer sun, with words tripping off too fast from her tongue, she couldn't be more different from Ophelia and the other women born to St. Giles.

But then, mayhap that was the appeal of her.

Why did that leave her oddly bereft?

"She was a friend when I escaped St. Giles." There it was again: friendship. "And then . . . I'd hoped there would be even more." He grimaced. "Expected it." *More.*

"You believed she was going to marry you," she finished for him, her heart tugging with regret for him.

"She promised to marry me. We'd spoken of it." He flashed a wry smile. "Then along came her duke, and a street rat with no title and few funds was no match for a viscount's daughter."

Something vicious slithered around inside, a sentiment nasty and vicious and wholly foreign.

Jealousy.

She scoffed. *Of course you aren't jealous. This is Connor O'Roarke.* Her childhood nemesis . . . *Who you also secretly admired for accomplishing what few outside Black's gang had managed.* "That was your first mistake." How could he have forgotten? "Never trust a nob," she said softly, this time without her previous levity.

Connor waved his hand. "Bethany wasn't . . . isn't like the lords we once feared." Bethany. His use of that woman's name deepened the level of intimacy between Connor . . . and his duchess. "She gives her time to foundling hospitals." As Cleo had pointed out. "She organizes events to raise awareness of the plight of the poor."

In short, a virtual paragon.

At his defense of a woman who'd proven unfaithful to him, when loyalty was the most valuable currency those in St. Giles had to offer, that stinging, insidious poison continued to spread. "She thought herself too good to wed you? Chose another?" She gave her head a shake. "Doesn't seem like she's the angel you make her out to be."

The look he gave her was faintly pitying. "The world doesn't exist in absolutes of black and white, Ophelia."

He'd pity her? When it was Connor who had the wrong of it. "Yes, yes it can. And does." She held up one palm. "People are good"—she held the other up—"or they're bad. They aren't like your angelic duchess. As such, I would say you're better off than being trapped with a wife who"—she ticked off on her fingers—"one, couldn't have the courage to choose you over her father's wishes, and two, lied to you, making you believe she would."

"And yet, with your brother's intentions to land a noble connection, are you any different from Bethany?"

"What?" He was comparing her actions to that of a fancy lady of the *ton*? It was both preposterous and insulting. It was—

He lifted one shoulder in a casual shrug. "Your families both determined the course you should follow, and you're both readily going along with their wishes."

She sputtered. "I-it is not at all the same." For it wasn't. It—

He winged an eyebrow. "Isn't it?"

Ophelia wanted to spit all the reasons he was wrong back in his face. She wanted to protest that he knew nothing of it. Remind him that she would never be anything like Lady Bethany or any lady, for that matter.

But God help her . . . she couldn't get the words out.

It is true.

In the end she was saved from forming a response in the unlikeliest way.

Connor held up a hand.

Then it met her ears, faint and distant: footfalls and an occasional giggle.

Connor grabbed her by the hand and pulled her into a room, then closed the door behind them.

She squinted, attempting to adjust her eyes to the unlit space.

Heavy gold frames hung throughout the room, with the only furniture a handful of King Louis XIV chairs scattered about the center. She tilted her head back, taking in the sweeping ceiling with a mural done in powder-blue and pale-pink shades.

The Duke of Somerset's portrait room.

The tread of footsteps grew increasingly close, and shoulder to shoulder beside Connor, there was a thrilling danger to being alone here with him, one doorway between them and the world and discovery. It was the same thrill that had gripped her as she'd picked a wealthy lord's pockets. Only this was an electrifying charge made more potent by the heat pouring from Connor's muscled frame, threatening to burn her.

At last, those steps continued on, and there was only the hum of silence.

"I would say this is a good deal more conducive to our arrangement than the ballroom," he whispered close to her ear. His breath stirred the sensitive flesh of her nape.

Her lashes fluttered closed. "O-our arrangement?"

Then she recalled the three questions.

The promise she'd made him if he danced with her.

"Of course, your three questions." What accounted for the disappointment that stabbed at her breast?

"How do you find the children you employ at the Devil's Den?" he asked, coming forward, a predator hunting its prey.

Unnerved for the first time since he'd entered, she backed up, continuing her retreat. "H-how do we find them?"

"Aye." There it was again: a lilting brogue that revealed one of the few traces of his past. It highlighted all the more that despite a path that had brought them continual clashing, they were strangers still. Two people, raised as enemies, who'd be wise to be suspicious of each other.

Needing to reassert her strength before this man, she forced herself to stop.

"Ya want to know?" She leaned against one of the Corinthian pillars better suited for a museum than a townhouse. "Oi find the most desperate ones. The ones hungry and in need, who've given up on loife and 'ope, and I take them under my wing."

Had she not been so intently studying him under hooded lids, she'd have missed the way his entire body jerked, like one who'd been run through with a serrated blade. When he spoke, his words came flat and emotionless. "Those are familiar words."

"Is that a question? If so, that'd be your second."

"It wasn't." He dipped his thick gypsy lashes lower. "I better than anyone know that vow."

It was on the tip of her tongue to ask him why he should believe himself one who'd know that more. Did he think he'd somehow suffered more than Ophelia or any other member of Mac Diggory's gang? *Present yar back, girl . . . it's toime far ya to feel the sting of moi rod.*

Her gaze slid over to the Duchess of Somerset's portrait, and she lingered on that jagged flesh forever marred by flame.

"And when you . . . find these desperate children," he continued, and she stared on with something akin to horror as he pulled out that same damned leather notepad and devoted his attentions to that book, "what do you do with them?"

That second query hit her like a fist to the belly, and as she dragged her attention from the duchess and put it squarely on the person who'd always excelled in insulting her and her kin, she sneered, "What do ya think Oi do with them? Send 'em out as pickpockets? Have Cook turn them into mince pies? Make the girls whores?" Her gorge rose. She gave thanks for the dimly lit space that bathed them both in shadows, for shadows in all places offered a person protection.

At last he lifted his head. "That will hardly suffice the terms of the agreement we struck."

She'd wager her very life he didn't question the motives of his angelic duchess. Damn him to hell.

"I give them work," she snapped. "A place to sleep and eat and wages, and in return they work the kitchens or serve as runners for our family." She omitted Gertrude's role in schooling those children, leaving him to his infernally low opinion, because to hell with him.

"You indicated overseeing the hiring of children has only recently fallen to you."

She watched him guardedly as he flipped through his journal. "Yes."

"Yet I trust these are boys and girls not unfamiliar to you. Rather, they were former gang members of Mac Diggory who've either been kept on in your employ in a new capacity or absorbed into the hold of another kingpin."

It was a detail only one of the streets could glean. A respectable runner or gent with a fancy background wouldn't know the inner workings of East London the way Connor O'Roarke did, and that surely marked just one reason he'd become so successful in what he did.

"I want the history of the children in your employ."

It was an expansive third question and yet a question all the same. Ophelia balled her hands. She'd be damned if she turned those boys and girls over to his questioning. "And have them lay bare their crimes before you?" she scoffed. "So you might threaten them and receive the information you seek?" She'd been jaded enough in life to know the only thing one could trust was the unreliability of others.

Ophelia turned to go.

"That is what you believe, then? That I'm some ruthless investigator who lives with the sole purpose of exacting misery on the masses?" Wasn't his opinion of her as low?

"Aren't you? Doing the bidding of a nob at the expense of anyone and everyone?" she spat. This was safe ground with Connor O'Roarke. A familiar one that steadied her. Reminded her of the great divide that had always existed, one that would always be there. "Look at you," she said, scraping a gaze over him. He stiffened under her scrutiny. "You claiming to care about others when you only ever thought of yourself."

A muscle jumped in his cheek. "You don't know anything of it."

"Don't I? You were too good to join the boys and girls in the streets." It had always stabbed at her.

A sound of disgust burst from him. "It was never about that."

"Wasn't it? Living in the shadows like a ghost, you'd take favors where you could get them."

"As we all did," he said quietly.

"Yes, you saved my life"—she jabbed a finger at him—"but I *never* pretended Oi was too good for others, either."

They locked in a battle, and Ophelia stood facing him, energy humming in her veins, as she at last laid bare every resentment she'd carried over Connor.

"My father was an Irishman, skilled with horses."

She cocked her head. What was he . . . ?

"My mother . . . she was a squire's daughter and fell hopelessly in love with a man her father could have never approved of."

Her jaw went slack. "You were born to the peerage." It was why he spoke like a gentleman . . . because he'd been born one. As such, it hadn't been outside the realm of reality that he might marry his Lady Bethany. Ophelia curled her toes hard in her slippers.

He shifted. "A squire isn't of the nobility. They have a coat of arms and are usually related to someone in the peerage, but . . ." Connor silenced his ramblings. "My parents set off to London to make a life for themselves. They struggled . . . we struggled . . . but we were always happy." His gaze grew distant, and a wistful smile pulled at his lips and filled his eyes, and she ached to see a glimpse of that happiness he spoke of. Because it was his. Because it was unfamiliar. Because she wanted to know that some children didn't always know strife. That Connor's life had once been filled with even a fleeting happiness.

He fished around the inside of his jacket and handed something over.

Head bent, she stared down at the rusty piece. A crimson jacket still marked the child's toy, a soldier. She accepted it, turning it over in her hands. It was an aged version of a similar gift presented to Stephen when Broderick had taken over the Devil's Den. Those toys had gone unplayed with and been packed away. Handling this token, so precious Connor kept it close to his own heart, opened further that window into his world.

"It did not matter how dire our circumstances were, they sacrificed for my happiness. There were child's games and books and lessons and food for me . . . even while my parents went without." The column of his throat moved. "Even as they insisted they weren't hungry and watched me eat my meals."

She braced for the familiar envy that came for children who'd known those precious gifts she herself had never had.

Only this time . . . it didn't come.

Ophelia looked up as Connor continued his telling. "My da and ma would make every and any sacrifice for me, and one day they did."

A chill shuddered along her spine, ushering in a cold. Because even though she didn't know the telling, she knew where life had ultimately found him—in the streets, on the run. Knew that the happiness had been snuffed out and, coward that she was, wanted him to freeze his story with the most joyous moments he'd known. Despite that, a question came tripping off her tongue anyway. "What did they do?"

"My da borrowed funds to feed our family through the winter."

She slid her eyes closed. Reflexively, her palm wrapped around his metal soldier, the metal cool against her hand, his tiny bayonet digging sharp into her skin. The moment one opened the door to the gangs in St. Giles, there was no forcing them out. They were in, and in they remained until one was gone from the earth. Only the most evil survived. "What happened?" she asked with a knot forming low in her belly.

"My da had been charged an exorbitant amount. An amount he could have never fully paid back in the time frame he'd been given. Then the day the debt was to be collected . . . the leader of the gang . . ."

Oh, God. No. Her mind screeched to a stop as a dawning horror rooted around her mind. She knew before he finished. Knew what he'd say. "Diggory came calling."

No. Her mind screamed. Her heart stopped. And then resumed to beat an erratic, frenzied pattern.

"He had a . . . sick fascination with my mother. The moment he discovered she was a squire's daughter, he wished to make her his wife."

Ophelia hugged her arms close to her chest in a futile bid to keep warm. "He had an obsession with respectability," she whispered. Helena and Ryker Black's mother. Connor's.

"My father . . ." Connor stared vacantly through her, and she knew it was the precise moment he'd forgotten her presence. "He loved her enough to battle the Devil for her." His Adam's apple bobbed. "And he did."

"He lost," Ophelia whispered. For in the end, everyone had always lost to Diggory. Even after he'd gone, his vile hold remained, haunting one's days and sleepless nights.

"We all did that day. He slit my father's throat." She squeezed her eyes shut, willing him to silence, but the methodical, deadened words continued coming. "He raped my mother and then broke her neck." Did that tortured keening come from Ophelia? She bit her lower lip and tasted the metallic tinge of blood flooding her mouth. "I saw it all."

No. No. No.

It was a litany. A mantra that could never, would never, take away the evil Connor spoke of. He hadn't been an orphaned bastard or an unwanted child sold off by a whore mother and nameless father. This had been a child who'd laughed and loved and known the gifts of true parents.

He lost it all . . . because of my father. Here she'd believed herself incapable of loathing him more, only to be proven so very wrong.

"Oh, Connor." She stretched her spare palm out for him. Except . . . what did one say? There were no words to drive back his suffering. And certainly no words from the child of his parents' murderer. Ophelia let her quavering arm fall to her side.

He palmed her cheek, and she leaned into it, selfishly taking comfort from the last man who should be offering that gift. "You always presumed to know who I was and what drove me." A sad smile formed on his lips. "But just as I don't truly know anything about you, Ophelia, you don't know anything about me." No, they'd not truly known anything of each other. "On that day, Ophelia, I vowed to rid the streets of men like Diggory. Instead, I was forced to join him . . . and when I broke free, I could not understand how other boys and girls made orphans by that Devil, children like . . ."

"Me," she finished for him on a whisper.

He gave a small nod. "Why should he have any person's loyalty? When for me the thought of bringing the Diggorys of the world to justice sustained me. It is why, despite the wealth given and promised me by my adoptive father, I still do the work that I do."

The moment she'd found him in Broderick's offices, she'd mocked him and taunted him for the role he'd taken on. Shame gnawed at her. Palm shaking, she handed over the last link he had to his family. "No wonder you hate me."

Connor curled her fingers around that piece. "I could never hate you."

Tears flooded her eyes, blurring his visage before her. "How can you *not?*"

"Oh, Ophelia," he said with a tenderness that threatened to shatter her. "You are not like him."

"But I am," she cried, spinning out of his reach. She didn't want his undeserved defense. "I've killed and robbed and—"

"And you freed me."

"That debt was paid."

"You never sought to collect," he insisted. She hadn't. It had been a fundamental rule of Diggory's she had always broken for Connor O'Roarke. "You followed Ned and me in the streets. Why did you do that?"

Ophelia looked away.

Large, comforting hands settled on her shoulders, forcing her gaze back. "Why did you do that?" he repeated with a quiet insistence.

"You're making more of it than it was, Connor," she whispered, overcome by the depth of his magnanimity.

When he spoke, he did so in hushed tones, gentle ones far more difficult to take than had they been filled with a rightful contempt. "You're still so stuck in the acts you were forced to carry out, you still blame yourself for the work you did for"—she wrenched away—"Diggory."

Ophelia clamped her hands over her ears, wanting to blot out that hated name. It was futile. Not a single one of them could fully purge his memory from their thoughts. Tears slid down her cheeks, and he caught them with his callused thumb. "But you do. You question my motives, believing I've some sinister man bent to hurt a child and help a nobleman because that is all you've ever known. Because of it, you cannot even acknowledge that in trying to reunite a father and son, there is good in what I do. Just as there is good in many peers."

Her throat tightened.

He couldn't be right.

Because if he was . . . what did that mean about everything else she'd taken as fact over the course of her life?

Chapter 12

The following afternoon, Ophelia sat in the Eve Dabney Foundling House as the founder, Mrs. Eve Dabney, spoke to the assembled gathering. This event was proving far preferable to other *ton* events she'd been forced to suffer through. Despite the lords and ladies also present, Ophelia found herself in contact with men, women, and children to whom she could relate and understand.

As Eve Dabney spoke in her flawless, cultured tones, her words shifted in and out of focus, blending with Connor's revelations.

"No child should know hunger." *My da made him an orphan.* "No child should be alone." *My da hurt his mother in ways no woman should ever know pain, and Connor witnessed it.* "No one should know strife . . . and yet so many do. Too many."

While Mrs. Dabney went on, Ophelia struggled to swallow around the emotion stuck in her throat.

They were cut down before my eyes by a ruthless, heartless scum of the streets, a man named Mac Diggory.

Diggory had killed his parents.

She briefly closed her eyes. Was it a wonder Connor should hate everyone and everything connected with that miserable blighter?

Since they'd been reunited, he'd been anything but hateful. He'd spoken candidly, letting her into his past. He'd defended her before a room full of highborn guests. He treated street urchins with concern when any other constable or investigator would have cared about nothing other than the information to be obtained, and to hell with how they got those details from a guttersnipe.

He doesn't realize you're not just any child bought or sold into the Diggory gang. She was one of Diggory's bastards. Sprung from his blood and loins, as a living testament to evil.

Would he have stepped in to save you all those years ago if he'd known who you really were?

Bitterness stuck in her throat.

She'd spent her entire life hating the nobility. Hating the law. Both of which represented her enemies—those who gave no thought to the oppressed and lived for only their own pleasures and pursuits. Yet she'd not truly taken ownership of the crimes carried out by her and her family. Instead, she'd separated herself from the truth.

Until Connor.

"The children of the streets," the young lady was saying, "are far more than the circumstances they were born to." The woman's voice rose in an impassioned plea. "We have an obligation to provide when the world has failed them."

A murmuring of assent went up about the crowded room; Mrs. Dabney's reminder was a near echo of Connor's from the evening prior.

"We are more than our stations and experiences," Ophelia mouthed. Mayhap the other woman was . . . correct. Mayhap the world—Connor—could see more in Ophelia than Mac Diggory.

"Wot did ya say?"

She started.

Her brother Stephen scrunched his nose. "Ya're talking to yarself now?" he demanded on an outraged whisper.

Stealing a glance about, she leaned close. "I am not talking to myself." She'd merely been repeating silently what Connor had reminded her of in the Duchess of Somerset's portrait room.

"Ya were." She set her teeth. God, he'd a stubborn streak to test a bloody saint. Stephen yanked at the side of her skirts. "And ya're dressed all funny," he said more loudly.

"Shh."

Several pairs of eyes swiveled to where Ophelia sat alongside Stephen.

At the front of the room, Mrs. Dabney paused. In contrast to the stern looks shot their way, Calum Dabney's wife caught Stephen's eyes and smiled before resuming her talk for the impressive crowd.

Settling in her high-backed Empire chair, Ophelia trained her focus again on the young woman speaking. She was known throughout London as amongst the greatest philanthropists, and the unveiling of their latest foundling hospital under any other circumstances would be a welcome shift from the tedium of *ton* functions.

If she hadn't been needled for the past thirty minutes or so by her youngest sibling.

"Ya smell funny, too," Stephen accused in blatant disregard of the guests assembled and the woman speaking.

"I do not smell," Ophelia said from the side of her mouth, keeping her gaze trained on Mrs. Dabney.

"Ya do stink. Loike the whores at the—"

This time Gertrude leaned over to glare. "Hush," she whispered, delivering a well-placed pinch.

"Ouch," their youngest sibling groused, shifting back and forth in his chair. "But she does."

"I most certainly do not smell any different than I usually do," Ophelia shot back, earning a sharp pinch of her own. "Bloody 'ell," she mumbled, rubbing her wounded side.

"Will you two be silent?" Gertrude hissed.

An older gentleman with greying hair at his temples turned to glower once more.

"Mind your affairs," Gertrude warned, favoring him with a fierce look that sent his head whipping forward. "And you two . . . enough. It is bad enough that the Blacks believe us uncouth scum who have no place here." As one, their stares traveled to the front of the room where Ryker Black, his wife, and the remainder of their brood frowned.

Except, those four couples were not all Blacks. There was one interloper who'd easily inserted herself in the fold.

"They did invite us," Ophelia felt compelled to remind her family.

Gertrude and Stephen spoke as one.

"What?"

"Wot?"

Ophelia shifted on her feet. "It's just that *Gertrude* said they believe we're scum."

"Uncouth scum," Gertrude reminded.

"But Mr. and Mrs. Dabney did invite me to dine," Ophelia went on, "and all of us to the unveiling of their new establishment." The couple didn't have to make any attempt to include them—the family who'd burned their once great club to nothing more than ash—*twice*.

"They've been glaring at us since we sat," Stephen pointed out, motioning to the group in question.

"Mayhap because you haven't stopped talking," Gertrude said.

"Why, even Cleo's glaring at us," Stephen gritted out, ignoring their eldest sibling's chastisement.

They looked as one to the front of the hall.

Except it was not Cleo who commanded her notice.

Ophelia's heart skipped a beat. *Connor.*

He is here.

Connor occupied a distinguished place in the front row on the left-hand side of the hall, sandwiched between his father and his duchess.

Her stomach lurched.

Just then, the dark-haired beauty lifted her head and whispered something to Connor. He angled his head. Sitting as a silent observer to that pair, with their heads bent and bodies bowed toward each other, Ophelia felt like an interloper in that private exchange. Whatever his reply, Connor earned one of those perfect pink blushes and a widened smile before the pair refocused on Eve Dabney.

Ophelia gripped the sides of her chair so hard her nails made indents on the oak.

The evidence of their closeness threatened to shatter Ophelia, and yet she was unable to look away.

"See, Oi told ya she was glaring," Stephen crowed triumphantly.

"As she should." Gertrude turned her thumbs out, pointing them at Ophelia and Stephen. "You are being unpardonably rude, and we are attracting attention."

"She's a traitor," Stephen muttered. "Taking up with the fancy nobs and Black gang."

Forcing her macabre attention from Connor and his duchess, Ophelia frowned at her youngest sibling. "They are doing good for the children here," she admonished and then started. Hadn't she herself been precisely like her brother, failing to see any of the good their rivals and the nobility were capable of? Blinded by her hatred, she'd allowed herself to see nothing more than the crimes of most and not the good of some.

"Ya, too, then?" Stephen shook his head, disgust rampant in that jerky movement.

"I'm merely pointing out—"

"Perhaps you'll do said pointing later," Gertrude interrupted in hushed tones. "People continue to stare."

This time, while her brother continued to make his displeasure known, Ophelia fell silent, noting with her gaze the latest attention they'd drawn.

Connor glanced over his shoulder. He held Ophelia's gaze, his steel-grey eyes piercing and teasing at the same time. The Duchess of Argyll followed his stare to where Ophelia sat, shattering the connection.

She bit the inside of her cheek.

Stephen jammed an elbow into her side, and she grunted.

"Wot are ya doing?"

"I didn't *do* anything."

"Ya'ar eyeing the Hunter." Ophelia curled her toes in her slippers. "That ain't nothing."

"That isn't nothing," Gertrude automatically corrected on a hushed whisper. "It is . . . oh, blast. Do I need to escort you out?" she warned.

Hope briefly lit Stephen's freckled face, which he swiftly concealed.

But not before Ophelia had detected the fleeting sentiments, and the truth slowly trickled in.

He didn't want to be here. His constant haranguing and bid for escape didn't have to do with the Blacks or the lifelong rivalry between their families—but rather his own insecurities. It was a sentiment Ophelia could see because she herself had experienced it countless times since she'd been banished to Cleo and Adair's fancy townhouse. Feelings which had been made all the worse by observing Connor and his duchess—a woman he called friend and had one day hoped to marry.

And by the lady's blatant intentions, one day would.

Ophelia jumped up. "I'll take Stephen," she whispered.

She was met with surprise by the pair of siblings flanking her.

"But . . ."

Before her sister could launch a protest, she grabbed for her brother's hand. Stephen hopped up with such zeal, his seat scraped loudly along the oak floorboards.

Wincing, Ophelia took her brother by the elbow and guided him down the long row of Empire chairs. "Excuse me. Pardon," she muttered as they made their way from their seats and out into the spacious, cheerfully painted corridors of the foundling hospital.

As they strode through the empty halls, her brother whistled a familiar tavern ditty while Eve Dabney's distant voice carried, some of her words moving in and out of focus.

"We should not, however, take on the care of these children because it is an obligation." Ophelia's ears pricked.

"Clever work back there," Stephen cut in, a grudging appreciation coating those few words. "Managing to wrestle us both free of that rot." He glared. "Doesn't mean Oi forgive ya for making eyes at a bloody investigator."

"Hush," she scolded, darting out a hand to swat him.

Stephen danced out of her reach and, revealing his tender years, skipped down the hall at a brisk clip.

"No," Eve Dabney was saying. "We should not look after these boys and girls because it is an obligation we have—even true as that may be—" Ophelia slowed her steps and then stopped. She strained to hear all of the other woman's words. "Rather, we should do it because we *wish* to. Because we see the cleverness of . . . the spirit . . . the potential of all."

As Ophelia listened, she stared at the portraits lining the yellow-painted walls, frames containing the likenesses of boys and girls, more babes than children, some near in age to Stephen and others older.

Since she'd overtaken the responsibility of the children in the Devil's Den, she'd done so with the need to spare them from the suffering she herself had known. It had been a single-minded mission in which she brought those boys and girls into the club, but then it had been Gertrude who'd overseen them in the ways that mattered. Their education and, through that, their futures.

Unlike Connor's angelic lady, who'd spent years working for the betterment of those children's lives. And Ophelia? She hadn't thought much beyond the simple task of saving them . . . until Connor. Saving, however, looked like many things, and it was not the neat one-time effort Ophelia had exerted since she'd taken on the hiring of those children.

A portrait of a pale-haired girl with dimpled cheeks beckoned, drawing Ophelia over. She lingered before the baroque wooden picture frame. The ornate carvings were a contradiction to the shyly smiling child's modest white frock.

No, she was nothing like Lady Argyll. Ophelia's efforts had been purposeful, yet how meaningful had they been? What thoughts had she put to who those same children would one day become? The opportunities that awaited them. Unlike the Connors and Eve Dabneys of the world.

The irony was not lost on her. All her life she'd reviled the people born to the *ton* when there had been those like Calum's wife, and men such as Connor's adoptive father, who didn't care for birthrights, whereas Ophelia and her own family had failed to see those struggling in the streets as anything more than new staff to hire. It didn't matter that they'd offered work. It didn't matter that they'd found security and safety in the Devil's Den. For how fleeting were those gifts? What of the women employed as prostitutes because there were no other options? Or the children when they became adults? Was the Devil's Den all they would know? Before she'd been reunited with Connor, she would have said that would be enough . . . for any person. It should be. For it was vastly preferable to the darker options.

Another wave of guilt swamped her.

"Wot are ya doing?" her brother called loudly, his voice pinging off the high ceilings.

She didn't blink for several seconds.

Then Stephen called out again, grounding her in the present. "Come on already!"

Reluctantly pulling her gaze from that portrait, she held a fingertip to her lips, urging him to silence.

Mumbling to himself, Stephen kicked the broad plank floors with his foot.

How very angry he was.

Just as Ophelia herself had been. As Cleo had been. And so many of them.

You have passed judgment on your sister for smiling, taking it as a sign of weakness. You've condemned her for changing. When it was really Ophelia who all along had been so very wrong . . . about so very much.

"Ophelia?" her brother urged, motioning with his fingers for her to come.

Ophelia joined him and ruffled his tangle of golden curls.

He ducked to escape that sisterly pat. "Wot ya doin'?" he demanded again, swatting at her hand.

Despite his grumblings, Ophelia gave his head another rub. "Come, let us explore." Ducking, she looped her arm through his and forced him to accompany her. They traced their steps through the earlier tour they'd received of the establishment and made for the outdoor gardens. "Talk to me of how you've been spending your time at the club." She started. How many times had she referred to it as a "club"? Never had she referred to it as a home, too. "What have you been doing there?" Stephen had once been used as an arsonist to set blazes for Diggory, and that dangerous passion had dogged him still long after a bullet had ended the Devil of St. Giles.

"Nothing's changed without you." A pang struck at what should already be a needless reminder of how expendable they each were. "Been watching the foights from the observatory," he said with a boyish enthusiasm that made her wince.

"What of your lessons?" she asked with the maternal edge Gertrude was noted for and had mastered years ago.

Her brother beamed. "MacTavish and some of the other guards taught me how to smoke a cheroot."

"Stephen," Ophelia choked.

"Wot? All the boys and men there do it. Some of the girls, too," he added with a shrug.

"Not those manner of lessons. Rather . . . *Gertrude's* lessons."

"Foine." He gave another one of his negligent shrugs.

In that instance Ophelia discovered a newfound appreciation for the impossible task her sister had taken on . . . motivating Stephen and the other boys and girls to value an education. Ophelia dusted her spare palm over her face. What future awaited him? Oh, he'd forever be a partner in the gaming hell . . . but was that all? Would the purpose of his and their existence be to build their fortunes as Broderick intended, without thinking of how they might benefit those people beyond?

"Stephen." She weighed her words carefully. A single misstep would shut down any and all discourse with her most obstinate sibling. "You have to also take time for your schooling." Never before had she truly appreciated Gertrude's role in educating Stephen and the other children in the club . . . until she'd seen the life Connor had made for himself.

Stephen groaned. "Oi think Oi'd prefer to listen to Dabney's wife run on about nonsense."

Gathering him by the arm, she steered him back. "Splendid. We'll just slip quietly back in while the—"

"All right, all right," he entreated, digging his heels in.

They locked in battle, and then, capitulating, they reversed course once more.

"Oi've been reading."

After a week apart from her brother Stephen, that had certainly been the last pronouncement she'd expected from him. She smiled, proud of his efforts . . . and relieved. "That is splen—"

"Ya know, those gossip columns Broderick's so keen to follow."

Her smile froze on her face. *Oh, bloody, bloody hell.* "Indeed?"

"Oi always thought reading, and those papers, was a waste of moi toime." They turned at the end of the hall and continued on to the corridor that led to Eve Dabney's gardens. "But it turns out there is useful information to be 'ad in there, after all," he went on as they reached the doorway.

Ophelia cast a longing look over her shoulder.

"All the papers are talking about how ya're smitten with that bloody investigator," Stephen hissed.

"Will you hush?" she ordered, doing a quick glance about. Ophelia grabbed the handle and let herself outside, and she welcomed the soft warmth of the afternoon sun on her face.

A bevy of giggles and laughter filled the gardens from where the children played.

"Ya didn't deny it," he charged, following close at her heels.

"Ya're being foolish."

"Ya just slipped back into yar Cockney. Mayhap ya'd all be wise to be loike me and not waste yar toime with hiding who ya are. Makes lying easier."

She scowled. "I'm not *lying.*" She wasn't smitten. "I . . . I . . ." Stephen stared expectantly back. Ophelia rubbed a hand at her throat. "I simply . . ." Enjoy being with him. *Oh, God.* Her mind balked. Her body trembled. Ophelia skittered a panicky gaze about, alighting on a wooden case. "Here . . ."

"Where are ya going?" her brother called after her.

Dropping to her haunches, she plucked out two rackets and a ball. She balanced her burden and shoved awkwardly to her feet. "Take this," she ordered, holding out one of the wood rackets.

Stephen whistled between his two missing front teeth. "Ya're mad." Nonetheless, with the child's curiosity he'd managed to retain, he came over and took the racket.

"Back up several steps. Two more," she instructed and then held up her filled hands. "Stop." Focusing on the white ball, she delicately tapped it toward him.

Stephen made no move to volley that shot; the ball landed and then bounced upon the grass several hops before landing at a little girl's feet. She set aside the small doll she'd been playing with, grabbed the ball, and tossed it over to Stephen.

He grunted as it hit him in the back of his knee. "Ya're just trying to distract me from talks about ya and that blighter."

Actually, she had been.

Ophelia called over her thanks to the girl and paused. The same little girl from the portrait she'd studied a short while ago waved back.

Ophelia froze, her gaze locked on the child's corn-silk curls and cherubic cheeks.

During her darkest, most frightening days, Ophelia at least had her sisters and eventually her brothers. Who did this little girl have? Or had she been like Connor? Alone without a friend or family member in the world?

"Hullo?" Stephen shouted, waving his arms back and forth, bringing Ophelia out of her musings. "Ya didn't answer my question."

"It wasn't a question," she reminded him as she scooped up the ball. She swatted it at him. It struck his racket, and they went back and forth, volleying the ball. "Furthermore," she added as Stephen cursed, flailing to keep the projectile in the air, "it was a statement. And an untrue—" Her gaze caught at the point just beyond Stephen's shoulder, where that angelic little girl now spoke with a visitor.

Ophelia's heart began to race.

A visitor who managed more silent steps than Ophelia or any of her kin.

Squatting beside the girl, a bag in hand, Connor briefly glanced up. The sun's glow cast a halo about his dark curls, giving him the look of a fallen Lucifer. He was—

The ball knocked her in the forehead.

She grunted.

Jerked back to the moment, she blinked wildly, pressing a finger to the bruised flesh.

"Untrue statement, my arse," Stephen muttered.

Chapter 13

She'd been playing with the boy.

Even her presence out here alone was an incongruity with all the other ladies present for the unveiling of Eve and Calum Dabney's newest foundling hospital.

From where he knelt, speaking with Grace, Connor bowed his head.

"Do you know her?" the girl whispered.

"I do." He had for most of his life, if only for fleeting moments in time.

Discovered by Connor when he'd been investigating a case several months ago, Grace now had a place in Eve Dabney's foundling hospital. So had begun his connection with the Dabneys . . . and the little girl Grace.

"She looks like an angel." Gracie spoke in awestruck tones of the young woman baldly staring back at them.

Connor reached into his jacket and fished out the bag of peppermints the child so loved and handed them over. "May I beg your pardon, Lady Gracie?"

The small child giggled. "You are pardoned, sir."

With a wink, he shoved to a stand. "Miss Killoran," he called over, redirecting his attentions, "we meet again."

"From wot Oi've read in the papers, it ain't really much of a surprise," the small boy beside her piped in.

Ophelia gave the child a discreet but still discernible kick to the shins.

The pair glowered at each other for a long while, exchanging equally black looks; a whole conversation played out between the combative duo without so much as a word spoken or needed.

Tamping down a grin, Connor wandered over, passing by another child at play, until he reached Ophelia.

She had the look of an owl startled from its perch. "You," she blurted out, sounding like one of those night creatures.

The boy nudged her in the side, startling her into words. "Forgive me. Con—Mr. Steele," she hurriedly corrected. Too late. By the dangerous narrowing of his eyes, the boy had detected that slip. "Allow me to introduce my brother—"

"Stephen Killoran," the boy cut in, puffing his chest. "Ya can call me 'Killoran.'"

Schooling his features into a somber mask, Connor delivered another bow, this time for the boy's benefit. As one who'd once been equally snarling and angry, he well recognized that pugnacity in the proud child.

"Stephen," his sister warned.

Connor waved off her attempts. "Respect amongst those on the streets is not dictated but rather earned. Isn't that true, Mr. Killoran?"

Ophelia's brother folded his arms across his narrow chest. "Ya're the bloody law."

"An investigator," he elucidated. "Somewhat different." There had also been a time when he'd been in possession of the same wariness for the men in Connor's position.

"Mr. Steele also lived on the streets."

Stephen's eyebrows shot up to his hairline. Then he lowered them swiftly back into place. "Ya funning me?" he demanded of his sister.

"I assure you, she's not."

"Ya don't sound loike me or Ophelia," he challenged, suspicion heavy in his voice. "Sound more loike Broderick."

Connor looked to where a blonde girl twirled a porcelain doll in a circle. He'd been near in age to that solitary child when the world had been cut out from under him. "Any child can be made an orphan," he said gravely. "And I was one of them."

"Where'd ya live?"

With the boy's tenacious questioning, he'd make for a skilled investigator someday.

"Mr. Steele lived all over," Ophelia supplied for him. "St. Giles. The Dials. Bond Street."

Stephen took a step closer. Squinting, he peered up at Connor as though he sought for proof of his sister's claim. "Did ya?" he asked. Some of the hostility receded from his voice. Then the wall of suspicion was back in place. "Oi never saw ya."

"Before I was adopted, I was an orphan on my own."

"Why were ya on yar own?"

Because there'd been no other alternative for Connor. *Nay, it's because you chose that fate.* Aye. How long had he shut people out? Ophelia had opened his eyes to that. "It was . . . safer." The choice had existed between his morality and killing on command, as his friend Niall had been forced into . . . or living in the shadows, a boy without a family or friend. "Your sister"—he looked briefly to Ophelia and then back to Stephen—"saved me from capture several times."

"Ophelia?" Connor might as well have suggested God himself for the incredulity there. "She would 'ave been a baby."

His lips twitched. Two years away from thirty, he'd not considered himself old. "She was just a girl." And she'd had a spirit greater than all Diggory's men combined.

"So ya were loike us." Stephen gave him a once-over. "But now ya ain't. 'elp the nobility." His was a statement steeped in condemnation. "Ya threaten our club."

Ophelia shot him a silencing look that the boy ignored.

So the child knew the terms Connor had put to Ophelia. "I help those in need of help," he said quietly.

"At the expense of who?" the boy charged with a world-wary wisdom far suited to one who'd attained two decades more of experience. How very much he sounded like his sister.

Connor had threatened Ophelia and her family. He had been so removed from how those in St. Giles lived, and for so long, that he'd used ruthless tactics of ensuring cooperation. All along, he'd not thought about the terror known by those children like Stephen.

"Stephen, run along while I speak to Mr. Steele."

The boy set his jaw at a mutinous angle.

"Here." She collected the rackets and ball and stuffed them into his arms. "Go play with that young girl."

Stephen blanched. Tossing up his palms warningly, he backed away. "She's a girl."

"She's alone," Ophelia insisted. "Unless you'd rather return and listen to the remainder of Mrs. Dabney's speech?"

Cursing, the child yanked the items from his sister's arms and stomped off.

"Remember to have fun," she called after him.

Stephen lifted one finger in a crude gesture.

Ophelia sighed and remained there, staring after him.

"Mrs. Dabney has since concluded her remarks," Connor said from the corner of his mouth.

"Hush, or I'll invite my brother back to continue his questioning."

They shared a smile; the moment was natural, relaxed. How much he preferred it to the contentious debates that had once riddled their exchanges.

Connor and Ophelia watched the playing children.

"Perhaps I should . . . smooth the way for introductions," she ventured, worrying at her lower lip.

"You needn't worry. The girl is more capable than most."

Ophelia glanced up quickly. "You know her? Is she—?"

"A subject of my investigation?" he drawled. What accounted for the pang of disappointment that she believed him incapable of good and driven by nothing more than the assignments he took on? "She is not. I . . . found Grace several months back. It was winter. She was begging . . ."

"And you brought her here," Ophelia correctly surmised.

"I'm a . . . benefactor of Mrs. Dabney's newest foundling hospital. I serve on the board for several of her organizations. When I'm able, I visit Grace."

Utter shock transformed Ophelia's features.

With a wink, Connor found a seat on the wrought-iron bench facing Grace and Stephen. Ophelia's indecision carried with it a lifelike force; he felt her hover, lingering in the spot he'd left her, and then with slow, reluctant steps, she stopped at his shoulder before sliding onto the bench beside him.

They settled into a comfortable silence, watching as Stephen attempted to provide Grace a lesson in tennis.

Periodically the boy frowned, rolling his eyes to the heavens.

"He's angry," Ophelia murmured, the first to break the quiet.

Connor studied the boy. "All the people who lived on the streets are." How long had he himself hated everyone, regardless of station?

She flattened her lips. "No. This is . . . *different*. He was a cheerful babe, always smiling. Each year, however . . ."

"Each year?" he encouraged.

"With Diggory's death, I thought Stephen would lose some of the hatred and anger in him." Her voice grew as distant as the gaze she now trained on her sibling. "Instead, he only became angrier. More . . . unpredictable." The boy hit the ball to Grace.

She made an ineffectual swat, and it sailed past her shoulder.

Stephen's loud grousing reached them as he sent the girl to fetch the ball. The pair resumed their slow-moving game.

"I was not unlike him in that regard. When the earl took me in, I hated the world and everyone in it. I trusted none. Eventually I learned to trust again. To smile. In time, it comes." Or it had for him.

Sitting here, their legs nearly brushing, amidst the sun-soaked grounds, it occurred to him how little he truly knew about Ophelia. Where he'd opened to her about his existence, she guarded her secrets and past. "And what of you?"

Her expression instantly shuttered. "What?" she repeated carefully.

A strand of hair fell over her eye. His fingers itched to brush it back, and yet at the same time he preferred that pale curl as it was: natural and unrestrained. "I've known you since you were as young as Grace," he murmured, more to himself. "And yet I know even less about you than the young girl I found six months ago."

Ophelia's thick, nearly white eyelashes swept low, but not before he detected the stricken expression in her eyes. "There's nothing really to tell," she ventured, clenching and unclenching her hands. "I lived on the streets with my three sisters, and eventually Stephen and Broderick." She gave a shrug. "That is all."

The paleness of her cheeks and the tension in her narrow shoulders belied the casualness of her words.

He took in that uneasy gesture, and she instantly stopped. She flexed her fingers and laid flat palms on her skirts.

Once, he would have left her to her secrets. Now, having known her these past weeks, he wanted to know more. "What was your life like before . . . ?" The name stung his tongue and hung there, briefly unspoken, because when one uttered that name aloud, it would add a chill to the spring air and usher in the darkness that had always accompanied it.

She tipped her chin. "Diggory?"

But then, she'd always been braver than Connor. Defying Diggory when she was only a child herself had stood as a testament to her strength.

He nodded.

Tension brought her lips angling down, and she held herself coiled so tight beside him, he felt the emotion spilling from her slender frame.

"I already told you . . . there is nothing to tell," she finally said, her tones gruff. "My parents died . . . I was part of Diggory's gang, and that is all I am."

His heart stumbled. That was what she truly believed. That those three sentences defined her existence.

Grace's boisterous laughter carried on an errant spring breeze. Had Ophelia ever known laughter as a child?

Connor gathered her hand in his, twining their fingers together. "That is not all you are, Ophelia Killoran. It never was nor will ever be all that defines you." He raised her knuckles to his lips and dropped a lingering kiss atop them. "Tell me about your parents."

"Wh-why do ya want to know?" she whispered, her voice cracking.

How suspicious she'd always been.

Across the way, Ophelia's brother and Grace played on, the innocent actions of two souls who'd also known darkness, but in this they may as well have been a pair of children innocent to the ugliness in the world. "I don't know why I want to know," he said quietly, his lips close to her ear. Perhaps it was a cowardly desire to know that at some point she'd experienced happiness. "But it matters."

It matters.

It had been inevitable, the question of her parentage.

Only, she'd convinced herself it was not coming. She'd allowed herself to believe that he'd already accepted that she was a bastard and nothing more . . . and therefore no queries were needed.

How easy it had been to delude herself. Restless, she pushed to her feet and wandered closer to where her brother now played.

Tell him. He's proven one capable of forgiveness. Far more than Ophelia herself. Yet seeing good in an otherwise dark world and in people of all stations was altogether different from speaking of the man who'd raped his mother and murdered his parents. Her mouth went dry . . . and God help her for being a coward, she could not drag the confession out.

Ophelia registered Connor taking a place at her side, and in the absolute absence of her response, she forced a chuckle. "Is this another debt to be paid, Steele?" she charged, erecting that small but necessary barrier. "Ya told me of yar past, an' Oi should tell ya moine?"

Hurt flashed briefly in his eyes, and shame—morphed with guilt—threaded through her. She hated herself for altogether new reasons.

"That was never why I shared my past with you, Ophelia." He spoke in hushed tones.

Why aren't you snapping at me? Why aren't you indignant and hateful?

Because there was only one hateful one between the pair of them, and it had never, ever been Connor.

He drifted closer. "I wanted to let you in . . ." *Please don't. Don't, Connor.* "Just as I want you to let me inside."

Her throat worked. *Oh, God.* He'd said it. A handful of words that spoke to more than a case and even hinted at something greater than friendship.

Ophelia closed her eyes, warring with herself. All the while Connor remained beside her, silent. He didn't pressure or probe further.

She rubbed at her arms in a futile bid to bring warmth back to those cold limbs.

"They . . . died," she finally settled for, her voice hollow.

Even that was only a partial truth. Her da had taken a bullet to his chest at the Duchess of Somerset's hand, but whoever had birthed Ophelia and her sisters was just any other mystery of the streets. Shame choked her airflow.

"How old were you?"

Ophelia gave a jerky shrug. "Oi don't know, Connor," she said, exasperated—with him . . . with her circumstances. "Oi wasn't"—she slapped the air with her hand—"loike ya. Me mum and da . . . they weren't fancy folk. They didn't know their ages. They didn't know how to read or write." When Broderick entered their fold, he'd transformed Ophelia and her siblings into more than their parents had been. As much as she resented his using her like a pawn on a chessboard, she'd forever love him for seeing in them more than street rats, incapable of, and undeserving of, better.

Stephen paused to look at her, his arm drawn back midswing. With the handful of paces between them, the protective glitter in his eyes sparkled in the afternoon sun.

She offered him a smile meant to reassure, and silently mouthed to him, "I'm all right. Have fun."

He pointed his eyes to the sky and then shifted his focus back to his game.

Ophelia sighed; the defensive fight had left her. "Gertrude was the eldest. We always knew that. She was always also the most clever." A wistful smile stole across her lips.

"I cannot believe she, nor any woman, for that matter, could be more clever than you." Connor's matter-of-fact pronouncement wrought havoc on her heart.

Her entire life, she'd been overlooked and underestimated. Oh, she'd managed to wrest some control of club business from her brother, but ultimately she'd forced his hand. Broderick hadn't trusted her the same way he had Cleo. Had even, by so easily sending her away, dismissed the significance of the work she did.

"Oh, but Gertrude is the wise one. In ways myself and Cleo never were." This was safe. This spoke to a world Connor O'Roarke, now Steele, could understand: a loving family who loved deeply in return. Kin who protected one another at all costs because of that love. "Gertrude," she went on, warming to the talk of her beloved family. "She could make sense of letters and numbers long before Broderick hired tutors and governesses for us." She chewed at her lower lip. "I would mock her for wasting her time. What use did any of us have of numbers and letters? We served only one purpose. Gertrude disagreed. One day she lined each of us up and explained that she'd determined an approximation of our ages." The stray laughter of children playing blended in a cheerful harmony of innocence. "I had on my usual scowl."

"I know the one," he said lightly, and she looked up.

They shared a smile.

"But all the while, I fought from grinning. Secretly, I wanted to know something about myself. She placed me in the middle between her and Cleo and reasoned through our ages. I was . . . in awe." She shook her head. "I'd forgotten all that until now," she said softly to herself.

Grace glanced over and waved excitedly at Connor. He returned that exuberant gesture. After she'd returned to playing, Connor spoke.

"And what of your parents?"

She knew nothing about the woman who'd given her life. Ophelia's da had been the Devil incarnate. Those were hardly the joyful details Connor had shared of his own departed parents.

Feeling his eyes on her, Ophelia looked up. *Tell him . . . tell him all.*

It would kill all the warmth he'd shown her these past weeks and destroy the unlikely bond they'd formed.

Selfish she was, and selfish she'd always been.

She wasn't ready for the end of what they'd known together. Nor could there be any denying that the inevitable conclusion to their relationship was coming. When he'd finished his case, he'd no longer have any need for dealings with her. Their paths would never again cross. He'd have his duchess and the fancy lifestyle he'd been born to and always craved.

And Ophelia? She would have some nobleman husband.

Never before had she felt more like weeping.

She hugged her arms close to her midsection and drew in a shaky breath. "My da . . . he knew I loved hot cross buns." How easily that lie had rolled off. "There weren't funds for them and yet . . . Oi always wanted them." Which was as much a truth. While out thieving, she'd passed so many bakery windows, her mouth watering from the scents and sights of those baked treats in the window. "Did ya ever 'ave them?" she asked curiously.

"Shrewsbury cakes were my choice treat."

Of course, he had owned a bit of the life she'd dreamed. Once she would have been riddled with resentment and hostility. No longer. Now, she took comfort in knowing one of them had been happy once.

Ophelia wandered over to a nearby marble rendering of three children playfully climbing within an urn. She trailed her fingertips along the sun-warmed stone curls of one girl. Plump, grinning, and playing amongst the flowers, it was a future she'd secretly longed for as a girl herself. There had been little reason to dream and hope for those in Diggory's gang, and ultimately those longings had faded. How much easier the fabricated life was from the truth. Warming to the pretend history she crafted for herself, she continued to weave her world of make-believe. "My da knew 'ow much Oi loved them. We'd 'ave no funds, and yet he'd insist my ma make them."

Eat it, girl . . . ya steal from me . . . ya'll eat it.

Perspiration beaded on her nape. *Do not let him in . . . Do not let him steal even the pretend dreams from you.* Or mayhap that was merely her punishment for the falsehoods she offered. She dusted her hand over the back of her neck and wiped it away. Sinning had always come far more naturally to her. As such, the lies continued falling. "My da, 'e'd 'ave me sit there, and we'd watch me ma together. Oi was always so hungry." She whispered that truth to him. "He allowed me to eat the whole plate. And then came the tea." She shivered. *Please don't . . . Oi promise Oi won't do it again.* Her own screams pealed around her mind. *Drink it, girl . . . drink it.* "Oi'd finish that whole cup quick-like."

Children's laughter echoed around the gardens, as if mocking the gamut of lies she'd fed Connor.

In the scheme of her crimes and sins, sharing a pretend past with Connor O'Roarke was amongst the least of them. So why did that not ease her deepening guilt?

A spring breeze stirred through the gardens, washing over her face, pulling at her curls. Several strands tugged free of her chignon.

"Here," Connor murmured, collecting those strands. Except . . . instead of tucking them behind her ear, instead of pinning them under her diamond shell-combs, he clung to them.

Her breath caught.

Or was that his?

In this instance, the whole world melted away so that there was only—*"Oomph."* Connor blinked and then abruptly released the strand. He rubbed at his temple.

What in blazes?

"'ands off moi sister, ya miserable blighter," Stephen thundered.

Her stomach lurched, and with it, reality. "Stephen, no," she commanded in stern tones as her brother came charging. Anticipating his intentions, Ophelia placed herself in the path of the nearly ten-year-old warrior rushing over.

Not breaking stride, Stephen hurled himself past her. His fist bounced off Connor's jaw, bringing his head whipping back.

Connor may as well have been struck with a feather.

Ophelia's heart hammered as around them shouts and cries went up from the previously playing children. "Stephen," she shouted, grabbing the back of his jacket. "That is . . ." He wrenched himself free and lunged again at Connor.

"Oi read the papers about ya. Panting after moi sister, and now putting yar hands on her. Oi'll kill ya," Stephen snarled and launched again.

Connor easily caught her brother and gathered him in a firm yet unthreatening hold.

"Let me go, ya bastard." Stephen bucked and thrashed. "Oi won't let moi sister be pawed by a bloody investigator. She ain't a whore."

"Stephen, that is enough," she bit out, taking him by the forearm.

He yanked the slender limb free. "And wot of ya? Panting after 'im loike one of the—"

"Not another word." Connor steeled that command in an ice that cut across the boy's rage.

Then she registered the absolute still that had quieted even the spring breeze.

From the front of the gardens, a cluster of guests stared on with varying degrees of horror and fascination.

Ophelia's heart plummeted as she took in her wide-eyed sisters layered between the Dabneys, Connor's father, and a stricken Lady Bethany. The duchess touched quivering fingers to her lips and then wordlessly bolted off.

Oh, bloody hell, she knew rot about propriety and decorum, but she knew enough that this was bad. *"I'm ruined."*

"Ophelia," Connor said in a hushed whisper.

Only, what was there to say?

"Let me go," Stephen cried, bucking back and forth like a wounded dog Gertrude had once taken in. "Oi'll kill ya. Oi'll—"

"Enough." Gertrude crossed over, effectively silencing their brother.

Even so, he stood, alternating a black glower between Connor and Ophelia.

"We're done here," Gertrude said.

Dread sank like a stone in her belly. "It is not—"

"Not here," her eldest sister bit out. "We're leaving."

"I arrived with Cleo—"

"And you are leaving with me."

Any other time she'd have gone toe-to-toe with anyone, kin included, who sought to order her about. Only they'd attracted a sea of stares, whispers, and gossip. Who would believe Ophelia would prefer facing questions from Cleo to this simmering eldest of her siblings?

"We're leaving," Gertrude repeated, her mouth not even moving as she spoke. Gripping Stephen by the shoulder, Gertrude gave Connor a once-over and marched off.

Ophelia lingered, wanting to apologize . . . for this day, for her father's treachery, for his loss, her lies. There were too many places for her to even begin.

He gave an imperceptible shake of his head, one that conveyed that all was fine when it wasn't.

The guests parted to allow her siblings their exit, and bringing her shoulders back, Ophelia marched forward with her eyes daring anyone to say so much as a word.

After an interminable march through the Dabneys' foundling hospital, cloak in place, bonnet in hand, Ophelia found herself back in Broderick's carriage.

No sooner had the carriage rocked into motion did Gertrude cry out, "What in blazes were you thinking?"

"It was not how it looked," Ophelia exploded, tossing the lace-trimmed straw bonnet on the opposite seat. It landed with a quiet *thwack* beside her sister. "As such, blame should be placed where blame is due."

As one, they looked to the waiflike figure on the bench beside Ophelia.

"Me?" he squawked. "Me? She's the one who was making eyes at Steele, letting him paw her in public."

"Stephen," her sister snapped.

High color flooded Ophelia's cheeks. "I was not letting him paw me."

"Liar," Stephen shouted.

Gertrude held up a hand just as Ophelia opened her mouth to launch into a tirade against the fieriest of her siblings. "Regardless, it is done."

It is done.

There was an air of finality that hung from those four words that chilled the carriage.

The eldest Killoran sister rubbed at her temples.

"Broderick is going to take him apart with his hands," Stephen said with a vicious glee.

"Stephen," Ophelia and Gertrude said together.

He kicked his feet out on the bench, hooking his ankles. "Wot? 'e is. 'e sent ya to Mayfair to nab a nob, not cozy up to an investigator who—hey," he shouted as Ophelia knocked his legs out from that insolent pose.

"There's no reason he will find out."

"Been reading the papers."

Of course he had been. He'd always been inordinately fascinated by the gossip pages that offered a glimpse into the lives of the nobility.

Ophelia caught herself just as she went to massage her own temples.

"And 'e ain't happy," he added, more cheerful than Ophelia remembered seeing him since . . . well . . . ever.

"First, nothing happened," she directed to her sister. "Second, aside from the children at the foundling house"—of which there had been ten or so—"no one other than Cleo, the Dabneys, and Mr. Steele's father and . . ." The woman he'd hoped to marry. A proper, respectable miss who still held feelings for Connor and wished to wed him. "No one will say anything," she said with a quiet confidence. Assuredly not the woman more than half in love with Connor. A fissure ripped across her heart.

"You cannot be certain of that." Gertrude remained in possession of her usual quiet pragmatism.

"I am confident."

"Ya're relying on trusting the Blacks and a fancy lady?" her brother piped in.

"She'll say nothing," she said more harshly than she intended.

The carriage came to a slow stop outside Ophelia's temporary home. She pushed the door open and jumped down.

"Stay in the carriage," she heard her sister warn their brother.

Ophelia made it no farther than three steps before Gertrude caught up with her. She took her by the shoulder. "What . . . ?"

"Do you care for him?"

Her mouth moved, but no words emerged. Not a hint of a sound or a sigh or a whisper.

Her sister repeated in quiet tones, "This Mr. Steele written about in the papers. Do you care for him?"

Did she care for him?

A denial sprang to her lips. It was madness. It was illogical. It was . . . impossible.

Yet she froze, fearing one of the occasional breezes this day would knock her down, God help her. She did care for him. More. *I love him.* She loved him for caring about the lives of the men, women, and children of all stations and not just his profits, as Ophelia and her family had been. She loved him for visiting a little girl named Grace and playing coin tricks with street urchins to ease their fear. "No," she rasped.

"Between that reply and the belatedness of it, that is hardly convincing," Gertrude muttered, jarring Ophelia back from the precipice of madness. "Listen to me." She took Ophelia by both shoulders. "If you love him, then nothing . . . not Broderick, not the club"—she paused—"not me, nor anything or anyone should keep you apart." Ophelia stared with horror at her sister, who'd lost the use of one eye because of Ophelia's actions.

"I can't," she said dumbly. She couldn't sacrifice Gertrude, not again. Nor for a man who'd been made an orphan by Ophelia's father. "Leave it alone," she warned, her voice shockingly steady despite the fact that she was splintering apart inside.

Gertrude searched her face. "It does not matter what Broderick—"

"I said leave it alone," she repeated, more firm in both her resolve and her command.

Her sister instantly fell silent. "I see."

No, she didn't. She couldn't. Because Ophelia had kept secrets of old and had only added new ones to them, and ultimately they all somehow came back to Connor O'Roarke. Ophelia was too much of a coward to share the truth with either of them. "I am doing this. Marrying a lord." Horror squeezed at her insides. These past three weeks, she'd lived in a world of pretend where only she and Connor had existed. Originally he'd been comfortable, safe, a link to her past and the lifestyle she knew, and not that of the peerage. Somewhere along the way, everything had changed, morphed into something more. "There is nothing between me and Conn . . . Mr. Steele."

Not allowing her sister another question, she darted up the steps of Cleo's townhouse and sailed through the front door, opened by the burly guard there.

Before it had even been shut, Ophelia raced abovestairs and didn't stop running until she reached her rooms. Panting from her exertions, she let herself in and pushed the panel closed.

She layered her back against the door and stared blankly at her temporary rooms.

Do you care for him?

How simple her sister's questioning had made it out to be.

When in truth there could never be anything between Ophelia and Connor. Too many lies, crimes, and hurts existed between them that made the dream of having more impossible.

But there was one thing she could do. One gift she could offer him. It had been the only one he'd ever sought. Once she provided it, they could be through.

Then she could move on and begin the process of forgetting Connor O'Roarke.

Chapter 14

"Are we not going to speak of it?"

It had been inevitable.

Striding through the halls of the Eve Dabney Foundling Hospital, Connor cast his father a sideways glance.

"I hardly trust this is the place for a discussion."

There had already been display enough with Ophelia and her brother and a host of guests . . . and Bethany. Connor would not delude himself into believing the tension spilling from his father's frame came from anywhere but Bethany's response.

Exiting the establishment, they fell into step and made for his father's waiting carriage. "Join me."

Connor spared a look across the street to where a small boy held the reins of his mount. He firmed his jaw. "My mount—"

The earl lifted a hand, and one of his footmen leapt from his perch beside the driver. "See my son's horse returned to his residence."

Oh, bloody, bloody hell.

Connor fought the urge to tug at his collar, feeling a good deal like the boy he'd once been, caught stashing the earl's fine silver under his bed in preparation for his eventual ejection from the household.

His father motioned him in and then pulled himself in behind.

The earl gave a firm command. Having always excelled in his studies and having succeeded in every endeavor he'd undertaken since he'd been adopted, Connor had only ever striven for his father's approval.

Taut, he steeled himself for something wholly foreign and unfamiliar—the earl's displeasure.

"Bethany is in dire straits."

Connor rocked back in his seat. Of everything and anything he'd expected from his father, that had certainly not been it.

"Her . . . husband wagered it all away. Mistresses, whores, drinking."

As a young man he'd been hurt by her betrayal, and yet he'd still not wished, nor ever would wish, ill will upon her. For she had been a friend to him . . . and still was. "What of her dowry? The viscount?"

His father grimaced, giving his head a slight shake. Connor's mind raced, trying to keep up with the revelations. "It does not make sense," he said to himself. He'd based his career and his cases on logic and reason, and nothing in what his father revealed made any sense. Both Bethany and her father were in deep, and yet . . . "It doesn't fit with the viscount." Through the years he'd proven himself measured and proper. The pieces did not fall into place.

"It was why he made the match between Bethany and Argyll, Connor. Poor investments, bad crops. The duke was willing to overlook a penniless bride." A penniless and stunning beauty deemed a Diamond of the First Water, she'd taken the *ton* by storm.

At that point Connor had been recent to London, just beginning to establish a career with funds given him by the earl. He'd have never made a sufficient match for the viscount. Not when he'd had a penniless daughter and a mountain of debt.

I would say you're better off than being trapped with a wife who, one, didn't have the courage to choose you over her father's wishes, and two, lied to you, making you believe she would marry you.

"She *needs* a husband," he said somberly. It explained why the young widow had made such pointed attempts at reestablishing their previous relationship.

His father frowned. "Do not make her out for a fortune hunter."

"Isn't that what she is?" he asked without inflection. "Twice now." At his father's silence, he winged an eyebrow. Granted, she was a woman with little choice in a world that restricted nearly all opportunities for women. However, she'd been driven more by the need for funds than by her feelings for him. At the very least, his father could acknowledge as much.

A vein bulged at the corner of his father's right eye. "Is that what you'd like? For the lady to suffer now because she chose another?" He dropped his voice to a whisper. "By God, she is my goddaughter, Connor. Stanley's daughter."

Now, both the viscount and Connor's father expected him to rescue the lady and her family.

How much his father had worried about the viscount's daughter, and yet, as Ophelia had pointed out, where had been Bethany's faithfulness to Connor? Where had been her courage and conviction to throw over expectations and marry the street rat he'd once been? "It is odd you should speak solely of the lady being hurt when she made the choice long ago to marry another."

An impatient sound left his father. "At last it makes sense."

Connor creased his brow.

"Your interest in that woman."

That woman. It was a snobbishly dismissive reference to the young woman that marked her as more object than person. Connor thinned his eyes. "What are you talking about?"

"With the attention you've shown that woman, you've done nothing but hurt Bethany."

Fury spilled through him. "That is what you believe? That I am *using* Miss Killoran as a pawn to incite the jealousy of another?" Did his father think so little of him?

"She made a mistake, Connor," he said, confirming that ill opinion. He whistled. "By God, it *is* what you think." He held his father's gaze. "Is it so unfathomable to you that I enjoy Miss Killoran's company?"

The earl winced; it was a slight, nearly indistinguishable twitching of the muscles in his face and body, and yet Connor saw it.

"I understand you must . . . *relate* to the young woman."

Still, his father could not bring himself to utter her name. Frustration knotted in his gut. "In what ways, Father? The fact that we were both thieves?"

"Stop it, Connor Steele."

"Oh, come," Connor spat out. "You know I speak the truth. It's why you"—despite Connor's protestations—"insisted I change my name and garments."

High color flooded the earl's cheeks. His silence served as a mark of the truth, further fueling Connor.

"It's why you provided me a fine education."

His father slammed his fist against his palm. "I *wanted* you to have an education because you were intelligent and deserving of a new beginning."

Connor scoffed. "You wanted to erase all hint of the streets from me."

"You are being difficult," his father gritted out.

"Tell me, do you hate her because she reminds you of what I am?" He put the somber question to him. "Not only a thief . . . but also a murderer."

His father clamped gloved hands over his ears. "It is because when you are with her, you can remember only what you've done, and I don't want you to think of the past," his father cried out, his chest heaving. The fight went out of him; his shoulders slumped. "I don't want you to remember your demons," he whispered, stretching out a hand. "I want them buried . . . for *you*."

Connor sank back in his seat. That was what this was about. "And you believe that in my having"—what . . . what was it he had with Ophelia?—"any connections with Miss Killoran, it will remind me of my past?" A past he could never truly forget. One that had been indelibly burned into his mind, heart, and soul?

"I remember you as you once were, Connor," his father whispered, his voice ragged, his eyes overfilling with anguish. "The day you first came home with me, I intended to feed you, clothe you, and send you on your way with a sizable purse. You were a scared, wounded animal, and I could not let you go back out into that world with those people."

He'd been four and ten. Already jaded in more ways than the Earl of Mar could have even fathomed.

Yet, despite his father's fears, with Ophelia—because of Ophelia— Connor had realized there was a world outside of his work. She'd made him dream of a life that included a family—with her. *I want that with Ophelia.* "Don't you see, Father?" He searched the harsh plains of a face showing signs of age. "All of that . . . it will always be with me."

"I know that."

Except there was nothing convincing in those three words, more rote reply than anything.

"Do you?" he quietly asked. Where his father had urged him to bury his previous life, including the parents who'd given him life and loved him, Ophelia had reminded him that Connor had known a fleeting time of happiness with them. It had been wrong to set aside memories of a mother and father who'd died protecting him. "You never asked about my parents."

His father frowned. "I know what happened to them." Again, "them," not "your parents," but rather an informal, aloof acknowledgment of those who'd mattered most to Connor. "That Diggory fellow killed them before you."

Yet he could drag forth that hated name.

"You've never asked what my life was like before that night. Who my mother and father were. What our life was like as a family."

"Because I wanted you to forget," his father exploded. "What good could come in talking about parents who were murdered before you, Connor?"

Yes, murder was ugly and messy and vicious. Certainly not fit for polite or impolite circles, and yet . . . no good had come to Connor in trying to forget, either.

"Do you know who she is?"

The earl shook his head once.

"You do not recognize her?"

His father frowned.

Dropping his palms on his trousers, Connor leaned forward. "The day you rescued me, she was the girl with me."

The earl went slack-jawed.

"I stepped in that day," Connor went on, "and intervened on her behalf. It should have been her you saved." His father groaned, a wounded sound of protest. "It should have been Ophelia who was educated and cared for and protected." *Not me.*

The earl didn't speak for a long moment, and then he touched a hand to his chest. "You didn't steal my coin purse that day." Connor stilled. "You sacrificed yourself to save her."

With that undeserved defense that painted Connor in one light and Ophelia in another, his father opened his eyes to charges Ophelia had made about those of the nobility: the sense of entitlement and their disdain for people outside their station.

A watery smile turned his father's lips. Leaning across the carriage, he patted Connor on the arm. "And *that* is why you are different from that . . . Miss Killoran."

Christi Caldwell

Connor shot up a hand and knocked hard on the roof.

The carriage jerked to a quick stop, and he planted his feet to keep from pitching forward.

Not waiting for the servant, Connor tossed the door open and jumped out.

"Connor?" his father shouted after him.

He paused. "Tell me, Father. When you say you wanted my past buried . . . was it for me? Or you?"

His father's face crumpled. "Where . . . what are you . . . ?"

Not looking back, he continued walking, ignoring the calls fading behind him.

He walked through the same dank cobblestones he had as a boy, passing alleys he'd hidden within and establishments he'd stolen from.

He just continued on.

Connor had been blinded by the good his father had done in saving him, helping others, fighting in Parliament for laws that sought to curb vice and lessen the suffering. He'd accused Ophelia of unfairly judging others when he himself had been guilty of the same charge.

Only where she'd seen darkness and disdain all around, he'd retained an unfair and unrealistic view of those like his father and other members of the peerage. For all the members of Polite Society like Connor's father and Bethany and the Viscount Middlethorne's attempts to aid those less fortunate, they'd ultimately treated those people as somehow less. Beneath them. While Connor had been separated from the masses because of one chance twist of fate.

All the while his inclusion in the world hadn't been unconditional. It had come at the expense of burying memories and hiding his past because that was far safer and cleaner than the truth of what he'd done.

Connor stopped outside the three-story limestone building. With its intricate mansard roof, dual redbrick chimneys, and black matte door, it was a sleek representation of elegance and wealth.

Two gentlemen rode up on equally expensive horseflesh, tossing those reins to diligent servants.

Instead of entering, the pair exchanged words, nodding periodically and motioning to the structure that when completed would be filled with patrons. An establishment to rival White's and Brooke's. They pointed at one of the gables.

From where he stood at the gas lamp across the way, Connor studied the two men engrossed in discussion. For despite the elegant cut to their cloaks and hats, they were not, by Society's standards, gentlemen.

Ya always thought ya were better than the rest of us.

That condemnation Ophelia had leveled at him, which he'd vehemently denied, now pinged around his mind, accentuated by his father's condemnations, muting sound, dulling all noise but that of his own breathing.

He took a step as a horse came galloping forward. Shaking a fist, the rider shouted, effectively jerking Connor from his tumult and attracting the attention of that pair.

They locked in on Connor, immediately training their pistols at his chest and head.

Recognition registered in Adair Thorne's eyes. He quickly tucked away his weapon. "Steele," Thorne called. His greeting came distant to Connor's ears as he remained focused on the other, heavily scarred figure coming forward. Suspicion still darkened those familiar eyes.

More than two feet taller than when they'd last met and at least four and ten stone heavier, all muscle and power, he bore little resemblance to the boy Connor had left behind in the dead of night.

"Allow me to introduce you to my brother Niall Marksman. Niall, Connor Steele. Steele is overseeing the investigation into Lord Maddock's lost son. He's also a benefactor of Eve's hospitals."

Some of the wariness receded, but it didn't leave the other man entirely. Yes, a man might leave St. Giles, but those dark deeds one had witnessed and taken part in would always remain. No matter how much a man tried to forget or a well-meaning parent willed it away.

His former thieving partner held out a hand. "Steele," Niall said in his coarsened Cockney.

Connor stared blankly down at those digits as scarred as his own.

He'd left. Without a word. Without asking Niall to accompany him so they might help each other survive in an uncertain world, and all because he'd been afraid. One boy could hide. A pair garnered notice. So he'd run. And he'd continued running—from his past, his existence . . . all of it.

Shame swamped his senses.

How much better off Niall had been with the new family he'd found.

The brothers of the streets exchanged looks, prompting Connor into movement.

He swiftly caught Niall's hand in a firm grip, his fingers curling reflexively around them. "Niall . . ."

The other man's eyebrows shot to his hairline.

Connor withdrew his hand.

Leave. Just turn on your heel, and do what you've always done best . . . hide. Remain the ghost you were. A person who'd relied on none and kept everyone out. Except he remained rooted there, unable to complete the steps to put this club, this family, this whole bloody day, behind him.

"We knew each other . . . once," he said gruffly, his voice hoarsened with shame and regret.

He felt his onetime friend sweeping his gaze over his face, frantically trying to place him.

"I'm . . . my name . . . I am Connor. We . . ." *Stole and killed together.*

The air hissed through Niall's teeth.

Adair Thorne looked between them and then quietly backed away.

"Connor." His former friend spoke and looked as one who'd been visited by a ghost. In a way that is what he'd always been. *Nay, that is what you made yourself.* "My God. I thought . . . I believed . . ."

He'd been killed. "I wasn't." It was a fate too many boys in Diggory's hold had met. Connor had left, putting himself before all.

While Ophelia had stayed.

All the breath in his body, lodged somewhere between his lungs and throat, stuck.

As long as he'd known Ophelia, he'd questioned her—nay, worse, he'd passed judgment upon her for remaining in Diggory's gang. When all along she'd been the loyal one. She'd never left a person behind, not as Connor had. He'd not even remained true to his parents' memory.

He was nearly crippled by the weight of his shame. "I left because I didn't"—Connor inhaled slowly, forcing himself to say it—"I didn't want to kill anymore. I thought of myself only. I was your friend, and you deserved more from me. You deserved better." Unable to meet his former friend's eyes, he bowed his head. "I wanted to say how sorry I am," he said hoarsely in a useless apology that could never right a wrong.

Niall's lips worked. He stuck a palm out. "There's nothing to forgive," he said gruffly. "We all did wot we 'ad to survive."

Connor eyed that offering and then again shook Niall's hand.

"'ow did ya survive?" There was curiosity there. After all, no one survived in the streets without help.

He chuckled. "Would you believe me if I told you a small girl saved my worthless hide more times than I deserved?"

"Oi would," Niall laughed, the sound rusty. "Oi've come to appreciate the strength in people Oi once underestimated."

The doors to the club were thrown open, and they both looked up. A pair of jovial builders stepped out, carrying a long beam between them. Their laughter and reverie stood out, a stark contrast to the solemnity of Connor's exchange with Niall.

Connor inclined his head. "I'll leave you to your business."

He took a step to go just as Niall called out. "Connor?"

He looked back.

A grin pulled at Niall's scarred mouth. "Oi'm glad ya didn't find yarself dead."

Connor returned that smile. "Me too."

As he began the long, slow trek on foot through London, a weight lifted from him. Time rolled together until he reached his Bond Street offices. He fished the key from his jacket and let himself inside.

The faint bark of a dog, forlorn in its loneliness, filled the London streets. Connor lifted his head from the lock and looked around.

A chill scraped along his spine as all his nerves went on alert.

Carefully edging the door open, he slipped inside.

And knew.

The faint glow of the candle filtered from the crack under his office door, the only light in his darkened office.

Heart hammering, Connor slowly brought the door closed behind him. He reached into his boot and removed the pistol tucked there. His gun close to his chest, he crept the length of the narrow corridor, stepping over aged floorboards given to creaking.

He stopped.

The faint rustle of parchment echoed within his office, followed by the sound of drawers systematically opening and closing.

Drawing back the hammer, he waited.

Chapter 15

Her neck ached.

Having sneaked off to Connor's offices and picked the lock to let herself in, she'd been since shut away, poring through his files.

Consulting details he'd written, she leaned over and made several notes on parchment she'd commandeered from his middle desk drawer.

Until, at last, she finished.

Stretching her arms above her head, she assessed her work. Each page was marked with the year at the top and neat columns; each row contained names and information Connor had desperately sought.

Ophelia silently mouthed the names of each child, searching her mind for any boy or girl she might have forgotten. She paused on the last sheet and stared down at those names there.

Twenty of them, now gone, existed as nothing more than a mark upon her page. Capturing her lower lip between her teeth, she trailed her fingertips over each one. There had been so little time to mourn. The only time permitted was that which one stole. Any expressions of grief or weakness were met with sound beatings and a lesson on just how much tears cost a person.

A single, solitary drop rolled down her cheek and slapped noisily upon the page; the tiny bit of moisture blurred that name.

The door exploded open with such force it hit the wall and then bounced back.

Gasping, she grabbed for her knife.

Her breath came hard and fast. "Ya scared the bloody 'ell out of me, Connor." Her own panic reflected back in his eyes. Tossing aside her blade, she pressed a palm against her chest in a bid to still her galloping heart.

"Ophelia?" His voice emerged hoarse. He swiftly lowered his weapon. "My God, I nearly shot you." Terror riddled that realization.

Praying he couldn't see her tears in the darkened room, she discreetly swiped at her damp cheeks. "Ya wouldn't 'ave shot me. Ya'ave more control than that."

Cursing, he shoved the door closed with the heel of his boot and stalked over. "I had a gun pointed at you." He alternated a horrified stare between the weapon in his hands and Ophelia. He blanched. "I pointed it at your head."

At the evidence of his worrying after her, her heart did a little somersault in her chest. "For what it's worth, O'Roarke, if I were forced to choose, I'd rather take a shot to the head than the belly."

He opened his mouth and then closed it.

Connor tried again.

Ophelia winked.

"Are you bloody mad?" he growled. He tossed his weapon down on a nearby side table. "Are you making light of me nearly killing you?"

Her confidence wavered as a memory intruded . . . of another charging forward.

"There is nothing at all humorous in that," he barked.

She blinked, finding him a mere desk length away.

Connor. It is just Connor.

He froze, and his gaze dropped to his files laid out. "What is this?" he blurted.

With shaking fingers, Ophelia stacked the scattered pages lying about. "Oi was going to clean it," she said under her breath. "Didn't expect ya to be here."

Connor folded his arms. "You invaded my office, broke into my desk, and examined my files."

Not long ago he would have been accusatory and suspicious. Deservedly so. So much had changed between them.

And yet . . . given your birthright, it is sure to be fleeting. A sheen blurred her vision. Dratted office. Tears for a second time this night. He really needed to dust his mahogany furniture.

"Nothing to say?"

"You really need better locks, Connor," she said with forced lightness. "As one who's lived on the streets, you know that flimsy locks are useless if someone wants in."

"There were three locks," he drawled.

She paused in her task to raise three fingers. "Three useless ones."

"Not everyone is as skilled at lock-picking as you."

She picked her head up and beamed.

Smiling, Connor reached across the desk and brushed his knuckles along her jaw. "You're the only woman I know who'd take that as a compliment, Ophelia."

Unlike his duchess. The girl he'd called friend, the young lady he'd hoped to marry, and the woman deserving of him.

Her smile froze in place, straining her cheek muscles until she feared her face might shatter.

Connor spoke, all teasing gone. "Why are you here?"

"Why . . . ?"

She followed his stare to the neat pile. Forcing back a searing jealousy, she gripped the pages in her hands, wrinkling the corners. *Turn*

them over . . . explain what you've provided, answer any questions he has,
and be on your way, so you can begin living a life without him in it.

Instead, she brought the stack close to her chest, retaining a death
grip on the sheets she'd meticulously compiled. "I hated the nobility,"
she confided. "I resented them for having so much when I wanted so
little. I hated them for not seeing me or, worse, for not caring about me
or my siblings." Ophelia glanced briefly at the stack she clutched. "It
was always there . . . the hatred." She drew in a shuddery breath. "Just
varying degrees of it. I use to read palms," she whispered.

Connor stitched his eyebrows into a single line. "I know—I—"

She shook her head, and he immediately fell silent. Everything was
jumbled together in her mind, forcing parts of her past out in an order
that made no sense. Counting to three, she tried again. "Diggory realized he could earn far more coin in me reading the palms and telling
the future of fancy lords and ladies than I could in snatching purses." A
brittle laugh bubbled past her lips, and her body shook with the force of
that empty mirth. "Imagine that? More coin was to be had from a street
rat making up fake fortunes for people who already had more than that
guttersnipe could have ever dreamed." Awkwardly angling her palms,
she studied the ink-stained, callused flesh. "The ladies yearned for love,
and the men, fortune. It didn't take me long to gather as much from my
clients. The grander the vision, the more exorbitant the prize." Coins
she'd had to turn over without so much as a pence for her efforts. "Cleo
still had to steal. It was learned I'd . . . seen you, and as repayment for
crossing Diggory, he punched Gertrude." Ophelia sucked in an uneven
breath. "She lost vision in one of her eyes."

Grief contorted his features. "Because you spared my life," he finished for her, regret heavy in that understanding.

"After I helped you, Connor. I didn't spare you. You were always
a survivor. You were destined to survive whether or not I intervened
those days."

"I don't believe that," he murmured, taking a slow path around the desk.

She held up her overflowing hands, and he instantly stopped.

"Then there was me . . . the gypsy." Ophelia chuckled. "A gypsy with white hair. It merely added to the illusion. Just like that, a shift in role, and my life was safe in ways Cleo's and Gertrude's were not." Tears flooded her eyes, and she blinked them back, but the misty sheen remained until she let them fall. "I even had a dress," she whispered. "It was so soft and pure white. It was laundered"—a task that had fallen to Gertrude—"every night until it frayed, and then I had another. And do you know what, Connor? Selfishly, I was g-grateful." Her voice broke. He reached for her, but she stepped back, needing space between them. "I was grateful that I didn't face the dangers that my sisters did and relished the small comforts I had. I accused you of looking after only yourself, and yet I was even guiltier of that charge." Her voice dissolved into a faint whisper. "Because I had sisters who relied on me."

"Hmm," he protested, closing the space between them. He cupped her cheek in a firm but gentle grip. "You are only human, Ophelia. You were just a girl, and even if you hadn't been, there is nothing wrong in wanting to be safe."

"But . . . there was shame in it, and I was rightfully punished for those sins."

He stiffened; his arm fell to his side. Had he prodded . . . had he asked a single question or made a hint of a sound, she'd not have gone on. Mayhap it was his skill as an investigator. Or mayhap he'd been the only true friend she'd had and innately knew that she wouldn't continue. But he met her silent tumult with an equal quiet.

"I had handlers. Two of them. Diggory knew my worth."

Ya're worth more than both yar sisters combined, girl. Don't ya dare get yarself 'urt.

Words from a father that hadn't been issued out of any concern but for the monetary value she represented to him.

"Oi 'ad a place down an alley in the Dials. 'ad to walk hours to get there because Diggory didn't want to risk that someone in St. Giles remembered Oi was just a pickpocket turned gypsy. A fancy lord came. Foine garments. 'ad a daughter loike me, 'e said. 'is wife 'ad just died, an' he wanted to know the future that awaited him." Another tear streaked down her cheek.

Unable to meet Connor's unnerving gaze, a gaze that saw too much, she turned away and wandered off several steps.

"It was going to be so easy. Oi knew precisely wot 'e hoped to 'ear. A new love, a new mother for his girl. Oi let my guard down. Oi didn't allow myself to see the hardness in his eyes, the way he looked at moi chest and not my eyes as he spoke." She forced her feet back around, forced herself to meet this man's eyes, needing him to understand why she'd spent so many years fearful of that lot he so trusted. "When I went down that alley, Oi learned real fast that Oi'd never been the lucky one."

When he was just a boy, he'd nicked his first pocket. His nerves had made him sloppy and careless. One clumsy grab had alerted the gent to his intentions. The shout had gone up, followed by a cry as hands shot out and a sea of strangers made to grab him. Until the day he drew his last breath, he'd recall the thundering of his heart, the absolute absence of sufficient air for his lungs.

Standing there, with Ophelia huddled within herself, her story unfinished, he felt very much the way he had then.

His pulse raced, and coward as he'd always been, he wanted to retreat once more, wanted to halt a telling, for he knew. Knew before she even continued what happened to girls who wandered down those alleys.

"What happened?" he forced himself to ask.

She lifted her slender shoulders in a stiff shrug. "He told me 'ow pretty Oi was. Told me moi 'air was beautiful. Then he touched it."

Oh, God. His stomach pitched as those imaginings slapped at his mind. Of Ophelia, a small girl, and some bloody nobleman collecting those silken strands in his fingers.

"'e wasn't the first," she said, her voice faint. "All the lords and ladies wanted to touch my 'air. They thought it was magic. Sometimes Oi even sold them an extra touch for a pence." Her throat moved rhythmically. "Oi sold him a touch that day. Oi thought Oi was so c-clever. He said Oi invited it. That Oi wanted it."

He moaned. "It wasn't your fault. He had no right . . . to any of it." He ached to take her in his arms but knew if he did, she'd cease her telling, and so he stood there, his arms hanging tense at his sides.

"He ripped moi dress." A half laugh, half sob tore from her; the pained sound shredded his frantically pounding heart. "That was the first thing Oi thought. And then it all happened so fast. Touched me . . ." She squeezed the burden she clutched harder against her chest. ". . . here. Then jammed a knee between moi legs."

Did that low groan better suited to a wounded animal belong to Connor? How was he even capable of a single utterance through her telling?

With trembling fingers, Ophelia set her papers down. "Said moi mouth was a whore's mouth that he couldn't kiss, that he 'ad other uses for it." As she spoke, her telling took on a methodical quality where each word she spoke hit like a lance to his chest. "Oi knew wot the girls did with their mouths. Oi'd even seen it. Oi'd always been sick at the thought of . . . it. 'e stuck 'is fingers in me first." A heartrending shame dripped from that whisper and cut him to the core. "It was real painful. Oi fought h-him." Her voice broke on that imagery that conjured Ophelia as she'd been—alone, riddled with terror, desperately fighting off the attack of a treacherous nobleman. "'e enjoyed it. Urged me on."

He concentrated on drawing in slow, even breaths, wanting to be strong, for she deserved that strength. She'd been strong when any other man, woman, or child would have cracked and crumbled.

"Then Oi let myself go limp." A triumphant grin curved her quivering lips. "That was 'is misstep that day. Oi grabbed moi knife while he was loosening his falls, cut him." She motioned to her thigh. "He screamed loike a stuck pig an' Oi took off running. Oi burned that dress," she added on a whispery afterthought. "Beat by Diggory for losing it. It was the first beating Oi actually wanted because Oi deserved it. Because Oi'd encouraged him."

Groaning, Connor came forward and then stopped. Not knowing what to say . . . afraid to touch her.

"Don't do that." Her voice broke.

He shook his head.

She lifted ravaged eyes to his, and those shimmering crystalline pools of despair hit him like a kick to the gut. "Please don't look at me loike ya don't know 'ow to be with me."

Taking the permission she granted, he folded her close as he'd ached to since she'd begun. She turned her head, layering it against his chest, and he continued to hold her. Resting his cheek against the silken crown of pale curls, he clung to her.

All the while a white-hot rage pulsed through his veins, a primal yearning to hunt down and find the stranger responsible for her nightmares and take him apart limb by limb.

Time melted away, ceasing to mean anything more than an irrelevant click on the mahogany wall clock, as Connor just held her. Since their first meeting, he'd touted the honor and goodness in the nobility, when every experience she'd ever had, every exchange, was tainted by ugliness. When one of those same gentlemen had attempted to rape her, and very nearly would have if it hadn't been for her own resourcefulness. "I am an arrogant, unmitigated fool," he said, hollow inside and out.

"Taking you to task for not seeing the good." A broken, cynical laugh rumbled in his chest. "All along I was the one who was so wrong."

She pushed away, and he mourned the space she erected between them. "No," she said, frustration lending her voice strength. She gave her head a shake. "That isn't why I told you . . . about that day. I told you because you were right."

He briefly closed his eyes. How in God's earth could that horror she'd recounted show him anything of the sort? "I couldn't have been further from the mark."

Ophelia sighed. "Part of me, I fear, will always be wary of the nobility."

How could she not? He wanted to toss his head back and rage at the world for what she'd endured.

"But you've taught me . . . you've shown me," she amended. "There are lords and ladies who are good. Like Eve Dabney and the Duke and Duchess of Somerset. They are all people who have included me in their lives, despite their knowing precisely who I am . . . and what I've done. And your . . . father . . ." His father was undeserving in this instance of that honorable placement she gave him. ". . . and Lady Bethany."

Connor palmed her cheek, and she leaned into his touch. "You are a remarkable woman, Ophelia Killoran."

"I'm not," she said simply. "I'm just a woman who realized you were correct." Her eyes held his. "I have not helped you in your investigation because I feared the intentions of the gentleman you work for. I'm not afraid anymore. I trust you, Connor. I trust that these children"—she picked up the forgotten pages—"will not come to any harm." Ophelia placed that burden in his arms.

Blinking, he looked at the stack. "What is this?"

"It is everything. All the children I've hired, the details I recall about their pasts. The boys and girls who belonged to Diggory's gang, those who remained on with us, those who died . . ." Her words trailed off.

His heart started as the enormity of her faith and trust slammed into him. Connor skimmed through the sheets in his hands and all the information contained upon those pages. "Ophelia," he said hoarsely.

She held up a staying hand. "A debt owed."

Required a debt be paid. He stilled, braced for the demand she'd put to him.

Ophelia breathed deeply. "I want you to make love to me."

Chapter 16

Ophelia's heart hammered, threatening to beat a path out of her chest.

She'd said it.

She'd put her request to him.

It was wicked and scandalous but surely no more wicked or scandalous than she'd been in the whole of her existence. A proper lady, a virgin at that, would never dare enter into a bargain with a request to be . . . to be . . . relieved of one's virtue, but she'd never been one of those proper ladies and had never sought to shape herself into the one her brother wished her to be.

All she knew was that before she forced herself to give up Connor O'Roarke, she wanted to know the pleasure to be found in his arms, to taste passion without fear, to experience desire without shame.

Connor remained as motionless as those carved statues outside the Devil's Den.

Ophelia shifted on her feet. "Th-that isn't altogether true. I . . . I wanted you to have it anyway. The information, that is." Ophelia wetted her lips, and his gaze immediately went to her mouth. His eyes darkened. "I wanted to help you in your case because it is right." She rambled on. "And I will still help even if you don't wish to . . . even if you can't bring yourself to . . ."

Abandoning the sheets he held, Connor cupped her nape and covered her mouth with his.

It was a tender meeting, searing for the heat of it and yet so very gentle. His lips, firm yet soft, explored the contours of that flesh she'd spent her life hating. Now she relished the attention he showed it. With each brush of his mouth against hers, sparks kindled, and warmth continued pooling low in her belly.

Her lids heavy with her hungering for him, she fought to keep them open. So she might imprint upon her mind and memory thoughts of this moment: the shadow of a day's growth upon his rugged cheeks, his own eyes weighted closed by desire, shielded by those thick gypsy's lashes.

Ophelia threaded her fingers through the tangle of his loose midnight curls, luxuriating in the satiny softness of those strands against her coarse palms. She met his kiss. Tilted her head and opened herself to each stroke of his mouth. Until the tenderness of that kiss slowly melted away, replaced by a straining need that she felt spill from his wildly taut frame.

She parted her lips, letting him sweep his tongue inside, and tasted only desire.

With a little moan, Ophelia layered herself closer, wanting more of his kiss. Of him. Of a night she wanted to go on forever.

Connor filled his hands with her buttocks, sculpting his large palms against that flesh. He brought her close.

His length, hard and hot and straining against the front of his trousers, pressed her belly, a marked sign of his want.

Ophelia stilled, a whisper of fear slipping in. Of another. Forcing her . . . touching her . . .

As though Connor sensed the tension building in her, threatening to carry her from this moment, he lightened his hold, gentling his kiss once more and then breaking it altogether. She wanted to cry out from the loss of it. Gripping him by the lapels of his jacket, she drew herself closer to him.

Except he didn't step away. He merely shifted his lips, trailing a path elsewhere: kissing the corner of her mouth, worshipping her cheek, the sensitive shell of her ear. On a breathy half moan, half laugh, she tipped her head, opening herself to those ministrations.

"You are so beautiful," Connor murmured against the column of her throat. His breath came quick, like one who'd run a hard race.

She arched her neck, allowing him access to the place where her pulse beat erratically for him.

He lightly sucked and then nibbled at the flesh. Working a hand between them, he slipped her dark jacket free. It landed noisily at their feet. Connor reclaimed her lips, and she parted her mouth, allowing him entry. Their tongues touched, met, and danced in a primitive battle, dueling as they reacquainted each other with the moist contours of those caverns.

Scorched again with the heat of his embrace, Ophelia melted against him. He caught her close. All the while he searched his hands over her hips, lightly sinking his fingers into that flesh. His breath rasped within her mouth, and she swallowed those desperate, panicky sounds of his hungering.

He kissed her deep in a kiss that went on forever and took with it time and left in its place only a burning-hot longing.

Ophelia closed her eyes, clinging to the heady magnificence of his embrace. "With you, I feel safe," she rasped between each kiss. *I want to know only your embrace.*

Regret for what would never—could never—be allowed began to slip in, threatening the stolen moment of pretend she'd allowed herself. A tear spiraled down her cheek, and she prayed Connor wouldn't see that token of her sadness. She wanted nothing to shatter this moment: not memory or nightmare or regret.

Panting, Connor angled back, putting a small distance between them. She moaned, gripping at his shirt to pull him close again. He captured that lone drop with the pad of his thumb and wiped it away. "Please," she whispered, her voice ragged. Ophelia raised heavy eyes to his. "Do not stop." How could she live the rest of her days without knowing Connor O'Roarke in every way?

He eyed her through heavy, dark lashes, caressing his molten gaze over every corner of her face. "From the moment I first met you, Ophelia Killoran, you captivated me." Connor held her stare and slowly reached for the corners of her wool shirt, his meaning clear: she was free to step away. He wanted her to see and know precisely what he did.

Her chest rose and fell quickly as he caught the fabric and slowly tugged her linen shirt free of the boy's breeches she'd donned. His eyes never breaking contact with hers, Connor drew the coarse garment over her head and tossed it behind him.

He paused, lingering on her bindings.

Drawing in an uneven breath, she nodded.

Without hesitation, Connor reached for the fabric and unwound strip after strip, until her breasts were bared to him.

She automatically hugged her arms close, protectively covering herself. This was Connor, who'd never hurt or harmed her.

With those assurances ringing around her brain, she let her arms fall to her sides.

His breath caught, and he stretched out a hand. Reverent in his regard and touch, he filled a palm with the heavy flesh. Then, placing his other against the previously neglected mound, he cupped them both.

Her pulse quickened as he weighed her breasts in his hands.

Then he brushed his thumbs over the crescent peaks, sending sparks shooting through her from that fleeting, forbidden, and delicious caress.

Ophelia bit her lower lip.

He made to release her.

She shot out her hands, covering his palms with her own, anchoring him in place, keeping him close, needing this, wanting it. "Don't . . . stop," she entreated.

Inhaling between tightly clenched lips, Connor caressed and massaged that skin. She fluttered her lashes; his touch was thrilling. This was what so many of the women in the Devil's Den whispered about. All along she'd believed them liars, mocked them in her mind, only to be proven so very wrong in Connor's arms.

He caressed his lips over the swollen tip of her right breast, bringing her eyes flying open. "What . . ." She breathed heavily; her words rolled together, incoherent. "Please . . . oh, God." What did she even ask for? She no longer knew. She was incapable of anything but feeling.

Then he closed his mouth around her nipple.

A gasp ripped from her throat.

He made to draw back, but she gripped his head, holding him firmly in place. "Do not . . . please . . . I want . . ."

He laid his cheek against her chest. Her heart thumped wildly under the very place his head rested. The sigh of his breath cooled her perspiring skin. "Tell me what you want," he whispered, his voice hoarsened by a restrained desire. "Do you want me to stop?" She loved him all the more for the pain in that question, one that said he'd release her no matter how much he wanted her.

"Do not stop kissing me," she whispered.

With a groan of supplication, he took that bud between his lips once more, lapping at the flesh, teasing it with his tongue.

"Connor," she rasped.

A slow-moving conflagration rippled through her, and she wanted to lose herself in the blaze, burn up like that sun, and know only the splendor of this moment.

He shifted his attentions to the previously neglected tip. Drawing it between his lips, he suckled.

Ophelia cried out, her hips arching with her need.

A sharp, searing ache between her legs begged for his touch. Through her desire-heavy mind, she registered Connor slipping off her trousers until she stood bare before him. The cool night air kissed her heated skin.

Connor swept her into his arms and carried her to the red Chippendale sofa in the corner of his office. He set her down and then straightened.

Ophelia shoved herself up on her elbows. With eyes laden with desire, she urged him on.

He brought shaking fingers to his jacket. He undid the handful of buttons there and rid himself of the fine woolen garment. He tossed it aside. The article joined the other forlornly thrown garments scattered about the room. After divesting himself of his shirt next, he reached for his breeches.

She held a staying hand, and he froze.

On unsteady legs, Ophelia rose. She joined him and rested her palms against his thickly muscled chest, thinly matted with whorls of dark curls. She slipped her fingers through it, testing its softness, feeling his strength.

"Ophelia," he groaned, her name a prayer and a command all at the same time.

"So beautiful," she whispered, sliding her fingertips over his flat stomach. The muscles of his abdomen were as crisply defined as his corded biceps and thick forearms. Tentatively, Ophelia caressed his nipple. That flesh puckered, and a hiss slipped from his throat.

Connor reached between them and shoved his trousers down, then kicked them aside so that he stood before her naked.

She froze as hunger warred with fear. All the ugliest memories slid in, and with them, the doubts. *I cannot do this . . .* Her breath came fast. *I cannot.*

Connor cupped her cheek. "I will never hurt you."

Those five words penetrated the slowly building panic, stopping it in its place. Warmth suffused her heart, healing and beautiful. "I know," she whispered, believing his vow. "You are"—and always would be—"the only man I've never feared." Even as she had no right to him, even as there could be nothing more, she selfishly wanted to take what he offered. Her mouth went dry, hungering for a glimpse of him.

Ophelia glanced down.

And then wished she hadn't.

His turgid length jutted proudly from a nest of dark curls; a pearly sheen pebbled on the tip.

Oh, God. Her stomach pitched. "Ya're going to put *that* in me?" She shook her head in denial and disbelief. "It ain't ever going to work, O'Roarke."

He took her lips in a brief kiss. "Do you trust me?" he whispered against her mouth.

She did. She always had. Even as a girl, when she'd learned nearly all were given to deceit, she'd implicitly trusted this man. "I do."

He swept her into his arms once more and laid her on the cool fabric of that sofa. Only this time he joined her, lowering himself above her, balancing himself on his elbows.

Then he again found her breasts, worshipping first one and then the other, until her fears and doubts receded and she was reduced to a thrumming bundle of nerves, capable of nothing more than feeling.

Connor slipped a hand between her legs and cupped her mound.

She cried out, her hips shooting up as the ache there throbbed and intensified.

He slid a finger into the moist heat, finding the nub there. He toyed with it until tears sprang to her eyes and words eluded her. For there was no shame. There was only a joyous, splendorous beauty in his touch.

"So beautiful," he breathed, that long digit stroking inside her, and then he slipped another inside.

"Connor," she pleaded, panting, hot, wanting something. Not knowing what, only that he could provide it.

Through the desire fogging all thought, she registered him slipping a knee between her legs, gently parting her.

Spread your legs for me.

Ophelia cried out as that cold reality of her past intruded on this blissful moment she stole from Connor.

"Do not think of him. Think of us. Think of only us," Connor whispered against her temple. His husky, rich baritone anchored her to the present, pushing back thoughts of another and leaving nothing but that deep, hot longing.

Us.

Who knew one word alone could seduce and tempt?

Refusing to mourn now what would never be, Ophelia let her legs splay open.

Connor lowered himself between her thighs. Sweat beaded on his forehead, and all his muscles strained with the evidence of his desire and the cost of restraint.

She stiffened, braced for him to batter at that thin piece of flesh she'd fought so hard to retain. She wanted both to cede that precious gift over to this man and to clamp her legs closed for fear of what would come.

His fingers again found her and tangled in the damp curls shielding the apex of her womanhood. "Connor," she managed, gasping. His butterfly-soft caress, slow and deliberate as he stroked her, stirred desire, and her speech dissolved into a blend of incoherent pleas, sighs, moans.

Connor lowered himself farther, and through the thick desire, she registered his shaft probing at her entrance. All the while his fingers continued to work their magic, teasing at that nub until she was beside herself with longing.

At last he stopped, the head of his enormous length poised, pressed against that bit of flesh.

His chest heaved.

How tender, how restrained, when painful need spilled from his eyes. "Do it, Connor," she said quietly.

His lips twitched in an agonized smile. "Ordering me about even here?"

They shared a teasing smile that quickly faded. Connor lowered his mouth and teased the tip of her right breast. She gasped, twining her fingers in his lush curls. He continued suckling. His ministrations brought her hips again arching.

"Forgive me," he pleaded. With a groan, he plunged himself deep.

Ophelia cried out as he battered past that scrap of skin. Tears popped behind her lashes. She made herself go absolutely still. His enormous length, buried to the hilt, throbbed, sharpening the sting of pain.

"I am so sorry," he whispered, kissing the trail of tears that slid silently down her cheeks.

"Oi told ya it wasn't going to w-w-work," she stammered.

"It will." He brushed his mouth over hers. When he pulled away, a tender yet agony-filled smile curved his lips. "We were made for each other."

His profession melted her from the inside out.

Wordlessly, he pressed another kiss atop her breast.

Her breath quickened as his ministrations stirred the earlier desire, and slowly the pain receded. Then he began to move, filling her, stretching her. With each deliberate stroke, discomfort faded and left in its place a throbbing ache. Ophelia lifted her hips, meeting his thrusts. Their bodies moved conjointly, their hips moving in perfect sync.

A shuddery gasp left her as the pressure built and the fire spread.

Their movements became frantic.

Ophelia wrapped her arms around him, clinging for all she was worth, sinking her nails into his back.

He groaned, a deep, masculine sound of approval.

Connor drove deeper, harder, faster, and she took all of him, wanting him. Wanting this. Wanting all of it.

A tingling pressure built at her core, as with each lunge he drew her up higher and higher until she feared she'd break apart, until she ached to shatter.

He thrust home, and she screamed her joy and surrender, splintering into a million beautiful shards of light and sensation.

Connor stiffened, back arched, neck thrown back, as he joined her, spilling himself in deep, rippling waves that stretched her pleasure on forever.

Then she went limp under him, panting, out of breath from the power and beauty of their joining.

Connor collapsed, swiftly catching himself on elbows that shook.

With the hot, reassuring weight of his body blanketing her own, Ophelia smiled.

Chapter 17

It was the cold that awoke Connor.

The absolute absence of Ophelia's warmth pulled him back from the heavy haze of sleep. He reached for her, searching, his fingers caressing only air.

Mayhap in a hungering he'd carried for her since she'd stepped into Killoran's offices, he'd only dreamed her being here now, in his office, in his arms, under him.

He forced his eyes open . . . and then found her.

Behind his desk, she examined two pages in her hands. She'd since donned her lawn shirt and breeches. Now, she alternated her attentions back and forth between those sheets. Seated as she was in his massive leather winged chair, there was a naturalness to her being there. In his office. In his life. As though she belonged there. As though she always had.

And I want her here.

I want her beyond how she might help me solve Maddock's investigation and more than the gift she gave me a short while ago.

His heartbeat sped up and then slowed to a near stop.

Ultimately, with her brother's expectations . . . she'd choose another. Just as Bethany had. Where that had wounded a younger version of himself, losing Ophelia would break him in ways no one and nothing had before.

Ophelia nibbled at her lower lip, an endearing hint of the concentration she devoted to her task.

Connor used her distractedness as an opportunity to study her: the tangle of her white-blonde hair like a curtain draped around her lush siren's frame. Delicate shoulders peeked out from between those luxuriant strands.

Except mayhap he'd come to matter to her, too . . . and mayhap Ophelia would choose him unconditionally for who . . . and what . . . he was.

She set down the pages and reached for another.

"I expect I should be offended that you prefer papers and files to me, Ophelia Killoran," he called over, his voice heavy with sleep.

She started and lifted her head with enough force to strain the muscles of that graceful neck he'd kissed only—he squinted over at his clock—thirty or so minutes ago. "You're awake," she observed quietly.

"And you've been," he ventured.

She nodded. "I didn't sleep. I've been looking through your files"— Ophelia glanced briefly to the work laid out before her—"about the marquess's son."

There wasn't another woman like her. Unlike the previous women he'd taken as lovers who'd craved baubles and wealth, Ophelia had instead carved a place for herself in the world. Connor swung his legs over the edge of the leather seat and stood.

Ophelia's eyes formed perfect circles, and a fiery blush stained her cheeks. She dropped her gaze to the pages in her hands. "Uh . . . yes . . . well . . ." she stammered, and his heart pulled. He'd been in awe of her spirit as long as he'd known her, captivated by her wit, and now so wholly enthralled by her innocence.

He crossed over and rescued each article of his garments. "What are your thoughts?" he asked, stooping to gather his trousers.

"M-my thoughts?" she squeaked, studying that page as if it contained the details to Blackbeard's lost trove.

His lips tugged. He stuffed one leg into his pants. "Of the information, Miss Killoran," he clarified after he'd pulled the article over his hips and buttoned the falls.

She blinked wildly and then lifted her eyes. "Oh . . . uh, yes, of course. I've been considering the timeline of events: the fire, the disappearance . . . or the death of the child." It was a significant concession from one who'd been adamant about the fate of the marquess's son. "I've immediately crossed off many of the children on my lists because they were in Diggory's gang prior to the fire. Others"—she reached for another page, with names inked through with a definitive *X*—"were born on the streets to women I know . . . knew. They are the babes of Diggory's men."

He grabbed a chair and carried it over.

Ophelia hopped up, but he waved her back.

Pale-white brows lifted with her surprise.

"Do you expect I'm so arrogant that I'd order you from your chair?" he drawled.

"It is not my chair. It is *yours*," she quietly corrected, fiddling with her papers. "I'd expect it because . . ." Because he didn't trust her.

Resting his hands along the arms of his chair, he leaned back. "I never distrusted you, Ophelia."

She snorted.

He offered a sheepish grin. "Very well. I was suspicious, but only because of what I do. I've been given reasons to question all." He held her gaze. "But never did I believe you capable of harming a child." It went against everything he knew of her, as a girl who'd saved him and even more so now.

Her lips lifted in a tremulous smile.

Edging his chair closer, he nudged his chin, encouraging her to continue.

She handed over a page. "These children. I've marked a question mark alongside their names because I believe they are too young, and yet I cannot determine with any real certainty. My sister Cleo . . . she's always appeared far younger. As such, one shouldn't rely on an illusion of age."

Connor studied her notes.

"What of the marquess's son?"

He paused, glancing up from his reading.

"Perhaps if I examine the research you've conducted, I might match it with anything I know of the children at the Devil's Den."

She wished to see his notes. Once such a request would have been met with an immediate and firm no. Once he would have also been riddled with suspicion at finding her in his office, alone, and only after having sneaked out in breeches and picked his locks.

Leaning over, he reached for the bottom drawer—which sat agape.

He gave her a droll look.

"That requires a more reliable lock, as well," she muttered matter-of-factly when most would at least feign sheepishness.

Connor rescued the file resting on top—a thick folio containing all the information he'd assembled on Lord Maddock's case. She'd not gone through it yet.

"Don't make more of my motives than there is. Oi would 'ave eventually gotten to reading through it," she said, shifting in her chair.

"Would you have?"

Ophelia shrugged. "Perhaps."

Or perhaps she'd intended to record her information and leave it for him? His mind slowly picked through that. It did not make sense. It would imply she'd no intention of again seeing him . . . His stomach muscles clenched.

Either way, he turned over the folder for her to peruse.

Ophelia proceeded to read the synopsis resting on top. Her eyes frantically worked over those words written there, and with each line read, the color seeped more and more from her cheeks.

"My God," she whispered. "The staff saw her . . . heard her . . ."

"Burning alive," he confirmed somberly. "Horrific stuff. Some of the servants who escaped claim she was searching for her child. A handful of others say she was screaming that her child had been taken. Whatever it was, there were conflicting reports that none could confirm. And the constables deemed their information unreliable because . . ."

"They were servants?"

Another time he would have disputed her on that quick assumption. But that had been before his father's display of self-aggrandizement and his disdain for Ophelia.

Ophelia looked to the page again. "No wonder the man went mad," she murmured without rancor. She resumed reading. "He claims the nursemaid set the blaze and made off with the child."

"The investigation concluded she'd also perished in the conflagration. No remains were ever discovered."

Ophelia finished scanning the top sheet and then turned to the next. "Why does he blame the girl?"

Connor rolled his tight shoulders, and his chair groaned in protest to that slight movement. "She came highly recommended, with commendations from her previous employers." The Marquess and Marchioness of Flint. "I was the first to question them regarding their opinion of the young woman. They never wrote references on her behalf."

Ophelia whipped her head up. "What?"

"They came upon the young woman arguing with another servant in their employ. She spoke in Cockney tones and brandished a knife. The marquess did not even allow her to pack her belongings. Several servants escorted her from the residence."

He could all but see the questions turning over in Ophelia's eyes. "And there were no inquiries made into . . . this . . . this woman . . ." She flipped through the pages. "Charlotte."

"There was no reason for it," Connor explained. "The investigation centered around the one person most believed responsible."

"The marquess," she murmured.

"Continue reading."

At his urging, Ophelia immediately directed her attention back to the page. She paused. "There was a fight."

"A terrible one, with him storming off to his clubs and the lady in tears." All hints of guilt had pointed squarely at the young husband. "He had no reason to question the nursemaid."

"Until?"

Connor cracked his knuckles. "He came upon the tale of Ryker Black and Helena Banbury and how they'd been stolen and given to Diggory."

Ophelia's entire body stiffened. Something dark flashed behind her eyes but was quickly gone. With measured movements, she placed his notes in their proper order, closing the leather folder. "And from that he believed . . . ?"

"Diggory had a sick fascination with the nobility that sent him in search of a noble son." He reached into his desk and withdrew another folder. He tossed it before her. "The boy's name was . . . is . . . August Rudolph Thadeus Stephen Warren, the Earl of Greyley."

"August Rudolph Thadeus . . ." She paused.

"Stephen Warren, the Earl of Greyley," he finished for her. "Quite a lot of name for any one person." He chuckled. "I always said the number of names one was saddled with was a mark of one's importance and place in this world."

She stared back at him through unblinking, stricken eyes.

On the heel of that, remorse flooded him. "I didn't mean . . . I wasn't . . ."

"No, it is fine." Ophelia brushed off his response. "It's true. To the world it is a sign of power. May I see it, your file on the child?"

He inclined his head in unspoken acknowledgment.

While she went through his notes about the marquess's lost son, Connor examined the papers she'd supplied him with.

They read, a companionable silence falling between them, as they scrutinized all the information thus amassed. Otherwise, but for the ticking clock, the only sound came from the periodic crackle of a page being turned.

After a lengthy stretch of quiet, Connor glanced over.

Ophelia tenderly caressed the small rendering that had been completed for the purpose of his case. The plump babe captured from a combination of the marquess's recollection and the handful of portraits throughout Lord Maddock's Grosvenor Square townhouse existed upon the miniature canvas as a child frozen in time. His cheeks full, a mischievous smile on his lips, the future Marquess of Maddock, right down to the glimmer of his eyes, exuded joy and innocence. "He was so very small."

"Aye." Through the melancholy of the moment, another thought slipped in. A welcome one. Another babe, loved and joyous and innocent. Only a blonde girl with Ophelia's spirit and courage. The tantalizing dream of it sucked all the air from the room, gripping him with the beautiful possibility of it.

"It could not have been Diggory." The mention of that demon effectively kicked ash upon the lighter musings that had distracted him. "Diggory had no use for children."

"He required them to pick pockets and build his fortune," he pointed out.

"Mmm," she said, noncommittal. "He did, but he took the children of whores and beggars. Those in foundling hospitals. He wouldn't risk his neck for a noble child when he could have a sea of common ones answering to him as the King of the Underworld."

"But according to this . . . he didn't."

Ophelia cocked her head.

He flipped open the folder she'd previously gone through, searched, and then found the page he sought. He turned over to Ophelia the detailing of Lord Maddock's son's last day as a cherished child. "This woman . . . the nursemaid would have risked her neck. Diggory was always clever enough that he'd thrust others into the fire and never himself. And he certainly had enough willing to sacrifice their own necks to help him achieve his goals."

Ophelia didn't refute his argument. Neither did she concur with it.

Studying that heartbreaking sketch, she worked her eyes over the description provided by the marquess and any staff who'd remained on about the child.

"Blond hair," she murmured. "It could be any English child."

Aye.

"It certainly would have been easier had he possessed red." Connor folded his arms behind his neck, stretching his strained upper-back muscles. "There were several distinguishing marks upon the boy. A birthmark to the right of his navel and a horn-shaped scar upon his left knee."

Ophelia whipped up her head. "Wot?" she whispered, breathless.

"It was not intentionally done." The horror they'd endured as children had left them surrounded by people who'd mark a child: Connor's brow, the Duchess of Somerset's cheek, Niall . . . the list went on. "By Lord Maddock's accounting, he entered the child's nursery when he'd been playing soldiers. In his haste, running to the marquess, the boy tripped and fell onto one of those metal pieces. The arms were thrust into the young earl's knee. I reminded Lord Maddock that as the wound had been relatively recent, he could not be confident either way that it had left a permanent scar." Connor let his arms fall. "Regardless, these are the only defining characteristics by which I have to identify a missing child nearly seven years to the date of his disappearance." Connor grimaced. "Nor would any sane boy living in East London be willing to lift his shirt and roll up his pants to expose himself because an investigator demanded it."

As such, Connor had found himself searching for a single needle in a meadow, as she'd charged weeks earlier. Until Ophelia, who with her information had at least narrowed down those paths which would have otherwise been a waste of his time and energies.

Chapter 18

It couldn't be.

There were a million reasons she was wrong and only one disconcerting reason she might be correct.

Fighting the tremble to her fingers, she tightened them upon the page in her hands, not seeing the words there, hearing only those that Connor had casually supplied.

Oi ain't scared of 'im . . . 'e's just a man . . . An' Oi'm a man marked by the Devil.

Except Diggory's mark had been left on many Ophelia knew, and it had always come in the form of a *D* or his name. Letters carved into a person's skin to remind them who their liege was and what their role was in serving him.

Her heart thumped an erratic rhythm. Of course, that single scar Connor spoke of that might not even be a scar all these years later served as no definitive proof of anything. She reached for the rendering of the missing babe. Briefly closing her eyes, she counted to five, not wanting to look closer, with the information Connor had supplied whispering around the back of her brain.

She didn't want to question the world as she knew it and the implications for all if what Connor supposed was truth.

Forcing her eyes open, Ophelia looked.

The smiling child, more babe than boy, stared back. Innocence in his eyes, trust in his smile, he was unlike any child she'd ever known in St. Giles. All those boys and girls had been born with a frown and hadn't an extra ounce to spare for the food sparingly provided.

A little whispery sigh of relief sailed past her lips.

So why did she not put the page down? Why did she retain her white-knuckled grip upon it, staring at a child who as she'd claimed earlier could truly be any English child? A nurtured and beloved nobleman's babe, that was.

Ophelia forced her gaze back over it once more.

He was a cheerful babe, always smiling. Each year, however . . .

Those words she'd casually confided to Connor not even two days ago slammed into her with all the weight of a fast-moving carriage. She ceased breathing; all the air remained trapped in her lungs.

It was impossible . . . it couldn't be.

Just because of mention made to a possibly scarred knee . . . and . . .

August Rudolph Thadeus *Stephen* Warren, the Earl of Greyley.

Even as her mind screeched in protest to the improbability of what she'd unwittingly pulled forth, bile climbed up her throat.

She stole a frantic look in Connor's direction.

His head remained bent, fixed on the pages in his hand.

How? How?

How could he not see she sat before him in tumult, questioning everything she'd known to be fact? Questioning her existence and the existence of a sibling she would have traded her life over to the Devil ten times to Sunday to prevent his suffering.

Think, Ophelia . . . think. Just because Stephen had once been a smiling child, plump, cheerful, with a mark upon his right knee . . . those details did not a nobleman's lost son make.

It was a fantastical leap that defied logic and reason when that had been the only tenet of life that guided her.

Before now.

Now . . . she could focus on nothing more than a scar, a lengthy name, and memories of Stephen as he'd been.

Again, she clenched her eyes shut, willing the memories of her past forward. Forcing herself back to the days when a new Diggory bastard had been thrust into their care.

'e's my roightful 'eir . . . a boy . . . if a single 'air on 'is 'ead is even combed wrong, I'll carve out yar innards. Are we clear?

Ophelia's stomach pitched. She and her sisters had assumed the boy was another Diggory bastard brought into their midst. As long as she could remember, he'd railed at the whores who'd given him daughters while lamenting their whore's blood. But what did she really know about Stephen's origins?

Think . . . think . . . when did Stephen join the fold?

They'd pegged him as nine, nearly ten. But none had known for sure. What if he were in fact a year older? Her heart stumbled, and ignoring that similarity in her mind, she inventoried the years.

The year would have been . . . 1819?

She jumped up.

Connor looked over with a question in his eyes.

"Water," she managed in even tones. Ophelia made a show of searching his offices. "Do you have water? A glass."

"Of course." He shoved to his feet with languid movements. Cupping her cheek, he placed a kiss on her lips.

When he broke that too-brief meeting, he tweaked her nose. "Don't go running off on me, Miss Killoran."

She forced a laugh. As soon as he'd gone, she bolted over and retrieved one boot. Heart racing, she yanked it on. Where was the other? Where was it?

Falling to her knees, she crawled around the room and found her missing boot peeking out from under the crimson-velvet sofa.

Where Connor had made love to her.

On a lie.

So many lies.

Had there ever been any truths between them?

A sob catching in her throat, she yanked on her other boot. Not bothering with laces, she slipped from the room, down the hall, and out into the night once more.

As she rushed alone through the London streets, the night wind tugged at her loose hair, whipping those strands about her face. Hers was no longer a veiled disguise. If she were seen running as she was without a chaperone, she'd be called out for the Killoran she was and ruined. There would be no match . . . a match she'd never wanted and still didn't.

But one made even more impossible given everything she'd learned in Connor's offices.

Ophelia continued walking and didn't stop until she'd reached the point where Finchley Road intersected with Hendon Way.

Stephen is not my brother.

Her heart squeezed.

Oh, he was and would forever be her brother in every way that mattered. But his life had been a lie.

All of it.

As soon as that thought slid in, she sucked in a shuddering breath. Mayhap she was wrong. There could simply be a collection of oddly connecting details that made it seem to be one thing, when it was really another.

She knew.

Knew in her heart.

Stephen's unhealthy fascination with fires. Diggory using him to set blazes, even when Broderick had gone toe-to-toe with their liege to end Stephen's role as an arsonist.

Ophelia hugged herself, rubbing at her arms.

'e's a boy of fire . . . 'e'll set my fires.

A boy of fire.

She'd not given much thought to that statement. Any thought. They'd all, after all, filled respective roles within the Diggory gang. That had been Stephen's. Now, with the files she'd read and the suspicions settling around her brain as more than suspicions, she heard the twisted, sinister relish in that long-ago pronouncement.

What now?

For Stephen? For their family?

Yet, for her and her siblings, the Devil's Den mattered more than anything for what it represented. Now she was proven so very wrong. All of them.

Another cold night wind stole across the silent London streets.

Her neck prickled, and she glanced about.

Someone is watching me.

It was an innate knowing that could come only from a lifetime of creeping through the darkest corners of England and living to tell of it.

Springing into motion, Ophelia quickened her steps until the sensation grew. Silently cursing, she glanced back and forth, heart knocking painfully against her rib cage as she lengthened her strides.

She broke into a full run, sprinting onward until the safe, familiar sights of the Devil's Den loomed ahead.

Not breaking stride, gasping from her run, sweating for her efforts, she bolted for the only home she'd ever known.

"Ya there, stop," a guard barked.

The barrel of his pistol gleamed bright in the otherwise dark. The faint click.

"Ellis," she managed to pant. Dropping her hands on her knees, she bent forward and drew in slow, steadying breaths. "It's me."

"Miss Killoran?" The burly bearded guard instantly lowered his weapon.

"The same." Offering him a weak smile, she looked down the alley, hesitating.

Do not think of it . . . do not think of it.

Connor had helped her to see the absolute control she had over her demons. She'd reclaimed her heart, body, and soul this night.

Lifting her head, she waved to the warrior who'd served with their family since Broderick had joined the Diggory gang.

"Killoran coming," he thundered behind her.

The guards stationed at the end of the alley dropped their pistols.

"Coleman. Aubert."

"Miss," they replied in unison from their positions flanking the doorway. As though it were entirely commonplace to find the head proprietor's sister down this particular alley. As though they were familiar friends exchanging pleasantries about the weather.

Ophelia fiddled with the handle and let herself in. The soothing scents of freshly baked breads and cinnamon permeated the air, filling her nostrils, bucolic scents better suited to a country kitchen. She closed the door behind her and made quick work of the three locks and special top bolt Broderick had installed years earlier.

She leaned back against the wood, taking comfort in the solid, reassuring weight at her back.

Several shadows whispered forward, breaking the brief moment of peace she'd allowed herself. Unsheathing her dagger in one fluid motion, Ophelia brought her arm back—and froze.

Her sisters glared back.

"Cleo?" she whispered, shocked. "Gertrude?" Then a sense of doom filled her.

An always clever Gertrude, who'd seen too much, examined Ophelia's garments, her flyaway hair. "Where in blazes have you been?" she exploded, and it was a sign of Gertrude's panic that her ever-in-control sister both cursed and raised her voice.

She shook her head. "I don't want to talk about it." She wasn't ready for a lecture from her sisters on propriety.

"You don't want to talk about it?" Cleo barked.

Before Ophelia could formulate another reply, Gertrude whipped over and took her so quickly by the shoulders, the blade slipped from Ophelia's fingers. The dagger clattered noisily upon the hardwood floor. "Oh, we are going to speak on it," her eldest sister rasped. "My God, do you know how worried we've been? I received word from Cleo two hours ago asking if you'd returned home. We've been tearing up London in search of you, thinking . . . believing . . ." Gertrude buried a sob in her fist. "Will you say something to her?" she ordered Cleo.

Cleo, however, just studied Ophelia with a quiet contemplativeness, far more unnerving than Gertrude's show of temper.

"Very well, then, I'll say something. You don't just disappear and not . . ."

While Gertrude continued her tirade, Ophelia glanced away.

She wasn't ready to talk to her sisters or anyone about anything. She needed to slink off, find her rooms, and make sense of what she'd uncovered. "I needed a walk," she said after Gertrude finally stopped with her lecture.

Cleo's dark eyebrows formed a hard line. "Do ya think I believe that yarn?" she demanded.

Tucking her knife back in her boot, Ophelia sighed. "Was it too much to hope that you would?"

"Ya were with Steele."

Ophelia's entire body jolted. Had Cleo announced that she'd discovered Ophelia was, in fact, born to the king and queen themselves, she couldn't have been more shocked by her sister's accurate supposition. "What?" she blurted. "How? Why?"

"How did Oi know?" Cleo drawled with some of her earlier outrage gone. "Oi'm yar damned sister, Ophelia. I know ya."

Gertrude rocked back on her heels. "What?" Sputtering incoherently, she looked to Ophelia. "You were with . . . Mr. Steele? You *lied* to me?"

For everything Cleo did know and was keen enough to gather, there was also so much she didn't. Horrible, ugly stories of a time long ago that Ophelia had only ever shared with Connor.

A man whom she could never, ever be with.

I'm the daughter of a murderer and kidnapper.

She briefly considered the path beyond her sisters to her rooms, and privacy, wanting nothing more than to shut herself away.

Except . . .

"Though that isn't the only reason I suspected where you might be," Cleo confessed, drawing her attention back. Behind her spectacles, a twinkle lit her brown eyes. "Given the fact you were making eyes at him the moment he entered Eve and Calum's parlor, I trust there's at least some grounds for suspicion."

Ophelia choked on her swallow. She'd seen that?

Cleo went on. "Surely you didn't believe I of all people would fail to see how you were looking at the man?" A frown lingered on her sister's lips. "I wasn't one of those fancy ladies in attendance."

Gertrude glanced back and forth between them.

Ophelia gave the doorway serious consideration. These were her sisters . . . but she didn't want to have this discussion with them. Nay, she didn't want to have it with anyone.

"Were you . . . watching him?" their eldest sister asked softly. She switched her gaze between Ophelia and Cleo.

Cleo didn't allow Ophelia an answer. "You were making moon eyes, and Oi also despised Adair Thorne and drew a knife on him. Things change," she said matter-of-factly. "Sit," she ordered, motioning to the long wood table.

As she briefly considered retreat once more, Gertrude stepped into her path.

Ophelia slid onto one of the benches.

Yes, as her sister correctly pointed out . . . things changed.

Only Ophelia had never truly hated Connor. She'd admired him . . . marveled at his strength and courage, even as she'd resented him—unfairly.

She'd been wrong about so much. Ophelia scraped a hand over tired eyes.

Her younger sister, the one Broderick had always had such faith in, and for so many rightful reasons, wandered over to the stone counters. She gathered a dish of sponge biscuits and carried it back, then set it down between them. Cleo sat. "You were with him tonight." She'd slipped back into her smooth, measured tones. Ones that hinted at her steadying control.

Why had her sister always been so blasted perceptive?

She studied the long, narrow treats, made for those equally narrow wineglasses. She desperately wanted liquid fortitude now. For there was little point in lying to one as perceptive as Cleo.

What was more . . . Ophelia had tired of lying. To her siblings . . . to Connor.

Her gut clenched; her mind shied away from all the truths she knew she needed to reveal to him.

"He seems like a nice enough gent," Cleo observed, dogged in her pursuit of information from Ophelia.

"Cleopatra," Gertrude snapped.

Their youngest sister shifted back and forth on the bench. "For an investigator, that is," she mumbled.

"He is," Ophelia said softly. To give her fingers something to do, she picked up a biscuit and took a bite. The flaky morsel sat like clay upon her tongue, and she forced herself to choke down that swallow. "He's not like the other investigators or constables we've dealt with," she defended, needing her sisters to know that about Connor. "Connor is a man who has known the same strife as us but who, with his career, seeks to make life better for others." Her voice grew impassioned. "He's fair and kind and good to children and . . ." At her sisters' piercing stares on her, Ophelia let her words trail off.

"Why do I take it you've known your Mr. Steele before?" Gertrude asked.

"Because I did." Her voice emerged faint. She set down her unfinished biscuit with hands that trembled. "I was a girl. He was . . . the one who got away."

Her sisters' mouths fell open. Cleo shook her head. Was it shock? Disbelief?

Ophelia nodded. "Connor O'Roarke. I found him . . . several times." Three. She kept her eyes trained on the nicked wood table, unable to meet Gertrude's gaze for the familiar guilt sweeping through her.

"You came across him and you didn't turn him over." An undeserved pride coated Gertrude's pronouncement, and Ophelia wanted to blot her hands over her ears to push back those misplaced sentiments.

Would she still be so proud when she learned what Ophelia's decision had cost her? Nonetheless, she'd been a coward too long. Her eldest sister had been deserving of the truth long ago. "The last time I saw him, I let him go. Went on my way to steal a purse." She swallowed around the lump in her throat. "I was s-sloppy." Ophelia paused a fraction of a heartbeat. "I was caught by a constable and the nob." Even years later, shame in admitting that misstep filled her.

So much shame. It was a stinging, burning, unwelcome sentiment that had grown increasingly familiar.

Cleo's gasp filled the kitchens. "But how . . . ?"

"How did I escape?" Toying with the plate, Ophelia searched for the strength to tell her sisters everything. "That night, Connor came forward. He took ownership of my crime and went in my stead."

"He sacrificed himself for you," Gertrude said softly.

"He did," she whispered. It was the greatest, most generous gift one had to give in St. Giles—that of one's life. And Connor had offered his over to her. It hadn't mattered the end result had found him safe and secure in a nobleman's home as a beloved adopted son; it mattered that he'd taken her place and marched on to what would have been any other person's grim fate of Newgate and a hanging. "He was adopted by that same lord. Given a home and a new beginning."

"The Earl of Mar." Cleo slid that detail into place.

What a life Connor had made for himself. He hadn't become the indolent, roguish, privileged child of a nob. Rather, he'd embraced a chance to begin anew, establishing a career as one of the most respected, successful investigators in England. He worked when the peerage looked down at those who made a living with their hands.

What did my family do? We operate the most wicked, scandalous den of sin in London. Coins a'plenty, respectability for none. Ophelia dropped an elbow on the table and rested her chin in her hand.

"You love him."

You love him.

There they were: three words that ripped through the heart of why Ophelia lay ravaged inside. *I do. I always did.* Tears pricked at her eyes. "Does it matter?" she asked, her tone sharper than she intended. "Oi 'ave to marry—"

"To satisfy Broderick's wishes."

"To save me," Gertrude quietly put forward.

"Yes. No." Because of both.

A thick pall fell over the kitchens. The revelries from deep within the establishment filled the rooms, the sounds muffled.

Gertrude was the first to again speak. "All these years you've all sought to look after me. Broderick, Stephen, Cleo, and you, Ophelia."

They had. When Ophelia had stumbled into their hovel, bruised under her tattered garments and riddled with terror, she'd hated Cleo. Hated both her sisters for failing to look after her. Hated herself with an equal ferocity for being unable to look after herself.

"Neither of you have ever realized . . ." A sad smile played on her lips. "I do not need you to look after me. I never did." The narrow lines of Gertrude's face contorted into a paroxysm of hurt. "And certainly not at the expense of your own happiness."

Ophelia swiped a hand over her face. "It has never been because I've doubted you," she said hoarsely. Even with her sister's dubious look, she still struggled to utter those words aloud.

Tell her.

"The last time I freed Connor, Diggory promised I'd s-suffer." Her voice cracked. "And I did. Just not in the ways I believed. In the ways we'd come to expect." Tears flooded Ophelia's eyes, blurring Gertrude's visage. "He beat you that day. Clubbed you in the head as a lesson to me. I—I am the reason you are partially blind." Her shoulders shook with the force of her silent tears. Remorse and heartache brought teardrop after teardrop.

Soft, tender hands collected Ophelia's coarser ones.

Gertrude squeezed her palms. "Do you *truly* believe I would hold you responsible for a single act that monster committed?" Hurt wreathed that question.

Another sob ripped from Ophelia. "I chose Connor." Unwittingly at the time. And God help her, then or now, she could not say she'd ever have done anything different. She wept all the harder.

"No," Gertrude said, vehement. "You chose goodness. Despite fear . . . despite knowing Diggory would undoubtedly beat you or worse . . . you defied him." Her voice caught. "There is only good in that, Ophelia."

She released her hands, came around, and took Ophelia in her arms. Just held her. In Gertrude's embrace, with Cleo silently watching on, there was at last a warm, healing peace. It slipped into Ophelia's heart, freeing and strengthening. Until her tears dissolved into a watery hiccup.

She rubbed her eyes against her sister's shoulder. "I am so—"

"Do not," Gertrude clipped out. "Your apologies imply there is something so very wrong with me." Yet that is how they'd each, in their quest to help Gertrude, inadvertently treated her. "Now, what of your Mr. Steele? And your nighttime disappearance?" her eldest sibling urged after she'd broken their embrace.

Tears welled anew. What in blazes was becoming of her? She angrily brushed them away. "He is not mine. He can never be mine."

Cleo frowned. "Because of Broderick?"

Worse. Because if it were only their brother and his grasping attempts at noble connections, she'd have thrown them over, just to have Connor in her life.

Restless, she jumped up. "Because of who I am." She owed him the same explanations and truths she'd given her sisters this night. Even when she did . . . which invariably she would, the divide between them was insurmountable.

Gertrude bristled. "What is wrong with who you are?"

Ophelia stopped, her back presented to her sisters. She stared at the unlit fireplace. "Diggory made him an orphan."

The air slipped past the lips of one of her sisters on a noisy hiss.

"Precisely that," she whispered, gripping her arms about her waist.

And there was the matter of Stephen, and Connor's investigation.

How was it possible for one person's entire life to crumple so very quickly?

"It is not to be."

"Alas, it is."

At that peculiar reply, she turned back.

Cleo brandished a thick sheet of velum. "This arrived earlier this evening. An invitation to an intimate dinner party . . ." She paused. "With the Earl of Mar and his family."

Oh, God. Ophelia's stomach muscles clenched. She was being invited to his father's household.

Happiness glowed in Gertrude's pale-green eye. "He is presenting you before his father."

"You simply need to tell him," Cleo said with such a matter-of-factness that the thin thread of control Ophelia had on her emotions splintered.

"You speak as though it will not matter to him. As though the fact that our father killed his father and raped his mother, before killing her, too, are minor infractions."

All the color drained from her sisters' faces. *Good.* Airing those words aloud should ground them in reality. "This is not make-believe. This is not 'pretend,' like the Gothic novels Gertrude reads."

"Adair forgave," Cleo intoned.

"Did Diggory make Adair an orphan?"

That effectively silenced both sisters.

"Ya're 'ere!"

They spun to the entranceway.

"All of ya!" Stephen stood framed there, a joyful glimmer in his gaze and a smile on his lips—an honest, unrestrained one that was such a marked copy of the one in Connor's sketch that tears flooded her eyes all over again.

In three long strides, Ophelia was at his side and had him in her arms.

His little arms folded around her, tearing a silent sob from her throat.

Just like that, he transformed into his usual belligerent self. "Wot now?" he groused, shoving against her. "None o' that. The crying nonsense or the hugs."

Ophelia only held him all the tighter. She ignored the confused glances exchanged by her sisters.

"Wot's the matter with 'er?" Stephen begged their sisters.

"I'm just so happy to see you," she whispered, at last allowing him the space he craved.

Eyeing her carefully, he retreated a step. "Wot's going on 'ere?"

No one said anything for a long moment.

"We just missed you and wished to see you," Cleo supplied for them.

He snorted. "Do ya think Oi was born on Tuesday? Oi've 'eard Broderick 'as men out searching for ya." He narrowed his eyes. "Where were ya?"

"I was coming here."

"But before she did," Cleo improvised, "she came to visit . . ." Her brow scrunched up.

"Eve and Calum Dabney," Gertrude added to the lie.

Stephen scratched at his golden curls. Those same sun-kissed strands in the miniature painting.

Mayhap she was wrong. Mayhap a lifetime of having only the worst happen was responsible for the suspicions that had sent her into flight, seeking out the club and her youngest sibling.

Oh, God, I cannot take this.

Ophelia crossed over and grabbed the sides of his fine lawn shirt.

"Wot in 'ell are ya—?"

She yanked it up, scraping her gaze over his small chest and belly. And finding it.

A birthmark to the right of his navel.

With numb fingers, Ophelia let the fabric fall back into place.

"Ophelia?" Cleo pressed.

"Forgive me . . . I . . ." She gave her head a shake. "Forgive me." It was all she could manage. Stephen belonged to another family . . . sired by a man other than Diggory.

"Where in blazes have you been?"

Broderick.

The Killoran quartet looked to the entrance of the kitchens.

With matching glares, her siblings filed past him.

Cowards.

"My God, Ophelia," he snapped. "I have had guards scouring the streets of London. Questions have circulated as to where you've been. If a single gentleman learned of your disappearance, your reputation would be ruined."

"How important that is to you," she said, sadly eyeing him. "Titles, connections, rank, and prestige. What of family?" *What of Stephen?*

A ruddy flush marred his cheeks. "Is that what you believe?" he snapped. "That I do not care about you?" A wounded edge underscored his question. "That you don't matter?"

For a long moment, she studied him—the brother who'd entered her life, first a hated stranger who'd gone on to protect her and her siblings from Diggory's cruel machinations. "I do not doubt your love." His flush deepened. Because regardless of truth being valued, one didn't speak of sentiments such as love . . . or any feelings or emotions. "And yet . . ." She took a step closer. "The first thing you spoke to was my reputation and how it affected a match." Surely he saw that.

His mouth tightened. "I'll not have us speak in the kitchens."

Without waiting to see if she followed, Broderick spun and marched from the room. From the moment Diggory had learned Broderick's value—one who could read, write, and speak like a gent—his rank had been elevated, and not a single soul—Ophelia and her sisters included—had dared question Broderick's authority.

She followed at a sedate pace behind her brother, passing guards stationed throughout the corridors. Another time she'd have gone toe-to-toe with Broderick, and witnesses be damned. Her stomach, still queasy, threatened to revolt at the discovery she'd made. Minutes ago? Hours? A lifetime? Time had ceased to mean anything or matter in any way.

What her respectability-driven brother didn't know . . . couldn't know . . . was that soon, no match would be possible. Their club, and their reputations, would never survive the charges they'd be held responsible for. That it had been Diggory who'd captured a nobleman's child, and that Ophelia and her siblings had been unknowing of his treachery, would be overlooked. They'd be held complicit.

As soon as they were shut away in Broderick's office, he folded his arms. "Have you been hurt?"

She opened her mouth.

"If some gentleman has"—fire flared in his eyes, a lethal glitter that would have terrified a battle-hardened warrior—"hurt you in any way . . . I'll have them taken care of."

Killed. He'd have them killed.

"It is not that," she demurred, rubbing at her arms.

"Steele?"

So he *had* been closely following the reports in the gossip columns speculating on Ophelia's relationship with Connor. But then, should she really be surprised, given how enamored he'd always been with the *ton*?

"Not Connor," she finally said, struggling to bring the admission forth. For once it was breathed into existence, everything would change. And they would lose a sibling. Tears filled her eyes. "Not in the ways you are worrying."

Broderick stilled.

A black curse exploded from his lips. "I'll kill him."

"I didn't say anything."

"You used his Christian name and cried when I can't think of a single day you've ever wept before me," he said in lethal, hushed tones that spoke of a violence she'd not believed him capable of. "That is all you needed to *say*."

"He's been a friend to me, Broderick." He'd allowed her to see she was so much more than that one night in an alley.

Her brother recoiled.

Despite the severity of their situation, a sliver of droll humor tugged at her. "Why do I believe you'd have preferred I say he hurt or offended me?"

"Do not be silly," he muttered, his color deepening. "I've never wanted you hurt. I've only sought to make our family more powerful so we have the security you deserve."

Her grin faded.

He worked his eyes over her face. "What is it?"

Ophelia drew in a breath. "You are aware of Connor's investigation into the nobleman's missing child."

"I am," he said succinctly.

"He's allowed me to view his files. He's spoken freely of his findings."

When previously no other man, including the one before her, had allowed her true power: within the club, over decisions made, over any aspect of life.

"And?"

Of course, Broderick would hear more in her words.

Ophelia briefly closed her eyes. When she opened them, she spoke in quiet tones. "And I've determined the child's identity."

Broderick sharpened his gaze on her. "Well?"

"It is Stephen."

That admission sucked the life, energy, and sound from the room, leaving in its place a tense silence.

Broderick shook his head.

She nodded.

He gave another shake.

"It is true, Broderick." Ophelia proceeded to reveal everything to her brother. By the time she'd finished, he was silent once more, his face carved of granite, his chiseled cheeks a sickly ashen hue.

He stalked over to his sideboard and poured himself a brandy, and with his back to her, he downed it. He filled another glass. When he faced her once more, color had been restored to his cheeks, and he had his usual, fully composed, master-of-his-emotions facade in place. "You're wrong."

"I'm not. You know I'm not."

"I know no such thing." He slashed the air with his spare hand. "So Stephen has a mark on his belly—"

"And his knee."

"It in no way confirms that he's—" Broderick wisely cut himself off and eyed the doorway. Yes, one never knew when someone was lurking about. "It confirms nothing."

He was seeing what he wished to see. Nor did she doubt his reason for doing so.

Ophelia joined him at the sideboard. "I love him, too, Broderick," she whispered. "I don't want him to leave, but—"

"He is not leaving," he rasped.

"He belongs to another," she continued over him.

He jerked, liquid droplets splashing over the rim of his glass. "This is because of your damned investigator." He set his tumbler down, spraying more droplets onto that immaculate mahogany.

She balled her hands into fists. "Surely you are not blaming Connor for this?" Blame belonged to only one—the devil who'd sired her. She'd be damned if Broderick twisted his frustration and hurt to suit his suffering. "Connor has done nothing but help." Once she'd so judged him, too. He'd shown her that not all were the ruthless lords she'd taken them for.

"You are to have no more dealings with him."

Ophelia blinked slowly. Surely she'd misheard him. Surely . . .

"Your damned sister has allowed you to run about with the last person any of you should ever marry, let alone keep company with. You're remaining here."

Odd. There'd been a time, not so very long ago, when living inside the Devil's Den had been the only request she'd put to Broderick.

Her brother moved to his desk, sat, and dragged a ledger over.

"Why . . . why . . . you are attempting to make me a prisoner." The revelation escaped her on a breathy exhale.

"I'm protecting you, Gertrude, and Stephen," he replied, directing his words to the books before him.

Ophelia stalked across the room and planted herself at the front of his desk. "This will not make the truth go away. It will not make—"

Broderick pounded the desk with such force his ledgers jumped. "Silence," he boomed. He inhaled. Flicking an imagined speck of lint from his sleeve, he went on. "Every decision I ever made and every decision I will continue to make is with the best interests of each of you in mind. Where Stephen is concerned . . . you are mistaken," he said simply. As if they spoke of some trivial detail. As if they didn't speak of murder, arson, and a stolen child. "It is, however, even more imperative that you make a respectable match with a nobleman. No more entertaining Steele. No more waltzes with an untitled gentleman. If those rumors come to light—"

"Those rumors?" She shook her head. "Who *are* you?"

"We're done here, Ophelia."

They were done here. "Go to hell, Broderick." Lest she do something like plant him a facer to break his perfect nose, she wheeled about and left him.

As soon as she had the door closed, and the panel between them, she stopped.

He was determined to let Stephen's life remain a lie . . . and have the Killorans continue to perpetuate it.

No more.

For even as it would shatter her heart to give him up, and even with the implications of what it would mean for their club and family . . . there was only one recourse.

And only one person to now help her.

Chapter 19

Connor raced through the streets of London.

In the span it had taken him to gather a glass of water and return, she'd disappeared like a phantom shadow, and he'd been left with his world upended.

All the while he'd searched for her, with the grimmest possibility of the fate awaiting a young woman alone, wandering the streets of London, he'd reassured himself with the reminder that no one knew these streets as well as Ophelia.

It hadn't helped.

Instead, he'd tortured himself with the darkest memories she'd shared. A testament of the peril that faced all people in London regardless of skill, strength, size, or knowledge of those well-traversed paths.

Ultimately, his searches turning up empty, he found himself in the same wrinkled garments, unshaven, and earning a bevy of stares from the handful of respectable lords and ladies awake at this early-morn hour.

Several hours after Ophelia had flown off, Connor thundered on the heavy black panel. That rapid, incessant, staccato beat matched the wild thump of his heart.

By her flight, she wanted nothing more to do with him. She'd been clear from the beginning as to what her brother expected of her and what she intended to do—find a titled husband. When most women would only ever put their own desires and interests first, Ophelia acted on behalf of her sister.

Even if she did not, what makes you believe she'd even choose you?

That jeering, vicious thought wound around his brain.

Bethany had ultimately chosen wealth and title. If it weren't Ophelia's sister and the bid to protect . . . it would no doubt be something else.

A vise cinched around his chest. He'd been thrown over before.

Then, he'd been angry, resentful, bitter . . . hurt.

This, however, this searing, stinging agony in knowing Ophelia would belong to another, and nothing he offered—himself, his heart, body, and wealth—would be or ever could be enough, cleaved him in two.

For with Ophelia, he'd never had to hide the darkest parts of himself, because she'd known the demons that haunted him and did not judge him for acts he'd committed in order to survive. He loved her spirit and her strength and her absolute courage that had allowed her to emerge triumphant from the prison Diggory had once sentenced her to.

There were only two places she could be—*KnockKnockKnock.*

Here. *KnockKnockKnock.*

Or—

The door was yanked open, and a bleary-eyed, equally haggard butler greeted him. "Wot?" he groused, giving Connor a quick once-over. "Beggars 'round back."

Connor shot out a hand to prevent it from being closed in his face. He fished inside his rumpled jacket and withdrew a calling card. "I am here to see Miss Killoran."

The man eyed the scrap a moment. "Ya're 'ere to see Miss Killoran?" Then his gaze snagged on Connor's name. Suspicion darkened his eyes. "Ain't 'ere for the loikes of ya." He made to thrust the door shut once more.

Connor thrust his elbow in the door. "Is she here?" he demanded, his heart leaping.

"Oi ain't answering to a damned investigator about whether she is or isn't. Get yarself off Thorne's doorstep or Oi'll beat ya beyond recognition." That threat was an inordinately bold one, given the amount of panting the butler was doing while they battled with the door.

At last Connor forced his way inside, knocking the burly guard on his arse.

The man immediately reached for a weapon.

Stepping on his wrist, Connor effectively disarmed the man. "Is she—?"

"Wot in blazes is this about?"

He whipped up his head.

Adair Thorne, his wife close at his heels, came charging forward.

That brief distraction proved costly.

The butler punched Connor behind his right kneecap, cutting his feet from under him. With a curse, he went down hard, reaching for the servant—just as Thorne bellowed.

"Waterly, enough."

His assailant instantly jumped to his feet and looped his arms at his back.

Ophelia's sister and brother-in-law stopped before them.

"Wot is the meaning of this?" her sister demanded, leveling them with a hard look, which even with her spectacles and waiflike size would be enough to alarm any sensible man.

"This one forced 'is way in. Asking questions about yar sister."

Connor steeled his jaw. "Is she here?" How did that query come out so even? All the while panic rioted through him.

Husband and wife exchanged a look. "That will be all, Waterly," Thorne murmured.

The servant hesitated, and then, with an uneven bow, ambled off.

Cleo Thorne gestured him forward. "Our offices." *Our offices.* It was a bold stake of ownership when the ladies of London more often than not ceded all control to their husbands. It was a mark of just how much like Ophelia this younger, darker, somewhat more hardened version of Ophelia was.

His heart twisted.

He fought to regulate his breathing in time to his even steps.

As soon as the door was closed, he demanded, "Is your sister here?"

Adair Thorne made to speak, but his wife held up a silencing hand. "Ya do realize that given the hour, your appearance, and yar questions, it implies ya were with her."

Because he had been. What had begun as an offer on her part to assist with his investigation had become more . . . and he wanted it to be even more.

A future. A marriage. A family.

His shoulders sagged. "Is she here?" he implored on a gruff whisper.

"She's not," her sister calmly stated.

He scrubbed his hands over his face. Her family's club. She had to be there. Except . . . how to go about forcing his way into the secured gaming hell that would take even less to Connor's appearance than Thorne's butler? He let his arms fall to his sides. "Thank you," he said hoarsely. "Forgive me for disturbing you at this hour."

He made it no farther than two steps.

"Oi didn't say Oi didn't know where she was."

Connor jerked to a stop. His pulse picked up a frantic beat as he spun to face her. *She is well. She is safe.* "The club?"

Cleopatra Killoran met him with a stony silence.

On the heel of that, the reality took root and grew . . . She'd fled him.

A debt owed . . . I want you to make love to me.

She'd not asked for more. Rather, she'd spoken of a favor asked in return of a debt.

Surely that wasn't all she had wanted. With every question, the weight pressing on his chest deepened. Her sister and brother-in-law continued standing there with the unnerving quiet stretching on.

"If you'll excuse me?" he said tightly. "I'm sorry to have stormed your household."

He made to go, but Ophelia's sister blocked the way.

She held her husband's stare. Some unspoken dialogue passed between them, and then Adair took his leave.

I know that intimacy. There was one woman whose thoughts had always moved in a synchronic accord with his.

"Well?" she urged when they were alone.

Connor shook his head.

Cleopatra Thorne pointed her finger. "Oi'd think again before Oi played the lackwit, Steele. My sister was sneaking about in breeches, and ya come searching for 'er not even six 'ours later. Wot's it about?"

By God, with the ferocity in her too-clever eyes, she'd the skill to rival him or any investigator. "She was . . . helping me with my investigation." He settled for that vague truth.

An inelegant snort burst from the lady. "And that's the reason you've come bursting into my home, smelling like ya rolled in pig shite with that thick beard on yar face?" She nudged her chin. "Try again."

He took a slight sniff, wincing. Aye, after hours of running aimlessly about London, rolling in pig shite was kinder than his scent warranted.

"I'm in love with her."

Cleopatra Thorne's jaw fell. "What?" she blurted.

She'd been expecting him to prevaricate. And why shouldn't she?

Connor scrubbed at his brow. "I want to marry her."

"Ya want to marry 'er?" A look of chagrin flickered briefly to life in her eyes. It was instantly gone, shuttered behind thick, concealing lashes.

"Aye, I do." He wanted to have children with her, and fill her life with laughter, and be the family they'd always both craved, but with each other. He'd always loved her. Even when she was just a girl, he'd loved her for risking herself for a boy who was nothing more than a stranger and saving him. He loved her even more for being a woman of unswerving strength, conviction, and courage.

At Cleopatra Thorne's silence, he glanced over.

She chewed at her lower lip, that slight distracted gesture so very much like her older sister. "'ow well do ya know my sister, Steele?" she finally asked.

"I've known her more years than I haven't." He paused, honing his gaze on her face. "And I know I want to marry her."

"Our life 'asn't been loike yars."

Standing witness to his parents' murder and his mother's rape, he'd wager they were more alike than she'd ever credit or believe. "You might be surprised by the life I've lived," he said somberly.

"And ya might be surprised by the loife we've lived," she shot back. "Wot, then? Wot 'appens when—if—you learned the darkest parts?"

He shook his head. "There is nothing that would stop me from loving your sister. I intend to offer for her." Before she could speak, he went on. "Regardless of whether or not your brother approves."

"'e doesn't," she muttered.

He furrowed his brow.

"Approve of ya." Ophelia's youngest sister stuffed her hands into the pockets sewn along the front of her gown, looking years younger than her age. "She ain't here, and my brother doesn't want her living here."

"I don't take you or Ophelia as ones who'd have Broderick Killoran or any man dictate to you."

Some of the worry melted from her narrow face; another wry smile replaced it. "Oi think Oi loike ya, O'Roarke."

O'Roarke. His back went ramrod straight. She'd not referred to him as Steele but rather the one name only one other knew of.

Twin splotches of color splashed the lady's cheeks. She realized her misstep. For the panic and misery that dogged him this day, a smile pulled. "Don't be getting smug, O'Roarke. We talk about a lot." She folded her arms. "There still remains the part of Ophelia now living at the clubs, and my brother wanting her nowhere near ya."

"I'm asking you to help your sister," he said quietly.

"Ya're assuming she needs help. That she wants it."

That reminder struck like a well-placed arrow. "I won't know what she wants"—*with me*—"until I can speak freely with her myself." So that he might tell her he loved her. And selfishly ask her to set aside her brother's plans for her and the entire Killoran family for him. "Thank you for your time, Mrs. Thorne. If you'll excuse me?" Connor dropped a bow and resumed his trek for the door.

"O'Roarke?" she called out, freezing him at the front of the room. "Oi'll 'elp as Oi can." Her eyes flashed a threat of death. "But don't ya dare make me regret doing so. Are we clear?"

His heart kicked up. He nodded. "You have my word."

In St. Giles, one's word was a sacred vow not to be broken.

She eyed him a long while and then slowly nodded.

A short while later, Connor was let into his Piccadilly residence at Albany.

"Mr. Steele," one of his three servants greeted.

The younger man, with Connor since he'd taken his own rooms years earlier, hesitated. His nose twitched.

"Have a bath readied, please," he instructed, shrugging out of his thoroughly wrinkled jacket.

"Yes, Mr. Steele." He hurried to take the garment and draped it over his arm. "A visitor arrived a short while ago."

Connor started down the hall. He stopped abruptly. *Ophelia.* "Was it a young woman?"

His servant choked. "A young woman?" he repeated, scandalized horror wreathing that echo. "Uh . . . no, Mr. Steele."

Aye, because women were forbidden from visiting the gentlemen's rooms at Albany, and Connor, once a slave to respectability, would have never done anything to break with propriety. "I'm not accepting callers."

"But, Mr. Steele," the persistent butler called after him, "it was your father, the Earl of Mar."

That gave him pause. "Should he return, please advise him I'm not home," he instructed.

Connor turned the corridor—and stopped.

His father stared back. Except this was his father as he'd never before seen him: cheeks ashen, his eyes brimming with sadness, he was a hollow version of his usually jovial, garrulous self. "Connor." Hat in hand, his gloved fingers toyed with the brim. He moved his gaze slowly over Connor, his eyes taking in every aspect of his unkempt appearance. "May we . . . speak?"

Wordlessly, Connor stepped aside, motioning for his offices.

They entered, not a word exchanged even after Connor closed the office door behind them. Moving around to his desk, he studied this man who'd adopted him. When the world had seen only a guttersnipe, this man had taken him in. He'd given him a new beginning and a future Connor had not even allowed himself a dream of.

The one unspoken request never explicitly stated but revealed by his father's lack of questioning was that Connor not speak of the life he'd left behind.

As such, with the greying earl glancing all around, anywhere except at Connor, he found himself at a loss as to what to say.

How was it possible to know someone so fully . . . and yet, at the same time, not at all?

"Would you care to sit?" he finally invited, motioning to the chair before his desk.

"Thank you," his father said, a formal acknowledgment that only further deepened the gulf between.

Connor claimed the chair opposite him . . . and waited. Contemplating his father, his future, his past.

Would the Lady Bethanys of the world who gave of their time and attentions put their own lives at risk for a child they didn't know, as Ophelia had?

The earl rested his hat upon the edge of the desk. "I trust you are . . . preoccupied with your investigation."

"Aye." Each case prior to the Maddock assignment had been a solitary endeavor. Ophelia had been the only person to ever demand entry into his work, challenging him along the way.

"But that is not all?" his father ventured with his usual astuteness.

Connor's jaw worked. "No." For everything that had come to pass, the earl's ill opinion of Ophelia, his unwillingness to accept Connor's future, he still loved him. As such, he could not feed him the lie, even as it would be easier to do so. "It is not."

"Is this about that wom . . ." At Connor's narrowed eyes, he swiftly amended his words. "Is it because I expressed my reservations with Miss Killoran?"

Connor leaned forward, erasing some of the distance between them. "It is because you cannot see that having her in my life has been good. She has been the one person"—his father included—"whom I've never had to hide my past from."

The earl pursed his lips. "Your past has been a secret to no one."

"But it has mattered to everyone." There'd been only one who'd never cared about his origins or the evil deeds he'd committed in the name of survival. Tiring of the exchange, Connor eyed the clock hanging over his father's shoulder. "If you've come this morning to speak on

Ophelia's *suitability*"—the earl's brows went shooting up—"or to debate me on a subject I'll not relent on, there is nothing further to say."

"That isn't why I'm here." The earl stretched his legs and crossed them at the ankles. It was the same casual pose he'd assumed when Connor had first entered his household and joined him in the library following the evening meal. "I'm here to ask you to join me tomorrow evening. Bethany's father and I will be leading a discussion with other members of Parliament. Bethany will be there."

Ah, the real reason for the visit, then. Yet again, another desperate attempt to matchmake Connor and his father's goddaughter.

Connor indicated the folders stacked before them. "I'm afraid given the work I have on my latest assignment, I must convey my regrets."

There was a time a lifetime ago when that was the only match you would have aspired to . . . or hoped for.

With Ophelia he saw how very empty his life would have been had he married Lady Bethany. Respectable. Predictable and safe. Because he'd been chasing safety since the moment Mac Diggory had hauled him by his shirtfront and forced him into his gang.

How bleak and empty your life will be when—if—Ophelia chooses another.

His fingers curled around the arms of his seat, leaving marks on the aged wood.

His father worked his eyes over Connor's face and then shoved himself up. "That is . . . unfortunate," he settled for. He collected his hat and placed it atop his head, adjusting the article until it sat perfect. "I am sorry I've hurt you, Connor," he said softly. "I am sorry that I've failed you with my unwillingness to talk about those days." Connor's heart squeezed. "But you are my son," he said hoarsely. "I love you as much as if I'd given you life myself. I would spare you any and every hurt if I could. And I would have you know that every decision"—his Adam's apple jumped—"has only ever been made with your happiness in mind."

"I know that," Connor said somberly. Even with this new glimpse he'd had of his father's character, it did not change his love for him. Ultimately, they were all flawed beings in their own ways and rights. "I am so very grateful for not only everything you've given but also who and what you've been to me." He paused. "Another father."

His father offered a shaky smile and made to go.

But then he stopped, lingering at the entrance of the room. Once more he fidgeted with his hat, adjusting it back and forth. Finally, he turned back to face him. "I would have you know I've extended an invitation for Mr. and Mrs. Thorne to join my dinner party." Connor's muscles jumped. "Along with Mr. Thorne's sister-in-law, Miss Killoran."

Every nerve thrummed to life.

"Father?" he called out.

The earl stopped and threw a questioning glance back.

"I will join you."

Something flared in his father's eyes and then was quickly gone. "I—I am grateful to you for coming. This is for you, Connor. I would have you know that, as well."

Connor stared after him.

His father, Ophelia's brother—they were both determined to keep them apart.

He steeled his jaw. He'd no intention of having either man, or anyone else, dictate his and Ophelia's future together.

Now he needed to convince Ophelia that she wanted him in her life.

Chapter 20

Ophelia had dwelled in a prison of her father's making for more than twenty years of her life. After he'd gone on to the fiery flames of hell, she'd believed she'd been eternally freed.

How easily her brother had resurrected a prison of a different sort.

"Is anything amiss?"

Across the small oak table on which she'd conducted her business in the club since Cleo's departure, her sister nudged her chin at the pages spread out between them.

Was there anything amiss? She growled. "My brother has made me a prisoner in my own home, no less."

Gertrude coughed into her hand. "Uh . . . yes, well, I referred to the work I'd overseen in your absence."

The work she'd overseen?

Ophelia blinked slowly, and then embarrassment stung her cheeks. Of course.

"I've not gone out and . . . found children hires as you yourself have," Gertrude went on hesitantly. "But MacTavish and Trembley have both surveilled the streets. I've also created a schedule," she explained, dragging one of the notepads over, "so that the boys and girls both can be properly instructed at various points through the day. I've interviewed each and matched their strengths to a suitable role for them. And . . ."

Ophelia pulled herself back from the frustration that had dogged her since she'd rushed to speak with Broderick and truly attended her sister.

Pulling back the same book her sister had been referencing, Ophelia examined all the improvements she'd made. All the well-thought-out changes that took into account details Ophelia herself had failed to think on. She'd been so fixed on saving children that she'd not given proper thought to creating assignments that aligned with their strengths.

Gertrude bit at her lower lip. "It is rubbish?"

"It is not," Ophelia said softly, lifting her head. "It is . . . the opposite. It is thoughtful and clever and . . ." She touched a finger to the neat columns and rows outlining the new schedule to be followed. "Perfect. It is perfect."

A slow smile tipped Gertrude's lips. "Indeed?"

How many reasons did she have to be suspicious of kind words? Mercilessly mocked by Diggory's men because of her partial blindness, Gertrude had carried on a quiet existence, never the recipient of deserved praise for her intelligence.

Setting aside her own resentments with Broderick and worries with Stephen, she covered her sister's hand with her own. "Oh, yes," she marveled. "I did not think of . . . all this."

Her eldest sibling glowed; that blush transformed her long, heavily freckled face, radiant in her happiness. They resumed their quiet study of the changes implemented in Ophelia's absence.

"You are not . . . disappointed?"

"Am I disappointed?" she compelled.

Gertrude shrugged. "That I've taken on all of . . . this."

Ophelia sat back in her chair. "Truthfully?"

Her sister nodded once.

"Three weeks ago I would have been," she confessed. She would have been gutted at how easily she'd been replaced and how effortlessly her role had been filled. "I felt this was the only way I might have control in life. I wished to prove myself . . . my worth." After a lifetime of feeling sullied and second to their youngest sister, she'd sought to establish her place in the Killoran family. "I felt I had an obligation to save those children living in the streets. But there are so many, and there are others"—like Connor and his father, and Eve Dabney and Gertrude—"who wish to prevent the suffering that we know." She managed her first smile since she'd fled Connor's offices. "And how many more people there are who might be helped."

Connor had shown her that. He'd shown her so much about herself.

"I was not referring to my work."

Ophelia glanced up from Gertrude's tidy notes.

"When I asked if anything was amiss, I referred to you. You no longer wish to be here."

"Yes." Ophelia jumped up. "No." She wanted Connor and her secrets at last laid bare and a new beginning together.

Gertrude's unimpaired eye twinkled. "Who would believe you'd bemoan being barred from living in Grosvenor Square."

"Indeed," she said under her breath. Except it had nothing to do with the location of that street and everything to do with the one person her brother had effectively barred her from seeing.

"Broderick does not approve."

She gave her head a tight shake. Their brother wouldn't have approved when Connor was simply sans the desirous ranking craved by Broderick. He approved even less now that Connor and his assignment represented the thin thread between the Killorans' continued success . . . and certain ruin.

Footsteps thumped in the hallway, followed by a perfunctory knock.

Before Ophelia could even call out with permission to enter, the door opened.

Cleo stormed inside. Their satin-clad sister with diamond butterfly combs and neck dripping with rubies was better suited to a fine lord's ballroom than the club. Once that would have grated on Ophelia's nerves. Now, she'd come to find that for the lavish wealth the *ton* was born to, there were those who did good and were undeserving of condemnation. Dropping her hands on her hips, she passed an assessing glance over Ophelia. "You are accompanying me."

Her heart thumped hard. "What?"

"The Earl of Mar has asked Calum Dabney and myself to speak before several members of Parliament composing legislation to benefit orphans in St. Giles."

The Earl of Mar. Connor's father. His actions to help proved again how very wrong Ophelia had been about the nobility. Her hope sank. Their blasted obstinate brother. "Broderick will never—"

"I've already spoken to him," Cleo informed. She kicked the door closed with the heel of her slipper, stalked over to Ophelia's armoire, and tossed the doors open. Mumbling incoherently to herself, she swatted dress after dress out of the way.

Ophelia and Gertrude spoke at the same time. "And?"

Their youngest sister briefly halted. "Surely you don't believe I'd let Broderick dictate which event you'd be attending?" She winked. "It certainly helped, reminding him that the Earl of Mar is still nobility." And, as such, he could be forgiven the slight of having an adopted son who could never inherit that coveted title. Cleo retrained all her efforts on the armoire. "This will have to do." She tugged out a pale-grey satin gown. "I'm speaking. I want you there."

Only Cleo could have managed to secure Broderick's capitulation. But now . . .

I'll see him. Soon she'd have to tell him everything, the truth of her parentage, when she'd previously given him lies. And Stephen. Her throat muscles bobbed reflexively. Despite the fact it would tear the Killorans apart and destroy the Devil's Den, she owed him the truth about Stephen. Stephen deserved to be reunited with his true father.

Cleo haltingly lowered the gown in her arms. "That is assuming you wish to accompany Adair and me?"

That sprang Ophelia into movement. She hurriedly presented her back to her sisters, and Gertrude came 'round and set to work on the neat row of buttons down her back.

While Cleo and Gertrude helped her from her dress and into the silken garment, her mind slowly picked around the reality of this night: this was not just any *ton* event, like those they'd attended together in the past, where they'd sneaked off and stolen private time alone from the rest of the world. Now, she'd seek him out with the purpose of telling him everything. Her stomach lurched.

Gertrude spun her about and proceeded to button the pearls lining the length of the gown. The soft, silken fabric fluttered about her ankles. As Cleo rushed to gather a pair of slippers to match, Gertrude whipped her around once more. "Here," she murmured, pinching Ophelia's cheeks hard.

Ophelia winced. "Bloody hell, Gertrude."

"You are pale," Gertrude said unapologetically. With even less remorse, she yanked the shell-combs from her hair and began dragging a brush through Ophelia's tresses.

"Ouch," she muttered.

A look of concentration fixed to her face, Gertrude set to twisting those strands into an intricate chignon. She held out a hand.

Cleo came forward with a gold-and-gem tiara.

"No." Hands held up to ward off their attempts, Ophelia backed away.

She no longer wished to be the Jewel of St. Giles or a woman playing at nobility. She simply wished to be Ophelia, carving out a new beginning where her past and her brother's hopes for the future did not define her.

"I hated mine, too," Cleo finally said, examining the gold piece, alternately studded with oval-shaped diamonds, amethysts, and rubies. A large, round yellow diamond adorned the center of the tiara. "It is so beautiful, is it not?" she murmured, a question not requiring an answer. When Broderick had first presented her with it, she'd immediately mocked his inexplicable fascination with the peerage. Except . . . her eyes had caught that pale-yellow gemstone. Soft and light, unlike the bloodred rubies of her dagger, punishing stones that conjured thoughts of death and murder. And despite the strong urge to tell her brother to go to hell with his expectations for her, a part of her hesitated, wanting to set that piece atop her head. "You should not wear it because Broderick expects it, but neither should you not let yourself don it because you worry about how the world views you, or us, or anyone else in St. Giles."

Ophelia hesitated and then gave a slight nod. Cleo urged her to the long bevel mirror and angled her before it. She set the jewel-studded tiara atop her curls. "There," she murmured. Capturing her by the shoulders, she gave a slight squeeze.

Ophelia stared at her reflection. The diamonds and amethysts twinkled in the candles' glow.

"Your Mr. O'Roarke came searching for you yesterday."

She jerked her head about with such force, she knocked the crown aside.

"Here," Gertrude chided, adjusting the jeweled piece.

"Wot . . . What did he . . . ? Did he . . . ?"

"He was terrified." Ophelia's heart squeezed. She'd simply run off without an answer or explanation because at the time she'd needed to sort through the discovery she'd made. "He . . ."—her eyes flew to Cleo's—"cares about you," her sister at last said.

"When he learns the truth . . ." Bitterness laced her tone.

"I had the same fears of Adair, and he was able to separate who I was from Diggory." She cupped her cheek. "From what I gather of your Mr. O'Roarke, he will be able to."

"If he cannot accept you for who you are, then to hell with him and his narrow mind," Gertrude exploded with an uncharacteristic display.

Startled, they looked at Gertrude in the mirror.

Her cheeks flushed. "What?" she muttered.

The door exploded open. Stephen stormed in with one of his usual fits of temper. "Ya're going to that bastard's," he thundered. "Oi forbid it."

He was a formidable boy. He'd only grow to be an indomitable man.

Or, rather, marquess . . . In everything but his street-roughened tones, he'd always worn his rank.

Her breath lodged in her throat.

While her sisters took him to task for his entry and words, Ophelia crossed over. Uncaring for the fine fabric given to wrinkling, she grabbed her brother and hugged him tight.

"Wot in blazes is that for?" he muttered, his words muffled against her chest.

"Just because," she managed to squeeze out.

He struggled against her hold. "Well, Oi don't loike it." He shoved away. "Oi loike even less yar being anywhere near that investigator and his family. They ain't to be trusted."

She brushed a sandy-blond curl from over his brow. It promptly sprang back into place, as stubborn as the boy himself. "You're right," she softly said. "Some of them are dark devils like Diggory and the henchmen who delighted in beating us and anyone else they could land their fists on." The small knot in his throat bobbed up and down. She stroked her fingers through his hair again. "But, do you know, Stephen, there are good ones as well. People like Connor and Eve Dabney and his father. It is so much more important that we focus on the good as opposed to the darkness."

Dirt-stained fingers swatted at her. "None of them are good. The moment you forget that is the moment they'll ruin ya." Snarling, he spun about and bolted.

She stared after him, a chill scraping her spine.

"Shall we?" Cleo urged, holding out an arm.

Fighting back the ominous foreboding at her brother's words, Ophelia followed her sister through the club that had been home, past the same burly guards and prostitutes who'd been more family than the parents who'd sired her. They'd reached the front of the club when a voice sounded through the raucous din. "Ophelia?" Ophelia stiffened, feeling her sister tense at her side.

Guests parted, making way for the king of London's greatest gaming empire. Broderick stopped before his sisters. "I've not changed my mind where he's concerned. I'll not support a match between you and . . . him. He isn't good enough for you."

She'd not debate all the ways in which he was wrong in this public way. "Mayhap we've just been so *mired* in bad for so long that we've lost sense of what is truly good and bad," she said softly.

He inclined his head. "We'll agree to disagree." Her brother looked to Cleo. "Do not make me regret this."

Cleo winked.

Broderick lifted a hand, and the guards stationed there immediately drew open the heavy black panels, allowing them to pass through.

From where he stood at the carriage, Adair lifted his head from the timepiece he'd been studying. As soon as his gaze snagged on Cleo, his eyes went soft. There was such a beautiful tenderness, so much love spilling unashamed and unchecked from his eyes, that it wrenched at Ophelia. *I want that. I want the same forgiveness Adair gave to Cleo . . . and a life together. All of it.*

How unfairly she'd judged Adair and her sister's relationship with their onetime rival. Regret sat heavy in her heart.

When they reached him, her brother-in-law gathered Cleo's fingers and raised them to his lips for a lingering, tender kiss. "Cleopatra."

A simmering passion blazed to life as husband and wife exchanged a look so intimate, so powerful, that Ophelia looked away. After he'd handed Cleopatra inside, he turned back. "Ophelia," her brother-in-law greeted with far greater warmth than she'd ever deserved from him.

She blinked back a sheen of moisture from her eyes. Going up on tiptoe, she kissed Adair's cheek. "Thank you," she said gently.

There was a question in his eyes.

"For loving my sister." For not allowing Cleo's blood to be what defined her . . . or any of them. "For . . ." Shame needled at her insides. She fisted the fabric of her silk cloak. "For being so kind to me when I've been anything but to you—"

He held up a hand. "We are family."

We are family.

A tear slipped down her cheek. *Drat.* She swiped it back.

Offering him a tremulous smile, she allowed him to help her inside.

A moment later the door closed behind them, and the carriage rumbled forward.

Drawing back the curtain, Ophelia stared out at the passing streets of St. Giles that had ruled the whole of her life.

How easily Adair had granted forgiveness.

It gave her hope that Connor would, too.

Chapter 21

In his father's parlor, with London's leading Parliamentarian friends and Whig counterparts, Connor was reminded once more of the things good in his father.

It made it infinitely harder to continue the icy wall of indifference Connor had erected.

Standing beside one of the ceiling-to-floor-length windows in his father's Grey Parlor, the buzz of conversation filling the room, Connor absently studied those gentlemen who'd already arrived.

Calum Dabney sat speaking with his wife. The young woman took her husband's hand and gave his fingers a slight, encouraging squeeze.

Glancing away from that intimate moment, he looked in his father's direction. At present he spoke with Bethany, that young lady Connor had once hoped to marry.

Connor had never loved Bethany. Not as anything more than a friend. And even that friendship had been forever fractured when she'd chosen to wed another—a man hand-selected as a suitable match by the Viscount of Middlethorne.

Periodically, his father glanced up from his conversation. His gaze would land on Connor, and he'd swiftly jerk his attention back to his goddaughter.

Never had the distance between him and his father ever been wider. But then, that had been the divide since Connor had left his father's carriage. Even his arrival a short while ago had been met with a stilted exchange. Unfamiliar.

How he hated it.

Hated that his father avoided his gaze and kept the room's length between them. As if he were ashamed, as if he didn't know how to be with Connor any longer.

"Plotting your escape, as you always do?" a teasing voice whispered over his shoulder.

In the crystal windowpane, his gaze collided with Bethany's. Disappointment stabbed at him, wishing she were another. He forced a grin. "I've been assured there is no dancing," he offered in a bid at levity.

Bethany snorted. "If it were a room full of Tories, that would be a certainty. With a gathering of Whigs, one never knows."

They shared a smile, and he did another search of the bustling street below for a hint of Ophelia and her family.

"But you do dance with some women, Connor," Bethany pointed out hesitantly.

Put your hand on my waist, O'Roarke. Oh, blast, I'll do it myself.

A grin tugged at his lips. Ophelia Killoran was a woman who'd never accept no and would take command of any and every situation, if she so wished.

"Miss Killoran seems like a lovely young woman," she said, following the path his thoughts had traversed.

"Aye." As no good could come in speaking about one woman to another, one who'd had marital aspirations set on him since she'd been widowed, Connor met her nonstatement with nothing more than a concurrence.

Bethany drifted closer. "Your father disapproves."

She spoke as someone who knew. The realization that his father had spoken freely and poorly of Ophelia to Bethany snapped his patience. "I'd hardly allow my father to make a determination for me, one way or the other."

She recoiled and stared at him with wounded eyes.

"You . . . care about her, Connor." Again, it was an observation stated more as fact than anything. *Nay, I love her.* "He doesn't believe she deserves you."

"He doesn't know her," he said tightly.

Bethany sighed. "Yes, well, they always believe they know what we need or deserve." She spoke from experience.

"Your father has not yet arrived."

She looked to the door. "No. He's not been well—" Bethany's lips formed a strained smile. "But he assures me he is fine and intends to be here for the lecture."

Yet this was not a scholarly lecture one might find in a circulating room or library. This was an intimate reveal from two people who'd lived on the streets like Connor and sought to share their experiences as a way of exacting change for the better. "I'm so sorry, Bethany." She'd been a devoted daughter and had enjoyed a closeness with her father that, at first witnessing, he'd envied and resented. Wanted for himself.

"If you'll excuse me? I would speak with Mrs. Dabney regarding the foundling hospital."

After she'd gone, Connor remained fixed in his place at the window.

"Hullo, Connor."

He stiffened.

Just over his shoulder, the earl lingered. Wringing his hands, he was one who waged a tangible battle with himself.

"This is a wonderful gathering you've assembled," Connor said gruffly, breaking the impasse. This was talk that was safe. The earl's philanthropic efforts and the good he sought to do.

His father made a dismissive sound. "It is important that one sees and hears with one's own eyes what is . . . all around us."

Nonetheless. "I'm grateful to you for inviting Ophelia and her family." He quit his spot at the hearth and moved to where his father stood. "Her brother wishes for her to make a match with a nobleman," he continued, "but if she will have me, I intend to make her my wife."

He may as well have run his father through. "Connor," he said impatiently, "this is hardly the time to speak on that . . . on Miss Killoran or your intentions for her." His father made to leave.

"I love her," he spoke in hushed tones, needing this man who'd adopted him and given him a new beginning to understand. Needing him to accept Ophelia as she was. But even if he did not, it still would not matter.

His father whipped around. "Connor," he managed, an entreaty in his hoarse tone. He lifted his palms. "You do not know what you are saying. You do not know her. Not truly. Come." He gave an impatient flick of his hand. "I've to speak to Lord Marlborough prior to Mr. Dabney and Mr. and Mrs. Thorne's words to the room."

The butler appeared with the next guests to arrive. "Mr. and Mrs. Thorne and Miss Killoran," he announced.

She'd arrived.

He immediately found her with his gaze. Desire lanced through him.

Clad in silver satin and a glittering tiara atop her crown of pale curls, she was Lagertha in every way.

As Thorne and his wife went to greet the Dabneys, Ophelia fell back, lingering at the doorway. She'd the look of a bird poised for flight.

Weaving through the throng of Parliamentarians assembled, he found his way before her.

"Mr. Steele," she greeted quietly.

Mr. Steele. They'd returned to formalities.

"Miss Killoran," he said with a wry grin, "it is a pleasure." He bowed over her hand and, bringing her fingers close to his mouth, whispered against them. "Given your hasty flight and subsequent disappearance, I'd feared you'd not be here."

She flinched. "I had . . . reasons for rushing off."

He angled his shoulders in a way that he cut off their exchange from prying eyes. "You had your reasons? My God, Ophelia, I tore through the streets of London, sick with worry of what might have happened to you."

"I'm sorry," she said somberly. "I returned home."

Home. The club owned by her family, passed down by Diggory.

And yet no man had ever made her flee. "What happened?" he asked quietly.

"I'd not speak on it here."

Very well. "Then, where? When?"

His father clapped his hands, bringing silence to the crowd. "Ladies and gentlemen, if I might invite you to take your seats."

Connor cursed that interruption and, holding his arm out, escorted her to the chairs arranged at the front of the room for those who'd be speaking this afternoon and their families.

After the guests had all claimed their seats, his father remained standing at the front of the room, delivering his formal introduction. "As you know, I dedicated much of my life to improving the plight of the children in St. Giles."

At his side, Ophelia remained with her attention trained forward.

"I missed you," Connor whispered against her ear.

She wetted her lips, stealing a nervous glance at her sister and Thorne. The pair seemingly engrossed, Ophelia shifted her focus back to the earl. "I . . . missed you, as well," she whispered from the side of her mouth.

"There have been conflicting opinions in Parliament regarding the fate of those children. Some contend . . ."

"What is it, Ophelia?" he asked, searching the cherished planes of her face.

"My brother believes you are a dangerous influence."

He didn't give a hell what her brother wanted or felt. "And you?"

His father's speech droned on as nothing more than noise in the background of the only discussion that mattered. "These members of Parliament will defend their legislation with tales of the dangerous aspects of those lives, too. It is imperative to listen to both and see that ultimately good . . ."

She lifted her eyes to his. "I believe I'm better only because of you." Ophelia dropped her gaze briefly to her lap, but not before he caught the flash of pain there. "But—"

"As such, allow me to present the Earl of Whitehaven."

All the color leached from Ophelia's cheeks. She sat unmoving as her dead, horror-filled eyes fixed on the lectern now abandoned by his father and taken over by the earl of middling years.

Connor narrowed his eyes, taking in the way Ophelia slumped in her seat, her tightly curled fingers on her lap.

"Many of you know of my recent attack in the streets of St. Giles."

All the room murmured their ascent.

"It is a trap," Ophelia whispered, scratching at her throat.

Her sister leaned over and looked at Ophelia, a question in her eyes.

"What?" Connor demanded. *What was she—?*

"I was attacked with a knife, and I've kept that piece, a reminder of the darkness in the souls of those people."

Lord Whitehaven brandished a heavily jeweled dagger, and the room exploded in scandalized whispers. Connor didn't need to inspect the blade, a slightly curved serpent hilt studded with emeralds for the snake's coiled frame and ruby eyes. He had felt the sting of that dagger against his flesh two times in his life.

Ophelia slid her eyes closed.

A chill snaked through Connor as a recent conversation flitted forward.

"I lost mine."

She'd lost hers. Lost a piece that had once been the defining part of her presence in St. Giles. His stomach muscles clenched in a thousand knots.

"I was attacked after I attempted to save a small girl from being taken at the point of a knife—"

"Lies," Ophelia whispered. She struggled to her feet. The earl froze midsentence.

"My God, it is her."

It was that voice. Familiar. Hated. That night came rushing back in a fury. *There ain't no mercy in these streets.* His pleas. His cry. The crack of his head striking the hard, cold earth.

Lord Whitehaven.

She struggled to draw breath.

It was a trap.

She'd walked directly into it on the arms of her sister and brother-in-law. Numb, she looked to Connor, her heart rending in two jagged shards. She searched for evidence of his treachery in this.

Confusion clouded his eyes.

"Stop her," Lord Whitehaven cried.

Ophelia bolted.

Straight into the arms of a sturdy footman. Panic knocked around her insides as she wrestled against the servant. Except her delicate slippers and thin satin gloves dulled her ability to strike. It had been likely she'd again see him, the man she'd attacked. Nor would a single lord or lady care or believe the reasons for her actions that day. They'd see only a street rat, an interloper who'd assaulted a lord.

Oh, my God, I'll hang.

She bucked and thrashed. "Let me go, ya bastard," she panted.

"Wot in blazes is this?" Cleopatra hissed, brandishing a knife. Cries went up. Several ladies wilted in their seats. "Unhand my sister."

"Unhand her," Connor boomed, stalking forward.

In this instance he was an avenging angel, more powerful than even that Devil Lucifer.

To the servant's credit, any other man, woman, or child, with the fury of Connor O'Roarke and Cleopatra Thorne, would have been reduced to a blubbering mess. The heavily muscled servant merely glanced to his employer.

"In my offices," the earl boomed.

Digging his callused fingers hard enough into her flesh to raise bruises, the servant wrenched her arm back and used it to steer her from the rooms. Tears stung her eyes.

At her back, the music room exploded into a hum of whispers and weeping.

Frantically, Ophelia searched about.

Connor was immediately at her side. "By God, remove your hands from her or I'll cut yours off with glee."

The footman instantly released her.

Her legs buckled.

Connor caught her. "Ophelia," he whispered. "What is it?"

"I . . ." There was too much to explain. She longingly eyed the path from this place. Her sister caught her other arm and edged Connor out.

"What is this?" she whispered, Adair close at their heels.

"Th-there was a girl. I intervened on her behalf."

Cleopatra cursed.

Yet with every step, terror receded, replaced with a righteous sense of fury. The age-old resentment she'd carried for the lying lords who took their pleasures and left a trail of misery in their wake surged forward.

The difference was she knew there were those who were truly good. As such, she'd not let this bastard reduce her to a quivering mess.

"Now what is the meaning of this?" Connor's father demanded as soon as the group had gathered in his offices.

"This woman attacked me."

All eyes went to her, none more searing than Connor's.

"That's rot," Cleopatra bit out. "Ya're a bloody liar." She surged forward, but her husband and Calum Dabney caught her by the arms.

For one sliver of a moment she considered lying about that night. However, she'd make no apologies. "I did," she quietly intoned, eliciting a series of gasps. "But only after I came upon him in an alley, attempting to rape a girl."

The Earl of Whitehaven went ruddy-cheeked. "Lies," he hissed. "Your type are capable of nothing but—"

Connor felled him with a single blow.

"Connor," his father cried, storming forward. He stepped between his son and his next attack. "Hear Lord Whitehaven out."

Hear Lord Whitehaven out. Those four words that confirmed this was no chance meeting.

"I've seen the work Miss Killoran does with children, and I know your reputation," Connor said sharply, jabbing a finger at the cowering lord on the floor.

That defense filled her heart with a healing lightness.

"We're leaving," Adair said coldly.

"Do you also know who her family is, Connor?" his father called out over Adair's interruption.

Her throat closed, and she struggled to breathe.

"What is this about?" Connor asked, looking to his father. "I know precisely who—"

"*Not* her siblings."

She dimly registered Cleo sliding her fingers into hers, and she clung to them, absorbing that support. So that was what this was about . . . destroying Ophelia before his son.

He turned to Ophelia.

"I wanted to tell you," she whispered. "I just . . ."

"Didn't, Miss Killoran," his father snapped. "You just didn't. Just as you fed lies about Lord Whitehaven, you also fed lies to my son."

"No," she begged. She ripped her hand from Cleo's and lifted her palms in entreaty, needing him to understand and, more, needing Connor to. "It was different. This was different."

"You don't need to do this," Cleo said quietly. "We're leaving."

Ophelia shook her head. She needed to have this finally said.

"I don't understand," Connor said slowly, turning agonized eyes to her.

"I didn't want to hurt you."

"Didn't want to hurt him?" His father stalked forward, and she forced her feet to remain rooted, forced herself to meet his condemning gaze. "But then, your father hurt him enough, did he not?"

A single tear streaked along her cheek. "I'll speak to you now, Connor. Alone."

"The time for that is at an end, Miss Killoran, but then, that's not truly your name, is it?"

Her heart thudded.

"Ophelia?"

At Connor's questioning, she shook her head. "That is not my name." She lifted her chin. "Just as yours is not Steele." In their quest for a new family and a new start, they were not unlike. "I'm not truly a Killoran, but that does not make me less."

Hideous splotches of crimson outrage marred the Earl of Mar's cheeks. "Don't you dare compare yourself to my son."

"Father," Connor bit out, but the earl lifted his hand, urging him to silence.

"Miss Killoran is not simply another member of Mac Diggory's gang."

"Not . . . ?"

Ophelia's heart knocked against her rib cage.

"She is Mac Diggory's daughter."

Silence hummed loudly in Ophelia's ears, muting the frantic pounding of her heart.

Connor shook his head.

"It is true, Connor," she whispered.

He reached for the high back of the oak chair and dug his fingers in hard enough to leave crescent marks upon the otherwise-immaculate wood.

"Her father killed your parents. Raped your mother. And with her ruthlessness, she is just like the monster who sired her."

A painful groan lodged in her throat. Did that tortured sound belong to her?

The door opened, and another gentleman entered. Connor's father waved a tired hand in his direction, and this time when he spoke, his voice sounded decades older. "If you wish further proof of her treachery, Stanley can stand as witness."

A dull buzzing filled Ophelia's ears, like a swarm of bees set free in her mind.

She could not move. She could not breathe. Around her the words raced in a nonsensical blur.

Years later, and more than ten years older, time had changed him, and yet one never forgot.

Her eyes closed.

He was fatter, fleshier in his cheeks, and rounder about his middle. A jovial-looking gentleman as soulless as Satan.

Only now—he had a name.

Stanley Alberts. Viscount Middlethorne. Lady Bethany's father. The man who'd attempted to rape her.

You want it, you little whore. Your kind always want it.

Biting her lip, she was still unable to keep the agonized moan better suited to a wounded beast from spilling out. Fighting the sting of bile in her throat, she searched her hands around for purchase. Anything to keep herself from collapse.

A hand wrapped about her lower arm.

Crying out, she wrenched away, tripping over herself in her haste to be free.

Adair. It is only Adair.

She scratched her fingernails down her cheeks. What was happening to her?

"Ophelia?" Adair urged, concern heavy in his voice.

"You," she whispered, staggering back, away from the handful of guests, witnesses to her shame and humiliation.

Looking around at the witnesses present with befuddled eyes, Lord Middlethorne nodded once. "This is the woman who once attacked me. Years ago. I'd always remember that hair."

Look at that hair . . . May I touch it?

Her stomach pitched. *I'm going to throw up.*

"Seems she has a history of it," Lord Whitehaven spat. "Attacking an innocent child, indeed."

Ophelia stood trembling. *Say nothing. Challenge him, this man who with his actions that night haunts you still.* Her tongue felt heavy in her mouth, and she tried to make it move, to form words.

Why, why can't I speak?

"My wife had died, and this one, a gypsy," Viscount Middlethorne spat, a grander actor than any London stage had seen, "offered to read my palms. Tell my future."

Connor's body went whipcord straight.

Motionless, pale, and most damning of all—silent.

That silence was a greater betrayal and condemnation than had he called her out before the room of guests. Icy rage froze her veins. Her fury grew, and she turned herself over to it. Otherwise she'd become lost to the misery and horror threatening to break her.

"Liar," she breathed. "Ya're all liars."

The Earl of Mar sputtered, "Madam, these are some of the most respectable, honorable gentlemen in England. Seize her."

The doors exploded open, and three constables stormed the room.

Adair and Cleo put themselves between Ophelia and the constables, and she took even more strength in that show of support.

She whirled around.

The footman who'd been stationed in the parlor leapt forward.

Panting, her breath coming loudly in her ears, she feinted left toward the window.

Strong hands wrapped about her waist. "No," she panted, kicking her feet.

"Ophelia," Connor thundered. His father and Viscount Middlethorne wrestled him back.

With her sister bellowing after the constables, they carted Ophelia off.

Chapter 22

In the span of moments, the world had gone insane.

And at the center of the madness was his father.

Ophelia dragged off, the explosiveness of her and her family's fight, left only a stark, empty silence in its wake. Damning.

Connor glanced to the trio of noblemen assembled—two of whom he'd long respected, one he'd wager was bound for hell for his vices.

"Get out," he ordered Lord Whitehaven.

"Close the door," the Earl of Mar called over to his friend after Lord Whitehaven scurried off. "I'll not have servants talking," he grimaced, "any more than they will be."

Connor jerked. "My God, that is what you now worry over? Gossiping servants?" Who was this man? He no longer recognized him. But mayhap, this was who he'd always been. One who'd wanted to erase the filth of the streets from Connor and transform him into something pure and good—something he would never, could never, be. "You did this."

"I did nothing," his father said tiredly, fetching himself a brandy. "I merely opened your eyes to what the young woman is."

*It is important that one sees and hears with one's own eyes what is . . .
all around us.*

His breath whistled through his teeth. His father's earlier words had
been a warning, and he'd been too blind to see.

While the earl poured himself a drink, Connor stared on incredulously. A drink. This man who'd adopted him now sought to sip fine
French spirits when he'd consigned Ophelia to—

His mind came to a screeching, jarring halt; even in silence, he
could not bring himself to complete the thought.

"What is that?"

His father froze, midpour. He looked over his shoulder quizzically.

"What *is* the young woman?"

The earl slammed his bottle down, and his drink alongside it. "My
God, Connor," he shouted, "her father slaughtered your parents. Raped
your mother."

"I know what he did," he cried, slamming his fist on the earl's desk.
"I know," he whispered. "I witnessed it. I heard their pleas. I saw their
throats cut. All of it." The color bled from his father's cheeks. "Mac
Diggory was the man who did that." *Not Ophelia.*

"Don't you do that, Connor," his father ordered. "I saw your reaction when you learned the truth about her father."

He sucked in a shuddering breath. Until the day he died, he'd recall
the shame bleeding from her eyes as she was held to blame for crimes
her father had committed. In his silence, he'd failed her. Shock didn't
excuse it. Nothing could ever pardon it.

At last his godfather, Lord Middlethorne, stepped forward. "It
brings me no pleasure to see the young woman hanged, Connor," he
said in even tones one might use when discussing the weather. "If I
might?" he ventured, lifting a finger. "I did see a possible solution to
Miss Killoran's dilemma."

This was the man who'd attempted to rape her. The man who
still haunted her. Connor clenched his hands into fists to keep from

snapping his neck. "Say what it is you'd say," he said brusquely. How was it possible to know so little of a person? His father. His godfather. Men he'd respected. Men he'd trusted.

"I understand your father explained my . . . circumstances. Bethany . . . and I . . . are in dire financial straits. Together, a union would at last join our families." Middlethorne reached into his jacket and withdrew a small stack of papers bound with ribbon. "If you enter into marriage with Bethany, I will, of course, see that the charges against Miss Killoran are dropped. An arrangement has already been drafted; it merely awaits your signatures."

My God. The air left Connor on a whoosh.

"Is that what this was?" he whispered, his mind slowly making sense of it. "An attempt to drive me from Ophelia? For what?" He spun to face the cocksure viscount. "So I might marry your daughter?" How easily they'd dispensed with Ophelia. They'd proven all her hatred and suspicion of the nobility well founded and deserved, and how he hated himself for his naïveté in failing to see the ugliness around him.

Viscount Middlethorne stared back, silent. Calm. Unmoved. Unaffected. The same person, more monster than man, who'd pinned Ophelia to an alleyway and scrabbled with her skirts as she'd pleaded.

A burning hatred scorched through Connor's veins like a vicious cancer, threatening to consume and destroy.

I'm going to be sick.

He swung back to face his father. "You have no qualms with him forcing me to whore myself to save an innocent young woman's life?"

His father flinched. "It is . . . not as bad as all that."

Connor stalked to the door.

"Connor," his father cried. "Do not leave. We are not through speaking on this."

Ignoring that order, he continued forward.

The viscount held up the formal documents. "I trust you'll see—"

Not breaking stride, Connor grabbed him by the throat and drove him against the wall. Those traitorous pages fluttered to the floor at their feet. The viscount's eyes bulged, terror spilling from their depths. *Said moi mouth was a whore's mouth that he couldn't kiss, that he 'ad other uses for it.*

The same primitive fight that had led him to kill and survive on the streets roared to life, and he reveled in the other man's weakness.

"Connor," his father shouted, "release him."

The viscount gasped and panted, clawing at Connor's hands. Tightening his grip, he choked him all the harder. "How does it feel?" he whispered. He brought back his left arm and planted his fist in the viscount's nose. The satisfying crack of bone shattering was followed by the spray of blood that coated Connor's fingers.

"Connor!" his father entreated, grabbing at his arm.

Connor punched the viscount again and again, until he was a limp mass in his hands. He released him.

Lord Middlethorne slid to the floor, sucking great, heaving gasps of air, scrabbling with his neck.

His body was a divide separating Connor from his father. "He is a monster," Connor said in emotionless tones. "He . . . attacked her as a child." How many other young girls had been so assaulted? How many more who'd been violated in every way by him?

"It is not possible," his father bit out. "He could not. He would not."

"Wouldn't he?" he thundered, and the earl recoiled. Connor swiped the contract from the floor. "He expects me, your son, to whore himself to save Ophelia, the woman I love." He ripped those pages and tossed them at his father. "You are too blind to see." He shook his head in disgust. "All these years I've admired you for being a champion of those unfortunate boys and girls like myself. I raised you in my mind as a hero. But you're not." His chest squeezed. "You passed judgment on Ophelia for no other reason than because of her birthright while you'd defend"—he spat on the viscount's prone but still unfortunately breathing body—"this man." With a sound of disgust, he stepped over the viscount and started for the door.

He yanked the panel open, and Bethany came spilling in. Her skin ashen, she pressed her palms against her mouth. "Connor, please wait. Don't—"

"Where are you going, Connor?" his father pleaded behind him.

He paused, his fingertips on the door. "I am going to fight for Miss Killoran's freedom. And God help you all if I can't win it."

With that, Connor left.

Chapter 23

Tucked in the corner of her dank cell in Newgate, with the date of her execution already set, Ophelia came to a realization: she hated satin.

It was a rather silly, nonsensical detail to note, given that the only thing between her and drawing no more breath was two more sunsets. And yet there it was. She despised the bloody fabric, and if she believed in miracles and the possibility of escape, she'd vow to never again don a blasted garment made of the damned stuff.

Oh, she hadn't always hated the whispery-soft, fine fabric. As much as her brother's obsession with the nobility had grated, she'd celebrated the day she'd shed her tattered, coarse wool garments for the fine satins and silks Broderick insisted they don.

Now, she appreciated how useless those expertly sewn dresses were. The heavy chill and dampness of the cell permeated her fabric, stinging her skin and freezing her from the inside out. Ophelia hugged her arms close to her chest and rubbed in a futile attempt to restore warmth.

How much easier it was to focus on one's clothing than the stench of death and decay all around. Pungent odors hung heavy in the air, clogging one's nostrils and threatening to choke off the last clean breath in one's lungs.

A bold rat scampered close to her slippers, and she shot out a foot, kicking him back.

He darted into the tiny crack in the wall he continually slipped in and out of.

Dragging her knees to her chest once more, Ophelia wrapped her arms about them. She rested her cheek atop the smooth fabric and eyed that rat's nest.

The irony of this moment was not lost on her. Her life with Connor O'Roarke had come full circle.

Since she was a girl, stealing the coin purse from a nobleman, and Connor had stepped in to spare her, she had been destined for this place.

Yet living a life of crime and sin on the streets, and dancing on the edge of discovery, nothing could have prepared her for the hell that was Newgate.

A vicious itching at her scalp threatened to drive her mad, and she dragged her ragged nails through the uneven tufts that had been left by the guards. She scratched furiously, until she registered the whisper of warmth on her fingers.

Yanking her hands down to her lap, she stared at the crimson stain left by her efforts. Absently, she wiped the blood onto the front of her tattered skirts.

"My God, no . . . please . . . Oi . . . no . . ." The incoherent, muffled cries of another poor soul reverberated around the prison until Ophelia wanted to clamp her hands over her ears and blot out all sounds: the squeal of rodents who'd feast on flesh, the moaning and weeping of prisoners who'd not yet accepted the truth: there was no absolution or salvation coming.

All that awaited was that iron-cased half door and the iron-bound, lattice-oak Debtor's door that led to the scaffold and one's public execution.

Ophelia slid her eyes closed as every nerve in her body twitched with fear, straining with her need to batter herself against the doorway in a useless bid to break down the barrier between her and freedom.

She knocked the back of her head against the stone wall, dislodging a small piece of plaster.

How close she'd been to having everything she'd ever wanted—everything she'd never known she wanted—until it had been too late.

Not even one month ago, she'd have cynically believed she'd stepped into a well-laid trap perfectly executed by Connor and his father.

How effortlessly he'd knocked down the guards she'd erected to keep herself safe. No longer the bitter, snapping young woman she'd once been, she had seen with clarity the shock, disbelief, and horror in Connor's eyes for the truth they were.

By God, you will not take her.

A shuddery sob started in her chest and climbed up her throat. She clamped her hand over her lips, blotting out the sound of misery that would alert the guards stationed nearby.

For once again, even knowing what her father had done, Connor had stepped between her and the path to Newgate. He'd brandished a weapon, threatening the constables, his father, the powerful peers in that room, when it would only shatter the reputation he'd earned as an honorable, respectable investigator.

A tear slipped from her eyes. She rubbed her cheek over her skirts, hiding that lone drop. He'd always deserved his Lady Bethany. Ophelia had hated the woman on sight for what she represented. Now, she could accept the truth—Lady Bethany was right for Connor in all the ways she had always been wrong.

Another tear fell. Followed by another. And another.

"Another one's making the march," one of the guards outside her cell called. The sound of spit landing on stone followed. "Wot's our wager on this one?"

"Ask the bitch. Fancy gaming hell owners, her sort know sumfin of it."

That mocking retort was met with a series of guffaws from the other brutes; their laughter echoed through the corridors and carried through the manacled cell.

Lisp, as she'd named one of them for the reptilian quality to his voice and the rasp of his tongue when he spoke, pressed his face against the bars. "Want in on the wager, fancy piece? An extra plate an' water . . . We get a piece of ya if ya lose."

Ophelia sat there, stone-faced, looking through him.

You want it, bitch.

Do not think of him. Do not think of them. Think of Connor. Think of the fleeting wonder you knew in his arms and with him.

"Wot?" one of the guards demanded. "Ya think yarself too good to part yar legs for us. Playing at lady. Not so pretty without yar 'air, are ya?"

Unwittingly, she slid her fingers through the sloppy tangle of short strands.

He laughed. "Ya and yar kind ain't no different from the other whores 'ere."

Refusing to give any of her taunting captors the satisfaction, she let her hand fall and met their questions and charges with a flinty silence.

"Too good to sit on 'er mattress," another guard piped in. "She ain't goin' to be so proud when she's making the march. Ya 'ear that, bitch?" He cupped himself through his wool trousers. "Maybe we should show 'er she ain't no different." He fiddled with the falls of his breeches.

Ophelia jumped up and held out her fists. "Try it, ya ugly, pox-ridden son of a whore," she seethed. "Oi'll rip the scrawny bit between yar legs off and feed it to ya for yar last meal."

Cheeks mottled red, her jeerer surged forward. "Oi'll give it to ya good, ya bloody bitch," he shouted.

His more-restrained friends grabbed at him.

"Get control. Ya know we can't touch 'er. She's off-limits."

Ophelia latched on to that.

"She's as good as dead," the toothless brute railed, bucking at them. "Ya got powerful enemies in the nobs ya put yar 'ands on." Yes, Ophelia's trial and sentencing had been swiftly pushed through with little effort on the part of Whitefield and Middlethorne. The guard eyed his friend hopefully. "Wot's the 'arm if we fuck 'er? 'e won't even know—"

"What won't I know?"

The pair released her determined attacker, and the three immediately sprang to attention.

The rhythmic click-click-click of his cane silenced even the rats and raindrops that penetrated the ancient stone roof.

In the darkened space, Ophelia squinted, straining to see the owner of those cultured tones, struggling to bring him into focus . . . and then wished she hadn't.

Attired in a garish brocade jacket with a diamond stickpin in an elaborate cravat, his garments were as out of place in this hell as his refined speech. It was not his fancy attire, however, that gave her pause.

She shrank back before catching herself in that reflexive response.

For the stranger before her, with his midnight hair drawn back at his nape, accentuating a face that didn't know if it was beautiful or hideous, had the look of Satan himself. At last he stopped before the three men.

Lined shoulder to shoulder, the trio silenced; they each kept their gazes wisely on the floor. After giving them a dismissive once-over, he turned his attentions on Ophelia.

"You are Diggory's daughter, then," he murmured in smooth, melodic baritones, his words casual as if he inquired after the weather.

"Only in the sense he sired me," she said evenly. Connor had helped her see that she was so much more than that vile, blackhearted bastard who'd roused terror in the hearts of all.

His lips quirked up. "It is not so simple to divorce one from one's blood." He spoke as one who knew.

Yet . . . with that admission, how very little he understood. She'd not debate the point with him. She studied him; his swarthy features, better suited to a gypsy, were carved in a cold, unfeeling mask. It was enough she knew the truth.

She realized that now.

Turning his shoulder dismissively, he glanced to his minions. "Who proposed violating terms of an agreement I struck?" he asked in lethal, ice-laden tones.

The men quaked; two of them looked to the one between them.

Lifting a hand that shook, he stepped forward.

"Tsk, tsk. What. Am. I. To. Do. With. You?" He clicked his tongue to the roof of his mouth as he wandered a path around him. Contemplating him. Toying with him. The nameless Devil lifted the head of his cane, close to his mouth, so close his lips nearly touched the gleaming gold metal. "To my offices, until I decide what to do with you."

The man swallowed loudly and dropped a bow. He tripped over himself as he ran away to an assured doom.

For there could be no doubting the man who stood before them was Wiley, known all through the Dials as the liege of this hell.

He lifted his spare, immaculate white glove.

The guards immediately faded into the shadows.

Wylie came closer to the bars. He raked a derisive eye over her person. "You don't have the look of your bastard of a father, Miss Diggory."

Inside, her body shook, and she battled down that fear, refusing to be cowed, refusing to spend the last days she had on earth pleading with a man incapable of mercy. She edged her chin up. "My name is Ophelia Killoran."

He chuckled, but the deadened sound was absent of all amusement. "I see you are quite special to some people that they'd unblinkingly turn over a fortune to make your last days . . . comfortable."

Her pulse jumped. *Who . . . ?*

A tall figure stepped forward.

Her hopes immediately plummeted. "Broderick," she said, her voice hoarse and raspy from ill use. Of course.

"Did you expect it was another?" the warden mocked.

Her brother took in every inch of her person before ultimately settling on her sheared tresses. His face contorted into a paroxysm which he instantly concealed as he cast a dark glower at the warden. Impervious to that icy rage, he removed a key from inside his jacket. "You have five minutes."

"Ten."

God, how she loved her brother for the fearless warrior he'd always been . . . on her and her siblings' behalf.

"Ten," the devil shockingly concurred. He let Broderick inside.

Her brother rushed forward and then stopped, again studying her. At last, he opened his arms.

Ophelia hugged herself close. "I . . . You shouldn't." As if a reminder of all the reasons she wasn't fit to be touched by anyone, the mites making a home in her scalp wrought havoc on the already rubbed-raw skin. She scratched again.

Groaning, Broderick came close and drew her against his chest.

She struggled against him.

"Do not . . . ," he whispered against her lice-filled scalp.

This was the last she'd ever see of him. Never again would she see her sisters, or Stephen, or Connor. "Broderick . . ." Then she wept, crying great, big gasping tears and wetting his jacket front with the misery she'd fought these past days. Only there were no other words. What was there to say, after all? Every decision she'd made, as a girl of eight and then as a woman of two and twenty, she'd have made all over again.

"I know," he said softly, cupping her cheek. He just held her, with the precious time they were allotted melting away. At last, she managed to gain control of her sorrow. She forced herself to back out of his arms.

"I wanted to come sooner," her brother explained hoarsely. "I offered a fortune." He cast a hate-filled look to the place Wylie had occupied a short while ago. "In the end, Steele made arrangements."

Connor.

Ophelia fluttered her hands about her throat. "Connor."

He'd done that. Despite knowing who her father was? Any other man would have let her rot alone for the secrets she'd kept. But then, that had never been the manner of person Connor was.

Broderick held her cheek, forcing her attention back to him.

"I cannot save you."

The hoarsened words should have cleaved her in two for the finality there and the fact that her fate had been sealed.

Except . . .

It was what she'd been expecting. She'd known the truth before he'd even said it.

"I know," she said softly.

"I am so sor—"

"Five minutes," the warden called out.

She pressed her fingertips against Broderick's lips, willing away his guilt. She was the owner of every decision she'd ever made. "You need to allow Gertrude a role in the club. She is intelligent. She sees so much. Do not underestimate her. Not anymore." They all had. For so, so long. He gave an unsteady nod. "And Adair—be kind to him. He loves Cleo and has a heart that is so wonderful." The column of Broderick's throat moved rhythmically. "It is time for us to be at peace with the Blacks." Why had it taken her so long to realize the good in them? *Because you needed Connor in your life to make you at last see.* "I'd have you make me a promise."

He caught her hands and raised her fisted knuckles to his lips. "Anything," he managed, his voice rough.

"I want you to end prostitution in the club." Her brother's pained laugh echoed around the stone walls, and she continued over it. "The

women we hire, they've had no choice but to sell themselves to survive"—
how narrow her views on survival had been—"but they possess skills and
strengths as great or greater than any man we've hired." Just as Ophelia
had been overlooked, so, too, had the women employed by the Devil's
Den. "Speak to Black and his family about what they've done. They will
guide you. Promise me."

A glossy sheen filled Broderick's eyes, nearly breaking her.

She bit her lower lip to keep from giving in to another fit of misery.

He offered another jerky nod.

"Promise me," she urged, demanding that he say it. Needing to
know there would be a new beginning for some women when there
wouldn't be for her. Oh, God. *I do not want to die.* Her heart crumpled.
I thought I was so much stronger. "Promise," she said. Her voice, tinged
with panic, pitched to the ceiling.

"You have my p-promise." His voice broke.

Ophelia patted his stubbled cheek. How many times had he taken
on the role of soother, assuring her and her siblings that all would be
fine? How those roles had been so transposed.

"Two minutes," the warden announced, stirring the panic in her
breast.

"There is one more thing." Ophelia drew in a slow breath.

"Do not," he begged, because of course he already knew. Ultimately,
she believed that deep in her heart. Broderick would do what must be
done.

"He is not ours, Broderick."

Broderick squeezed his eyes shut and then covered his face with
his hands.

She wrestled them back to his side.

"We cannot lose h—" His voice cracked. "I cannot lose you both."

Her already broken heart ripped all over again, bleeding from the
agony in her brother's tone and ravaged eyes.

"Oh, Broderick," she whispered, squeezing his hands in hers. "He was never ours."

"Your time is up, Killoran."

They both looked to the iron bars.

Nonetheless, her brother remained. "Until I draw my last breath, I will regret that I sent you away. You belonged with us. If there hadn't been a Season . . ." His eyes slid shut.

"If there hadn't been a Season, there would have been no Connor, and my life was incomplete before him," she said with a surprising strength.

The door opened.

Her brother stretched out a hand, brushing his fingertips against hers, and then he was gone.

There was nothing more to do but wait until her walk to the gallows.

Chapter 24

Connor had stalked the halls of Newgate many times before.

Countless cases had carried him within the miserable gaol to put questions to men and women who'd murdered or stood accused of murder. To interrogate rapists and thieves.

One never forgot the stench of feces and rotting bodies, the metallic tinge of blood and sweat. As a once young investigator, he'd despised every trek he'd been forced to take down the rotted corridors. He was never more grateful than when he finished his questioning and was able to step outside and suck in the fresh air to drive back the fetid odors that clung to a person.

Not a single one of those visits could have ever prepared him for this one . . . to this woman.

Swallowing the bile at the back of his throat, he kept his gaze forward, on the guard escorting him through the dank, dark corridors.

From somewhere deep in the belly of London's most ruthless prison, a sharp, keening cry echoed throughout.

His breath rasped loudly in his ears, and he fought to shield those sounds.

She was here. She was deserving of more than his weakness.

With each step that brought him farther into the abyss that was the hell of Newgate, panic clawed at his mind, stealing reason and logic.

"'ere we are," the guard lisped.

A rat scurried over his boots, and Connor stared after the enormous rodent.

She is living here. She is living with rats and rapists and—

The guard opened the door.

It took a moment for Connor's eyes to adjust to the dark, narrow space. Then he found her, and his heart cracked, bled, and died there.

Ophelia lay in the corner. With her back presented to the door, her gown in tatters, and those glorious blonde tresses now shorn unevenly about her head, it was the absolute stillness that ushered in the truth.

She had given up on hope.

It invariably struck all forced into this place. But the evidence of it, from this woman whose life mattered more to him than even his own, destroyed him in ways he would never, could never, recover from.

He dimly registered the guard closing the door at his back, and Connor and Ophelia were left alone inside.

Connor went down on a knee beside her, hovering his hands over her, wanting to take her in his arms, afraid to force her. Afraid that despite the deal he'd struck with the devil who ran this place, she'd suffered anyway. "Oh, Ophelia," he whispered, his voice catching.

Her slender frame stiffened, but she made no move to face him.

"Has anyone hurt you?" For if they had, Connor would find the ones responsible, gut them with a dull blade, and gleefully watch as they choked out their last breath.

She gave her head a slight shake, and a wave of relief so strong assailed him it brought his eyes closed.

"Why didn't you tell me?" He finally asked the question that had haunted him since the moment she'd been hauled off. Had she not trusted him? Had she believed so little of him and his love for her?

But then, you never told her that you loved her.

At last she forced herself upright. When she faced him, the sight of her hit him like a kick to the chest. Dirt and grime stained her ashen cheeks, her crimson lips a stark contrast to their pale hue. But it was the wide pool of her blue eyes—haunted, hunted, tortured.

He ached to make her suffering his own.

"How could I tell you that?" she whispered. "How could I have told you, the only man I ever loved"—*oh, God,* her words splayed him open—"that my father was the one responsible for every suffering you and your parents knew?"

"Did you know me so little that you believed I should hold you accountable for his sins?" His question emerged harsher than he intended, and he immediately regretted it.

Tears pooled in her crystalline eyes. "At first the lie was just . . . easier. Easier than admitting that when we first met, I didn't even have a name. That I was simply 'Girl.'"

I will not survive the pain of this. "It is why you never gave me a name?" That agonized question came, dragged from him. A low moan seeped from his lips.

"I created a world that I'd wished was mine," she said softly, steadier in that explanation than he could manage. How much stronger she'd always been. "I offered you the world I'd secretly dreamed of."

"But I wanted all of you, Ophelia." Wanted . . . a tense that marked the end of what could never be. *I won't survive this.* Losing her would leave him hollow and deadened in ways even his own parents' deaths had not. "I didn't want the imagined; I wanted all of you." He reached for her.

She recoiled, scooting away from him until her back knocked against the wall. "Don't," she whispered, threading her hands through those shorn locks. Of all the agony and misery of her being here and what would come, and what he'd been powerless to stop, he mourned the loss of those pale-blonde strands. The ones that had lain draped about him like a silken waterfall were now jagged, greasy wisps.

Had it really been mere days since his world had fallen apart? How, when it felt like an interminable lifetime had come to pass?

"Oi've got the creepers."

With a groan, he pulled her into his arms, and she went unresistingly. "Do you think I would let that keep me from holding you?" When the time between them was so short. The air trapped in his throat, strangling him. All the while he was deluged with panic and something more crippling—helplessness.

They remained that way, still in each other's arms, on the dank cell floor.

Ophelia was the first to move.

She turned her head and layered her cheek to the place where his heart pounded. A soft, even sigh, a peaceful one, sifted from her lips. She grazed her fingertips, in a butterfly caress, over the front of his chest. The tenderness of that touch threatened to break him all over again.

Gathering her onto his lap, Connor simply sat there on the floor of Newgate, wanting to remain forever as they were, because then at least she would be in his life, still breathing. As long as they were together, he could survive anywhere.

Tears pricked behind his lashes, and he squeezed his eyes tight, wanting to be strong for her. "My Lagertha." Connor touched his lips to her right temple.

Ophelia edged back. "Tell me the story of it . . . that name."

There it was. For the first time since they'd met as children and he'd used that name, she asked.

The cinch squeezed all the more. "There was once a man named Ragnar Lodbrok. He went to war with the king of Sweden. Amidst the battle, a warrior emerged, an Amazon woman, braver than all the men on that entire field. Her hair hung about her shoulders as she fought. At the battle's end, captivated, Ragnar made her his wife." Just as Connor had wanted a future with Ophelia. He swallowed the ball of emotion in his throat. "And from then on, when he went to war, they fought at each other's side."

At her silence, he stole a glance down.

A wistful smile hovered on her lips. "I love that story," she said softly. Slipping her fingers into his, she joined them, connecting those digits. Ophelia raised his knuckles and placed a kiss upon them and then urged him to unfurl them.

"Your hands," he hissed, noting that detail he'd failed to previously see: the blood staining her fingers.

Ophelia made a dismissive sound. "It is the lice." She caressed her fingers over the palm of his hand and then trailed a jagged nail down an intersecting line over his left hand.

"This is the line of fate," she said, drawing his eyes to the perpendicular one that crossed his hand.

That was the last palm I ever read. Now, she'd read those lines upon his hand. There was a heavy shadow of finality to her actions. His stomach clenched sharply. "I don't want to know—" She briefly lifted her eyes, quelling him with a look. She returned her scrutiny to his hand. "You'll find yourself in possession of great wealth."

Connor stared blankly at her bent head. He *had* a fortune, built with his own hands, as well as the unentailed wealth and properties awaiting him at his father's passing. What good was any of it? All of it had proven useless thus far in trying to free Ophelia from this hell.

Ophelia continued. "This is the line of love." She trailed a jagged nail over the one in question. "This tells a person whether love is in your future . . . and who it will be."

You. There will only ever be you. His throat worked painfully. His eyes slid closed. Desolation swept cold through him.

"There is a woman—"

"Don't," he begged, wresting his hand back, but she retained an unrelenting grip.

"She'll remind you how to smile and laugh . . . and"—Ophelia's voice caught—"love."

He shook his head hard. "There will only be you, Ophelia. I—"

She covered his lips with her hand. "These lines show your future, Connor." Her eyes moved over his face before holding his gaze. "I cannot be part of it."

"Then the lines lie," he rasped, yanking them back.

Except Ophelia gripped them, imploring with her eyes to let her continue her telling. Even as each word she uttered knifed at the shards of his broken heart, he could no sooner deny her this than he could deny her anything.

"There'll be a babe," she whispered achingly, tapping a finger against several indents in the skin there, inaudibly counting. "Many of them. At least f-four."

"Time's up, Steele," the guard called from outside the cell.

No. I'm not ready. It isn't enough time. But then, a lifetime with Ophelia still wouldn't be enough. Connor gathered her face between his hands, tenderly stroking his fingers over the dirt-stained flesh. "I will get you out of this place. I—"

Her rosebud lips formed a quivering smile. "You always were smug, Connor O'Roarke."

A half sob, half laugh lodged painfully in his chest at that echo of long ago.

The guard called out again. Ignoring him, Connor stood and brought Ophelia up with him. Shrugging out of his jacket, he draped the too-large article over her narrow shoulders. The enormous fabric swallowed her smaller frame. As she huddled deep into it, there was a childlike innocence to her standing there. "I will get you-ou—"

"Don't," she quietly cut him off. "You were always truthful and forthright. Don't lie to me now." Her arms hung limp at her sides, the openings of his jacket dwarfing her delicate limbs. "I was going to tell you about my parentage."

"At . . . the earl's . . ." He could not even bring himself to call the Earl of Mar his father. Not in this moment. Mayhap not ever. For how did one move beyond the neatly laid trap that man had set, all to prove Ophelia's unsuitability and to preserve a union between Connor and Bethany?

Burrowing deep within herself, Ophelia nodded. "I was. I waited too long. I don't want any lies between us before . . ." His heart buckled. "Before."

The guard again shouted. "Oi said yar toime is up."

"By God, shut your bloody mouth or I'll have Wylie make your tenure here even more of a misery."

That effectively silenced the guard. As soon as he'd slunk off, Connor dropped his brow to Ophelia's. "What is it?"

The tip of her tongue darted out, trailing the seam of her lips. "I've solved your case."

"My . . ." He stilled. He'd not even thought of Maddock or the marquess's missing boy since Ophelia had been dragged from his father's home.

Leaning up on tiptoe, she placed her mouth close to his ear.

Her whisper brought his eyes weighted closed.

No.

Oh, God. His mind raged against the truth. He shook his head.

Ophelia nodded. "It is true." In hushed tones, she shared all. When she'd finished, pain bled from her eyes. "I have no right to ask you for anything."

"You do." If she wished for the stars, he'd climb to the heavens and gather her a handful. "Tell me what you want, Ophelia."

"Look after him." Her selflessness in even this brought his eyes briefly closed. She didn't speak of herself or plead for her salvation. Rather, she thought of her brother. "The marquess, he'll not allow my family anywhere near him after this." It did not escape his notice that she took care to omit specific names and details in her telling. Her cautiousness came only to those like them who'd lived on the streets. "See that he's cared for and safe, Connor. Please see that he's never harmed by his f-father." That slight tremble was the only hint of her despair.

God, she was breathtakingly remarkable in her strength. He raised her hands to his lips and kissed them one at a time. "You have my word."

Ophelia's throat moved. Then, going up on her toes, she touched her mouth to his.

He immediately folded her in his arms, slanting his lips over hers again and again in a violent, primal meeting.

This embrace, unlike any to have come before, was different for the faint thread of desperation to it. This prison was an acknowledgment of how tenuous their time together was.

He broke the kiss; their breaths came hard and fast together. "I love you," he whispered, placing his lips tenderly against her brow.

"If ya aren't out in one minute, Oi'll fetch Wylie myself an' let ya answer to 'im about why ya're still in there."

"Go," Ophelia urged, releasing his hands.

He went cold at the loss of her, and with the information she'd revealed knocking around his mind, Connor forced his feet to move.

Training his stare forward, he focused on Ophelia's revelation and the details she'd offered as proof. Any other person would have likely taken that information about one's brother and buried the secret forever.

She, however, wanted what was right to be done. She . . .

He slowed his step.

She'd ultimately found a nobleman's lost son, a young earl and future marquess. It was an act of bravery and valor deserving of a pardon.

For the first time since she'd been carted off, a sliver of hope took root and grew.

Resuming his walk, Connor all but sprinted through the halls of Newgate. As soon as he'd raced down the steps of the famed prison, he hurried over to the street urchin holding his reins.

After guiding his horse through the bustling streets, Connor found himself at the Marquess of Maddock's. As if on cue, a young boy bolted over.

"Watch my mount." He tossed a guinea to the child. "There will be more," he promised.

Hope fueling his footsteps, Connor raced to the marquess's door front and pounded hard. The door was immediately opened; Lord Maddock's devoted butler stared back. His eyes took in Connor's jacketless frame. "If you'll follow me?" As he ushered Connor through corridor after corridor, his mind whirred.

He should be solely focused on his upcoming meeting.

Instead, he thought of Ophelia, and the future he dreamed of became so real it was tangible.

He wanted to take her from St. Giles. Far away from Newgate and London. He wanted them both to begin again. This was the last thread of hope he had to save her.

The butler glanced back briefly and then urged Connor down another wide, dimly lit corridor. Portrait after portrait of images were draped in heavy black satin . . . except for one partially concealed portrait.

Slowing his steps, Connor stopped before the blue-enameled-and-jewel-encrusted frame. A thick black sheet had been artfully hung, neatly hiding the figure or figures there.

He drifted closer, pulled forward by the plump babe reflected on that oil canvas. With big cheeks and a wide, dimpled smile, the child radiated joy contradictory to the frosty cold that lived on in this household in his wake. Balanced between two people, the subject of the picture had one leg perched on the leg of his father; the babe's other disappeared sadly behind that curtain.

Connor diverted his focus to Lord Maddock's image: one relaxed hand curved softly about his son's waist while his left thumb had been seized by the babe. His head was slightly bent toward the child squeezing that digit. From the positioning of the marquess's body down to the more measured rendition of the grin worn by the child, the artist had expertly captured a frozen moment in time. It was a tableau of a bucolic family with a proud, loving papa.

Selfishly, Connor had thought only of how Stephen might secure Ophelia's freedom. Now, he looked at the boy, the brother so very loved by Ophelia, and the enormity of what this upcoming meeting portended slapped at him.

Had the boy in the portrait truly been happy? Had mother and father been equally blissful? Or had theirs been like so many other unions, riddled with resentment and faithlessness and disdain?

The butler cleared his throat. "Mr. Steele?"

Ignoring that unspoken question, Connor reached for the corner of the black satin.

Lord Maddock's loyal servant surged forward. "Mr. Steele . . . I must warn you—"

Not bothering a glance in the uneasy butler's direction, he lifted a palm, commanding the other man to silence.

Details mattered. Every single one of them provided a clue. Drawing the sheet back, he revealed the other persons in the portrait . . . or in this case, the one.

Clad in a pale-pink creation and her chestnut curls piled high upon her head, the young woman there could not be more than twenty years of age. A timid smile graced her lips, as she, too, with her head bent toward the child, evinced motherly warmth.

> I saw a fair maiden
> sitten and sing:
> She lulled a little child,

A sweete Lording
Lullay my liking.

He pressed his eyes closed as those lyrics of a forgotten lullaby echoed hauntingly around the chambers of his mind, sung in the clear, bell-like tones of his mother's voice.

Pray we now to that child,
As to His Mother dear,
God grant them all His blessing
That now maken cheer
Lullay my liking.

His throat constricted as he let the memories come rushing back in. Of joyous, peaceful times he'd forced himself to forget. Of a mother's and father's tender touch, a gentle smile. Stephen should have known that. Perhaps together, he and his father, two broken souls, could heal each other.

A lone floorboard creaked, and Connor forced his eyes open.

"That will be all, Quint." The marquess ordered his butler away.

The hasty beat of footsteps indicated the younger man had complied, leaving Connor alone with the reclusive lord.

Lord Maddock joined him at the portrait and, clasping his hands at his back, simply studied it. Silent. Unmoving. His expression revealed nothing, his eyes even less.

The quiet stood out so stark, so unforgiving, the faintest tick of Connor's timepiece, buried as it was in his pocket, audibly marked the passing time.

"The day of his birth," the marquess finally said, his voice hollowed of emotion, eerily deadened, "he remained turned. For hours the doctor waited for the babe to turn himself. Just . . . waited," he whispered.

"Her agony came in waves. I sat outside her rooms, head in my hands, simply listening to the cadence of her breathing and the shrillness of her cries, until I could not take it anymore." Lord Maddock drifted closer, so close his nose nearly kissed the canvas. "I stormed the rooms, ordered the doctor to do anything to save her. Threatened him by death at my hands if he didn't deliver the child, and when he remained there, wiping a nonexistent smudge from his spectacles, I grabbed him by his unwrinkled jacket and tossed him out of the room on his arse."

Yet the lady had lived.

The marquess grazed his fingertips along the ghost of a smile on his late wife's face. "I ordered Quint to fetch the village midwife. My mother, living at the time"—his lip peeled in a sneer, a hint of his feelings for that now departed figure—"forbade it as beneath a vaunted marquess to allow a commoner inside the birthing room of his heir. Tossed her out on her arse, too."

Connor remained silent through the telling.

"The midwife had to . . ." Lord Maddock's face crumpled, and Connor averted his gaze, allowing the other man his privacy. When he looked back, the mask was firmly in place. "Turn the babe. She claimed it was the only way to save my wife. So she turned him. The screams," he whispered. "They reached into my soul and forever remained." The marquess dusted his fingertips over the curls piled high on the young woman's head. "When I lie abed at night, I am kept awake with the question of her screams the night she was taken in that fire. Were they as tortured?" His throat bobbed. "Selfishly, thinking of only myself, I want to believe the smoke consumed her while she slept before she burned."

Reluctantly securing the satin fabric back in place, Connor covered the young marchioness as she'd been in happiness.

With a tilt of his head, Lord Maddock encouraged him to follow. They fell into step, not another word spoken, until he'd been ushered in and Connor had been seated.

The marquess made for the sideboard. "A drink?" he offered the way he might a casual friend come to chat and not an investigator who'd called in the dead of night.

"No, thank you."

The delicate clink of crystal touching crystal, followed by the steady stream of liquid hitting the glass, filled the rooms. "Your child has been found."

The tumbler slid from the marquess's hand and thumped the edge of the table. As the amber droplets spilled a path down to the floor, the marquess remained motionless. "What?" His voice, a ragged whisper steeped in disbelief, reached Connor. He turned slowly back. "Did you say—?"

"Your son has been found," he repeated, the admission the right one, and also heart-wrenching in what it would mean for Stephen and Ophelia and the entire Killoran family.

Lord Maddock gripped the edge of his sideboard, that white-knuckled grip keeping him upright. "I don't believe . . . I . . . How?"

Connor proceeded to reveal every detail recently shared by Ophelia. When he'd finished, the marquess said nothing. He remained rooted to the floor. Then a dark glint flickered in his eyes. "It is a trick," he whispered.

For a long moment, Connor didn't move. "I beg your pardon?" he finally asked.

Lord Maddock clenched and unclenched his fists. "They are hoping she'll be named a savior and her life spared."

Connor's neck heated at having his own hopes and thoughts so readily identified. "She wished to do what was right. She only just discovered—"

A chuckle laced with bitterness shook the marquess's frame. "How very *convenient* the young woman should share that information *now*." Fury spilled from Lord Maddock's taut frame. His lips formed a harsh sneer. "I may be more than half-mad, but I'm no fool. They'd foist that child off on me in the hopes a pardon will be issued, and I'm saddled with another one of Diggory's bastards who'll take flight the first moment he can." Lord Maddock grabbed the bottle and poured himself another glass. He slammed the crystal decanter down hard enough to shatter it.

"He has the marks." That gave the widower pause. "Upon his right knee and a mark on his belly."

Lord Maddock downed the contents of his snifter in one long, smooth swallow. His lips pulled. "I understand you've become quite taken with the young woman."

At that abrupt shift, Connor cocked his head. "I beg your—?"

"All the papers have commented on your infatuation with the Jewel of St. Giles, the diamond who took the *ton* by storm."

He narrowed his eyes. "Say what it is you'd say and be done."

"As one in possession of details about my son's identifying marks, you would be in a position to share with anyone. Including Miss Killoran. Would you not?"

The air slipped from Connor on a loud hiss. "My God, you are mad."

Lord Maddock grinned coldly. "Yes, I am. But then, having one's wife burned to death in a fire and one's child stolen has that effect." He swiped his bottle of French brandy and snifter and carried them to his desk. "Get the hell out, Steele. I no longer have need of your *services.*"

Fury roared through his body, and he curled his hands tightly to keep from bloodying the marquess senseless. The marquess was known in all respectable circles as a madman. One whose guilt had driven him insane. Though Connor would wager his very career and security that the man hadn't killed his wife and child, neither did he believe for a moment the man who'd employed his services was in full possession of his faculties. With madness oftentimes came ruthlessness. "Aye, you are correct. I am in love with her," he coolly acknowledged. "Orphaned by Diggory, I have no love or loyalty to the bastard who ruled East

London. But the young woman now imprisoned, I know her. She saved me as a boy. And she has found your son. You've become so twisted by your hatred that you'd let it keep you from your child."

Grief had clouded the marquess's ability to see reason. Nonetheless, Connor made a final attempt. "Ophelia Killoran would not hurt a child."

Lord Maddock winged an eyebrow. "Would she steal one?"

"The Killorans have the most prosperous gaming hell in London. They have power, wealth." And now sought noble connections. "What reason should she, or any of the Killorans, have to harm a child?"

"It is in her blood."

It was those five words that indicated a truth he'd not realized before now: Connor could not help this man. Nor reason with him. "I believe we've reached an impasse," he said tightly.

As Connor took his leave, the last flicker of hope went out.

Only . . .

His steps slowed, and he stood frozen outside the marquess's townhouse.

There had been *one* offer presented—one that would see Ophelia saved.

Connor's eyes closed.

He knew what had to be done.

Chapter 25

At best, Ophelia had an idea of her age because of her clever sister. There was not, however, a birth date, no one single day that had commemorated Ophelia's entry into the world. She'd simply been another bastard of a whore and gang leader, celebrated by none and unwanted by all.

There would, however, be a date to mark the last day she'd draw breath.

The 12th of April, 1826.

Lying on the unforgiving floor, she remained as she'd been since the evening before—on her back, staring at the stone ceiling overhead. Until the inky black of the night gave way to the faintest hint of light through the narrow window that looked out to the grounds below.

Mayhap it was exhaustion that contributed to her detachedness, but she did not feel like one who in several hours would be marched through the Debtor's door to the gallows and have a noose looped over her neck.

No, in this instance she felt . . . nothing.

Ophelia dragged Connor's jacket higher, covering her mouth and burying her nose. She inhaled the sandalwood scent that lingered there still.

Or mayhap it was not exhaustion. Mayhap it was finally that she'd found peace with every decision she'd made and trusted that when she was gone, Connor and her family would continue on, and all the wrongs done would be at last righted, including the feud with the Blacks which had morphed into a tense peace. What had it all been about? Or for? There was room enough for each of them in this world.

Stephen would leave behind the wicked gaming hell which had served as his home and be restored as the rightful heir to a powerful nobleman. He'd be educated, and in time would hopefully be healed of the suffering he, too, had known.

And Connor . . .

Tears flooded her eyes, blurring the ceiling overhead.

One day he would find love, be it with Lady Bethany or another, and marry and have a family and dreams Ophelia had never even allowed herself.

God help her for the selfish creature she was. In this, she was filled with a twisting regret. Wanting to be that woman. Hating the nameless stranger who'd capture his heart.

The clink of metal keys resonated from outside her cell, and the bottom fell out from her stomach.

Just like that, with the approaching footfalls, she was proven a liar.

I am not ready. I am not immune.

Her teeth clattered together with such ferocity, pain radiated up her jawline all the way to her temples.

Then the owner of those shuffling steps halted outside her cell.

It is time.

She scrabbled at the inside of her cheek, giving her teeth purchase, drawing blood and welcoming the pain. *I'm going to be ill.*

"Ya got company, Jewel," he said, tossing that mocking title.

Company.

Connor.

As the guard shoved the door open, Ophelia's heart lifted. Perhaps he'd coordinated her release. She shoved herself shakily to a stand. Perhaps . . . "Oh." That foolish organ, duped into hope, slithered down to her belly and sank all the way to her toes.

Wholly elegant and so very regal, the Duchess of Argyll hovered at the entranceway.

Had the Virgin Mary returned and paid a visit to Newgate, there couldn't be another woman more unsuited for the rot of this place.

"Hullo," the young widow ventured.

Ophelia looked to find her wanting. She wanted to see weakness in the woman whom Connor had intended to make his wife and who'd likely find herself his bride after Ophelia was . . . gone. Yet it was so very hard to pass judgment on a lady who hadn't already dissolved into a blubbering mess at the misery around them. Ophelia wanted to cry all over again at the sheer perfection of this woman.

The guard closed the door at her back, and the stunning beauty jumped.

"What do ya want?" Ophelia finally brought herself to ask. Had she come to gloat? Taunt her?

The duchess took a step and faltered. "I trust you despise me." Her faint whisper threaded around the cell, echoing like a thunderous roar in the quiet of Newgate. "For what my father did to you." Lady Bethany looked at the tips of her delicate pink-satin slippers. "After . . . after . . ." She wrung her hands together and then tried again. "After you were escorted off . . ."

Ophelia's lips quirked with a wry grin. "That is one way to describe it." Those fancy nobs, polite even on talk of prisons and eventual hangings.

•

The duchess flinched. Bringing back her shoulders, she again spoke, and when she did, there was a greater strength to her lyrical voice. "My father offered Connor an arrangement."

Connor. Just hearing his name fall so effortlessly from this flawless beauty's lips burned. "An arrangement?" Ophelia repeated gruffly. Jealousy stabbed at the very core of Ophelia's soul.

Lady Bethany nodded. "My father promised to coordinate your release"—her gaze locked with Ophelia's—"if Connor married me."

Oh, God.

A silent scream echoed around her mind, and Ophelia wanted to blot her hands over her ears and drive back those four words. "Oi won't sacrifice Connor's freedom for moi own," she said coolly. "We're done here." She turned. When the other woman spoke, her admission brought her back around.

"After you'd been taken by the constables, I listened in on a . . . fight between my father and Connor." *Connor.* That intimate grasp at his Christian name threatened to shatter her. "I heard the charges he leveled against my father."

Understanding dawned. "Ah, so this is why you've come." To challenge Ophelia's version of that long-ago day.

"I am to blame," the duchess whispered. "I'd heard the maids whisper and the servants talk about how he l-liked to be with young g-girls." She pressed a white-knuckled fist against her mouth. "I said nothing. I did nothing. I am complicit. As it is, I expect you hate me."

She did despise the Duchess of Argyll. Abhorred her with every fiber of her still-breathing body. She hated her for having broken Connor's heart. She hated her for someday having what Ophelia so selfishly wanted for herself. "You are not to blame for the actions of your father." The words slipped out, freeing and healing. And in them there was an absolution of sorts. Connor had taught her forgiveness. It was a gift not given her by the sisters who'd been with her since the beginning of her life, or the brothers who'd come along later. It had always been

Connor who'd opened her eyes to the best parts of the world. She briefly squeezed her eyes closed. *Oh, how I am going to miss him.*

When she opened them, she found the duchess's unreadable gaze on her. Ophelia steeled her spine. "If you allow Connor to trade his freedom for my life, then you, however, are to blame."

Tears glazed Lady Bethany's eyes. "Connor is so very in love with you. I wanted to find you undeserving of him, and yet you are his match in every way." She examined Ophelia contemplatively, as if she were an oddity on display at the Royal Museum. "My father insists it does not matter. That Connor will forget you. He believes in time Connor and I can be happy together again."

Again.

Misery strangled off Ophelia's ability to formulate words. The duchess quite easily filled the void.

"When I had my Come Out, I served as a lady-in-waiting to the queen." Of course, in her flawlessness, she'd have links to the king and queen of England themselves. "I was"—her cheeks reddened—"one of her more favored ladies. Often, she'd tell me she abhorred most of them."

"Why are you telling me this?" Ophelia asked tiredly, cutting into those ramblings.

"I spoke to the queen . . . on your behalf. I explained how you had been wronged. A pardon was issued."

A dull buzzing filled her ears. She shook her head, trying to clear the fog. What a cruel game. To have her future dangled before her as a reality . . . with Connor neatly cut from it. "Wot are ya saying?" she demanded hoarsely, her mind in rebellion.

The duchess crossed to the front of the cell and stretched a delicate, gloved palm through those metal bars.

Broderick and Wylie instantly appeared at that wordless command. The door was opened by the warden himself.

"You are free, Miss Killoran," the duchess said softly, and then slipped out.

No.

Ophelia briefly closed her eyes.

Broderick opened his arms, and on unsteady legs Ophelia stumbled over and collapsed against him.

It is done.

St. Giles
One week later

Not even a spare seat to be had at the tables, the Devil's Den was filled to overflowing with patrons.

Cups had been flowing and bore no hint of stopping at the early evening hour.

The clink of coins striking coins as men tossed down their fortunes echoed throughout.

Ophelia had been restored to her rightful home at the Devil's Den, moving about the gaming hell as naturally as if she'd been deeded the properties by Mac Diggory.

In short, the world had returned to normal.

Yet nothing would ever be the same again.

Standing in the glass observatory overlooking the gaming floors, Ophelia stared out at gentlemen whom only a few weeks ago she'd been skirting dances from. Once, she'd resented Broderick for forcing her out into Polite Society, craving the familiarity of the club and her purpose here.

How very wrong she'd been. Her ability to make a difference in the lives of children in East London had nothing to do with her place-ment in this club. Connor and the lords and ladies she'd since met had proven that change could be implemented anywhere. No, all this time Ophelia had told herself one thing, but ultimately she'd always been driven by fear.

Fear of men, a product of that long-ago night.

In a short time, she'd reclaimed every aspect of her life in every way that mattered.

Because of Connor.

Ophelia touched her forehead to the cool glass plate that offered a window out to the floors below.

Connor had been the one bright spot of joy she'd found in that oppressive world. In the end, he'd bartered himself for her freedom. She closed her eyes. Or mayhap that had been what he'd truly wanted anyway, deep down—a proper lady, which Ophelia would never be.

The mirror's smooth planes reflected back the regret contorting her features, and she took a step away to keep her misery her own.

The door opened.

Her sister Gertrude, a stack of notepads in hand, closed the door and made her way to one of the desks in the corner of the room.

Absolutely still, Ophelia studied her partially blind sister as she set up a place. With precise, efficient movements of one who'd carried out the same task multiple times, Gertrude stacked the folders and reached for a pencil.

It was a position of power Ophelia had once craved, conducting formal business on behalf of the Devil's Den with a defined role carved out.

As Gertrude made to sit, Ophelia announced herself. "I see our brother has become wise enough to use your strengths for the good of the club."

Her sister slapped a hand to her chest and jumped up. The walnut armchair skidded along the floors. "You scared me," she chided, faintly breathless.

Abandoning her spot at the window, Ophelia joined her. "My apologies," she said softly. The moment Gertrude had lost vision in one eye, there'd been an unspoken understanding that out of respect, one never took her by surprise. Ophelia reached for Gertrude's chair, but her sister waved her off and saw to righting the chair herself.

Ophelia passed her gaze over the work laid out. "What is this?" she murmured, more to herself. She reached for the top notepad.

Gertrude clasped her hands. "Broderick has tasked me with inventorying the strengths of each prostitute within the club and reassigning them new roles based on those skills. As well as educating them and the children . . ." Her words trailed guiltily off. "I should have asked beforehand whether you wished for the assignment. Given you are the reason for the change. But I—"

Ophelia waved a hand. "It is fine, Gertrude." Once, it wouldn't have been. Once, Ophelia would have been so very focused on establishing her place and demonstrating her worth. She'd learned that the only thing that mattered was impacting the lives of those who'd suffered and deserved new opportunities. She offered a gentle smile. "It is better than fine." At last, Broderick had seen each of their values.

"You're certain?" Gertrude put forward tentatively.

"I am." She motioned to the books. "May I?"

"Of course," her sister said quickly.

Sitting on the corner of the walnut Davenport desk, Ophelia flipped through the pages, skimming the detailed accounting her sister had thus far assembled of the women at the club.

Each page contained a comprehensive write-up of each girl, along with her skills and strengths and a mark about her individual hopes. She brushed her fingers over one young woman's name. They'd always taken Gertrude as soft-hearted and dismissed her as weak because of it. How much wiser she'd been in so many ways.

"This is just half of the women," Gertrude explained, cutting across her musings. "I hope by the end of next week to have charts assembled with not only their skills but also a schedule for their lessons."

She fell silent, and Ophelia continued reading her sister's work.

"You've not visited the gaming hell floors." Gertrude's quiet observation gave her brief pause.

"No." She hadn't.

"You've hardly left your rooms," Gertrude noted.

Ophelia toyed with the edges of the leather notepad in her hands. No, it was rather hard to make oneself go through the motions of caring when one's heart had been so thoroughly shattered.

"Broderick worries you went mad during your time there."

She stared vacantly down at the names inked upon Gertrude's book. For in a way, Broderick was not far from the mark. Any person who spent time in Newgate and lived to see light beyond the cell walls carried with them the horrors of one's time there. "It was hell," she softly whispered. Ironically, the day she'd been sprung free by the duchess had thrust Ophelia into an altogether different and yet more agonizing hell.

Small but steadying hands covered her own and lightly squeezed. She stared down at Gertrude's ink-stained fingers. "Is that why he's taken to avoiding me?" Since she'd returned, not a single guard or servant had been able to meet her eyes. "Or is it that he can't see past the hideousness of . . . of . . ." She fluttered a hand about her head. Though Regina, a master with scissors, had done an admirable job with the viciously shorn curls, the wisps were better suited to a boy than a woman.

"You are not hideous," Gertrude said, a frown in her voice. "You could not be any more beautiful."

Her sister lied, and she loved her for it. How ironic that she who'd lamented the wicked attention shown her by men should grieve the loss of her hair. However, those strands merely marked one more thing that had been taken from her: Connor, her happiness, her heart.

"Broderick has been . . . otherwise busy."

Since he'd joined the Diggory gang, Broderick hadn't known a moment's rest. He had, however, taken time for his sisters. "Oh?"

"What? He is," Gertrude said defensively. "He's been shut away in meetings." Her sister went tight-lipped.

That abrupt cutoff was too suspicious, and her eldest sibling's avoidant gaze was even more so. Ophelia narrowed her eyes. "What business?

Gertrude shrugged. "I've been occupied with my work."

So much so that she'd not paid any attention to those engaging Broderick in business? Her suspicion deepened, and along with it, her worry. "What aren't you telling me?"

Gertrude's cheeks went red. "I am *offended*. Very, very offended." Her poor liar of a sister spoke quickly, her words running together. "You're suggesting that I'd keep anything from you to protect you. I wouldn't have such a low opinion."

Ophelia folded her arms at her middle. "I did not say anything about your protecting me." Even as she struck a calm repose, on the inside, panic set her heart into a double-time rhythm. What if the decision to free her had been rescinded? What if . . . ?

"D-did you not?" Gertrude squeaked. "I was so very certain that you did."

"I didn't."

"Oh." Her sister went to sit.

That was it?

"That is all you intend to say on it?"

"Yes?" At Ophelia's narrowing gaze, she amended, "No?"

Secrets were being kept. "Who is he meeting with?"

When her sister remained mutinously silent, Ophelia spun on her heel. Secrets were being kept from her.

"Ophelia!" Gertrude cried. The echo of her footfalls followed Ophelia in her flight.

I want these men found . . . I want justice for . . . She damned the heavy oak panel that muffled her brother's words, pulling them in and out of focus.

"Ophelia?" her sister said on a furious whisper, this exchange feeling so very much like another one of a month ago. A meeting between Broderick and Connor. That first moment he'd reentered her life and flipped it all upside down.

The debt must be paid.

Gooseflesh dotted her skin as Broderick's ice-cold voice delivered that hated pledge that had been such a part of their existence.

It was done. It was time to let go of the resentment and quest for justice and wealth.

"Ophelia," her sister whispered, frantically reaching for her just as Ophelia shoved the door open. She instantly found two pistols leveled at her person.

"We don't . . ."

All words fled . . . and along with them, the air in her lungs.

The pair of men stationed behind the heavy mahogany desk stared back.

Connor.

Oh, God, how I missed her.

The sight of her, a Spartan warrioress ready for battle, she was Lagertha in every way.

Not taking her eyes from him, Ophelia pushed the door closed behind her.

That faint click snapped him back to the moment. He holstered his pistol.

It was the lady's brother who broke the tense impasse. "Bloody hell, Ophelia, how many times have I told you not to burst in when I'm seeing to busin—"

A single look effectively quelled the remainder of that warning.

With the steady, sure steps of one who owned these offices, Ophelia came forward, joining them at the desk. "You . . . have business with . . ." Her eyes briefly met his before she moved them over to Killoran. "Mr. Steele?"

Mr. Steele.

Two words that imposed formality, and given everything his father and those whom he'd respected through the years had brought to her, she was in her rights to be wary around him.

"I do," her brother was saying. "Business I was seeing to before you stormed my offices." He paused. "Again."

Ophelia's mouth tensed, those rosebud lips tight with her annoyance.

Connor had always been selfish. From the day he'd abandoned his only friend and thieving partner, Niall, to the day he'd unrepentantly lived a life of ease with the Earl of Mar while Ophelia had been left behind, it had been the greatest flaw to his soul.

In this instance, with Ophelia before him, hands akimbo and her eyes a mystery, selfishly he wanted her anyway. He wanted her despite the fact that he was the reason she'd been thrown into Newgate and he'd been unable to spring her from that hell.

Then Ophelia stole a glance at the door. When she looked back, worry darkened her eyes. "Is it time? Is he leaving?" The faintness to those questions stood in stark contradiction to the steely set to her shoulders.

Broderick hesitated and then shook his head. "Steele presented his . . ." Her. It had been Ophelia who'd pieced together details he'd likely never have himself. "Findings to the gentleman, and . . ." He gestured to Connor.

"And the gentleman was suspicious. Suspicious enough to doubt the boy is truly his son. I've asked him to eventually meet the boy, but he has . . . declined."

Shock spilled from Ophelia's eyes. "What?" She shook her head. "He's held out faith and hope that the child still lives, and when presented with the truth, he . . . ?"

Connor knew the precise moment that understanding set in.

Her lips moved, but no words came out.

How Connor hated it for her. Despised a world that had always passed judgment on her and her kin for crimes they'd been forced to commit. Once, he'd not seen that. He'd judged, seeing them as different from even himself. What a narrow-minded arse he'd been.

"That is why you're here then. To discuss Lord Maddock's case?"

Was it merely hope that conjured the regret in her tone?

He looked to her brother.

The other man hesitated and then motioned to the chairs at the foot of his desk. "After you'd shared with me . . . your suspicions," he said once he'd taken his seat, "I didn't believe you. I didn't believe you because I didn't wish to." Killoran's gaze fell to the stained, aged leather folders before him.

Ophelia leaned forward, studying those books. She jerked, gripping the arms of her chair. "Those are—"

"Diggory's books. Yes." The proprietor dug free a book tucked in the middle of his pile. He flipped through it and suddenly stopped. "Here," he murmured, holding it out.

Ophelia hesitated, then took the ledger.

"It contains the names of his wives from that year, along with their children."

"I don't under—" And then she stopped. Her slender frame turned to stone in her seat.

"It contains Black's name and his mother," Killoran confirmed. "A duke's by-blow, Ryker and Helena Black were perfectly suited children for one as obsessed with—"

"Noble connections," Ophelia finished for him. She glanced briefly in Connor's direction; their gazes locked, and then she cut him out once more. "I do not understand," she said to her brother. "What does any of this have to do with your hiring Mr. Steele?"

Again, Mr. Steele. His stomach clenched. Not Connor. Rather, a stranger and nothing more.

With more reluctance, the head proprietor slipped free the book at the very bottom of the pile. "Your allegations led me to search through his papers and books. And I discovered this." He handed it over.

Ophelia read through those pages, and then her gaze locked at the center of the page. "My God," she whispered.

"Your brother discovered Diggory's net had been cast far wider, and the children he'd once sought to make his heir were actually young babes born to the nobility."

The leather journal shook in her hands. "He always desired a nobleman's blood. Wanted it for his own."

"And he took it," Killoran said gravely.

"Not it," Ophelia whispered. She lifted ravaged eyes. "He took ch-children. Are there others? Than these?" She glanced back down.

"Three," Connor murmured. "Your brother discovered three in that particular accounting kept by Diggory and . . ." His words trailed off, and he glanced regretfully over at Broderick.

The proprietor's throat moved spasmodically. "Stephen in another." Grief contorted his features in a raw show of emotion.

Ophelia caught her brother's hands in hers, and Connor briefly looked away. Not only would Ophelia and her family be shattered by the loss of their brother but they'd also be raked through every gossip page and shunned by Polite Society.

Clearing his throat, Broderick released Ophelia's hands. When he again spoke, he was restored to the unaffected figure of Connor's first meeting. "Whether there are more children, I cannot say for certain."

He rolled his shoulders. "It is why I've hired Mr. Steele. He'll conduct the search to find their whereabouts . . . or the fate of each of them."

Ophelia gasped. "You believe they are alive?"

It was unlikely that they'd lived more than twenty years on their own in the streets of London. And yet . . . Stephen had survived. As had Connor. As such, there could be others.

"He marked the deaths and murders of those in his gang," Connor supplied.

Ophelia again studied the pages in that book. "For Diggory, it wouldn't have been affection that led him to mark the passing of those children," she said quietly to herself.

Aye. Everything Diggory had done in his hateful, evil life had been driven with a thought to his empire in mind. The poor souls in his book had been mentioned only in death because of the income lost and the need to replace them with others to fill their roles.

"There are no marks made on the fate of these children," she finally said, looking up from the pages.

"That is correct." Killoran, with greater reluctance, offered one final book. "It is why I suspected they managed to escape." And might be alive, even now. "The one other name thus far I'd found so marked was . . ."

Ophelia trailed her fingertips over the letters of one name. *Connor O'Roarke. It is his name.* "Connor's," she whispered.

The agony of loss gripped him all over again. It was a pain that would never go away. Ophelia had shown him that even as he'd sought to bury his past, it would always be there: the suffering . . . but also the love he had known with his parents.

Killoran broke the quiet. "It is the only explanation I could otherwise surmise."

Ophelia's eyes slid closed, and she shook her head. "That bastard."

"After he'd taken me in, with my"—he grimaced—"birthright and abilities, I was as close as he could come to respectability. And so I sufficed. We each served each other's purposes." Something dark lit the other man's gaze but then was swiftly gone. "I cannot erase Diggory's wrongs, but I can try to right them. Steele will be overseeing the investigation. It will be fully funded by the club."

"Oh." Ophelia dropped her eyes to that book. "I see." Wordlessly, she turned the aged journals over to her brother.

What did she believe she saw? The question raged around Connor's mind.

A knock sounded at the doorway, interrupting their meeting.

"Enter!" Killoran boomed.

A heavily freckled young woman ducked her head inside. "Forgive me. Your presence is required on the floors," she murmured. "A fight has broken out between two of the patrons, and they're demanding a word with you."

A black curse exploded from Killoran's lips. He shoved to his feet. "I'll be along shortly. Ophelia. Steele." He stretched a hand out, and Connor shook it. "You've your other business to see to." A dark glint iced his gaze. "Do not make me regret my decisions."

With that, the head proprietor stalked off, and Ophelia and Connor were left alone.

Chapter 26

Ophelia should have found peace in Connor's presence here. Her brother hadn't sought to bury away Diggory's evil—and because of their connection to that monster—their complicity.

The *ton* would gossip.

The club would likely suffer.

There'd certainly be no connection to the nobility for Gertrude after this.

Yet he'd put the lives of three lost boys—now men—before all of that.

That should be enough. It had long been the one hope she'd carried: that Broderick would abandon his Diggory-like obsession with the peerage and be content with his grand empire.

Selfishly, it was not.

Connor had come only on a matter of business.

He closed the notepads and folders he and Broderick had previously been studying. She followed each careful movement as he neatly stacked them.

"You have been . . . well?"

No, she'd been miserable—empty and aching and tortured by memories of Newgate, and riddled with a horror that would never leave. "I've not," she offered instead, unwilling to lie to him.

His face crumpled. "Oh, Ophelia." He reached for her. "I wanted to come to you," he said, his voice ragged.

Ophelia pushed his hands away. "And yet you didn't." She jutted her chin. She didn't want his pity. She wanted him in her life. She wanted his heart. "I th-thought you were at the very least a friend that you might . . . visit before . . . this." What a pathetically weak gift to settle for. A visit from him. A mere visit when she wanted all of him, forever.

"Is that what you believe?" he murmured, drifting around the side of the desk. "That we are friends?"

"Yes. No." For she had . . . she'd also, however, after his visit to Newgate and every intimate exchange before it, deluded herself into believing that mayhap they were *more*. "I . . . I . . . aren't we?" Because even as he'd been her lover, he'd first been her friend—a truth she'd denied all these years.

He dusted his knuckles over her cheek, and she leaned into that soft caress. "I wanted to see you." His hand fell back to his side, and she silently cried out at the loss of his touch. "There was business, however, I needed to . . . *wanted* to see to before I came here."

"Business?" she echoed hollowly. The irony was not lost on her that they'd come full circle. Business was that which had brought him back into her life.

"My father wronged you. He's since expressed regret for his treatment of you." A muscle jumped at the corner of his eye. "I'll not begin to explain for him or make apologies on his behalf, but . . ." His fingers curled into tight balls. "He proved your worst opinions about the nobility correct, and for that I am sorry."

Disappointment threatened to overwhelm her. Connor had come to apologize for crimes that belonged to another. "You are no more responsible for his actions than I am of my father's," she said simply. "You showed me that." He'd opened her eyes to the truth. Some in the nobility were as evil as Satan, but there were those who were good—not unlike the men and women born to the streets.

Connor sat forward in his seat. "I have operated the better part of my adult life believing I could right injustices." Regret flashed within his eyes. "And yet Lords Middlethorne and Whitehaven—they'll not rot in Newgate as they should for their crimes. They'll not hang." A seething rage spilled from his frame, and her heart ached anew with her love for him. His visceral reaction, that shared outrage—was for her.

She plucked at the fabric of her skirts. "Some are untouchable." Those dark lords who'd sought to ruin her were amongst them. "You can never change that. No one can."

He nodded. "Yes, some are. But everyone has weaknesses." Connor's gaze locked with hers. "Their reputations matter more to them than anything." Ophelia stilled. What was he saying? "I made clear to Lords Middlethorne and Whitehaven that every scandal sheet would sing with the crimes they were guilty of . . . if they didn't leave England." Her heart quickened. "I promised them the moment they set foot on English soil, everyone would know their sins."

The air exploded from her lungs. "You saw them exiled." *For me.*

Connor cleared his throat. "It is less than they deserve, and I wished I could . . . do more."

"Thank y-you," she said, her voice catching. This man had shared in her fury and managed what no one else could . . . or ever would, for a girl born to the streets. She wanted to hurl herself in his arms and live in that embrace forever. And yet . . . "That was the business you were seeing to," she murmured to herself. That had been the reason he'd not come sooner.

Connor took her hands in his and trailed his thumbs over the sensitive skin of the top of her fingers. That back-and-forth stroking sent little shivers from her palms all the way up her arm. "I had additional matters I needed to attend."

His betrothal.

Her heart ached all over again. "I understand an arrangement was reached between you and the duchess," she managed, her voice hoarse. With every admission, she left herself more and more exposed before him, but God help her, she'd no pride where this man was concerned.

Connor turned her closed hand over and brushed her palm open. "Have you ever had your future read?"

Blankly, she stared at their connected hands. Actually, she hadn't. She'd always been too busy telling the futures of others. Incapable of words, she shook her head.

With the tip of his index finger, he trailed the intersecting line that met her wrist and followed it up to the center of her hand. "This is called your fate line."

She studied him, wholly fixed on her palm. "What are you—?"

"There was a boy you once saved. You were destined to again meet."

Aye, it had always seemed that way where she and Connor O'Roarke had been concerned. Their paths had been meant to cross and their fates to be inextricably intertwined. Only to be so neatly severed by Lady Bethany and her father. Several tears slipped down her cheeks.

"And this," he murmured, grazing his fingertip over the horizontal line that met below her pinkie and following it to the middle of her hand, "is your love line."

"Stop it," she whispered, struggling against his grip, but he held firm.

"And in it I see a man who's loved you so hopelessly and helplessly from the moment you entered his life as a mere child. A man who loves you even more now, as a woman of strength and courage and compassion."

A little sob burst from her, and tears flooded her eyes, blurring his visage. "What game are ya playing?" she cried.

"There is no game," he said, so collected. He lifted his gaze, meeting hers, and then resumed his reading. "This man will remind you how to smile and laugh and love." *Oh, God.* Tears slid unchecked down her cheeks. "And there'll be a babe. Many of them. At least four."

A ragged sob tore from her throat.

"I offered to marry Bethany," he said quietly.

Ophelia bit down hard on the inside of her cheek and struggled against him. She exploded to her feet. Wanting to flee. Wanting to escape him and this moment and the future.

"I did it to save you—"

"You don't get to sacrifice yourself to save me," she cried, tossing her arms up. "Not again." Only he had.

"That reading," he went on, motioning to her palms.

"You cannot steal my reading, Connor." She knew precisely what her future would be without him in it: empty, bleak, with her married to a nob her brother approved of, and now it wouldn't even matter. It wouldn't matter because her heart had died in that cold Newgate cell.

"Ah, but you see, Ophelia." Connor brushed back the moisture from her face, but there were other tears to take their place. "I can use that reading you gave me. Because our lives, like our hearts, have been forever intertwined. That future you saw for me . . . was true. Because it was linked to you."

She covered her hand with her mouth, catching another sob.

His eyes grew somber. "Bethany freed me from her father's expectation."

Ophelia's entire body went ramrod straight. Heart thudding wildly against her rib cage, she jerked her gaze to his. "What?"

"She explained that my friendship meant too much to ever keep me from the woman I love. That even as desperate as she was, she herself was unwilling to enter into another cold, empty union."

She pressed a hand over her chest, willing his words to make sense. "What are you saying?"

He gathered her palms again and raised them one at a time to his lips, placing a lingering kiss upon her knuckles. "I am saying we are both . . . free. As such, the other business I spoke of . . . was with your brother."

"My brother?" she echoed, desperately trying to follow.

He sank to a knee.

Ophelia gasped, jumping back a step.

"I am asking you to marry me. Even as I have no right." *No right?* "My father wronged you, and because of him," he went on hoarsely, "I'm the reason for your suffering—"

Ophelia buried the remainder of that admission behind her fingertips. "You are not allowed to take ownership of the actions of another, Connor. You rightfully wouldn't allow it of me, and I'll not allow it for you."

"There will be only you, Ophelia," he repeated, and this time, where she'd halted his profession before, she now needed it from him. Wanted it. "I love you."

Joy exploded in her breast, but she hesitated.

"What is it?" he asked, his tone somber.

For all the time they'd known each other, from when she was a girl to this moment now, he'd made decisions that defined her future. Each time at the expense of his own. "I can't have you like this," she finally said, taking a step back.

His features contorted. "What? I . . . I don't . . ." Connor shook his head.

She lifted her chin, needing him to see and understand. "You don't get to sacrifice yourself for me, Connor. Not anymore. If you had married h-her . . ." Her voice broke, and she struggled around the despair stuck there. "There are many deaths a person can suffer," she whispered. His marriage to Lady Bethany would have left her forever bereft. Ophelia stared beyond his shoulder. "I would have preferred the hanging."

A sound of agony spilled from his lips. "I wanted you alive, even if it meant you'd never belong to me."

Lifting her hands imploringly, she willed him to see. "I don't *want* you to save me. I just want you to love me, Connor."

"I do," he said hoarsely. "I will not make decisions for you. Not any longer. Together, we'll make them. No matter how difficult they may be, and no matter how much I might—"

Ophelia hurled herself into his arms. "I love you," she rasped.

Connor grunted and fell back, taking her with him. "Will you m—?"

"Yes," she breathed against his lips, cutting off that request.

As their laughter, free and unrestrained, spilled around the room, they released the chains on their past and embraced their future.

Acknowledgments

I had certain plans for Ophelia's story. I had it all mapped out. I'd plotted, planned, and pitched it to my fabulous editor. I even had a number of chapters written.

And then one day . . . the story changed. Ophelia whispered in my ear, insisting *her* story be told, demanding I tell the story the way it needed to be written. One never knows how one's editor might react to a shift in story.

Alison Dasho, you are amazing. Thank you for trusting my vision and not putting constraints upon me. There is no greater gift an author could have than an editor she can trust.

About the Author

Photo © 2016 Kimberly Rocha

USA Today bestselling author Christi Caldwell blames novelist Judith McNaught for luring her into the world of historical romance. When Christi was at the University of Connecticut, she began writing her own tales of love—ones where even the most perfect heroes and heroines had imperfections. She learned to enjoy torturing her couples before they earned their well-deserved happily ever afters.

The author of *The Hellion* in her Wicked Wallflowers series, Christi lives in Southern Connecticut, where she spends her time writing, chasing after her son, and taking care of her twin princesses-in-training. Fans who want to keep up with the latest news and information can sign up for Christi's newsletter at www.ChristiCaldwell.com or follow her on Facebook (AuthorChristiCaldwell) or Twitter (@ChristiCaldwell).